The Brighter the Light, the Darker the Shadow

by

Verlin Darrow

The Brighter the Light, the Darker the Shadow

Cover Art by *The Wild Rose Press, Inc.*

The Wild Rose Press, Inc.
PO Box 708
Adams Basin, NY 14410-0708
Visit us at www.thewildrosepress.com

Publishing History
First Edition, 2026
Trade Paperback Print ISBN 978-1-5092-6413-1
Digital ISBN 978-1-5092-6414-8

Published in the United States of America

Dedication

To my wife Lusijah and everyone else who has supported me on my life path and my writing career. We're all in this life deal together, aren't we?

Chapter 1

Like most of us, my dog Zeus was a creature of habit, responding with patterned behaviors even when he encountered novel stimuli. He rarely surprised me after our six years together. So when an unprecedented howl suddenly returned me to the world on an April morning, leaving behind a dream that might've been more than a dream, I wondered why.

Zeus sounded close by in the small meadow surrounding my yurt. Loath to leap out of bed to discover what was happening, I rolled over and languidly speculated. Perhaps a stray female dog in heat had wandered onto the property. Maybe a dead animal had offended Zeus's keen nose. Was he injured? This latter possibility propelled me to rise, hurriedly pull on clothes, and rush outside.

Not thirty feet away, still howling, Zeus stood beside a prone human form. It appeared to be a woman. My first thought was that one of our members had snuck off the land, gotten drunk, and passed out. We had a handful of people in our community who were recovering alcoholics—some more recovered than others.

Barefoot, I strode closer. The recently risen sun cast long shadows from the neighboring redwood trees onto the dewy grass, stopping just past the body. The woman was obviously dead. The back of her head was a mess from what appeared to be a gunshot wound.

Here was a challenge to my ability to weather a horrific event without becoming untethered from my core self. Could I fully experience *this*? Could I stay alert and drink it in? I try to open up to everything that comes my way instead of line editing what doesn't suit me. But *this*…

I flunked the test and averted my gaze. Then I gestured to Zeus and he came to my side, facing the body, panting as though he'd been chasing an uncatchable critter.

I focused on him, delaying the next step I needed to take—calling 911. That was going to up the reality quotient of the murder, forcing me to squarely face what I still didn't want to face.

To a dog lover's eyes, Zeus looked half Alaskan malamute and half Newfoundland, which he was. To someone unfamiliar with jumbo breeds, I heard comments such as "Is that a bear or what?" Zeus only abandoned his gentle disposition when he was provoked by a good-sized dog. Little dogs could yap at him, and even nip him all they wanted. He responded with the canine equivalent of a smile.

I worried at first that furry Zeus might suffer in the Northern California summers. But other than a continuously lolling tongue, he managed. It helped that the redwood forest beside the meadow was always much cooler than the rest of the mountain.

Finally, I pulled the only phone allowed on the property out of my pants pocket and punched in the number. I carried it at all times ever since an incident with a young mountain lion. This was the first time in weeks I'd needed to use it.

"What is the nature of your emergency?"

The woman's voice was low-pitched and completely calm. The meta-message was that whatever represented an emergency to me wasn't likely to mean much to her. I liked the timbre of her voice. It reminded me of a girlfriend in college who had smoked enough to develop a slight burr when she spoke.

"I just discovered a dead body," I told the dispatcher.

"What is your name, sir?" she asked hurriedly. Clearly, I *was* reporting something significant.

"Kade Tobin."

"Are you sure the person is deceased?"

"Yes. Apparently, she's been shot in the back of the head."

"Where are you? What is your address?" she asked with increased urgency.

"We don't have a formal address. We're up in the Santa Cruz mountains. Let me give you directions, and you can pass them on to the police."

"That would be the sheriff's office, sir." She seemed happy to have had an opportunity to correct me. Perhaps she'd been a middle child or was in a one-down position in her marriage. On the other hand, perhaps I was overthinking to insulate myself again from the horror in front of me.

"Fine," I told her. I provided directions, answered a few more questions, and ended the call. Then I told Zeus to *Stay!* by the body to protect it from other animals. If I didn't state the command itself at a higher volume than the rest of a sentence, it didn't take.

By now, Jim Murikawa was striding toward me. I held my hand up to spare him a close-up sight of the body and met him near the far side of the meadow, where a particularly tall grove of redwoods sheltered most of our buildings.

"Trouble?" he asked. "We heard the howling in the dorm. What an unearthly sound. Who is that over by Zeus?"

Jim performed most of the administrative functions of our community. While not being particularly far along his spiritual path, he'd held a similar job at a private school.

Jim was a third generation Japanese-American who didn't identify with his heritage despite resembling a stereotypical Asian actor in an old black and white movie. His round face sported clunky black plastic glasses, but at least he'd been spared buck teeth.

"I'm afraid it's a murdered woman," I told him. "The police are on the way."

"Oh, my God." His face scrunched up, forming a cluster of more diminutive features in the middle of it.

"Tell everyone to stay away from the meadow and let them know they'll probably be questioned," I told him. "Make sure no one talks about the project."

"Yes, yes."

"Thanks, Jim."

He ran back into the redwood forest to enact my instructions. Overweight, out of shape, and clearly no athlete in the first place, Jim's retreating figure retreated rather gradually.

My mind wandered to murder mysteries I'd read as I walked back to the body. Often the killer was an unlikely candidate. Could Jim be a suspect? Had he acted the way an innocent person would act? I had no idea. I let go of that.

I couldn't imagine any of my students committing the murder, but like all of us, my imagination was often superseded by what the universe came up with.

Take me, for example. If there was such a category in high school, I surely would've been voted least likely to have become a spiritual mentor. And could I have envisioned the murder itself?

I pulled myself back into the moment. The deputies would come and do their job. Who had killed the woman, for what reason, and why she was on our land wasn't my job to discover.

Zeus began howling again, so I hustled to return to his side to soothe him. Already, the shadows had receded a bit and direct sunlight rendered the scene even more grotesque.

The dead woman lay face down. She wore a black T-shirt, worn jeans, and one red flip-flop. Her bare foot was quite tan, more so than her visible arm, which sported a plain silver bracelet. The discrepancy in skin tone struck me as odd. Whose feet received more sun than the rest of her? Her other arm was tucked under her, high on her chest, below her hidden face.

I would've had to truly look at the gore that was the back of the victim's head to describe the fatal wound. I looked at anything but that.

Zeus snapped at a fly that veered too far in his direction as it maneuvered for its share of airspace over the body. A slight wag of his bushy tail told me he enjoyed the effort, despite his failure to snare his prey.

Zeus was a constant reminder of the benefits of living in the moment. He was happy, or at least content, a great majority of the time, escaped flies be damned.

Most of us humans are burdened by the tyranny of

continuity—the ongoing, sequential storylines we feel compelled to construct. What about directly experiencing life—letting it tell us about itself?

I returned to my yurt to put on socks, boots, and a light sweater. Late April in Santa Cruz County was still cool in the mornings and evenings. I also brought a towel to sit on as I meditated beside the body. A wet butt wasn't going to help my day go any better.

After a half hour, two deputies arrived. I watched them as they strolled unhurriedly from our dirt driveway to the meadow where Zeus and I sat.

One deputy was tall. He walked with a slight limp. His graying hair reflected his years, which I put at late fifties. The other man was shorter, stockier, and quite young-looking. The bounce in his step hinted at an athletic career. He was gleamingly pale, like a stereotypical Irish milkmaid.

The tall, older deputy looked to be a Latino based on his skin tone, although he could've been a member of a host of other ethnic groups. In our area, when in doubt, it was sensible to assume Mexican or Central American heritage.

As they drew closer, I saw that this man's wrinkled uniform created a wonky chessboard across his chest, with more wavy horizontal lines than vertical ones. The younger Anglo man's outfit could've been pressed a half hour ago, and his cap sat so squarely on his head that I wondered if he'd spent some time in front of a mirror that morning.

I rose to my feet and offered my hand when they reached me. Neither of them shook it.

"Regulations, sir," the younger one told me. "The department is currently limiting skin-to-skin contact based on recent worldwide viral outbreaks."

His colleague frowned at this formal cop-speech. "Good morning, sir," he greeted. "I'm Matt Hernandez, and this is Jason Dearborn. Could you ask your dog to stand down?"

I glanced at Zeus, who sat quietly beside me, watching the men with friendly interest. I didn't see the harm of humoring the deputy.

"Stand down," I told Zeus.

Since this phrase was not in his vocabulary, his interest turned to me and he cocked his head to puzzle out what I meant. He gave up after a few moments.

"The forensic team and a detective are on the way," Hernandez continued. "In the meantime, why don't you tell us what you know about this." He glanced around, studiously ignoring the body that was three feet away. I think he was even better at it than I was. "Is there somewhere you and I can sit and talk?" he added.

I nodded. "Sure. In my office."

I gestured across the verdant meadow to the weathered cabin that was just visible through a gap in the trees. The colorful mural over the door was a blur in the shade. This array of obscure spiritual symbols floating in a blue sky hadn't been my idea. A committee had formed itself, settled on the details, and then painted it without any feedback.

Before I could turn to lead the men to my office, Hernandez spoke to his colleague. "Jason, cordon off the area and keep people away." He turned to me again. "There *are* other people here, correct? This is some sort of ashram or something?"

"More or less," I told him. "That's not a term I would use. Twenty-three people live on the property.

Unless it's twenty-two now."

Hernandez finally glanced at the poor soul that lay beside us. "I see what you mean. There's no way to identify the victim."

We began walking. Zeus ambled beside me, wagging his tail again. We were going for a walk, and I'd even brought along a new friend.

"What's your role here?" Hernandez asked in a neutral tone as we reached the trees. He had to work at it. I wondered what he'd sound like without the self-discipline he was exerting.

"I'm a teacher."

"Yeah? Did somebody put you in charge or did you just tell everybody you're someone special?" he asked, unsuccessfully masking his feelings this time.

I glanced at him and didn't answer. Not engaging with that sort of energy was often the best way to calm it down.

As we drew close to the soaring redwoods, the temperature decreased markedly and a pine-like odor wafted our way. Zeus snorted the way he always did as we passed the first tree. I guess the smell became stronger at that point.

"I asked you a question," Hernandez asserted with even more energy.

So much for my strategy. "You want to know how I ended up here, doing what I do," I answered. "The answer is long and complicated. I'm sure we have more important things to talk about."

We reached the veranda of the diminutive cabin.

"I hope your answers about this body are more forthcoming, Tobin."

"They will be," I assured him.

Chapter 2

Once we'd settled into the two elderly rattan chairs in my office—mine behind an ancient wooden desk—and Zeus had lain near the door, still hopeful about a longer walk, Deputy Hernandez let me speak without interruption. Periodically, his attention ebbed, and his eyes fixed on various features of the room. Perhaps he believed he could learn more about me from what I'd chosen to surround myself with than from what I said. And perhaps he could. I couldn't read him well enough to know something like that.

The office decor wasn't especially memorable. A side wall was only barely visible behind floor-to-ceiling shelves packed with books. The opposite wall displayed three black and white photos of Western Canadian landscapes. Behind where I sat at my Goodwill desk, two sash windows overlooked the wide trunk of a redwood tree that had gradually blocked the view that must've been visible when the original summer camp had been built in the 1930s.

After I'd finished outlining my experience, Hernandez asked a series of increasingly irrelevant questions about the Brethren of Congruence. Why in the world would someone want to live out here in the middle of nowhere? Did the women in the community have equal rights? What kind of food did we eat? He seemed less interested in my answers than he did in diving into his next question.

I was beginning to understand. A significant backstory prompted his digressive interest—even in the midst of a murder investigation.

I was rescued by a detective in a shiny navy-blue suit. When he opened the door to my office without knocking, Zeus leapt to his feet, ready to defend me if the intruder happened to be another large dog. As it was, he sniffed the air desultorily and lay down again.

The detective's alert green eyes created a contrast with Deputy Hernandez's duller brown eyes. Slim, with wide shoulders, a long neck, and an equally long face, his energy impressed me. A block at his fourth chakra marred an otherwise impeccable meridian system. This indicated difficulty creating or maintaining relationships. I placed him in his mid-forties.

"Bill Cullen," the detective told me. "Matt, go round up everyone and get them in whatever room is big enough to hold them all."

"Okay." He strode out, more purposeful now that a colleague, or perhaps his boss, was watching him.

I marched around the desk and held my hand out. "Kade Tobin."

He shook it. "I know who you are. I know about this place." Cullen's tone and facial expression were effortlessly neutral.

"Sit," I suggested. "Why is that?"

"Susan Burke." He lowered himself carefully into the rickety-looking chair and watched my face.

I returned to my seat behind my desk. "I don't understand."

"She's one of your students. Correct?"

"Yes."

"She's also the district attorney's daughter," he told me.

"Ah, I didn't know that."

"So the DA asked me to look into you."

"I see," I said, matching his neutral tone. Apparently, emotions didn't have a place in real life police interviews, unlike all the TV shows I'd seen before sequestering myself on the land. Of course, concluding such a thing from an N of one didn't make a lot of sense. These thoughts tipped me off that I was a bit nervous. And overthinking again.

Hernandez had been enough of a lightweight not to trigger any major concern. He didn't pass the threshold of mattering to me emotionally. Cullen was another story.

"Aren't you curious what I found out about you?" Cullen asked. "And for that matter, how I did? There's not much out there, is there?

"I already know who I am. And we purposefully keep a low profile here."

"Why is that?" He leaned forward as though this was the first answer he truly cared about.

"We don't recruit," I explained. "People find us through word of mouth and the universe's will. And outsiders tend to misunderstand the nature of communities such as ours."

"Okay, that's enough about that." He waved his hand dismissively, as though I'd sidetracked the interview. "Tell me what you know about the body."

"Certainly. I'll try to go into more detail than I did with Deputy Hernandez. He seemed more interested in other things."

"His son recently converted to a sketchy

fundamentalist Christian church and moved to Tennessee. It's on his mind. He's a good man, though. Don't underestimate him."

I nodded and began telling him what I knew, this time including my inner monologue at the time. Cullen was an excellent listener. And his ongoing prompts were far more pertinent than the deputy's questions.

"Why do you think someone would dump a body here?" he asked when I was finished.

"She wasn't shot in the meadow?"

"Did you hear a shot?"

"No," I told him.

"Was there blood on the grass?"

"Not much."

"Do you think she walked here with only one shoe on?" Cullen asked.

I shook my head. Did he expect me to have deduced all this? I suppose I could've if I'd tried.

"Well, then. Why here?" Cullen asked.

"I can't imagine," I said.

"Someone with a grudge?"

I paused and considered that. "We've had several people leave the community when they've violated our rules. And one poor soul began believing I was a demon."

"Where is he now?"

"It was a woman, and I have no idea," I told Cullen.

"I'll get her information later. What rules did these other people break, and why might they hold grudges?"

"Sexual harassment in one case. Theft, in another, believe it or not. Why come here to steal?"

"With some people, it's a compulsion," Cullen said.

I nodded. "That's true. The third rule breaker—a

woman—attempted what you might call a coup."

"A coup? You mean she tried to get rid of you and take over?"

"Yes. She had certain impressive powers and a great deal of ambition," I told him.

"Powers?"

"Esoteric abilities—things that would just sound weird to you. Trust me."

"So what happened?" Cullen leaned back. His forward and back movements now seemed random. Perhaps he had a sore back.

"She and her followers—all eight of them—decided to leave and establish a new community at the south end of the county—a farm outside Watsonville."

He paused and cocked his head a bit like Zeus, who was now asleep in a corner of the room. After all, this conversation hadn't yielded any words associated with eating or walking.

"You don't appear to farm here," Cullen said.

"No, the land doesn't lend itself to that, and I don't know anything about it."

"So what do you do for money?" Now he leaned sideways.

"We're a non-profit that relies on donations," I told him.

"I see." Cullen nodded as though I'd confirmed something he already knew. "Well, I'll get all the details of these people you mentioned later, of course."

"Sure."

"Where were you last night?" Cullen asked.

"I led a meditation until nine, and then I retired to my yurt for the rest of the night."

"Alone?"

"Yes," I told him.

"The yurt is that thing that looks like a tent?" he asked, pointing quite accurately at the spot on the wall that corresponded with the yurt's location.

"Yes."

"In your story, you said your dog was outside and his howling woke you up." This time he gestured vaguely toward the door behind him. "Why didn't he bark earlier—when the body got dumped?"

"That's a good question. I didn't think of that." I was beginning to feel foolish.

"Maybe the murderer was someone he knows," Cullen said.

"Anything's possible, of course," I conceded, although that seemed unlikely.

"Hmm, we'll have to get back to that later. As you heard, I'm going to speak to your group after this, and then I'll conduct interviews with individual members."

"Sounds good."

"Is there anything you can do that will help with that?" Cullen asked.

"Let me introduce you and ask everyone to cooperate."

"Okay. Shall we?"

I nodded. We rose and headed out. Zeus trudged behind this time, his tail still. He'd figured out we were no fun. As soon as we were outside, he sprinted deeper into the forest to chase whatever he could find.

Chapter 3

From the veranda outside the cabin, I saw two men across the meadow examining the body. Hernandez's partner, Jason, had rigged up yellow tape suspended on tall metal spikes surrounding the forensic team. One of members of the forensic team wore a red polo shirt and khakis as he took photographs with an elaborate rig. The other one wore a white biohazard suit and blue plastic booties. This man kneeled and rolled over the body. Thankfully, I was too far away to make out any details.

Cullen placed his hand on my forearm to keep me moving, which I didn't appreciate.

"Your group is waiting for us," he reminded me.

In fact, every member of the community sat cross-legged on round, gray cushions in our multi-purpose Quonset hut. Had there been an empty one, I'd have readily spotted it as we strode through the rows of members, skirting a few who hadn't left enough space between them. It would've been easy enough to walk around the gathering since the room was far larger than we needed, but Cullen led the way and I followed.

Since it was expensive to heat the high-ceilinged structure, we had the furnace on a timer which wouldn't kick in for another hour. It was chilly. Many of our members wore hoodies or sweaters.

A squirrel scurried across the corrugated metal roof, startling the detective. The first time I'd heard that, I thought a deer had managed an impossible leap since the sound echoed so strongly in the building. Recovering quickly, Cullen waved Hernandez and Dearborn away from the raised wooden stage in front of us. They retreated to the rear doors, each folding his arms as though they'd practiced synchronizing their stances.

In the meantime, Cullen and I clambered up the three stairs to the stage.

"Good morning," I began after bowing my head to the community. "As you know by now, an unfortunate soul has been killed on our property, and the authorities are here to sort things out. As Jim instructed you, please cooperate with them in the manner he requested."

I phrased this carefully to remind them not to speak of our project while they otherwise cooperated. Hopefully, Cullen wouldn't be able to decode this.

I continued. "There is no reason to be fearful. It appears that someone brought the body onto our land. The murder has nothing to do with us, and no one here is in danger. Now I'd like to introduce Detective Cullen from the sheriff's department."

I moved to the side, and Cullen spoke, much louder than necessary, given the acoustics.

"First of all, I want to make it clear that despite what Mr. Tobin has stated, we have no idea at this time if the murder is connected to this organization or any individual in this room. In the early stages of an investigation, we do not rule out any possibility. That said, don't worry about your safety. We're here. We will catch the killer, and your community can go about its business as usual once we do." He paused to survey the room. I did too.

Everyone except two members sat still in lotus

positions. Carol was a classic hysteric—a prime candidate for Dr. Freud's practice. She rocked, shook her head furiously, and grimaced as though someone had jabbed her with a red-hot poker. I had been tempted to do the verbal equivalent of that on several occasions—she brought out the worst in me. My commitment to working with everyone who asked for help precluded my simply sending her on her way.

Ruth was another story altogether. Due to a neurological disorder, she shook and even convulsed sometimes when stressed. Needless to say, that interfered with her day-to-day functioning. At the moment, she wriggled like a fish suspended in the air on a hook, which discomfited several people sitting near her.

"In the meantime," Cullen continued, "we will be briefly questioning each of you, and we would appreciate anyone who heard or saw anything unusual last night to come forward at any time. You may approach me or either deputy that you see standing behind you."

Several heads swiveled. Most did not. Jason, the younger man, waved and smiled. He reminded me of a garrulous crossing guard who had demanded my attention as I sauntered to middle school. The elderly man's monologues always started with a similar wave.

Cullen turned to me and spoke softly. "Is there a room we can interview people in?"

"Sure. I'll show you when we're done here."

He addressed the community again. "Please remain in this room until we come to get you for individual interviews. After that, you may move freely around the property."

He turned to me again. "I didn't see any cars when I

arrived. Can your people go into town if they want? Do I need to tell them not to?"

"It's not necessary. We have a couple of vans parked at the back of the property where there's another driveway, but no one would use one under these circumstances."

Cullen glared at me. I didn't know why. "We need to talk," he growled.

I instructed the community to meditate on mortality while they awaited their turn to be interviewed.

Then Cullen marched me back to my office. Zeus rejoined us for the short walk, then peeled off at the doorway. It was a beautiful day. Why would he want to be indoors again? At the moment, I shared that attitude for other reasons.

This time, Cullen stood to the side in front of the wall of books and turned to glare at me where I sat at my desk again. He had morphed from good cop to bad cop, or maybe it would be fairer to say reasonably friendly cop to cranky cop.

"You didn't think to mention there was another access point to the property?" he asked.

He stood more erect now, which seemed like an attempt to loom over me. Since I was sitting and Cullen was already standing, the maneuver constituted overkill.

"I'm sorry." I told him. It was hard to project a sincere apology when my minor omission scarcely deserved such a strong reaction. I switched from appeasement to defense. "I thought you knew since I mentioned we had two vans and they aren't parked by the road where you came in."

He frowned. He didn't like that. His response was to become louder and a bit more aggressive, although still within the bounds of civility.

"What else have you left out?" he barked.

I thought that over. "I guess it would be helpful to know that a couple of members have police records. I assumed you'd look into that if you thought it was relevant. I don't."

"Why not?" Cullen asked.

"What does it matter if someone embezzled money twelve years ago? Or was convicted of drunk driving?"

"Do you think either of these criminals might've been violent in the past in some way you don't know about?"

"It's certainly possible, but I can't share what I don't know, can I? And labeling them as criminals is a stretch."

Cullen's eyes narrowed, and he moderated his tone. I couldn't tell if this was a strategy to manage me or a belated awareness that he was overreacting—letting his emotions drive his behavior.

"Look, Tobin. I have no reason to trust or mistrust what you say at this point. I can only hope you're being straight with me, and my instincts say you are. Nonetheless, you need to know you're a suspect. If I find out you knew the victim or you've lied to me, you're heading to the top of the list. And as far as I'm concerned, omitting information is lying."

"I understand. But to be clear, I didn't say I didn't know the victim. I said I didn't recognize her, which is not surprising given both the condition of the body and the way she was lying. Also, all of our members were present and accounted for in the assembly, so the victim couldn't be one of them."

"How do you know they were all there?"

"All the seats were taken."

"Okay, fair enough." He thought for a moment, looking down and to his left. "What if one of your people *is* the murderer?" he continued. "He could've removed his pillow before he took off. Pillows aren't the best way to take a head count, are they?"

"No, you're right. I'll get someone to check that out."

Cullen received a phone call, which he took while he turned his back to me. Perhaps he didn't want me to see the expression on his face as he listened to the caller.

"Yes? Uh-huh. Got it. Okay."

"News from the forensic team?" I asked.

"How did you know that?"

I shrugged.

"There's no harm in sharing this. They didn't find any ID on the body, but her face isn't totally ruined, so we'll probably find out who she is even if her prints aren't in our database."

"That's got to help find the killer."

"Of course." Cullen paused long enough that I thought he might be finished with me. He wasn't. "So tell me more about the Brethren of Congruence. For starters, I thought brethren means a group of men."

"Originally, yes. It was associated with monasteries. Now it has a broader definition."

"Which is?"

"Members of any organization, especially religious or spiritual groups," I told him.

"You're making a distinction there—using the word 'or' between religious and spiritual," Cullen pointed out. I was impressed by this perception. "Aren't religions spiritual, and vice-versa? Aren't those just words for the same thing?"

"Mostly, but not always. We're a spiritual organization, but we aren't religious, for example. We work toward advancing along individual spiritual paths—becoming closer to Oneness by achieving congruence with the big picture. That overlaps with some religious beliefs, of course."

I always try not to adopt a professorial tone when I explain things. That day, I didn't do a very good job of it.

"In plain English, please," Cullen requested.

I assumed the concept of congruence had been the sticking point. Someone capable of noticing an "or" in a sentence surely could've understood the rest.

"Sure," I responded. "Spiritual congruence is the concept of rearranging ourselves to come into harmony with the bigger picture around us. The world isn't going to adapt to suit us. We need to transform ourselves to match it as best we can in order to step away from an adversarial relationship with it. That doesn't serve anyone."

"Don't fight reality, in other words," Cullen responded.

"Exactly. Well put. But it goes deeper than that."

I was once again impressed that Cullen had not only immediately grasped the concept, but had also rephrased it more succinctly than I had.

"Okay, fine," he said, returning to his baseline neutral tone. "I don't need to know any more about that. I get the idea. As I told you earlier, I already did some research about you and your group, so I got my lid loosened about this stuff. What can you tell me about the population here? Who are these people?"

"Hmm. Let me think about that." After a time, I

continued. "Many people discover us because they're troubled."

"Uh-huh."

"At first, they're seeking a remedy for whatever their problems are, usually because everything else they've tried has failed. I'd say this represents about half of the Brethren. Unfortunately, this make for a rocky start since having specific goals isn't what I teach."

"Don't people have to aspire to be better if they want to get somewhere?" Cullen asked. "Don't they have to solve their problems?"

"Absolutely. What you and I have said isn't contradictory. To my ears, anyway. Aspiring is something I encourage. We all need to aim ourselves in beneficial directions—in a general way. But striving, craving, or becoming overly focused on specific outcomes are very different animals. They're based on the idea that we're in charge—that our ideas about how things should be are trustworthy and that we can shape life to suit us. The point I'm making is that you may be surprised to find a more screwed-up population than you expect."

I paused and realized what I was doing. "Sorry about the diatribe. I'm accustomed to talking to my students, not to the likes of you."

Cullen nodded his acknowledgment of my apology. "Screwed-up, huh? That doesn't sound very holy."

"No one's holy here, Detective."

He nodded his acknowledgement of this as well. It looked to be a go-to move for him. "What about the other half of your people?" he asked.

"We have seekers of all varieties—all shapes, sizes, and stages of development. There's no way to characterize them. See for yourself."

"I will. Speaking of which, I better get to it." He took a slow step toward the door. "It's going to be a long day with so many suspects."

"I understand."

He took another step toward the door, even slower this time. Perhaps he was giving me a chance to get the last word in.

I spoke up, pleased to have the opportunity. "It might be helpful if I sat in on your interviews," I told him. This was important to me for several reasons. If he didn't immediately agree, I was prepared to push back.

He pivoted. "Why's that?"

"I know these people quite well. I think I'll be able to tell if someone's lying. And my presence will make it less intimidating for the members. As you can imagine, they trust me. My being in the room validates what you're doing—making it more likely they'll share what they know."

The words fell out of me. I was mildly surprised by how articulate I sounded. Ordinarily, I had to ponder a bit to construct a list of reasons about anything. In my experience, this type of flow meant that Spirit was at work—that whatever the topic was, it was too important to the big picture to leave the nuts and bolts to me.

Cullen cocked his head and then nodded it while it was still a bit sideways. "All right. Let's try it. But strictly as an observer."

"Of course."

Chapter 4

We set up in Jim's office, which had three chairs versus the two in mine. The roomier, but darker room was in a corner of a worse-for-wear building beyond the community's well. It also housed a small library, a private meditation room, and a storage area. Originally, it had been a floorless shed that smelled like manure. One of the first things the community had teamed up to do was turn it into a usable space. At that time, our finances dictated salvage materials and only a modicum of attention to aesthetics.

The office was distinctly cheerless, sporting only one thing on the dingy sheetrock walls—a framed diploma from Jim's long-deceased dog's obedience school. When I'd asked him about this, he'd told me that it was emblematic of what hard work could accomplish.

Papers were strewn all over Jim's gray metal desk and the tops of two wooden filing cabinets that sat beside it. Jim believed that at any moment hackers could erase everything from the ancient computer we'd inherited from the previous owner, so he'd relegated it to the worn linoleum floor. It sat underneath a casement window with a makeshift metal crank—a pair of pliers with the handles duct-taped together.

In our counseling sessions, I worked with Jim on the remnants of his paranoia, which he came by honestly in his family of origin. His father had been a fugitive, always looking over his shoulder as he moved the family from state to state.

Cullen surveyed the room once he'd lowered himself onto a plaid upholstered chair that had once sat in the waiting room of a dental clinic. We'd found the other two weathered wooden chairs at an auction liquidating a defunct high school in Salinas.

The detective sniffed the stale, musty air in the room, and I found myself following his lead. I immediately wished I hadn't. Did Jim ever open a window or wipe down the specks of dark mold I spied on the baseboards?

"This is the Brethren's admin office?" Cullen's tone reflected surprise; he accentuated the higher pitch of the implied question mark. What did he expect?

"Yes."

By chance, the first interviewee was Ralph Edevane, who had also been my first new student after arriving in Santa Cruz from Washington State. We met while he was in college at the UC in town. I would've said we met by chance if I believed in the concept.

Ralph's acne-scarred cheeks conveyed a fierceness à la a film villain—why were they always ugly?—and his pugnacious tone sometimes supported that impression. His eating disorder rendered him severely underweight, and he was prematurely bald. I was quite fond of him.

"So, Mr. Edevane," Cullen began after I introduced the two, "tell me about yourself."

"That's a rather open-ended question, isn't it?"

Cullen's eyebrows lifted, which opened his brown eyes a bit. "Yes, is that a problem?"

"No, I'm just commenting. That's how a lot of job

interviews start." He leaned back in his chair and squinted. Ralph wore contact lenses, but only when he was in the mood.

"Are you going to tell me about yourself or not?" Cullen asked impatiently. Once again, the detective had suddenly flipped from one intonation to another, more negative one.

"There's no reason to get hostile," Ralph said. "It would help if you told me what you want to know. Do you want to know about my childhood? My former career? My relationship history? Maybe you want to hear about my spiritual path. All of these are 'about me.' "

Cullen turned to me. "Is he always like this?"

I smiled. "Pretty much."

Ralph didn't seem to mind this digression at his expense. In fact, he smiled, too. I think he took pride in his ability to insert obstreperousness into pretty much any conversation.

Okay," Cullen said to Ralph. "Tell me what brought you here and what it's like for you living here. How's that?"

"Excellent. I'd be happy to." He didn't look happy at all. He'd probably been looking forward to more verbal jousting. "After nearly dying from an earthquake overseas, I became interested in metaphysics. After all, what's the point of sleepwalking my way through life when it could end at any minute? Also, I realized I wasn't in charge the way I'd thought. Something greater than me was out there, and I wanted to know about it. I read whatever I could get my hands on. Then I met Sri Tobin and I knew I'd found my teacher."

"Sri? I thought Mr. Tobin's first name was Kade."

"It's an honorific—like Pastor Dave or…"

"Saint Francis?" Cullen suggested, frowning.

Ralph laughed. "Hardly. Sri Tobin would be the first to say he's just a man—a man who's farther down the road than the rest of us. That's all. Everyone will get there in their own time. Anyway, I'm the only one who calls him that."

"What about this death experience? Did you go into the white light and all that?" Cullen asked, leaning forward as he had with me, but hadn't yet with Ralph.

"What's that got to do with the murder?" Ralph asked.

Cullen shrugged. "Nothing. I'm just curious."

"Well, in my case, I passed out and then I sort of woke up but I wasn't really awake, and I was surrounded by absolutely nothing—a void so expansive and profound, I couldn't begin to describe it. I was nothing, too." Ralph smiled wanly as his eyes unfocused.

The detective's eyebrows shot up. "And you liked that?"

He couldn't reconcile the expression on Ralph's face with what he imagined the experience would be like.

"There wasn't anything to like or not like," Ralph told him.

"Okay, never mind. What's this about metaphysics? I've heard that word, but I want to know what you meant when you said it."

I was struck by how Cullen had regressed to Hernandez's approach to questioning. Why would he be interested in the answers to these questions? Could he tell subtle things about people when they talked about what was important to them? Maybe he was educating himself so he'd better understand the rest of the day's interviewees.

Ralph was happy to explain. He'd been an education major before transferring to computer science. "The dictionary says metaphysics is the branch of philosophy that deals with the first principles of things, including abstract concepts such as being, knowing, substance, cause, identity, time, and space."

"Did you memorize that?" Cullen asked.

"Yes," Ralph told him, smirking. His ego was identified with being the guy who could quote things verbatim. Whenever he did it, that smirk appeared.

"As I said before, what's it mean to you?" Cullen asked. "I don't care about the dictionary definition."

"That would take some time to explain."

"Fine. Avoid the question if you want. Just know that dodging questions doesn't reflect well on you."

Ralph raised his voice. "So now I'm a murder suspect because I choose not to share my personal philosophy? Does that make any sense? Do you hear yourself?"

Cullen waved that away. "What about the second thing I asked you?"

"Are you testing my memory?" Ralph was calmer now, but he'd be easily triggered back into annoyance.

"Actually, yes I am," Cullen told him. "Do you remember everything?"

"Not quite, but mostly," Ralph told him. "To answer your question about life here, it has its plusses and minuses. It's peaceful for the most part, although we all endure several challenging personalities that, frankly, I wouldn't tolerate if I were in charge."

"So you wish you were?" Cullen leaned sideways now, and his mobile eyebrows danced upward. I decided he did suffer from back pain.

"Oh no. It's a thankless job, and I'm nowhere near qualified."

"It seems like a cushy gig to me. Tobin sits around and shares what he thinks is wisdom, and everybody acts like he's the best thing since sliced bread."

"Oh, I love that," Ralph said, clapping his hands. The sudden noise startled me, and I flinched. "Sliced bread!" he exclaimed. "Did you know they invented toasters before sliced bread was commercially available?"

Cullen held his hands up in surrender as if to say "You win, I'm not going to keep trying to get what I want from you about all this." "What do you know about this murder?" he said out loud.

"Absolutely nothing."

"If someone in your community did it, who do you think that would be?"

"No one."

"You have nothing at all to offer?"

"That's right."

Cullen took a deep breath and shook his head. "Go get whoever was sitting next to you, would you?"

"Sure. Good luck, detective."

When he'd left, Cullen spoke. "You work with this guy? You can talk to him without wanting to slap him around?"

I laughed. "My slapping days are over. Ralph's a good guy. You just have to learn how to bring out the best in him."

"I'm beginning to think your job isn't as easy as I thought," Cullen said.

"Among other things, it's a great deal of responsibility." I thought about the interview. "Why didn't you ask if Ralph had an alibi?"

"Honestly, I forgot. I'll talk to him again later."

Wayne Robbins was up next. A burly, working-class guy who was a mainstay in the kitchen, he rarely spoke beyond a question or two following one of my talks. That morning, he was only wearing a faded black T-shirt and brown corduroy jeans, despite the cool air.

"Tell me about yourself," Cullen began.

"I'm here. I'm working on myself." His voice was pitched as low as anyone I'd ever heard. At one time, I'd toyed with the idea of starting a chorus or a barbershop quartet, inspired by the rare pitch of his voice. Unfortunately, Wayne was tone deaf and completely uninterested in what he called "high school clubs."

"Where were you last night?" Cullen asked.

"When?"

"Let's say from ten until the morning."

"It's lights out at ten in the dorm," Wayne told him. "Then I slept until five thirty."

Wayne puffed out his chest and tilted his head back so he was looking down at Cullen. He wasn't quite in a defiant body posture, but it was close. I wondered if he'd had negative experiences with law enforcement in the past.

"Any witnesses to that?" Cullen asked.

"How would I know? I was asleep." Now his wide, toothy mouth frowned, and his deep-set eyes narrowed.

"What's your background?" the detective asked.

"That's none of your business," Wayne told him, transforming his frown into a scowl.

"I'll be the judge of that," Cullen said.

"Judge all you want." He crossed his arms, accentuating his biceps. All in all, the compendium of movements and posture constituted a strong nonverbal message—"Back the hell off, buddy."

"Why don't you want me to know?" Cullen asked, employing a quiet, chummy tone.

"Why should I?" Wayne replied, maintaining his belligerence.

Cullen looked at me, so I spoke up. "This is voluntary, Wayne," I told him. "I know you don't like to talk about yourself, and you don't have to. But I'm sure we all want this murderer found, so if you know anything that might help. Please speak up."

"I don't," he said, and stood. "Is that it?"

Cullen nodded, and Wayne took off.

"What's with him?" Cullen asked me, shifting once again in the chair I knew to be quite comfortable. "Is he that way all the time?" Cullen continued.

"I don't know Wayne very well. He's quiet. He's private. And clearly, something about you rubbed him the wrong way. That's all I can tell you."

"Tobin, we're two for two with pain-in-the-ass people." He shook his head slowly. "Can I expect more of the same all day long? Do I need to go get a cattle prod or something?"

I smiled. "Like I said, a lot of people are here to remedy their problems, but that takes different forms. You're going to have an easy time with most people. And aren't you accustomed to uncooperative witnesses?"

"Hey, if anybody witnessed anything, I'll be happy as a clam whether they're a pain in the ass or not."

"Why do you think clams are happy?" I asked, trying to change the mood. Cullen's current energy was mildly toxic.

"I know that one. The full idiom is 'Happy as a clam at high tide.' That's when no one can get at them. When you taste good, you've got to have protection."

"Ah." I actually knew that, but Cullen's had energy shifted. Mission accomplished.

Next up was Phil Karanos, a former trial lawyer and a respected member of our community. In his forties, his gray hair notwithstanding, he was probably the fittest Brethren member. I often spied him running the perimeter of our property.

I asked Phil once about his last name since he didn't even slightly resemble any Greeks I'd ever known. He'd told me all his brothers were short, had black curly hair, and looked nothing like him. The family joke was that Phil resembled the mail carrier. He might've even believed this, he told me, except the carrier was a woman.

All in all, his squarish, flat face inspired confidence. His deep-set brown eyes were alert; the rest of his features were unremarkable.

"Mr. Karanos," Cullen began once I'd introduced the two, "Mr. Tobin tells me you have a legal background."

"Yes."

"Does that give you any special insight into the crime here?"

"I don't see how," Phil answered. "If you have any specific legal questions, I'd be glad to answer them."

More than most, Phil was dedicated to being in service whenever he could. Another Brethren member called him a junior bodhisattva, referencing a Buddhist concept. Half a dozen members came to us from various Buddhist backgrounds. None of my teachings clashed with that tradition.

"You've been here a long time?" Cullen asked Phil.

I didn't know why he assumed that. Perhaps Phil's mature, reasonable responses contrasted so sharply with Ralph and Wayne's that he seemed to be an advanced student.

"Two and a half years," Phil told him.

"Why did you come?" Cullen asked.

"I was burnt out in my career, my wife left me, my son moved to Indonesia, and I knew I had to make a change." He stated all this matter-of-factly. He'd long since let go of his pre-spiritual angst.

"But why here?" Cullen persisted.

"Actually, it was because of a dream I had," Phil told him, a faraway look in his eye.

"Okay, let's move on." I think Cullen would've rolled his eyes if he thought that wouldn't interfere with the interview. "Are you aware of anyone here who might be capable of violence?"

"No." Phil shook his head emphatically.

"Do you know of any reason someone would wish to discredit your organization?" Cullen asked.

"Yes, actually. I briefly came out of retirement to defend the Brethren against accusations that we had inherited our land improperly. We won in court."

Cullen turned to me. "Do you know about this?"

"Of course."

"And you didn't tell me?" Aggressive cop was back. "Okay, I'll get the details from you later. We need to keep moving here. I've got a lot more people to talk to." Cullen turned back to Phil. "So you think these people in the lawsuit might've committed this murder?"

"Absolutely not. Who would kill someone to

discredit a community such as ours? It would be tremendous overkill. Just a juicy scandal of some sort would do us in. And we're talking about a grieving family here—not a pack of criminals. I was just answering your question as you asked it."

"So you think these people would be happy if your group was discredited, but you don't think they're involved in this crime?" Cullen asked.

"That's right."

"How about you, Mr. Tobin? What do you think?"

"I agree," I said. "I think that's a dead end."

Cullen asked a few more questions, and then sent Phil on his way. The detective briefly questioned a dozen more people before he met a member he truly grilled—Jasmine Hammond. From the start, it was clear to both of us she was lying.

Jasmine's skin tone was arresting—the darkest I'd ever seen—and she had no African roots. Apparently, there are several ethnic groups in India with that pigmentation. Her small features, including a notable snub nose, could've been attractive in a girlish sort of way. On a fifty-year-old, they looked misplaced—as though her face had been someone's first effort to create a photoshopped image. As always, she smelled like her name—Jasmine.

"So you say you were alone last night?" Cullen asked Jasmine again.

"Yes, sir."

"The others told me about the dorms you live in. Why weren't you in the women's dorm?"

"Like I said, I was sick so I went outside to throw up and then I fell asleep under that big tree behind the dorm."

"Was there dew this morning?" he asked.

Jasmine vigorously nodded. "Sure, there's almost always dew down there."

"So you got wet? Maybe you have stains on your clothes?"

"It's a pretty leafy tree," Jasmine replied. "And I changed clothes."

"So we'll find wet ones in the dorm?" Cullen asked.

Jasmine didn't respond. Her eyes darted toward the door. For a moment, I thought she might bolt.

"There was a full moon last night," Cullen continued. "Did you see it?"

"Oh, yes. Beautiful." She'd recovered already, happy to be able to agree with Cullen about something.

"So if we went over to the tree, we'd see vomit on the ground?" he continued.

"Oh, I cleaned it up."

"How?"

"What do you mean how?" Jasmine asked, stalling.

"What did you use to clean it?" Cullen asked.

"Uh, sticks and leaves."

Cullen was doing a masterful job of trapping Jasmine in her lies. I couldn't imagine she'd committed the murders, but then why was she lying?

"Jasmine," I broke in, "this is a murder investigation. You're turning yourself into a suspect by lying. There was no moon last night, and you're not very good at lying. What is it you don't want us to know? How bad could it be?"

"Pretty bad." She hung her head and slumped in her chair.

Cullen and I waited.

"I took one of the vans to see Greg." Jasmine began

to cry into her hands.

"Who is this Greg?" Cullen asked her.

I answered for Jasmine. She needed a few moments to gather herself. "He's her abusive ex—the reason she's had to visit the emergency room multiple times. We had an agreement about this. One more time and Jasmine agreed to leave the community to move in with her mother in Detroit—where she'd be safe from Greg."

"So her motive for misleading us is her desire to remain here?" Cullen asked.

"That, and shame. Jasmine, look at me. This is a relapse. You're going to let go of Greg. I know you will. You're just not ready to yet, that's all."

"I hate my mother. She's a horrible woman," she told me between sobs. "I can't go back to Detroit."

"Then why did you agree to our deal?"

"I thought I was really through with Greg. I never thought I'd have to leave." She looked up, her dark eyes open wide despite her tears, and her mouth twisted sideways.

I thought about it and then offered her a gentle half smile. "I'll tell you what. If you cooperate with the detective and promise not to tell anyone I didn't follow through on the consequences we agreed on, I'll forgive this transgression."

Jasmine's tears continued to leak onto her convex cheeks, but now the rest of her face looked hopeful.

"You will?"

"Yes. Now tell Detective Cullen everything. If you were out and about, you may have seen something important."

"I think I did," she reported.

"What was that?" Cullen asked.

"There was a car going by the property really slowly as I was driving away. When the driver saw me, he sped up toward the highway."

"Did you get a good look at him?"

"No." Jasmine shook her head. "I guess saying it was a man doesn't narrow it down much, does it?"

"This could be a big help." Cullen told her. "What about the car?"

"I think it was white."

"A sedan, an SUV, a pick-up truck?"

"Not a truck. Other than that, I don't know. I'm not a car person." Jasmine shrugged as she told him. Then she sat up straight and looked Cullen directly in the eye for the first time as he spoke again.

"Now, did you get a sense that this person was arriving or leaving the property?" Cullen asked.

"Neither one. He was just driving by in the middle of the night. I'm not saying he was the murderer or anything. Maybe it was someone who was lost."

"Then why would he take off when he saw the van?" Cullen asked. "Wouldn't he have stopped and asked you for directions?"

"I guess so."

The detective talked to Jasmine for another ten minutes but garnered nothing else helpful.

When we were alone, he asked me if the keys to the vans were available to anyone.

"Yes, we operate on the honor system."

"You know, Tobin, I was impressed with the way you handled Ms. Hammond. That little smile you came up with when you were forgiving her was really effective. I've got to put that in my repertoire."

"You don't think it sincerely reflected my emotion

at the time?" I tried to project sincerity again, having been busted the first time with Jasmine.

"Nope. Where'd you learn it? I either smile or I don't. Yours was right in-between those two."

"Look at most any statue of Buddha. He had it down." I half smiled again.

"Yeah, I can see that. Put on a little weight, get more followers, and maybe with that smile you'll get a statue someday, too." He tried a half smile, which wasn't half bad.

I was tempted to offer pointers—just use the corners of his mouth, make sure his eyes matched, and soften his voice while he did it.

"No, thanks," I said instead. "Once the statue phase starts, the teachings go out the window." I could see I'd lost him, and he didn't care that I had. "It's interesting to watch you work, too," I told Cullen. "I can see you're picking up more than I am. How long have you been doing this?"

"Too damn long."

Chapter 5

Only two more interviews yielded relevant results. By this time, we'd eaten lunch in my office—stir-fried veggies and tofu—and Cullen was beginning to leak further frustration since he wasn't getting what he was looking for. Answers invoking energy fields and other dimensions weren't the meat and potatoes of a police investigation. Quite a few members were enthralled with esoteric concepts such as these, working them into most conversations. I'd given up trying to discourage this.

Interesting interviewee number one was Alize Zugasti, who was a Basque illegal immigrant from the Spanish side of the Pyrenees. She'd overstayed a tourist visa eight years earlier. Naturally, she was suspicious of authorities and guarded in her responses. Cullen, ignorant of this backstory, interpreted her reticence as something more sinister.

It probably didn't help that Alize was sweating profusely, with the accompanying odor that one would expect. I'd gathered this was some sort of glandular condition.

Visually, Alize reminded me of a former partner. Both were wiry with long, taut muscles. In Alize's case, I don't think she was a rock climber, but she must've done something to earn her musculature before she came to us.

The resemblance ended there. Melanie had been

Norwegian. Alize looked just as I would imagine if someone told me she was from the Spanish side of the Pyrenees. Her long, rugged Hispanic face was easy to picture while she herded sheep on the side of a mountain. This Basque stereotype was probably apocryphal, but tell that to my imagination.

"Look, Ms. Zugasti," Cullen began again, "I'm sensing you aren't interested in helping me." His tone implied he was genuinely puzzled. "Why is that? Did you have negative experiences with authorities back in Mexico?"

"Cullen," I broke in. "That's offensive. Why do you assume that anyone with a Spanish accent is from Mexico?" Of course, I did the same thing all the time. I said this for Alize's benefit.

"I'm sorry. You're right. I apologize," Cullen told her. "But I still want to know what's the deal with you, ma'am?"

That riled her more than the Mexican reference. "I'm *not* a ma'am, thank you very much. You are an irritating man. That's why I don't want to talk to you."

"My job isn't to get everyone to like me. It's to solve crimes."

Cullen turned to me, so I stepped in. "The detective is only interested in the murder. If you know anything, I'm requesting that you tell him."

"All right. I don't know if this is important, but when I got up to use the restroom last night, I saw that Martha's bed was empty. I don't want to get her in trouble. I'm sure she's not involved in this."

"Why are you sure?" Cullen asked.

"She was a nun," I intervened. "Martha is a very gentle soul—a role model for other members."

"I see. And that's all you know?" he asked Alize.

"I had a dream which may help you."

"Oh, really?" He started to roll his eyes and then restrained himself.

"Listen to her, detective," I said. "Some of her dreams are prescient."

"They're what?"

"Predictive," I told him.

"You mean your dreams tell the future?" he asked her.

"Sometimes."

Cullen waved his hand. "Okay, go ahead."

"I saw a man in black standing over a woman by the side of a very straight road."

"That's it?"

"Yes. I think there will be another murder," Alize told him, "I think that was a dead woman on the ground."

"That's your interpretation?"

"That's what I knew in the dream when I saw them," Alize corrected.

"Okay, thank you for your help. Please send Martha in."

When we were alone, I said, "If there's another murder, please don't assume Alize is involved because she predicted it. This ability of hers is real. There's a lot that goes on that you don't know about."

"I'm sure. Right now, I don't care. What else can you tell me about this Martha?"

"She really is the least likely candidate in the community to commit a crime. To be clear, I'm sure no one here is a murderer, but if someone is, it's definitely not Martha."

"So where was she last night?" Cullen asked.

"Let's find out. We won't have to worm the truth out of *her*."

Martha always wore denim overalls over a white waffle-knit thermal shirt unless it was truly hot. Then she switched to no shirt at all, revealing the sides of her breasts under the overall's bib. This had always seemed wildly out of character to me. An African-American, Martha was short and stout, with a round face topped by a 1970s-style afro. By virtue of her protuberant ears and a noticeably asymmetrical nose, Martha may have originally sequestered herself as a nun in response to a lack of social success as a teen.

Following introductions, Martha began sharing her story before Cullen asked her to. Her voice didn't match her appearance. It belonged on a fifteen-year-old girl.

"I woke at two thirty-five with an urgent need for prayer."

Cullen raised his eyebrows and glanced at me. "You have them pray?"

"Folks here do as they please," I told him. "Many members retain their original faiths while they study here."

"You're still a Catholic?" he asked Martha.

"I never was. I'm a Buddhist."

Martha had lived on the grounds of a temple on Kauai for seven years. She'd told me that even there, after several markedly negative experiences in Asia, being Black lowered her status. It was one of the reasons she'd searched for a new spiritual community and found us.

"I heard you used to be a nun," Cullen asked. "They have those?"

"Indeed they do," Martha told him, smiling. This

wasn't the first time she'd run across Cullen's misconception.

"I didn't know that," he told her. "Please continue."

"My mind was full of impure thoughts last night, to use Catholic terminology you may be more familiar with."

"It's okay. Talk Buddhist-style if you want," Cullen told her."

"All right. I was ruminating about a particular sexual encounter from before I took vows, and I was having trouble stepping away from these unhelpful thoughts."

"Unhelpful thoughts versus impure thoughts? Buddhists think about this differently?" Cullen asked.

"Exactly. I don't judge. I attempt to be observational without attaching right or wrong to anything."

"Surely you think this murder on your doorstep is wrong," Cullen said, frowning.

"Well, there are limits, of course," Martha told him, "but generally, I try to accept whatever happens without adding my spin onto it."

"Interesting. Please continue. I'm sure what you're telling us is a delicate matter. I appreciate your candor."

"Not at all. The truth is what matters," she said. "If telling it brings up feelings for me, it's my job to manage those internally. I've found that when I avoid something that's uncomfortable, it just sets up a day of reckoning. That usually ends up worse than whatever the original experience would've been."

Martha's discourses were always a pleasure to listen to, no matter the topic. And when she spoke, her dazzlingly white teeth drew my eye to her smile.

"It sounds like you should be running this place," Cullen told her, glancing at me to see how I reacted to this. "That's some heavy-duty philosophy there."

"She could," I said, smiling.

"At any rate, I prefer to pray in the assembly hall," Martha said.

"Why is that?"

"The energy from years of group meditation has rendered it conducive to connecting with Spirit."

"Here's this energy deal again," Cullen said. "It's hard to buy into, no matter how many people here talk about it."

"Would you like a demonstration?" I asked. I don't know why I said that. Some things just bubbled up. Usually I found out why afterward.

"What would that look like?" His skepticism was obvious on his face.

Martha watched us with interest.

"It's better if I don't tell you that," I explained. "Your subconscious might resist if it knows more about it."

Cullen looked back and forth between Martha and myself. "All right, what the hell."

"Martha," I instructed, "let's send chi to Detective Cullen's heart chakra. Not too much—just to give him a taste."

She nodded and formed her hands into a particular configuration, as did I. We closed our eyes and let the energy flow through us and out our fingertips. The practice required no effort at this stage in our respective paths. We just had to get out of the way and let it happen.

After a minute or so, I said, "That's enough," and opened my eyes. A sweet, authentic half smile was on Martha's face. Cullen look dazed, slumped in his chair with glazed eyes, his head lolling to the side.

"Oh dear," Martha said. "Perhaps Mr. Cullen is more sensitive than we thought."

Cullen snapped to attention, sitting up ramrod straight as he blinked furiously.

"Holy shit! It's real. That was amazing. Wow." He started to stand.

"Sit a minute," I recommended. "Your system has been jolted—in a good way—but it'll take a few more minutes to adjust. How do you feel?"

"I feel great! I'm not tired anymore. Thank you."

Cullen stretched his arms up and jiggled his legs as though he were dancing in his chair. I don't think he was aware of this.

"I have more to tell you," Martha said. "Are you alert enough to hear?"

"I believe so." He nodded furiously and seemed to be having trouble stopping. An infusion of chi often freed up bound energy. Our bodies aren't sure what to do with it at first.

"When I was coming out of the building after praying," Martha began, "I heard Zeus growl around the side of the building. I assumed he'd encountered an animal since I'd heard that before several times in daylight—once with a stray cat and once with a family of raccoons. In hindsight, perhaps it was someone who was involved in the murder."

"I need to take a minute here," Cullen said. His gaze moved upward and he breathed slowly and deeply as he relaxed his body.

"Tell us how you're feeling." I said. "If you're having difficulties, perhaps we can help."

He waved away my concern. "It's just strange. It's like something loosened in my chest."

"Something did." I let Cullen breathe for a while. "Do you need to keep talking to Martha?" I finally asked him.

"I dunno. Have you got more, Martha?"

"Just one more thing. As I was lying in bed after that, I heard someone crying."

Chapter 6

When we'd finished the rest of the interviews, I asked Cullen if he wanted to stay for dinner, expecting him to refuse my offer.

"Let me take you out," he said. "You like Thai?"

I was surprised, but I recovered quickly. "Sure. That would be great. I'll just talk to Jim so he can run the evening program for me."

Cullen drove us in his electric car. I'd never been in one before. I expected it to be totally silent. It wasn't. Cullen was.

He turned left on Highway 17—away from Santa Cruz toward the Santa Clara Valley—in order to drive against the flow of commuter traffic. A lot of tech workers lived on the coast and traveled over the mountains to Silicon Valley for work, returning en masse on a mountain road never designed for so many vehicles.

Even so, the traffic was heavy with commuters who'd figured out where to live and work without adding an extra hour to their commute. Almost all the fast-moving cars were single occupancy, and most were expensive makes and models.

I imagined that Cullen was processing the most out-of-the-box experience of his life. For many, receiving an infusion of esoteric energy was sufficient to launch an individual into a metaphysical quest. After all, if *that* was real, what other extraordinary phenomena might be out there?

I knew this wasn't Cullen's life script. I was curious what was. It wasn't until we'd sat and ordered at an elaborately decorated Thai restaurant in downtown Los Gatos that he finally spoke to me.

"This energy thing doesn't necessarily mean you're the real deal," he said, toying with a package of throwaway chopsticks on his paper placemat.

"No, it doesn't," I agreed. "Many people can manipulate energy. Some study to do so. For others, it's a side effect of their spiritual progress. It's rarely important. It's more of a parlor trick."

"Then why did you do it?" He leaned forward, his eyes locked on mine.

"I thought you'd treat my people with more respect if you experienced energy for yourself," I told him. "Despite your granting us permission, I see now it was presumptuous of me." I'd thought about this on the drive. "You couldn't know what you were signing up for. I probably shouldn't have asked Martha to help, either. We nearly overwhelmed you. Her chi is smoother and less powerful, so I thought the combination would be easier to assimilate."

"No, no. Don't apologize," he said. "I'm grateful—just confused. Weren't *you* a mess when this happened to you?"

"Sure—much more than you. I was thirty-two, and it came out of the blue. I was already pretty shaky in the mental health department."

"What *is* that energy?" he asked after a diminutive server took our orders. "You called it chi."

"It's life force—what animates the world," I told him. "The same way there's electricity—an invisible force—there are other subtle energies in play. Most people aren't tuned into them."

"This could be some sort of trick," Cullen said.

He was doing his best to dismiss a destabilizing experience and losing the battle. This was a common reaction to any spiritual emergence or paradigm-defying event. If whatever happened could be discredited, we wouldn't have to change to accommodate it, would we?

"Yes," I agreed. "It could be a trick. Did it feel like one?"

"No. While the energy was flowing, it felt realer than anything ever has."

"There you go."

"Let's talk about the murder," Cullen suggested, shaking his head. He wasn't ready to meet this head on. He'd get to it when it was time.

"Sure.

"What's your take on the murder after all these interviews?" Cullen asked.

"I'm not sure if any of this derives from the interviews, but it seems as though an intruder was on the property," I said. "Perhaps he found some way to disable Zeus. Perhaps he has a grudge and chose our land to dump the body as a disruption to the serenity we've created. The bigger question is: why shoot that woman in the head in the first place?"

"Yes, motive reveals a great deal," Cullen agreed.

I paused and then spoke again. "Why are you discussing the case with me?" I asked. "Why are we dining together? This can't be standard procedure. You said yourself that I'm a suspect."

"You know, I'm not sure," Cullen responded, cocking his head sideways. "After the energy thing, I just feel a connection with you. And you're obviously sharp about people. The other thing is that my partner is out on medical leave. I'm not used to working cases by myself."

"I hope it's nothing serious," I said.

"Unfortunately, it is." There was pain on his face. It was clear the two men were close.

"You might bring him up to our land sometime. We have a healer," I told him.

"A healer, huh? Well, I'm not discounting anything anymore. We'll see. Anyway, what do you say? You want to keep helping me?"

"Sure, if it's okay with your boss," I said.

"What he doesn't know won't hurt him," Cullen told me.

"That's your call. You can change your mind if the arrangement threatens your career."

He nodded. "Yeah, I can. Don't worry about it."

Our food came, and it was delicious. Even the smells in the place made my mouth water—a combination of ginger, coconut, and garlic. I hadn't eaten in a restaurant in a long time. I even had dessert—mango sticky rice.

****

In the morning, Cullen texted me the preliminary forensic report, which I read after Zeus and I walked in the state park forest beside our property. Once again, I was struck by his willingness to collaborate, despite Cullen's explanation at the restaurant.

The weapon was a large caliber handgun, employed at close range. The shooter had to have been at least six feet tall, based on the angle of the entrance and exit wounds. The victim had been shot between two and four a.m. She'd have died instantly.

She was a fit, fair-skinned Caucasian, about twenty

years old. There was no evidence of sexual activity. She'd eaten Mexican food for dinner. She wore a cheap digital watch. Her teeth were poorly cared for. She was mildly diabetic, and she'd broken her arm as a child.

I was quite surprised that all this information had been gathered in less than a day. I texted this to Cullen, who replied that both the sheriff and the DA were up for reelection and a quick arrest in a high-profile case would help them at the polls. The sheriff had ordered the coroner to work all night.

While I meditated in my yurt a couple of hours later, Cullen called. Normally, I wouldn't have answered, since before I gave my number to Cullen, no one knew it, guaranteeing that a call was from a telemarketer.

"Good morning," Cullen greeted. "What do you think about the text I sent?"

"I'm sure you gleaned more from it than I did. For what it's worth, I would check local Mexican restaurants if I were you. Not that many Anglos make Mexican food at home. If someone could make a sketch reconstructing what her face had been and show it around, you might get a hit, and if she paid with a credit card, there's your ID."

Cullen paused before continuing. "I didn't send any photos. How do you know what the bullet did to her face—that it needed reconstructing? All I said before was that it wasn't totally ruined."

"I saw the back of her head."

"And?"

"I know what a face looks like on the other side of a head wound like that," I told him.

"You were in the military?"

"No, I was an EMT in a big city," I said.

"You must've been a lot different back then."

"I certainly was," I agreed.

"You liked that kind of work?" he asked.

"For a while."

"Okay, what else did you get from the forensic report?" Cullen asked.

"The murderer was probably a man," I said. "Very few women are that tall and they generally don't use large caliber handguns,."

"I'm with you on that," Cullen said.

"I was struck by the watch," I continued. "Who wears something like that these days? Maybe she didn't have a cell phone."

"Everybody does."

"I suppose so," I conceded. "But you didn't find one on her, I gather. That could be significant."

Cullen nodded.

I continued. "Crappy teeth makes me think of English people, although I know that's unlikely. Maybe she grew up poor—in some rural area without much in the way of medical services."

"That's a stretch, but keep it coming," Cullen told me.

"A close-range shot to the back of the head suggests that the victim knew the killer. Would she let a random person get up close, let alone turn her back on the guy? I don't think so. Any progress on identifying the body?"

"We're working on it," Cullen said. "Other agencies don't have an impatient sheriff running the show."

"I understand. What do *you* make of the forensics?" I asked.

"We're thinking along the same lines—to your credit. Are you sure you don't have a background in law enforcement?"

"Nope. I read a lot of police procedural novels, though. I like the step-by-step way the plots unfold."

"Yeah, I read them too. My wife thinks that's nuts. She says she doesn't read romances now that she does software for a dating app. Anyway, I'd guess we're looking at a boyfriend here," Cullen continued. "If a murder isn't gang-related—and I'm not ruling that out—that's who it usually is."

"You think a fair-skinned twenty-year-old woman might have been executed because she was in a gang?"

"Drug gangs come in all colors, Tobin. And she could've been a mule or a lookout or something. Maybe she was going to rat out her boyfriend."

"Now who's stretching, Cullen?"

"Call me Bill. All I'm saying is that it's not a good idea to totally rule out anything."

"Got it. So if you can identify the victim, you think that'll lead you to the killer."

"Sure," he responded. "We haven't had an unsolved murder in the county in years, and the last one was a serial killer who picked his victims at random as he traveled around the country. Murderers are impulsive or stupid for the most part. The elaborately planned murders you see on TV don't happen much, and when someone tries that, there are usually too many moving parts to get everything perfect."

"What are the odds you'll identify the body?" I asked.

"Very high. We're checking missing persons across a tristate area. If that doesn't turn anything up, we'll go to the press and get the public in the loop. All that's assuming we don't find out some other way first."

“Well, I hope you do. Any clues about why she was dumped here?” I asked.

“Nope. No idea. There are plenty of more isolated spots along Skyline Boulevard, so I don’t think it was by accident. Are you sure no one has it in for you?”

I reconsidered that. “There are those former members I mentioned, and several families were upset when their kids or partners chose to move here.”

“Kids? You have kids there?”

“No, I mean adult children,” I explained. “Everyone is over eighteen.”

“Text me the names of these members’ relatives.”

“Sure. I’ll find out. I don’t remember,” I told him.

“What about that first guy we interviewed?” Cullen asked.

“Ralph?” I asked. “What do you mean?”

“Just ask him. He remembers everything, right? I’ve never run into that before.”

“Me neither,” I told him. “I don’t know if it’s a curse or a blessing.”

“In my profession, who wants to remember?” Cullen said.

Chapter 7

After hunting up information on a laptop in the project building, I sent a text to Cullen—Bill—with all the possible suspects I'd mentioned to him. The list included the member who'd harassed other members, the one who'd stolen, the woman who'd founded another community after failing to take over ours—as well as her eight followers—and five people who'd showed up at one time or another to try to retrieve family members. Ralph did, in fact, help with compiling this latter list.

After leading a meditation and giving a talk about how to squeeze the learning out of what we were all going through, Zeus and I ate our lunches on a wooden deck that spanned what had been a swimming pool back when the property had been a summer camp.

Several shade trees whose name I always forget arched overhead, sending dappled light down onto us. Through the hefty branches, I saw the rocky peak of what passed for a mountain in our area. Compared to the Sierras a hundred and fifty miles to the east, we lived most of the way up a modest foothill.

Zeus was sullen at first because I hadn't spent much time with him since discovering the body. A bowl of leftovers—the same stew I was eating—won him over.

Cullen showed up as we finished—well, as I finished. Zeus had wolfed down his food in about thirty seconds before staring intently at mine.

"I've been wandering around looking for you," Bill told me as he approached the rusty patio chair beside me.

I was struck again by how alert his green eyes were. The moment he sat down, Bill began taking in his surroundings, including me, with keen interest. I wasn't accustomed to seeing someone so mindful—so focused and in the moment—outside of a spiritual setting. Of course, there was a lot to be mindful to that wasn't visual or verbal. I doubted Bill was tuned into the full spectrum of possible experience.

His long face and neck, even seated, gave Bill the appearance of his being taller than he actually was. His legs, stretched out in front of him, told the real story. If anything, they implied he was shorter.

Zeus snuffled Bill's pants leg, slobbering a bit.

"Sorry about that," I said, nodding at the wet hemline.

"No worries. He's smelling our boxer, who spreads saliva all over the house. It drives my wife crazy."

"You could've asked someone where I was," I told Bill. "I often eat out here with Zeus. Sometimes I need to reset my configuration after working with people."

"Reset your configuration? Never mind. I don't want to know. After we solve the case, I'll pick your brain about things. For now, I'm still wrestling with the whole energy deal."

"I understand. I give public talks on the first Sunday of the month," I told him. "You're welcome to come."

As soon as I said this, I realized how condescending it must've sounded. An expert in his field had graciously allowed a rank amateur to work alongside him, and now I was flaunting my own area of expertise. I vowed to keep the hard-to-swallow content to a minimum. At the least, that could serve as penance for my energy demonstration.

"Yeah, maybe I'll start with that," Bill said desultorily. "Anyway, I got a better feel for this place from walking around by myself and informally chatting with people. It's quite a spread. What do you use that building past the dorms for? I notice it was locked."

"We don't use it. The floors aren't safe in there, so our insurance company told us we need to keep people out."

"Ah." Bill reached up to rub Zeus behind his ears. When Zeus hovered in front of a seated person, awaiting his due in the petting department, he was tall enough that only an NBA center would reach down.

"Any interest in going down to Ann Marin's commune?" Bill asked.

She was the member who'd broken away after leading a failed revolution.

"Why there?" I asked. "I thought you were going with the boyfriend theory."

"I can't just sit around waiting for an ID to lead us to him—or her, for that matter. In the meantime, I need to pursue all the leads we already have. We can kill multiple birds with one stone down in Watsonville, suspect-wise, and one of Marin's followers has a record. Two felonies."

"I didn't know that. Who do you mean?"

"Gar Brindisi."

"That surprises me." I paused and thought for a moment. "I'm not sure I'd be welcome at Ann's."

"I'm not welcome anywhere, Tobin. I don't let that stop me." He smiled grimly. "I can recall several times I was especially unwelcome. I could show you the scars."

"Call me Kade, please. If you're Bill, I'm Kade."

"No Sri?"

"That wasn't my idea. Ralph came up with that, as well as several devotional chants. It's silly, really, but I guess it serves to keep some of the members focused on Spirit. If that needs to be through me for now, that's an intermediate stage I can tolerate."

"How do you keep from being too full of yourself? It must be a occupational hazard."

"Oh, I definitely have a grandiose streak, which I keep in check as best as I can. It's not the only thing I have to keep an eye on. It's not always easy being celibate, for example."

"Celibate? Really?"

I smiled and nodded.

"Don't sign me up for that. So you'll come with me?" Bill continued, still communing with Zeus as he spoke.

"Sure. Once again, let me make arrangements here. I've found that if members don't stick to a routine, they backslide in a hurry. It's like doing physical therapy exercises. If you take a break while you're on vacation, you might not pick them up again when you get back."

"Yeah, I did that."

"Can I bring Zeus?" I asked. It felt odd to ask permission. As the leader of a community, it had been a long time since I'd done that.

"Why?" Bill asked.

"He likes riding in cars. And there are a lot of good smells on farms."

"I'm sorry, but those aren't compelling reasons," Bill told me. "He'll be a distraction."

"What if he stays in the car after we get there?" I

tried.

"Fine."

****

I told Jim to tell certain members to work on our project while I was gone since it seemed unlikely that any deputies would return. The project was designed to support ourselves financially beyond our dwindling donations. Mainstream people might think it was inappropriate for a community such as ours.

The fifty-minute drive south gave Bill and me a chance to chat about our lives and outlooks. We had more in common than I would've suspected. Among other things, we'd both played lacrosse, which wasn't common in California. Also, our first jobs had been grunts on construction crews. I carried lumber; Bill wheelbarrowed bricks.

I liked the guy, despite his flare-ups of frustration early on. Perhaps those had been part of his vetting process—to see how I'd react to being pushed. Now that I'd passed whatever tests he'd thrown at me, Bill was almost convivial.

I'd opened a rear window for Zeus to stick his big, shaggy head out of, even though a bug had once collided with the corner of his eye, necessitating an expensive trip to the vet's. I couldn't deny him the pleasure of the treasure trove of smells as we passed through a variety of scenarios, some of them worthy of a few barks.

Zeus's voice was deep and throaty—nothing I minded hearing. I can't speak for his targets—a herd of goats, a black Lab in an SUV at a stoplight, and fieldworkers stooped over strawberry plants. One of the latter gave us the finger, so I guess I knew the story there.

Ann's commune sat alongside a narrow country

road just past a wholesale nursery featuring long rows of exotic succulents. A handmade wooden sign by the dirt driveway read Unity Farm in emerald green cursive.

Bill turned into the rutted driveway, kicking up a cloud of dust as we passed a bare field. Eventually the rutted track led us beside an old white farmhouse sorely in need of a paint job. The clapboard on the side facing us was pitted from insect activity, and the sole window was old enough that the discolored glass sported horizontal ripples at the bottom.

Through the car window, I smelled manure and hay, and as a light breeze wafted by, the odors grew stronger. Zeus snorted. When I left him in the car, his snort morphed into a prolonged grunt.

Ann strode out of her front door as we walked around the corner of the house and approached the wonky front porch. At first glance, it looked as though she'd slide right off the end of it.

Ordinary-looking in many respects, Ann nonetheless commanded one's full attention, even from those who rarely gave it. Perhaps it was her eyes—dark, almost black under bushy black eyebrows. Her posture probably contributed. She'd once shared that she'd been a successful gymnast in high school. That had surprised me, given her height. All the gymnasts I saw in the Olympics were tiny.

Ann's spiky black hair stood up unevenly and draped over her small ears on the sides. Her mouth was a thin line that sat just below a long, narrow nose. The gap between the two was remarkably small. If she were a man, a pencil-thin mustache would be all she could fit on her upper lip.

"Well, look who's come to visit," she greeted,

standing on the top flagstone step below the porch. "Who's your friend, Kade? No, let me guess. He's a cop, isn't he?"

We halted our progress just in front of her. "Hello, Ann. This is Detective Cullen. There's been a murder on our property. He thought you and the others might be able to help with his investigation."

She thrust her hand out to Bill, who climbed the first step to shake it. "Welcome. I'm Ann Marin, as you already know. We're suspects, right? That's fine. Investigate all you want. We have nothing to hide."

As usual, she spoke quickly in a clipped tone. I wondered if Bill could read her well enough to know that wasn't aimed at him in particular.

"Thank you," he responded. "For starters, I'd like to talk to you, and then if you could point me at Gar Brindisi, I'd appreciate it."

"Gar. I get that. He's not who he used to be, but you need to find that out for yourself."

"Yes."

"Come on in," Ann said.

I climbed the slightly less wonky steps, carefully navigated the porch, and followed Ann and Bill inside. As I passed through what had been the parlor, a couple of things stood out for me. The raggedy-looking sleeping bags on the worn fir floor were arranged in a wheel, their openings barely a foot apart. And a very expensive-looking set of floor-standing speakers flanked a cabinet stuffed with audio equipment.

In the kitchen, we sat around a modern, glass-topped table with straight stainless-steel legs that didn't belong in the otherwise Goodwill-furnished house.

As modest as our buildings were back up on the

mountain, our kitchen was a cut above Ann's place. The yellowed linoleum floor was buckled, with several rips visible from where I sat facing the doorway into a long hall. The walls were painted plywood, and their light green color did nothing to hide their peeling layers. Even the overhead light fixture had seen better days. This embossed glass globe hung down on a broken metal chain, a multi-colored bungee cord spanning the gap between links.

Someone had been baking. An earthy, sweet aroma suggested bread. I inhaled deeply, enjoying the scent, wishing I were eating its source.

"Have at it," Ann said to Bill once we'd settled in.

She'd chosen the power seat, where the energy was strongest. Every room has a power position, usually in a corner. Almost everyone was subtly influenced by this phenomenon. At this point on my path, I was not.

"Who do you think would shoot a young woman and leave her body on the Brethren's land?" Bill began.

"Obviously, I have no idea," Ann replied, "but let me see what I can channel."

She closed her eyes. Bill looked at me and I shrugged. I'd explain what she was doing later.

After a minute of silence, Ann spoke. "Raphael says it wouldn't be helpful to tell you anything about that at this time. He did say I should tell the detective that his partner is healthy now."

Bill stared at her. "Who's Raphael and what does that mean?"

"I assume you have a partner with some sort of illness, *n'est-ce pas*?"

"Yes."

"Bill," I explained, "Raphael is the name of a

bodiless entity who knows things we can't access on this plane."

"He's an archangel," Ann added.

"Hold on," Bill said. He pulled his phone out of his pocket and speed dialed. "Michael, any medical news?" He listened for a bit, then said, "That's wonderful. I'm so glad. Listen, I'll call you later to hear more about it."

Ann watched him with a smirk as he put the phone down. His raised eyebrows, wide open eyes, and tight mouth suggested confusion, with a hint of fear.

"That's a neat trick," he told her as he gathered himself and settled into a more neutral baseline expression.

"I just channel. You make of it whatever you want."

Bill nodded. He'd recovered. "What else can you tell me?"

"Nothing." Ann shook her head. "I'm not going to pester Raphael again with something like this, and as I told you, I don't know anything about what's going on back on the Brethren's land. We stay busy here—ten-hour workdays. There's no time for much else."

"So you don't have any contact at all with your former colleagues?" Bill asked.

"Colleagues? Hardly. Sheep is more like it." She pointed at me. "This one is leading them down a dead-end path."

"How's that?" Bill asked.

"You can only bring spiritual students along as far as you are yourself," Ann told him. "Kade is deluded. He sincerely believes he's hot shit, and he isn't. Not even on a personal level."

"What do you mean by that?" Bill asked.

"Oh, he didn't tell you?" She turned to me with a

crooked grin. "We were lovers."

Bill glanced at me, and I nodded. I had hoped that wouldn't come out and muddy the waters.

"What happened?" he asked.

"I don't even know," Ann answered. "One day we're together, the next day he's a fucking celibate. Pardon the oxymoron. I think he read a book about it or something. That didn't work for me."

"What has this got to with the murder?" I asked.

"Beats me," Ann answered. "I'm just answering questions, aren't I?"

"We're on a fact-finding mission," Bill said. "It's a fact, Kade."

"I'm surprised you're letting Kade tag along," Ann said. "Did he dazzle you with an energy transmission? Did he seem like some kind of junior detective? Don't be fooled. This guy knows how to manipulate people."

"Could you be the proverbial woman scorned?" Bill asked.

"I could be, but I'm not. There are eight more perfectly intelligent people not a hundred yards from here who also left his ashram. That's what it is, whatever Kade wants to call it. He's a guru, and they're sheep—fucking sheep."

By keeping her tone and voice under control, Ann's words landed with more impact. I felt her energy penetrate my chest for a moment before I protected myself.

"Is being angry something that's okay for a spiritual person?" Bill asked her.

Ann didn't like that at all. "You don't know anything, do you? You've gotten your ideas about all this from Kade, I'll bet. Go see Gar. He'll be over behind the barn."

Ann abruptly stood, marched out of the kitchen, and climbed creaking stairs around the corner. We'd been dismissed.

"Well," Bill said to me, continuing to sit. "You're full of surprises, aren't you? Ann's lover…What else are you still hiding?"

"Am I supposed to tell you my entire life story?" I responded. "I'll keep sharing whatever's relevant once I know it's relevant. Do you really want me to waste time telling you about my love life?"

"Of course not, but let me decide what's relevant. If it's about anyone connected to your community, I want to know."

"Okay, fair enough," I conceded. "You should know Ann is the one who's manipulative—and very good at it. She seduced me to find out more about how we acquired our land, how the deed is held, and what our finances are."

"To help her take over?"

"I assume so. It could be something else. Anyway, once I realized what she was doing, I broke it off."

"And became celibate? That seems like a drastic overcompensation, Kade."

"I learned from my mistake," I told him. "Even if Ann had been sincere, it's still wrong to become involved with a student. There's a power imbalance."

Bill nodded. "Okay, now tell me more about Gar."

I crossed my legs and leaned back. I'd been quite tense and hadn't realized it.

"He's a good guy," I told Bill. "He'd never do anything violent. I think he became disenchanted with me when I confronted him about his addiction to enemas."

"You're serious?"

"Unfortunately, yes. Twice a day. Special formulas he orders from Norway. The cost is at the expense of his child support back in San Diego."

"Jesus, I've never run into that one," Bill said. "I wonder what a shrink would say."

"I wondered, too. That's why I told him the Brethren would pay for sessions with one."

"Let me guess. He didn't go?"

"No. So I let him be. There are worse addictions, aren't there? But things were never the same between us after that."

Bill cocked his head and looked up and to his left. "Before we go further, I want to ask you something else about Ann Marin. And about you. It may sound accusatory, but remember, that's part of my job. It's nothing personal."

"Go ahead."

"Was all that denigration about you really just an attempt to manipulate me? Is there any truth to what she's saying? Are you sometimes manipulative yourself?"

"Do you feel manipulated?" I asked, aware of my defensiveness, but unable to derail it. "Do you think I'm deluded or exploitive? Which of us is a more reliable source of information—Ann or me?"

"Okay, okay. Let's go talk to Gar. I'll try not to picture his ass."

"Say what? Oh, I get it."

We rose and strode out of the house. Striding turned out to be the wrong way to maneuver on the decrepit porch. I almost fell as I lost my balance trying to find the top step.

Zeus was loose outside, chasing and being chased by a boy about twelve years old, who must've let him out of the car. I glanced at Bill, who was smiling. Apparently, this sort of distraction was okay with him.

The boy wore worn, dirty jeans and a black hoodie with the hood down. His orange work boots looked new. His hair was a proverbial bird's nest, and his sharp nose dominated his flushed face.

The boy wasn't very fast. When he was being chased, Zeus overran him after only a few yards, and then they switched roles. My dog's tail wagged furiously as he turned to tease the boy by lowering his front legs, play-growling, and then taking off. The boy, of course, never caught up with him. H didn't seem to care; he smiled continuously.

Gar strode around the side of the barn. "Oliver! Don't—Hey, is that Zeus?"

Hearing his name, Zeus glanced toward Gar, recognized him, and raced toward him. The two had been close up on the land.

Gar sprinted forward himself, instigating a game of chicken to see who would lose his nerve and veer off first.

"Watch this," I said to Bill.

At the last minute, Zeus and Gar both turned to the same side, collided, and went down in a heap with Zeus on top. His face loomed above Gar's.

"What are you feeding this monster?" Gar called out as we strode toward them, the boy joining us. He looked Zeus in the eye. "You're fat, Zeus. Very fat. And if you drool on me, I'll get my revenge. Remember when I glued your food to your bowl? Don't make me do something like that again."

Gar talked at length to every animal he encountered—and quite a few lived in our forest. He even anthropomorphized trees, claiming he could communicate with them as well.

"Zeus!" I called, and he disentangled himself and ran over to me. Gar hung back. He seemed hesitant to meet Bill. The boy—Oliver—stuck with us, standing beside Bill now. Because he was winded, Zeus allowed me to put him back into the car without a fuss.

I turned to Oliver when I returned. Bill was silently studying Gar across the compacted dirt that led to a green field behind the barn.

"Is that your dad?" I asked the boy.

"Yeah, he's an idiot."

"I didn't know Gar had a son."

"My mom dumped me here so she could run off with a bass player," Oliver told me. "It's hell. There's nothing to do. And they want me to work out in the field. It's like they never heard of child labor laws."

"That's enough," Gar said when he finally approached us. "Go find Henry, and see if he needs any help."

Oliver sighed dramatically and scurried away.

"He's been here a few weeks," Gar told us. "I don't think it's going to work out."

Gar towered over Bill and me. His broad shoulders were far wider than his torso, creating a distinct vee shape. Shaggy black hair loomed over a wide, indigenous-looking face, with chiseled cheekbones and eyes almost as dark as Ann's. A wide, toothy mouth belied this fierce countenance.

"Anyway, it's good to see you, Kade." Gar gave me

a huge hug, nearly lifting me off my feet. "I never really thanked you for all you did for me."

"It was my pleasure. Listen, this is Bill Cullen. He's investigating a murder up on our land, and he thought you might be able to help."

Gar's face darkened. "I'm tired of this shit, officer. I've been clean for six years now and I did my time. Anyway, I was never violent."

Bill's eyebrows shot up. "Really? I've seen your file, Brindisi. Resisting arrest? Wasn't that one of your crimes?"

"That was bogus. They tacked that on to strengthen their case so I'd make a deal. All I did was try to grab my coat while this asshole was pulling my arm at the front door. Shit, it was cold out."

"The detective has to explore all the possibilities, Gar," I said. "I told him you'd never be involved in anything like a murder. But maybe you know who would, or how we could find out."

"Cuz I have a record? That makes me a font of information?" He looked down and then spoke in a softer, calmer tone. "Look, I'd help you if I could. All I can say is nobody up there could've done it unless there've been newcomers in the last four months."

Bill looked at me, and I shook my head.

"I know every person in the community, and I knew killers in Folsom," Gar continued. "You're talking about opposite ends of the spectrum. Look elsewhere."

"Okay, thanks," Bill told him.

The remaining farm people had nothing to add. It was good to see them, even though several expressed bitterness, and one was outright hostile.

We stopped at a taqueria on the way home. I paid

this time. Watsonville is primarily an agricultural town with a majority of Spanish speakers. The Mexican food reflected regional specialties and was excellent across the board.

"So what did you make of all that back on the farm?" Bill asked between a mouthful of handmade tortilla chips.

"Believe it or not, I trust what Ann's disembodied source tells her. I don't believe it's Raphael or anyone else we might have ever heard of, but its track record is flawless."

"It?"

"You think there's gender wherever it is?" I asked.

"Beats me." Bill shrugged. "Do you really think someone without a body is withholding information from us?"

"I wouldn't put it that way. I don't think withheld is the right word. Look at it this way. If a source could tell you when you'll die, would it be in your best interest to know?"

He had to think about that. "You're saying that knowing more about the murder at this stage might not actually be beneficial in the long run?"

"Right. Suppose it's information that sent us off on a wild goose chase or you'd sustain a horrible injury because you took a different action than you otherwise would've. There's no way to know the why of it except occasionally in hindsight. We need to trust this entity. Anyway, what choice do we have? You can't bring it into an interview room and interrogate it, can you?"

Bill shook his head. "Already, this case is a hundred times weirder than any other, and I've worked some doozies. What's next? Ghosts?"

"We'll see."

"They exist?"

"How would I know? I'm a teacher, not a paranormal researcher."

"People do that? Research ghosts?"

"Yup."

He shook his head again and then dug into the Oaxacan-style enchiladas that had just arrived.

After we'd finished eating—another rare treat for me—Bill asked me if I thought Gar was being truthful.

"I do," I told him. "And the others, too. I know these people. Whatever our differences, they're not liars. On the other hand, I don't think it makes sense to give much credence to what Ann says. I mean, when she's speaking for herself."

"Tell me more about that."

"On the land, her methods for recruiting followers were sneaky. She slandered me, offered incentives she never followed through with, and used her powers to boost her status. Those types of abilities aren't bestowed on people to help them pursue personal ambitions."

"So you're well rid of her," Bill pointed out.

"Yes, but the same can't be said for her students. Their presence here represents a painful detour on their spiritual paths."

"They seemed happy enough when we talked to them," he said.

"For now. There's always a day of reckoning for posers. And then the posees fall hard."

****

The older woman who believed I was a demon lived in Santa Cruz near the Monterey Bay. I would have preferred to return to the land, but Bill wanted to interview her next and he was calling the shots. I hoped she wasn't home. She was.

Esme Dahl's diminutive frame was more hunched over than the last time I'd seen her. Other than having slightly more pleasing facial features, she could've played the role of a witch in a fantasy film. Her elongated head was framed by spiral-permed auburn hair which draped onto her sloping shoulders. As she stood in the doorway of her pink Craftsman-style house, I noticed dark circles under her eyes. That was something new, too.

Esme shrank back, her eyes wide, when she spied me. Bill stepped in and took the lead.

"Ms. Dahl?"

"Yes?' She retrieved a gold cross from inside her cable-knit sweater and held it out toward me.

"I'm Bill Cullen from the sheriff's office. I'd like to ask you a few questions."

"Let's see a badge." She'd gathered herself, and her voice reflected that. She still held the cross firmly at arm's length.

Bill showed her. "May we come in?"

"Absolutely not. Do you know what is standing next to you?" Her loud, raspy voice rang out at us.

"That's Mr. Tobin."

"No, it isn't. It used to be," Esme said.

"What if he stayed out here?" Bill asked.

She thrust her arm forward even more. "Anyone under his power will never cross my threshold. Say your piece."

"Where were you two nights ago?"

"At bingo. I won, too." Esme smiled for a moment and then caught herself and reverted to a glare.

"There's been a murder on the Brethren's land," Bill told her.

"I can solve your case right now, officer. The killer is standing right next to you. You wouldn't believe the things it does. With my own eyes I've seen unnatural, evil acts."

"Yes, ma'am. I'll look into that. Is there anything else you can tell me?"

"You should arrest the lot of them. They're planning something—something bad."

"I see. Well, thank you for your time."

Esme slammed the door before he'd even finished talking.

"Evil and unnatural, Kade?" Bill asked as we walked back to the car.

"Here's the deal with Esme," I said. "So far, you've found a way to gracefully accommodate the out-of-the-box experiences that have come your way—what you probably think of as weirdness. She couldn't. The only way Esme could make sense out of it all was to fall back onto her religious upbringing." I paused to consider whether I wanted to take this further. I decided to go ahead. "The takeaway here is that trying to make sense doesn't always make sense."

"Isn't that a paradoxical thing to say?" he asked as he climbed into his car.

"Sure. Here's some advice, Bill. If you want to know truth, you have to find a way to accommodate paradox."

"Gimme a break, Kade. I don't even want to think about that."

I'd gone too far and lost him. "Sure. Sorry."

Chapter 8

That evening, while an out-of-season light rain fell, I led a guided meditation in the multi-purpose room and then answered questions from my students. As usual, it was cool in there, and my voice bounced around the walls and convex ceiling, joining the high-pitched staccato of the rain. Quonset huts were designed for military purposes—storing equipment and such. The design didn't lend itself to talking, but we made do.

"Why do people kill one another?" someone asked. "Like with this murder. That seems out of synch with…Well, the big picture, I guess. Why does the universe allow that?"

"The big picture is a mosaic of all the little pictures," I began. "These two aspects of the universe work together to create personal life curriculums. We are here to learn—to eventually develop into individuals in congruence with Spirit."

The woman who'd asked the question spoke up again. "I don't understand. What's this have to with killing—with the murder?"

"I'm getting to that, Lucia. We live in a benign universe that doles out lessons that serve everyone's best long-term interests in terms of spiritual evolution. What we need to do, whether it's killing or loving or anything in between, has been determined by our actions in previous lives. Everything works toward creating balance.

"So how could the murder on our property be a subset of that? I have no idea, but is it my role to second-guess the universe? Either it all makes sense on some unknowable level or it doesn't. How could there be exceptions, no matter how awful something might seem to us?"

"That sounds cold and uncaring—no offense," Wayne Robbins called out.

"I don't need anyone to agree with my point of view," I told him. "I hold it. It works for me. Does any of this resonate with something inside you? Do your life experiences support these notions? I want everyone to think for yourself. Don't adopt my perspective simply because I'm the one saying it."

Martha spoke up. "Doesn't all this depend on what level you look at things from? Are words like cold and uncaring valid at a spiritual level?"

God bless her. She was lobbing me a softball question to help my audience understand. I couldn't pick her out of the group at first because she'd happened to sit between the dark-skinned Indian-American woman and our Basque member. The threesome represented a gradation of brown coloring that momentarily distracted me.

"Yes, everything is level-dependent," I said. "That's the key to this. At a human heart level, some things are virtually unbearable to us. From other vantage points—Spirit's or even that of a that of a criminal—there are equally valid perspectives—truths—given the givens embodied in these levels. People do what makes sense to them based on their back stories. These perspectives are compatible, not contradictory, unless one only views life from one fixed point—one level—which we tend to do."

"So we're supposed to look at life from a variety of vantage points?" Susan Burke asked. She was the DA's daughter. Of all my students, she might've been the brightest. I knew she already understood what she was asking. She was also helping to clarify what I said to the other members.

"More or less," I responded. "We need to expand ourselves to accommodate all the back stories that drive behavior. If you were the other person doing whatever they do, would you do it too if you shared all that led up to it? Suppose you had the same genetics, childhood, and life events? What then?

"Until you experience all this—and you won't in a given lifetime—how can you judge it? From a spiritual perspective, even a terrorist's life just embodies a really different curriculum than ours. These folks are learning firsthand about victimhood, hate, and violence. At some point in your incarnations, you've struggled with these, too. We all experience everything. These are the ingredients it takes to fully bake us."

I walked away and read a thriller in my yurt.

Why am I including all this? I confess I'm sneaking in what I consider to be wisdom in an effort to help whoever reads this memoir. I hope I haven't bored anyone with my philosophy.

Also, I offer this material so you'll understand how and why this particular spiritual teacher agreed to keep playing amateur detective. Would I have ventured into this realm if I held a different point of view—if I were a Christian minister, a rabbi, or an imam? Nope.

A murder fell into my lap, and I agreed to adopt the role I'd been assigned by the universe. I trust my curriculum. That has been my credo for many years—ever since a near-death experience and a fateful meeting with a spiritual teacher of my own. I dance the steps the master choreographer in the sky has created for me—happily, for the most part. I could live no other way.

Chapter 9

Bill called me in the morning. I was doing paperwork in my office. “We’ve identified the body. Althea Curtis. Ring a bell?”

“No.”

“Let me text you her driver’s license photo.”

“Sure.”

He did. She’d been an attractive young adult with long blonde hair, fair skin, and a smattering of freckles across her slightly crooked nose. Her eyes were alert. The rest of her expression seemed to be the product of a long wait at the DMV—a little tired and a little frustrated.

“Still no,” I told him once I examined the photo.

“She’s a student at a college in her hometown in Pennsylvania,” Bill told me. “Her family doesn’t know why she came out here. We’re contacting her friends to see what they can tell us.”

“It could’ve been a vacation,” I suggested. "Santa Cruz is a resort town, isn’t it? Or maybe she was visiting a friend—someone her parents don’t know about.”

“Maybe. I won’t need your help about this. It’s going to take good old-fashioned police work to find out. I think your involvement ought to be centered around the body’s location on your land. Why there? What does it mean? Any new ideas at this point?”

“No,” I told him. “We’ve still got a few people

associated with the community to check out, though," I said. "There's the thief and the harasser."

"I was thinking about that. How would you feel about doing that on your own?" Bill asked.

"Really?" I was surprised. "Why would you suggest that? I'm not a policeman. You'd trust me with interviewing suspects?"

"Yeah, it sounds strange to me when I say it out loud, too. There's just something about you, and we're stretched too thin in the department right now to cover all the bases. I don't want less likely suspects to get ignored. If you don't do it, they're going to fall through the cracks."

"There's only so much of me to go around, Bill. I have responsibilities here—people that count on me," I told him.

"I understand. It was just a thought. I'm not even sure why you've helped so much so far."

"That would be hard to explain without going into my ideology. I'll spare you that." I paused. "Let me think a minute. Maybe there's a way I can manage this."

I checked in with my intuition. Was I supposed to back away or keep pursuing the investigation? Sometimes a shift in the choreography was hard to read.

I could certainly keep turning over some of my community duties to Jim and Martha if necessary. I had done so in the past when I was ill.

"I'll find a way," I told Bill. "At the least, I'll meet with Janet and Paul—the two members I asked to leave. I don't think the families of students who believe I'm brainwashing their loved ones would be receptive."

"Let's keep them in our back pocket. It's hard to imagine someone committing a random murder simply to discredit a spiritual community. The usual thing cult families do—if they're desperate—is to grab their relative and have a deprogrammer work them over."

"Does that succeed?"

"Sometimes. Stay in touch," Bill said, "and the sooner you can rule out these ex-members the better."

"Sure. Oh, and how is your partner doing? Michael, was it?"

"Yes, he's still a little weak so he's probably a day or two away from coming back. Thanks for asking."

****

I wasn't looking forward to crossing paths again with Janet Trumbull, the thief, or Paul Chang, the harasser.

Janet was sneaky and a great liar, among other things. It's not easy to fool me, and she did so for several weeks. Paul, on the other hand, confessed his history in our first meeting, which I treat as though it's a job interview. He knew he had a problem. He wanted to work on his relationship to women in a safe space while he pursued his spiritual path. I never doubted Paul's sincerity, so I took a risk with him.

Two of my members paid the price, which, thank goodness, wasn't a high one. By Paul's standards, he probably believed he was behaving within acceptable parameters.

I called Bill back when I was unable to locate either one online.

"I'll get right on it," he told me.

And he did. In ten minutes, I had addresses—both were local.

"We have access to databases you don't," he explained.

I decided to enlist a young member to drive me in one of the vans—I don't drive. Mark was chatty en route, telling me how happy he was and how much he appreciated being a member of our community. I got a whiff of "he doth protest too much," but I let it be.

Janet's address turned out to be the county jail, which Bill could've mentioned. The buildings—there were two—resembled a college dorm, minus the windows. Two-story brick walls created long, parallel rectangles, with an imposing razor-wire-topped cyclone fence creating a courtyard of sorts between them. The flat roofs sported an array of silver vents, air conditioning units, and antennae. The border of the property was delineated by a tall, dense hedge.

Fortunately, I arrived during visiting hours and Janet agreed to see me, probably out of boredom versus any genuine interest in what I might have to say to her.

I sat by myself for twenty minutes in a remarkably uncomfortable plastic scoop chair in an empty classroom-sized room. These slippery torture devices were grouped around half a dozen metal tables that were bolted to the floor. The walls were bare except for a giant sign with a list of curious rules for visitors. Among other things, we were not to exchange bodily fluids of any kind, visitors were prohibited from having weapons or "any weapon-like equivalent no matter what other purpose it may serve," and—this one was my favorite—we weren't allowed to sing or dance.

When I read that rule, I suddenly had an urge to break into "Somewhere Over the Rainbow" while waltzing around the room. To be fair, many of the other rules made perfect sense. I would not care to have a chair flung in my direction, for example.

"What do you want?" Janet snarled as she finally strolled in the room.

We were still the only ones present, which seemed odd. Didn't anyone visit these people?

Janet was amazingly obese, to the point that you wondered how she managed to fit into any chair. In this case, she didn't. She stood behind one and leaned on it. It did its best to stay intact, and I wondered what would happen if it snapped instead of continuing to flex.

I remained seated. "There's been a murder up on our land," I told her.

"So?" Her belligerent tone matched the aggressive energy she was leaking across the stainless-steel table. Deep-set blue eyes reflected that as well. I think she was intentionally not blinking as she narrowed them and stared.

"Aren't you going to maintain the fiction that you're a seeker, Janet? You were so good at it."

I'd taken the bait and responded without a shred of compassion, which I instantly regretted.

"Thanks. I had you going for a while, didn't I?"

"You sure did," I agreed. "I don't know if I would've ever figured it out if you hadn't been caught red-handed."

"I'll bet you wouldn't have," Janet said. "I used be an actress. I was in three commercials. I was slimmer then."

"Good for you," I said. "You know, I'm curious about why you chose us to rob?"

"I didn't rob. I stole. There's a difference."

"Okay, why come to the Brethren to steal?" I asked.

"A guy I know said there was a really rich guy up there," she told me.

"Who was that?"

"Who was the guy who told me or who was the rich guy?"

"Who was the guy who told you?" I asked. "We both know Jack is wealthy, although he has very little of value with him."

"Well, I didn't know that. Anyway, it's none of your business who told me. Now what's this about a murder? I've been in here for three months, so it wasn't me, if that's what you're thinking."

"I'm simply questioning everyone the police weren't going to able to get around to," I told her.

"Why?" Janet asked. "You're a teacher. You aren't a detective."

"It's kind of like you and I were recruited to be in a play. I've been assigned the role of a detective, and you've been cast as a prisoner. Both of these are temporary—only as long as the play runs."

She tilted her head and frowned. "You know, that's a stupid thing to say, Tobin. Even for you."

"Anyway, what can you tell me that might help us catch the killer?" I asked.

"You should take a look at that lady who's always shaking. I think she's faking," Janet said.

"Why's that?"

"I caught her holding real still for a couple of hours once. When I said something, she made up some crap about new medication. I'm sure she was lying. I know liars."

"Why would she pretend to have a disorder like that?" I asked.

Janet looked to the side for a moment. "For sympathy? Maybe she's trying to get close to Jack.

Whoever marries him is going to have access to millions. She could be on the lam, too. The Brethren is a great place to hide out."

"Why didn't you try seducing Jack yourself instead of stealing from him?" I asked.

"Look at me," she responded, gesturing at her oversized body. "You think someone like him would want me?"

"Don't sell yourself short, Janet. The world doesn't revolve around looks."

"That's easy for you to say, pretty boy. You gotta be in your forties, and you could still play the lead in a miniseries."

I raised my eyebrows and smiled. "Not a feature-length film?"

"Get real, Tobin."

Chapter 10

Paul lived in an apartment complex just across the San Lorenzo River from downtown Santa Cruz. Homely in a way I found endearing, his building's stuccoed walls were an attractive shade of ochre, but only in the areas that hadn't been water damaged. The landscaping represented a sincere low-budget effort to brighten the property, but here the effect was marred by the opposite problem—not enough water. They hadn't chosen drought-resistant plants, and there had been very little rain for the last two months now that we'd entered the dry season. I could see the moisture from the previous evening on the ground and was thankful on the shrubs' and ground covers' behalf.

I expected Paul to be home, although there was no logical reason to think that. He answered the door in a gaping gray terrycloth robe, although it was ten thirty in the morning. Underneath the robe, he wore plaid red pajamas. Paul's most noticeable feature was his paunch, a half globe of a pot belly that contrasted sharply with his slight build. His neck was especially skinny, looking as if it couldn't support his bald head. Otherwise, Paul was a good-looking guy in a dissolute kind of way. His square jaw and resolute gaze implied an inner strength he didn't have.

"Oh hi, Kade. Thanks for stopping by," Paul said. "I was wondering if I would ever see you again."

"It's good to see you, Paul. I hope you're well."

"Come on in. You want some coffee or something?"

He held the door open for me, and I walked in. "Tea would be lovely," I told him.

"No tea. Sorry. Have a seat."

The living room I entered looked like a furniture store staging area, replete with matching light-colored wood pieces and lamps, artificial ferns, and an enormous breakfront filled with action figures in sealed packages.

"That's quite a collection," I commented, pointing at the crowded shelves.

"Thanks. They're an investment. You wouldn't believe the return I get on them. I have lots of other collectibles. Do you like comic books?" He pointed toward another room.

"That's okay."

"Sit, sit," Paul told me.

I hunkered down onto a couch that was more comfortable than it looked, and he sat in a similar-looking chair across a truncated coffee table from me.

"I'm afraid this isn't really a social call," I said, "although I'd love to hear how you're doing. Did you attend that group I recommended?"

"Not yet. What's up?"

"I found a murder victim on our land—a young woman," I told him. "The sheriff's department asked me to talk to any former members on the off chance that someone might know something that could help them find the killer."

"How would I know anything?" Paul asked.

"That's what I'm here to find out. I'm sorry to bother you with this, but the authorities are shorthanded, and they asked me to help. I'm sure you'd rather see me at your doorstep than a detective."

"Well, yeah. Give me a minute." He got up, walked away, and began rinsing dishes in the compact kitchen next to the living room. "I think better when I'm doing something," he called.

He returned after a few minutes. In the meantime, I studied the room more. It was hard to believe someone lived in it. Everything looked new, and there were no wall decorations, books, or anything else on any of the surfaces. If Paul had a TV or a stereo, they weren't in the living room. The area was spotless, as well, as if he'd just vacuumed, dusted, and polished the blond wood furniture.

"Okay," Paul said, standing in the archway between the rooms. "Here's what I came up with. There's one guy up there I never trusted. I'm not sure why. You told us to rely on our intuition—that everyone knows things they have no business knowing, so this was like that."

"Who is it?"

"That Jim guy who runs the office," Paul told me. "You know how I say or do things that are out of line sometimes? Maybe that gives me radar for other guys with problem attitudes about sex. You ever catch him doing anything he wasn't supposed to?"

I shook my head.

"You said the victim was a woman," Paul continued, "so I'd look into him if I were you. And maybe he's shady in some other way. I don't know. There's just something about him."

"Okay. Anything else?"

"Well, I just want to say I understand why you had to ask me to leave. I didn't at the time, but I do now. And you'll be happy to hear I haven't given up on becoming enlightened. I'm with Lama Rinchen now."

"That's great," I told him.

This was a guy named Elliot Rosenstein before he proclaimed himself to be the reincarnation of a Tibetan lama. From what I could gather, his teachings were generally helpful despite his self-appointed spiritual status. Many of these guru types were sincere but deluded.

Paul and I chatted for a bit—he had been close to several men on the land and wondered how they were doing. Then I headed back to eat lunch with the community. My people needed to stay connected to my energy.

****

At lunch—I ate with the others that day—Zeus visited his friends in the dining hall, giving approximately the same amount of attention to each of the dog lovers willing to get slobber on them while they ate. He never begged, even as a puppy, which is why I allowed him in there.

Martha—the former Buddhist nun—provided the same dose of compassion to Zeus she extended to everyone, rendering her first on his itinerary. Her essential goodness transcended the likes of slobber. She wore her usual overalls with a white waffle-knit shirt. The shirt contrasted with her dark skin, making it look freshly bleached.

Ralph—the first interviewee with the remarkable memory—was next on Zeus's lunchtime itinerary. I think Ralph related better to animals than humans, forgiving them their behavior even as he chided fellow members for simply being who they were and doing what they do. I'd been working with him on this. People were more like the weather than he thought—outside his ability to influence, let alone to train to match what suited him.

Ralph actually abandoned his plate of couscous and tofu to crouch down to Zeus's level and let him lick his face. I saw several other members grimace. One of them had complained to me about the behavior. I'd encouraged her to talk to Ralph directly since discussing the matter with Zeus was unlikely to get results. As far as I know, she didn't.

This happened frequently. Members asked me to be a policeman, or a boss, or any number of other roles that relieved them of a responsibility they wished to avoid. I taught—à la AA—that although we didn't cause all our problems, we're the ones who have the task of facing and working through them.

The other notable Zeus friend was Susan Burke—the DA's daughter. Her communing was more circumspect—eye contact and gentle pats on the head. Despite this minimal interaction, Zeus was quite fond of her, singling her out at least once a day, usually at an inconvenient moment such as when she was in the bathroom. He'd discovered a way to shove the bathroom door in the women's dorm inward even when it was locked.

Susan had mentioned this to me, and I'd tried to communicate her concerns to Zeus, but, alas, the concept, like refraining from licking faces during meals, was beyond his abstract reasoning ability. That ability was pretty much limited to the usual canine concerns—how to rip away a stick from a bigger branch, how to track said stick as it bobbed in the Monterey Bay waves, and anything associated with hunting, eating, or finding just the right spot to lift his leg.

The others Zeus visited were less familiar to me. If members didn't ask for a one-on-one meeting, they remained someone who sat with the group and meditated, occasionally asking questions after my talks. I remain puzzled why a handful of members had adopted this limited role. Why not take advantage of all the opportunities in our community?

The food wasn't up to our cook's usual standards. No one complained, least of all me. I knew Wayne and his helpers were doing their best with the available ingredients. In a way, this was a metaphor for our lives. Weren't we all doing what we could to be our best selves, given all the ingredients in our lives? Admittedly, many of us manifest a very dilute form of "best."

After lunch, I headed to my office and called Bill to report, filling him in on who Janet and Paul suspected.

"So now I've got two more people to talk to," I told him. "The woman with the neurological condition—Ruth, remember her?—and my administrator, Jim. I can't imagine this will lead us anywhere useful, but you never know."

"*I* certainly don't know. We're getting nowhere fast on our end," Bill reported. "None of Althea's friends have a clue as to why she came to California. She was seeing a shrink, but so far that woman has stonewalled us about why. Althea's parents said she wasn't anxious or depressed. They also told me she was shy and never got into trouble, but what parents really know their kid at that age? Althea's best friend did say she'd been preoccupied lately, and there'd been some traumatic event in her past she never talked about. That's something, I guess. If we dig into her past, maybe we can find out what that was. That might help."

"Did she have a boyfriend or an ex?" I asked.

"No boyfriend. One ex we know of. I've got a video call with him later today. On the phone, he sounded like a good guy who wants to help. We'll see."

"Okay. I'll keep at it and let you know what I find out," I said.

"Great. I really appreciate this, Kade."

"No worries."

I loved that phrase. I first encountered it when I dated a lovely woman from New Zealand in my mid-twenties. "No worries" conveyed two things that aligned with my core values: a wish for the recipient to not suffer from worrying, and an assurance that I'd handle whatever was being discussed—once again banishing any associated suffering. At a certain point in one's spiritual development, most ambitions and in-the-world priorities fell away, and being in service to reduce suffering became the primary modus operandi.

From my front step, I asked a passerby to find and send Jim to me. I met with him in my office. His Japanese heritage, even several generations removed, lent him a formal air. In this instance, my rattan chair that forced almost everyone to slouch was no match for his ramrod straight posture.

"How are things going with you—personally. I mean?" I asked.

"Fine. No complaints." His face was placid, and his words carefully enunciated.

"Any friction with other members?"

"Nope." Jim was a man of few words.

"How are your relationships with the women in the Brethren?" I asked.

"What do you mean?" His brow tightened down, and his lips formed a tight line.

I tried to put his mind at ease. "I'm asking open-ended questions on purpose. I don't mean anything in particular."

"Well, you know I'm gay, right?"

"No, you never mentioned it," I told him.

It made sense, though. I had terrible gaydar, but once I knew someone was gay, it always made sense to me.

"I should've told you, I know," Jim said. "I'm mostly still in the closet, and I figured you'd know, anyway."

"It's none of my business," I said, "unless it plays a role in your spiritual development. Does it?"

"I don't know. Maybe. But I'm sure it tells you something about my relationship to the women here. I'm certainly not lusting after them like some people."

"I want to hear more about your thoughts on these lustful members," I said. "Why don't we look into that when we have more time, Jim?"

"Sure. I better get back to work on the budget, anyway."

"How's that going?" I asked.

"It could be better."

So that was the secret Paul sensed, and it was nothing that made Jim a viable suspect. I was glad.

Ruth's shaking was especially pronounced as she sat in my office. Her rattan chair shook slightly out of sync, and I'd guess the rough fir floor below them both was absorbing some of her movements as well.

She was usually intimidated in my presence since she placed me on a towering pedestal. As a result, my words had more weight than they deserved, despite my efforts to convince her I was just someone farther down the same road she was treading. Once I even intentionally spilled soup on myself and swore. It didn't make a dent.

So slim that a casual observer unfamiliar with her medical condition might think she was anorexic like Ralph, Ruth was otherwise a stunning redhead. She'd been an elementary school librarian prior to her spiritual emergence and her illness. She maintained a sexy librarian look, replete with gold wire-rim glasses and prim clothing choices. She'd been divorced twice.

That day, Ruth wore an ankle-length black dress with a white lace collar. Her Mary Jane black shoes and a series of oversized barrettes matched it. She'd constrained her hair as though it was composed of sentient strands eager to slither away.

"Thanks for taking the time to come in," I began.

"Of course. However I can serve you, Master Tobin."

I couldn't help but sigh. Ruth had spent several years in a hierarchal Hindu cult in Montana, which didn't exactly lend itself to egalitarianism. And her squeaky voice always annoyed me. It was the human equivalent of chalk on a board. I girded my loins.

"I appreciate that, Ruth. I wonder if you could fill me in a bit more about your medical condition."

"Sure. What do you want to know?"

"Are there respites from the shaking?" I asked.

"No, it's continuous, but the magnitude varies."

"And that's determined by stress?"

"Well, that's one thing that triggers it," she responded, shaking harder now. "There are others—a poor night's sleep, certain foods, and if I'm in pain from something else."

"And the convulsions?" I asked.

"They're awful." Her face scrunched up. If she hadn't said anything, I would still have gotten the message. "They used to send me to the ER all the time. Now I take a med that keeps them from getting so bad."

"How long have you been on the med?" I asked.

"Three years now."

That predated Janet's stay on our land. Ruth was lying if Janet could be believed, since according to her, Ruth had stopped shaking for hours and had told her it was because of a new med.

I wasn't sure how to proceed. Of the two, Janet was much more likely to lie to me, but why would she? Did she hold a grudge?

I decided to broach the topic with Ruth. "What would you say if I told you I know you weren't giving me accurate information?"

Ruth bowed her head and began to cry. "Don't kick me out. Please. I need to be here. I really do."

"Why would I kick you out?" I asked softly.

"The same reason why Sri Ramanana kicked me out. I smoke pot to get relief from my condition. I know it's wrong, but I just can't stand shaking sometimes."

"What's wrong with that? It's not even illegal now," I pointed out.

"Sri Ramanana said I was befouling myself with an impure substance."

"Fuck Ramanana," I barked with uncharacteristic energy, shocking Ruth's tears away. I'm not sure how I knew strong language would help her.

"What?" Ruth's face froze as she tried to process

this.

"I think you heard me. It's reprehensible that you were treated that way. I know you to be a committed seeker who never lets your disorder hold you back. You're an inspiration to everyone in the community. I'm so glad you're here."

"But…but I lied to you."

"You think you're the first?" I said. "It's not the end of the world, Ruth. Let's just make a deal that you won't do it again. And I will never punish you for telling me the truth. Have you ever seen me do that?"

"What about Janet?"

"She stole money," I told her.

"Oh, I didn't know that."

"We all love you. Know that," I told her gently. "Now I want you to meditate on this for the next hour. The deck over the pool would be a good spot. Sit in the chair on the right." If she sat where I spent so much time, the energy might be healing.

"Yes. Thank you." Her tears now demonstrated gratitude. "I can't believe you're doing this."

Ruth needed a hug, but hugging female members was not something I ever did—for obvious reasons.

"Go see Martha first and ask her for a hug," I told her.

"I will. Thank you." She bowed almost to the floor upon arising, shaking all the while, but not as much as when she'd arrived.

Chapter 11

I returned to my duties at the Brethren for several days before any new developments appeared in the case. Bill called me after lunch as I stood on the sidelines of a dorm versus dorm soccer game on our undersized field, AKA the meadow beside my yurt. This was always quite a spectacle. Hardly anyone ever scored a goal and quite a few players stood and chatted as the ball whizzed by them. It was hard to do much, anyway, when there were so many players on the diminutive, uneven field.

"Kade, I've got news," Bill told me. "We've discovered that the victim—Althea—flew in just two days before she was killed. We would've found out sooner, but she flew into Sacramento for some reason.

"After spending a day up there, Althea stayed at the hostel on Beach Hill in Santa Cruz, where she told Greta, a girl from Germany, she was in town 'to get justice.' When Greta asked her what she meant, Althea said something along the lines of 'he's not going to get away with this.' Greta's in Seattle now—it was hard to track her down. I spoke to her on the phone. Her English is half decent, but she may not have understood Althea perfectly."

"That's great," I said. "So if you can find out how she'd been wronged, you might find the killer. It sounds like he could be a criminal, right?"

"Yes. We're hunting whoever she knew who has a

record—especially something sexual. At her age, the most likely thing that happened would be a rape or some sort of assault. According to her mother, Althea didn't travel much, so the Pennsylvania state police are looking into this in Harrisburg—at her college. Outside of other parts of the state, she just visited New York a few times, and once she spent a week in Montreal."

"The killer could be someone she knows?" I asked.

"Yes."

"Her friends aren't any help?"

"No, she didn't share any details with them," Bill told me.

"Have you convinced Althea's shrink to share what she knows?"

"No," Bill replied. "In Pennsylvania, whoever controls the estate is the one who can give permission for that—not the doctor. Since Althea didn't have a will—and what twenty-year-old does?—the state has to step in, and you know how slow those wheels turn."

"That sounds strange," I commented.

"Here. Let me read you what I found: 'When a person dies without a will, they have died "intestate." In cases where someone dies intestate, the Register of Wills will appoint someone to administer the estate. Usually, the estate administrator is a spouse or child of the person who died.' So we're stymied there for now. The Registry of Wills won't even return my calls, let alone appoint anyone any time soon."

"Bummer," I said. "But the rest of what you told me still represents substantial progress, doesn't it?"

"Sure," Bill agreed. "And that's not all. We looked into Paul Chang once we got a line on this 'I want to get justice' deal. A guy who harasses women at a spiritual center probably has a history of worse behavior."

"He does. He's talked to me about it. But it's not anything criminal."

"Well, he didn't tell you everything, Kade. He's had two arrests for forcing himself on dates. Charges were dropped both times since they were classic he said/she said situations. If there were a third time, we could establish a pattern and wouldn't need more evidence to indict him. Don't ask me why, but the DA doesn't think twice is a pattern. I do."

"I agree," I said.

"Maybe we couldn't get a conviction in court on that basis," Bill continued, "but most of these guys fold and take a plea deal once they're in custody."

Something occurred to me. "Speaking of the DA, is she taking a special interest in this investigation because her daughter Susan is here?" I asked.

"You bet your ass," Bill said. "I get a phone call every day. And the sheriff's on my case even more because of the upcoming election."

"I'm sorry to hear that. I wouldn't want your job."

"Sometimes I think I don't either." His tone didn't reflect his words. Bill definitely liked his work.

"So what are you going to do about Paul?" I asked.

"A colleague talked to him. He's got an alibi—we checked it out—but it's not ironclad by any means, so we're trying to dig into that."

"What's his alibi?"

"A woman he supposedly spent the night with," Bill told me. "I'm thinking that when we tell her about his past and maybe show her a photo of the victim, she'll recant if she's lying."

"How would Althea and Paul have met?" I asked.

"There's a good question. I have no idea. I asked Paul if he'd ever been to Pennsylvania and he said once—to visit museums in Philadelphia. The guy loves Rodin and Monet. He went on and on about them. I'll be dreaming about big statues and lily pads for weeks. Anyway, this was eleven years ago. Althea would've been nine."

"Do you think Paul was lying?" I asked. He'd omitted some of his sordid history to me. Lying to a detective wasn't a big stretch past that. And, sadly, even nine-year-olds get molested.

"He didn't seem to be lying, and Althea's parents say she wasn't in Philly at that time, anyway. But I haven't ruled him out. He fits the profile."

"Are all investigations this complicated and frustrating?" I asked.

"No, not at all. The interstate aspect makes it more challenging. Dumping the body doesn't help. We've got no murder scene and no weapon. And like I said, we're shorthanded. It's not just my partner, Michael. Thank God he's back at work."

"You know," I commented, "we haven't talked about DNA, fingerprints, fibers, or any of that other stuff they always have on TV shows."

"I would've filled you in if any of that had helped, Kade. We've got two DNA samples, and it takes forever to find out if they match anyone in the system. You wouldn't believe how backed up the lab is."

"That's a shame," I commiserated.

"It sure is," Bill continued. "There were various fibers, some of them suggesting she was lying on a beige carpet at some point. There's one in the hostel living room, but no one remembers her lying on it. Another fiber matched a sweater we found in her suitcase there. Then there were two unknown ones—light blue cotton and black wool.

"The fingerprint thing is a fiction. You don't usually find usable prints on a body or clothing. You don't even find them on gun handles very often. It's handy that criminals don't know this. We can bluff them into confessions."

"Can I help with any of this?" I asked.

"I don't see how. I'm just keeping you in the loop as a courtesy."

"I appreciate that. Maybe I'll do a little more digging on my own if I have the time," I told Bill.

"Sure."

Chapter 12

The next morning, Zeus's howling woke me up again. It was uncannily identical to what I'd heard when he discovered Althea's body. I feared the worst. Had Alize's prediction of a second murder come true? When our Basque member had told Bill about her dream, I hadn't expected it would, despite her track record.

The worst is what I found—another young woman's body lying in almost exactly the same spot, in the same position, with the same gunshot wound.

My gut tightened, and my stomach roiled, threatening to send its contents up and out. I'm not sure why, but I was enduring a much more visceral reaction to this murder.

What the hell was going on? Two young women killed and dumped? Would there be more?

I called Bill and told him the news while Zeus and I stood next to the body. Once again, I averted my gaze from the bloody mess, watching a hawk being chased by three crows. This time I didn't admonish myself for failing to pay mindful attention. Now it made sense to me to keep a horrific image out of my head.

"I'll be there as soon as I can," Bill told me. "Secure the scene. Don't let anyone leave."

"You got it."

This time it was forty-five minutes before a deputy I hadn't met before named Adele Somebody came to hold down the fort until Bill arrived ten minutes later.

Adele's attempt to compensate for being quite short by wearing black combat-style boots with substantial heels wasn't entirely successful. While boosting her height, it drew the viewer's eye to the gimmick it represented. Her medium-sized frame described a straight line from her shoulders down to her ankles. If Adele had hips, they were well-hidden behind her wide leather utility belt. Her friendly, heart-shaped face sat under a navy baseball cap that read "Deputy Sheriff" in embroidered yellow thread.

Instead of questioning me about the case or exploring the crime scene, Adele stood next to me and asked if I knew the meaning of life, followed up by questions about how to be more mindful.

Bill arrived in mild disarray. His customary shiny blue suit was wrinkled and dark stubble stood out on his cheeks.

After Adele and I greeted him, Bill told me, "It's no longer my case. Jeff McCall is in charge now, and he wants to see you at the station."

"You're staying here?"

"Yes. Jeff's orders. I'll question people again and report to him. He outranks me, and he's close to the DA. I'm sorry, Kade. I thought we worked well together."

"We did," I agreed.

"Adele will drive you. Try to stop her if she starts telling jokes. She gets them out of a book. They're awful."

"No, they're not," she asserted. "They're funny as hell."

In fact, terrible jokes tumbled out of the young deputy's mouth for most of the trip. I sat beside her in the front seat. Her profile reminded me of a comic actress whose name I didn't remember.

"I find humor relaxes suspects," Adele told me when she spied me involuntarily grimacing.

"I'm a suspect?"

"Well, I generally don't take people in for questioning if they aren't," she answered.

"I agree that humor might relax your passengers," I told her. "You should try some."

Here was another remark I regretted. Events were eroding my ability to remain kind.

"Ouch. Good one, bro. Have you heard about the zebra and the rabbi that walked into an auto parts store?"

The exterior of the sheriff's headquarters, just off Highway One in mid-county, resembled the backside of an Old California mission, with wide arches breaking up a long stretch of burnt orange stucco.

Jeff McCall met me in the lobby, a surprisingly compact area with padded benches along two walls, a restroom alcove, and a glassed-in counter manned by an older woman with purple hair. I think she must've seen Adele pull up and alerted McCall. I couldn't imagine he'd stand and wait for me when there were two murder cases pending.

McCall's gray suit hung off him as though he'd lost a lot of weight. His black cowboy boots weren't something you saw in northern California much, outside of certain bars. He'd slicked back his thinning brown hair, revealing a pronounced widow's peak. Alert blue eyes peered at me with a mixture of curiosity and false sincerity.

McCall offered his hand. "Thanks for coming in. I wanted to meet the man who's helped so much, and I need to ask you a few questions, too."

"Sure. I've been around enough dead bodies lately to last me a lifetime, so I'm happy to be somewhere else right now."

I expected McCall to escort me farther into the building. Instead he continued to stand in the middle of the lobby as he spoke.

"I get that," he said. "Sometimes I feel the same way. I hope you understand why I had to pull Bill from heading this investigation."

"Actually, I don't," I told him.

Two Hispanic men walked by us on the way to the counter. One of them sported a fresh bruise on his forehead.

"It's pressure from up above," McCall explained. "Bill is a great detective, but he's made very little progress on the first murder. The sheriff wants new eyes on this one, now that we've got a serial killer on our hands. Follow me, please."

He led me through a door beside the counter to a maze of blue-walled cubicles and then to a corner office. The department did seem shorthanded; most of the work stations were unmanned.

McCall's office overlooked a creek that ran behind the station. Several live oaks competed for sunlight with a huge sycamore, which sheltered a patch of blackberries. Unfortunately, just across the riparian scene, a tire store's parking lot displayed the elderly cars of its employees.

The interior decor was dated but had once been state of the art for a government building. The chrome and faux leather chair he'd gestured for me to sit in was quite comfortable. Dark wood wainscoting formed a visual perimeter that made the room look smaller than it was. The carpet was wall-to-wall taupe Berber, a recent addition from what I could tell. Oddly, the room smelled like a new car.

"So let's get started," McCall said from across his broad oak desk. "Why is it that I can't find out anything about you beyond six years ago?"

"I took a spiritual name when I lived in Baba Ahimsa's ashram. I've only been using it for six years."

"Kade Tobin? What's spiritual about that?"

"It was assigned to me," I told him. "I don't actually know what it's supposed to mean. Baba was going to tell me when I'd been at his ashram longer, but then he died."

"And who was this Baba character?"

"You can look him up online. Baba Ahimsa was the real deal—an Indian saint."

"All right. What was your birth name?" McCall asked.

"I'd rather not say."

"I'd rather you did," he insisted. His tone was cordial, but his eyes were steely.

I sat and gazed at him. His expression didn't change.

"So you've got something to hide," he finally said. "That doesn't bode well for you, Tobin. I'm not a friendly guy like Bill. You're going to have to level with me sooner or later. Or face the consequences."

He'd morphed his features into what he must've believed was an intimidating look—pursed lips and narrowed eyes. To me, it looked more like what a child might do when he'd eaten something unpleasant.

"I have my reasons," I told him, "and those are none of your business, either. I'm here voluntarily to help, not to be grilled about my past. When I committed to a spiritual path, I became a new man, and I've devoted myself to helping others on their paths ever since. I don't identify with who I used to be."

"The law does," McCall asserted, abandoning his contrived expression while he leaned forward and nodded. "The law holds everyone responsible for what they've done, regardless of how disconnected they think they are from their younger self. You ever hear of a cold case? We've convicted felons on DNA evidence thirty years after their crimes."

I shook my head. "Like a hammer that views everything in the world as a potential nail, McCall, you're seeing me through the lens of law enforcement. If I don't want to tell you something, it must be because of something illegal—something that implies guilt in this current investigation. That's very shortsighted."

He thought about that. "Okay, let's say we let that slide for now. Maybe it's not important. Maybe it is. Tell me about your dog."

"Zeus? He's a wonderful companion. What do you want to know?"

"He didn't bark and wake you up the night of the first murder, did he—I mean before you heard him howl?"

"Not that I heard," I answered.

"You don't think you'd hear him if he were outside near your yurt?"

"I guess I probably would," I conceded.

"I've seen photos of the yurt. It has canvas walls, doesn't it?"

"Yes."

"And I'm going to guess there was no barking last night either, was there?" McCall asked.

"Once again, not that I heard."

"Not that anyone heard, I'll bet," he said, raising his voice slightly. "Not one out of twenty-three people the first time. They couldn't all be heavy sleepers, could they?"

"No."

"And at least one or two were fully awake at the time of the Curtis murder, weren't they?"

"I'll tell you what," I told him. "Let's conditionally stipulate that Zeus didn't bark."

"Why do you think that was, Mr. Tobin?"

"I can't figure it out."

"Do you think your dog knew the person who dumped the body?" McCall asked. "Do you think he was drugged?"

"Perhaps," I conceded.

"We had a vet come out to your land while you were busy that first day. Your dog's blood sample didn't show any drugs." He smiled in a decidedly creepy way. McCall was hard to like.

"I don't think you had a legal right to do that," I told him.

"I don't care what you think." He glared at me. "You were our prime suspect at that point. Several things you said didn't add up. And they still don't." He paused again, this time softening his eyes and mouth. "So let's agree that your dog knows the murderer."

I just sat and gazed at him again.

"I think your dog knows *you* pretty well, doesn't he?" He stared me in the eyes.

"Do you really think I did this—murdered two young girls? If I did, why would I kill them somewhere else and then drop them at my own doorstep?"

McCall was happy to answer that. "So you could keep an eye on the investigation, or even manipulate a detective into letting you 'help.' That's why."

"There are so many holes in this story you're spinning," I told him. "It's nothing more than a string of assumptions. Are you thinking I'll be bullied by what you're doing? I might be if I were guilty, but I'm not. Talk to anyone in my community—see if they think I'm capable of murder."

"I don't need to. I talked to Ann Marin. She knows you are," McCall said.

That surprised me. I paused to consider what to do. "It strikes me that the more I defend myself, the more you're going to think I'm guilty. Why don't I go ahead and explain some things instead of just responding to your innuendos and accusations."

"Feel free." He waved his hand as if he were giving permission to a journalist to ask a question at a press conference.

"You're going to find out all this anyway now that you're focusing on me," I said.

"Go ahead. I'm listening."

"The reason I changed my name and didn't want to share my history is that I'm an illegal alien. I moved to the US from Canada to join Baba's ashram, and I never returned."

"Go on," McCall urged.

"I don't have a driver's license, I don't have a social security number, and I'm off the grid as much as I can manage. I'm sure you've noticed that other spiritual communities maintain a strong online presence to attract members. We don't. And there are no recent photos of me online that I know of, either."

"So you've been concerned we'd discover this and alert immigration to have you deported?" McCall asked.

"Yes, that's one of the reasons I got involved with Bill's investigation—to keep an eye on that."

McCall frowned and tilted his head down to accentuate what he said next. "I don't give a shit if you're from the moon, Tobin. All I care about are these murders."

"I'm very glad to hear that," I said.

"What about your dog? Are you going to come clean on that?" he asked.

"I didn't want to share this either, because it sounds unlikely and I can't prove it. Zeus has epilepsy, and that puts him out of commission sometimes. For some reason, his seizures tend to happen at night."

"Why is that something to hide?" McCall asked.

"He bites people. He gets disoriented when he's coming out of an episode and then he bites. He's already over the limit as far as the county is concerned. They'd euthanize him if they knew he's still doing it sometimes."

"You can't prove this?" McCall asked. "Why not? What about his medical records?"

"Our vet died and his partner closed the practice," I told him. "I know how that sounds, but it's the truth."

"Who was that?"

"Louis Gadsden at the Live Oak Animal Care Center."

"That's damn convenient, Tobin. We'll look into it," McCall told me.

"Thank you. Please do."

"You think that confessing to these little things gets you off the hook for the big ones?" McCall asked.

"They're not little to me. And they explain your concerns, don't they?"

"Mostly—if they're true," he conceded. "Now it's time to tell me your original name, where you came from in Canada, and what the hell you were doing before you supposedly got enlightened or whatever."

"My birth name is Carl Steubens," I said. "I lived in North Vancouver. I've never been in trouble with the law. I used to be a middle school counselor. Before that I was an emergency medical tech."

"That wasn't so hard, was it?" McCall said, smiling insincerely again.

"I see now I should've been more forthcoming. It never occurred to me I'd be a suspect for more than the first few hours. Can you think of a less likely profession for a murderer?"

"Certainly," McCall said. "Plenty of cult leaders have been murderers."

"Hasn't Bill explained that the Brethren is not a cult?" I asked.

"That's his perspective. Marion Burke and I look at it differently."

"The DA?"

"Yes," McCall confirmed. "Susan Burke has talked to her about you and what goes on up there on the mountain. If it quacks like a duck, Tobin…"

"So the DA pressured you to come after me?" I asked.

"Along with the sheriff, who I already told you about. You know, Tobin, you'd be surprised how much Bill was stringing you along while we investigated you. We saw you as a flight risk. I already know your real name and that you're Canadian."

"Then you were just seeing if I'd tell the truth?" I asked.

"Yes. Did you really think we wouldn't contact people in your old ashram in Washington once we heard about it from one of your members? Did you think no one there would tell us you're Canadian—from Vancouver? It was easy enough to send your photo to the authorities in BC and establish your true identity."

"Don't you have better suspects than me?" I asked. "Where's my motive? I didn't know Althea, and I'll wager I don't know the new victim, either."

"Some serial killers choose their victims at random," he said.

"Give me a break, McCall. Now I'm a serial killer?"

"I'm just saying. When you state inaccurate information, I'm going to correct you."

"Fine. Are we done?" I asked. "I need to get back to help my people deal with this."

"We're done for now. Don't go anywhere."

Chapter 13

Perhaps I should've leveled with you, the reader, as well. But I wasn't aware that any of this was relevant to my narrative. It's been easy to pass as a US citizen, and I haven't had to assimilate into mainstream culture to obtain a job or drive a car. Were I from Mexico, I'd probably be back in Jalisco or Michoacán by now.

Some of the original members of our community do know of my background from when we lived at the ashram. Seekers came from all over the world to Washington State, and many, like me, didn't officially migrate. It wasn't important at the time, and my in-the-know followers still don't care.

More history: when I left the ashram after Baba dropped his body, a dozen of these members followed me and one of them owned the land we occupy now. Unfortunately, Frank Dawson has since passed way. Fortunately, he willed the deed to the nonprofit corporation our lawyer member—Phil Karanos—established. As Phil told Bill in his interview following the first murder, Frank's family had been fighting this for years until recently. Their lawyer was ruthless. I was glad Phil dealt with him.

In British Columbia, my counseling career was satisfying, and I was content living with a loving woman. But when you die for twelve minutes and you meet God, your life changes. Enough said.

****

I was shook up as I ride-shared back to the land. McCall refused to authorize a lift home, even though one of the department's SUVs passed us on Skyline Boulevard a few miles from our destination.

I knew McCall was just doing his job—giving me a hard time on several fronts for the department's purposes. Nonetheless, it was hard to muster the compassion for him that I try to extend to everyone. And, in turn, that was hard to face.

More importantly, McCall had peeled back the disavowed layers I'd tried to bury. I confess I did abhorrent things when I was younger. But an over-attention to youthful foibles isn't healthy.

Even talking about the past can hold us back. It can breed regret, guilt, shame, and rumination. How do any of these serve us as we live our lives in the present?

Specifically, how could I help my students if I revealed my illegal alien status to the authorities? Would they follow me to Canada once I was deported? Some would, some wouldn't. The ones who stayed would be cheated out of what could've been.

I'm not so grandiose that I think my teachings are the only path to becoming more congruent with the universe. And were I to leave the country, most of the students who stayed would be presented with other viable paths. The universe can certainly manage it all without me—without *any* particular person or circumstance.

That would be plan B. Plan A was what was already in place—what the universe had arranged for all of us with exquisite timing and numerous synchronous events. Insofar as we could all cooperate with this—make it work no matter the odds—we'd gain the benefits of congruence. This dance between free will and the big picture's guidance, of course, can be hard to master.

You might be wondering what the benefits of congruence are? Why do I keep mentioning it? Why pursue this path? Here's a partial list: good luck, peace of mind, loving relationships, long life, the ability to serve others at a deeper level, and the satisfaction of living an honorable life. Those are merely what one experiences en route. The ultimate payoff is unknowable to the likes of anyone I've ever met—including myself—and would probably be ineffable, anyway.

Of course, referring to all this as a benefit or a payoff belies the spirit of, well, Spirit. It simply represents the human mind's vantage point. And our language limits us even more. We don't speak Sanskrit—a tongue designed from scratch to express spiritual concepts.

Sorry for all the proselytizing. It's an occupational hazard.

****

Back on the land, Jim met me in the meadow and walked me to my office. The body had been removed and the only sign of the sheriff's department was a lone SUV in the driveway.

Jim squinted behind his thick black glasses in the sunlight despite having pulled his straw wide-brimmed hat low on his forehead. He swayed a bit as he stood. He was still shook up.

"The police went through the same things they did the first time," he told me, "except Detective Cullen only interviewed certain people, and not as long as last time. Then they all left, except for a deputy who just got here. He's in the men's dorm. I don't know why."

"How is the community handling this?" I asked.

"Better than last time, but the fragile ones are doing what they do when they freak out—you know who I mean."

"Yes."

"I'm worried some of them may leave," Jim said, wringing his hands as though he were in a melodramatic silent film. "They came here to work on things in a safe environment. We haven't really provided that, have we?"

"It must be clear to them it's not our fault someone's dumping bodies here," I said, shading my eyes from the sun. "Maybe I should address this with the entire community."

He nodded. "I think that would be a good idea."

So Jim gathered everyone in the multi-purpose building, and I spoke.

"We're all sickened by what's happened. If we can stay tethered to our truth—trusting the universe despite the murders—we'll come through this without regressing on our paths.

"We can go down kicking and screaming as we face what doesn't suit us or we can learn how to yield gracefully to something greater than ourselves. That's the meta-lesson behind challenging life events.

"In terms of the violence brought to our doorstep, I want each of you to focus on what there is to learn from what you're going through. This will vary from person to person. If we don't pay attention and allow ourselves to be shifted by what we go through, we stagnate. Our growth halts.

"So don't stay rooted in your first take on what happened. There are always alternative perspectives that add nuance and understanding. There is always Spirit guiding us.

"No one expects you to do this well. We are facing a tough test right now to keep the faith, so to speak. But if you can manage it with murder, you'll be able to do it with everything. You'll have one of the most powerful tools to navigate life under your belt. This is a blessing."

I strode away before anyone had a chance to ask questions. Spending any more time addressing this wasn't going to help. Ultimately, everyone needed to let go and move on.

****

I called Bill after meditating. "What do you have to say for yourself?" I asked. "McCall says you've been stringing me along."

"Not the whole time, and it's nothing personal. I was just doing my job—following orders."

"What fascist movement does that sound like?"

"Let me put it another way, Kade. Your bio and a few other things didn't check out, making you a prime suspect. Does it make sense for me to be straight with a potential murderer? Don't I have a higher duty to the law?"

"You don't really believe I killed those women, do you?" I asked.

"No. I just heard the recording of your interview with McCall, and I know you. I was pretty sure you were hiding something, and now I know what. But what I believe doesn't matter much."

"What does?" I asked.

"Whatever matters to the higher-ups. I can tell you this, which might ease your mind. They'd need a whole lot more evidence to move on you. If there isn't any—if you're innocent—you've got nothing to worry about."

"Well, that's a relief," I said. "You don't think the DA would try to frame me to free her daughter and wrap up the case to get reelected?"

"Free her?" Bill asked.

"You know what I mean."

"Well, I suppose it's possible. Marion is ambitious, very protective of her two daughters, and kind of ruthless on a personal level, but to go so far as to put an innocent man in jail…No, I don't think she'd ever do that."

"Tell me about the other daughter," I said.

"Why?" Bill asked.

"It might give me more insight into the DAs mindset. Right now, that's something rather important to me."

"All right. But that's it. I can't talk about the case with you anymore, even though you actually have been very helpful. Deborah Burke is a student at Stanford. You'd think that would be enough to convince her mother she could manage her life on her own. They turn down valedictorians, for God's sake, including my niece—who's a friend of Deborah's.

"Marion still keeps Deborah on a tight leash. She has to call every day. She can't go off campus without her mother's permission. It's kind of ridiculous."

"Parents control their kids as an external method of managing their own anxiety," I told him. "I'll bet Deborah goes wherever she wants, anyway."

"You bet she does. But you get the idea."

"Yes. It must drive the DA crazy that Susan has broken away and come here," I said. "Marion is probably projecting her controlling methodology onto me. When you have that tendency, you tend to assume other people do too, even if they're not demonstrating it in some overt way."

"I can hear the counselor in you now, Kade. That makes sense. But getting back to what you're worried about, nobody's going to frame you. The more we talk, the more ridiculous the idea sounds. Maybe Marion will send people up there to find code violations and try to force you to close down, but if she wanted to do that, she would've by now, right?"

"That makes sense. Okay, thanks. I appreciate your sharing all this."

"Goodbye, Kade. And good luck."

Chapter 14

I slept restlessly, still concerned about becoming a suspect and how the DA might respond to hearing my interview. For all I knew, McCall might not have believed me about any of it and reported that to her. They'd check it all out, but that would take time. How quickly would Canadian authorities respond? In the meantime…

McCall could certainly report me to ICE. For now, he wouldn't want a suspect to leave the country. When the case closed, though…

Also, the fact that Zeus's medical records weren't available certainly seemed suspicious. What were the odds his role in a murder investigation would happen to be unverifiable? How often did veterinarians die or close their practices?

I don't believe odds or statistics are particularly meaningful since I don't view the world as mechanistic. There are other "reasons" things happen. Unfortunately, law enforcement sees it differently.

In the morning, I found Susan Burke at breakfast and asked her to join me in my office when she'd finished eating.

"It's about my mom, isn't it?" she asked once we'd seated ourselves ten minutes later.

In her late twenties, Susan looked younger. Her skin was remarkably smooth and clear. She'd probably eaten all the chocolate she wanted as teen without any facial repercussions.

Susan's small and symmetrical features sat under mousy bangs. Her elfish ears stuck out from the rest of her hair, and bright green hoop earrings hung from those. Even across my desk I could smell her characteristic rosewater scent.

"I'm concerned that the authorities may regard me as a suspect in the murders," I told her.

Susan frowned and raised her voice. "That's outrageous! Those idiots. How can I help?"

"I'm not sure you can, beyond shedding a little light on the subject. I was told your mother is the DA?"

"Yes, she is." She nodded. "And she's good at it."

"You have a lot of respect for her?" I asked.

"Yes—professionally. She was a crap mom growing up—putting her career first and always being scared something would happen to me and my sister. But I've made my peace with that after two years of therapy. And now, of course, I see things from a spiritual perspective. My mother is just doing the best she can with the hand she got dealt—just like everyone else. *Her* mother was a piece of work. Even as a toddler I didn't want anything to do with her."

"How does your mother feel about you?" I asked.

"That's more complicated. On the one hand, she sometimes seems pleased that I've worked on myself and stand on my own two feet now. On the other hand, she keeps trying to lure me back home. I mean I'm twenty-seven years old. Why would I want to do that?" Susan shrugged as if the answer to her rhetorical question was unknowable.

"I imagine she thinks poorly of me?" I asked.

"Well, yes." Susan's tone told me she regretted she had to tell me that. "She thinks what we believe is nonsense and that you're convincing people to buy into it so you can avoid having a real job. She says you've never had one, which is ridiculous."

"I was a school counselor. Before that, I worked as an EMT in a big city."

It felt odd to repeat what I'd just told McCall when before the murders I hadn't shared my history in years. I thought for a moment about what else might be helpful to tell Susan to refute her mother's claims. "I've spoken about my near-death experience. That's why I left the workforce." Susan nodded, and I continued. "Do you think your mother would regard me as a murder suspect simply because you're here?"

"No, that's not her. She's by the book—to a fault, I'd say. If you're a suspect, it's because there's some misleading evidence or someone's lying to implicate you. My mom would never break the law herself. It's sacred to her."

"That's ironic, isn't it? It's sacred to her. Yet her attitude toward us…"

"Yeah." Susan cocked her head and tossed a strand of dislodged dirty blonde hair behind her ear. "You know, I could talk to her. I've defended you in the past—we email sometimes on the community computer—but I've never proactively given a testimonial about your character or anything. Do you think that would help?"

"I don't know," I replied. "Would she hear it as you being my puppet, or would she think you were acting as a reliable, independent reporter?"

"The first one, I guess." She paused for a moment. "I did date one of her assistant DAs for a while. I could try emailing him. It's not like he makes any decisions, but he might know the inside story, and he's still got a thing for me."

"That might be helpful."

"Great!" She hopped up. "I'll tell whoever's got the computer time slot that you said I should get on it right away."

"Fine. Thank you."

As Susan scurried away, I noticed that my gut had relaxed, and I was breathing more deeply.

****

The deputy who'd disappeared into the men's dorm the day before came back mid-morning to interview me about the second murder. I was surprised they'd taken this long to find out if I had an alibi, what I'd seen or heard, and all the rest I'd been subjected to the first time. Why hadn't McCall asked me about all this when I'd been at the station?

Tim Schmidt was the first law enforcement officer I'd met who looked as though he could be a model in a clothing catalog. It was easy to picture him in a puffy jacket and a patterned ski cap standing in front of a Chilean mountain range. In fact, I could see him as the lead in an action movie.

He was also quite tall, but his lack of grace made it hard for me to picture him on a basketball court. He almost missed landing in my rattan chair and didn't seem to know what to do with his legs when he did.

"Have you read a report about the first murder?" I asked, preempting whatever he had in mind.

"Yes, sir."

"Then you pretty much know the story with me the night of the second murder. My dog woke me up a few minutes later this time. Otherwise…"

"So you were sleeping alone in your tent and heard nothing until you heard your dog howl?" he asked.

"That's right. It's a yurt," I said.

"Isn't that a type of tent? Don't Mongolian nomads put them up and take them down as they wander around?"

"It sounds like you know more about it than I do," I said.

Tim nodded. "Anyway, here's my next question. Do you always sleep alone?"

"Yes."

"Are you sure? I hear there's a lot of hanky-panky at these places."

"Hanky-panky?"

He grinned. "That's the word my grandmother uses about what happens at her nursing home."

I smiled back at him. I liked this guy. "I'm sure there's some of that old-fashioned intimacy here, too, but I'm celibate."

"Bummer," he responded. "Now about your dog. I heard he has a disease that puts him to sleep or something. He must be a pretty lousy watchdog, huh?"

"That's true, but we don't have much that needs watching here."

"Other than murderers and the bodies they tote around," Tim pointed out.

"Right. Other than those," I said. "Look, why don't I just tell you what I think might be helpful. I worked this case with Bill Cullen. I know a lot about it."

"That was the first murder. This one is different," Tim told me.

"How's that?"

"Different gun. Identifiable victim. A suspect in custody."

"Really? Who?" I asked.

"I'm not at liberty to say. I can tell you who the victim was, though. And I have her photo to show you. Obviously, we want to know if you recognize her."

"Okay."

"Her name was Chloe Valois," he told me. "Take a look."

When he handed me his phone, I was struck by how long Tim's fingers were. I was distracted for a moment as I pictured him playing the piano.

Chloe must've been a year or two older than Althea. In the photo, taken on a crowded beach somewhere, dark eyes peered out from a distinctly triangular face. She was slightly built with a Roman nose and a long neck.

"I know her," I told Tim. "She called herself Lily when she came here to check us out a few weeks ago, but she decided not to stay. She said she was heading to Big Sur to investigate a community there."

"What else can you tell me about her?" he asked excitedly. I don't think he expected much from our interview.

"You may already know this from the coroner, but she had a few burn scars on her arm and neck. You can't see them in the photo. I would guess she was in a fire quite a few years ago."

He scribbled notes on a small pad. "How did she behave? Was she weird or something?"

"On the surface, she seemed kind and friendly. I could easily see her living here, although, of course I was planning to interview her at length first."

"One bad apple spoils the barrel, eh?"

"Right," I agreed. "Here's one other thing. Usually my right hand man Jim gives interested people tours, but Lily—I mean Chloe—insisted that I be her guide. I think she wanted to check out who was running the show right off. She asked me a lot of questions about myself. Oh, and she had a slight French accent."

"This is really helpful," Tim said. "I want to call it in right away."

"Sure."

"McCall will want to talk to you more about this," Tim told me.

"I don't doubt it."

****

Sure enough, McCall called a half hour later while Zeus and I strolled on a path that wove between the rugged limestone outcroppings near the southern boundary of our property.

Zeus avoided the warm sun by seeking whatever shade he could find along our route. I did my best to let the spring sun bask my head and shoulders, occasionally tilting my face up as well. A slight breeze rustled the scrubby bushes that had managed to take root in the rocky soil. It was remarkable that just a few steps beyond soaring redwoods, another ecosystem could be so markedly different.

"You knowing this victim is an interesting development, don't you think?" McCall began. "Is it okay if we record this call?"

"Interesting? Sure. And record away."

"So you think Ms. Valois was French?" he asked.

"I have no idea. I just heard a slight French accent. There are many parts of the world where it's spoken."

"And you say she was in a fire?" he asked.

"That's just an interpretation based on what I saw. I can't say for sure. During my time doing emergency medicine, I saw my share of burn victims, but not what they looked like five years later."

"So you're saying she was in this fire five years ago?"

"Are you doing this on purpose, McCall?"

"What?" His tone tried unsuccessfully to sound as though he no idea what I meant.

"Trying to get me on the record saying definitive things when I'm just trying to report what I observed."

"Sorry about that," he responded, not sounding sorry at all. "Some people fall for it. Then we can catch them out later when they contradict themselves."

"You think I'm a more likely suspect since I met this second victim, don't you?" I asked, sidestepping an animal dropping.

"Not necessarily," he protested.

"I suppose it wouldn't do any good to ask for more details about Chloe," I tried.

"That's right. It wouldn't. Now I've been told—by Bill Cullen—that you're pretty sharp about people, so I want to hear more impressions about Ms. Valois. Use your intuition or whatever special powers you think you have. Just give me more."

"Okay, but to be clear, none of this is fact. It's just impressions and speculation," I told him.

"Fine."

"I got the sense there might be more going on with her than just seeing if she wanted to join—some sort of hidden agenda. Maybe she was a journalist or something along those lines. And her interest in me was peculiar. At one point—when I was pointing out features in our kitchen—I caught her staring at my profile as though to commit it to memory."

"Well, you are a good-looking guy. Maybe she had a crush," McCall suggested.

"Maybe. And she could've been a bit intoxicated by my energy. One of the reasons I don't usually give tours is that it's better if newcomers have a chance to gradually assimilate my energy—spending one-on-one time in small increments."

"Yeah, whatever," McCall said.

"Another impression I had was that she was repressing anger," I continued. "Underneath her sweet personality, she was processing old trauma that she was still angry about. Of course, underneath that was her essential self that I could've helped her get in touch with."

"Are *you* doing this on purpose, Tobin? I don't need the mumbo-jumbo, do I?"

"Sorry."

McCall sounded almost reasonable and genuine when he spoke again. "So maybe this injustice that Althea told Greta about at the hostel was some kind of trauma like Lily's," McCall said. "Maybe the two victims are connected about that."

"That's a stretch."

"That's what we do—stretch," he told me. "We try things on for size. What do you think?"

"You're asking me?" I was surprised. Was he stringing me along the way that Bill had?

"Yeah," he replied. "Maybe you're involved in this and maybe you're not. Either way, it's going to help to hear what you have to say, Tobin."

"Okay. I think it's possible the victims knew each

other, but not likely. What about your suspect?"

"Actually, we had to let him go. His alibi for Althea's murder is airtight, and we've only got circumstantial evidence about the second murder. Marion said he'd walk in about an hour if he had any kind of lawyer at all, and he has a good one."

"I've got more, but it's even more speculative," I told McCall.

"Go ahead."

"Lily—Chloe, sorry—was afraid of dogs, or at least my dog."

"I haven't been up there yet. Is he aggressive?" McCall asked.

"He's big, but he's super friendly and sensitive to whoever prefers him to keep his distance."

"So what does the dog deal matter?" McCall asked gruffly.

"Do you want to hear what I noticed or do you want me to do your job for you? I have no idea what the value of any of this information is in your investigation."

"Whatever. Go on."

I pictured McCall waving his hand in the air. His whatevers annoyed me. If he chose to dismiss what I said, he could do that internally without voicing it.

"Just one more thing," I added. "Chloe mentioned she was visiting the area—not a local."

"Like Althea. Why didn't you tell all this to the deputy?"

"He walked away before I was finished. He said he needed to tell you what he'd learned and let you follow through."

"Sorry about that," McCall said. "We didn't figure you had anything much to add, so we sent the new guy."

"Give Tim time. He's personable," I said.
"So what?"
"You like saying things like that, don't you?"
"Yeah, I do."

Chapter 15

Later, I read more about Chloe's murder online after bringing one of the laptops from the project building into my office. She turned out to be Canadian too, here in the US on a full academic scholarship at Notre Dame. She performed with a swing-dancing troupe and majored in psychology. Like Althea, no one back East knew why she'd flown here from Indiana several weeks ago. At least, not so far.

Before I'd learned much more, a well-dressed woman and a burly man with a video camera on his shoulder threw the door open and brusquely strode in.

"Are you the one in charge? We need to talk to you," the woman said. Her makeup completely masked her face. She could've robbed a bank, then cleaned her face, and survived a line-up identification at a police station. Her medium-length blonde hair was frozen in place. I tried to gauge how hard the wind would have to blow to budge it.

"I am janitor," I said in a thick Russian accent. "You need to find Japanese man. He will talk to you."

"Okay, thanks."

They were out of the room as suddenly as they'd stormed in. Ten minutes later, Martha came in.

Her normally placid face had tightened with stress, revealing wrinkles at the corners of her eyes that I'd never seen before. The situation was getting to her, which said a lot about the magnitude of recent events. I'd seen Martha weather all sorts of stressors with remarkable equanimity.

"They're not buying it," she told me. "Jim doesn't impress them. How shall we handle this?"

I handed her my phone. "Ask them to leave while you hold the phone. If they don't immediately move, ostentatiously pretend to dial 911 and report trespassers. If that doesn't do the trick, get Wayne to escort them out by gently holding their upper arms."

"Right."

A few minutes later, Wayne showed up. I expected him to report success. His phlegmatic, intimidating presence—even with Bill Cullen in his interview—would surely discourage unwanted visitors.

"These people are like lampreys or something," he told me. "I can't get rid of them without getting really physical, which I don't think you want. Can't you come out and make a statement or something?"

"No," I told him. "Tell them we'll email them something juicy if they leave—inside information about the police investigation."

"Okay." He marched out, treading heavily, as usual.

I finally finished reading the various overlapping news stories online about the second murder without learning anything I didn't already know.

Ten minutes later, Martha was back. "It worked. Here's their email address."

"Thanks. Sit down a minute. Do you understand why I don't want to be on TV?"

She sat. "Yes, you have a problematic past, don't you? Were you a criminal?"

I stared at her. "Why would you think that?"

"Lots of things."

"Do other members think that?" I asked.

"Not that I'm aware of. You didn't answer my question."

"No, I didn't," I agreed.

I thought it over. I knew I could trust Martha to hold something in confidence. It went against the grain, though, to tell anyone about my immigration status.

"I'm not using my original name. I'm an illegal alien," I told her.

"From what planet?" She smiled radiantly.

"I wish. We're both marooned on this one, aren't we?"

Martha nodded. "That's the truth. You think someone might recognize you?"

"Yes. Better to be safe than sorry."

"What are you going to email to those two?" Martha asked.

"I haven't decided, but I guess I better get to it before they come back," I replied.

"We could station people at the driveways to keep the press out."

"No, but tell Jim to suspend working on the project for a few days," I told her.

"Sure. I'll tell him."

I emailed the reporter, revealing that the police had released their suspect and Chloe had been afraid of dogs. I hoped that would do the trick. I also suggested she find a way to make her hair look more natural. Vengeance was mine.

As I was finishing, Susan Burke walked in. "Oh, sorry. I didn't realize you were busy."

"No, come on in."

Susan sat down across from me. Buzzing with energy, clearly she had something she was impatient to share. Her hair had snaked away from an ear again, and she hadn't even fixed it.

"Mark—the guy who works with my mom—told me a couple of things that might be important. I didn't know if he'd call back when I contacted him, but he did after a while. The police found a possible connection between the two victims. I think it's kind of sketchy, but Chloe Valois is from Montreal and Althea once spent a week up there when she was twelve."

"It's a big city. Why would they have met?" I asked.

"I don't know. I'm just telling you what Mark said."

"Yes, of course. What was the second thing?"

"A week ago, Chloe deposited ten thousand dollars into a new bank account," Susan reported. "Her old one only has three hundred dollars in it. How about that?"

"Now, that sounds significant," I told her.

"That's what I thought."

"Anything else?"

"Mark admitted my mom has a hard-on for you," she told me. "He didn't think she'd railroad you either, but she's going to be aggressive about finding more evidence and maybe deporting you."

"You said '*more* evidence?' " I asked.

"He said they had some. He wouldn't tell me what it was. Sorry, Kade."

"Why do you think he told you what he did?" I asked.

"I said I'd go to dinner with him if he did—you know, to talk about maybe getting together again. Can I go? I might find out more."

"How do you feel about saying you'd go out with

him?"

"Crappy," Susan reported. "I didn't want to lie, so the way I said it wasn't exactly a lie. I *will* talk about taking him back, only I know I'll say I won't."

"So you misled him?" I asked.

"Yes. Was that okay? It seemed important to you to find out all that."

"You did great. I appreciate it. Sure, enjoy your meal with the guy. Take one of the vans. When is this?"

"Tonight, actually," she told me.

****

How would someone suddenly acquire ten thousand dollars? Winning a lottery? An inheritance? I considered Chloe's age and life situation. How many college students inherited money? And lotteries were basically a tax on ignorant people. She had an academic scholarship.

When I looked at it from the perspective of something shady, I came up with theft, embezzlement, blackmail, and fraud. I was sure McCall was looking into all these possibilities, so I let it go.

The possible Montreal connection was certainly worth investigating. I wouldn't rule it out if I were in charge. But if visiting a populous city meant you were likely to be connected to one of millions of residents, then most of us are in trouble.

Mark's comments about his boss were troubling. Not unexpected, but troubling nonetheless. Who wanted a DA as an enemy? I considered contacting Marion Burke directly to employ conflict-resolution techniques with her. If she had a chance to get to know me, perhaps she'd realize the absurdity of the idea that I'd commit murder. I tabled that idea for now. It could make things worse.

I decided to check on the security of the project while no one was working on it. I needed a break from the murder case. After a short walk with Zeus, I locked the door behind us and turned on the row of annoying fluorescent lights.

Three of the latest, most powerful laptops perched on three battered wooden tables. Another folding metal table held a coffeemaker, a microwave, and a pint-sized refrigerator against a side wall.

One by one, I fired up the computers and checked on the safety screens. The first innocuous placeholder site was dedicated to converting our non-profit into a religion, thus providing us with additional tax breaks. It was a logical project that an outsider or an outer circle member might find odd, but not truly troubling.

The Brethren of Congruence hadn't seemed like a religious enough title to Jeremy—the member tasked with developing this decoy project. I saw on his monitor that he was currently applying to the IRS as the Church of Divine Congruence. Also, according to his recent browser history, he'd accessed bondage porn that morning. Oops.

The second bogus project was a long-odds attempt to establish a new crypto-currency. A woman with a background in that field thought she could manage to create a realistic simulacrum. When I perused her laptop, I understood almost none of what she was supposedly working on. Blockchain architecture? Full stack development? I don't know why I bothered. Hopefully, if the police ever searched the building, they'd be similarly baffled.

The last work station belonged to one of my favorite members, due to his quirky sense of humor. Dan was ostensibly working on developing algorithms based on chaos theory to make money gambling online. When he first proposed this, I was opposed. What “system” has ever beat the odds?

Dan knew one. He’d been a physics professor at a major university where a colleague had won hundreds of thousands of dollars in Las Vegas at roulette tables using a similar method. The guy had even written a book about it. No wheel was perfectly round and balanced and that could be exploited. No “random” number generated by a computer was truly random, either. When Dan tried to explain why in detail, he lost me.

“I’ll use my own money to run experiments,” Dan told me. “If I don’t win, I’ll stop. If I do, I’ll transfer the money into the community’s account and keep going. The Brethren have nothing to lose. This could be a real project we run on the side. I’ll still be free to work on the main one most of the time. Anyway, Jeremy and Lisa do the heavy lifting on that, don’t they?”

On that basis, I let him give it a try. I have nothing against games of supposed chance per se, mostly because I don’t believe there is such a thing as chance. Everything mutually arises according to causes and circumstances we rarely understand. If that stew of life ingredients added up to winning in this instance, we would. If not, we wouldn’t.

Dan’s laptop yielded a lot of math, convoluted charts of gambling website histories, and ever-shifting screensavers of his four adult children. Once again, I didn’t think anyone else would understand or be alarmed by it.

I felt it was important to create these misleading and slightly off-putting sites to support the notion that we needed to keep the work behind locked doors. My people had done an exemplary job of coming up with red herrings.

Chapter 16

The rest of the day passed uneventfully. The next morning was another story.

McCall rousted me out of my bed. “This is definitely a tent,” he said, standing in the doorway.

“That’s an interesting way to wake someone up, Detective,” I said.

I’d actually been half awake, musing on a talk Baba Ahimsa had once given on what the opposite of love was—ignorance.

“We need to talk,” McCall told me. “First, I want you to show me around this place.”

“Sure. But unless you’re a voyeur, you might want to step out while I get dressed.”

He turned on his heel and strode away. I met him where he stood beside the still blood-stained patch of grass in the meadow.

McCall once again wore an ill-fitting gray suit and black cowboy boots. This time I noticed why. He was short.

If anything, his pronounced widow’s peak had slid down his forehead. At any rate, the point of it was lower than I remembered. His blue eyes contrasted sharply with his tan face. In another context—maybe at a golf course—his broad face would’ve made me wonder if he was some sort of captain of industry—an old school CEO.

McCall swiveled his head to study my face. "Why here unless it has something to do with you, Tobin?"

"There are twenty-three other people on the property. This meadow is the least lit place at night. Where the bodies were found probably has nothing to do with being near my yurt."

"It's a tent," he said, smiling his creepy smile. "So you're saying somebody else up here is the murderer? First you swear they're all saints, and now that you know you're a suspect, you're throwing them under the bus? Do I have that right?"

"No. I'm pointing out that narrowing your focus—keeping it solely on me—doesn't serve you. There are a lot of other possibilities, aren't there? I was just naming one of them as an example."

"You're quick on your feet, Tobin," McCall said. "I'll give you that. You've got an answer for everything."

"Let's go eat breakfast," I suggested, gesturing toward the door. "I can't show you much yet because people are still sleeping. Why did you come up here so early?"

"I'm asking the questions, and screw breakfast. Take me around where you can for now. After that, we'll wake people up if I feel like waking them."

"Whatever you say," I replied. I didn't see the value of upping the ante by meeting his belligerence with my own energy.

So I escorted McCall on a tour. He seemed interested in all of it, even basic things like what was in the array of refrigerators in the kitchen. Wayne was there assembling breakfast ingredients, and he obviously resented the intrusion, trying unsuccessfully to hide a scowl. As a big-time introvert, I knew Wayne liked his early morning solitude.

By the time we'd finished all the nonresidential buildings, most of the male members would be awake, so we visited their dorm.

"The women's dorm has the same layout," I told McCall as we walked in. "Men aren't allowed in there."

"Maybe that's where you're hiding your gun collection, Tobin."

I stared at him. "Really?"

"I like to see how people react when I say things like that," he told me.

"I think I'll try it," I told him. "Let's see how you react to my outrageous comments. The weapons cache is stored in a blimp that's tethered with an invisible rope to my ankle."

He waved his hand in the air. At least I was spared a "whatever."

The dorm wasn't much different from the ones soldiers are billeted in while in basic training—at least in the movies I'd seen. Brethren members had personalized their allotted spaces, though, which helped the long room be both more pleasing to the eye and more comfortable. The most common complaint I heard about the dorm was the inconsistent temperature that we'd never been able to regulate properly. If I slept there, I'd be most bothered by the lighting—more low-end fluorescent tubes.

"Next," McCall said after strolling through, "I want to see what's in that building you skipped on the tour—back by the vans."

"Why?"

"Why not? Do you have something to hide?" he asked.

I decided to make a stand. Acknowledging the truth of what he said, but not being forthcoming about it was a way to seize power in our interaction.

"Yes," I responded. "I have something to hide."

I knew I'd frustrate McCall as well, and frustrated people also lose traction in a conflict situation as their behavior becomes driven by their emotions.

"That's where the guns are?" he asked.

He didn't display any frustration. In fact, his jocular response indicated the opposite. My efforts had bounced off him.

"Will you stop with that, please? It's getting old," I told him.

"So what's the big secret?" he responded.

"I'm showing you around in the spirit of cooperation. You don't have a search warrant, and I'm under no obligation to even let you on the property."

It was time to even more firmly draw a line in the sand. McCall was getting on my nerves. He was in a position where he was obliged to take no for an answer, and he wouldn't.

"That's true," McCall acknowledged. "I'm asking you to voluntarily let me into that building in the interest of clearing yourself. If whatever's in there has nothing to do with the murders, why hide it? That doesn't look good, Tobin."

I couldn't help but sigh. I hated to admit it, but he had a point. "Fine. Follow me."

McCall was visibly disappointed when I unlocked the door to the project building and let him in. It was a time of day, fortunately, when no one would be working in there.

"That's it? Three computers? Why didn't you want

me to see them?"

"I guess it's a boundary issue. We ought to be able to keep something private if we want to," I explained.

"Bullshit," he said. "Let's see what's on these."

"Fine." I went to Dan's chaos theory laptop first and brought up the screen we kept as a placeholder.

"What the hell is this?" McCall asked.

"Beats me. Some math project I can't understand either. The member working on this asked that no one else see it. I guess he's concerned about someone appropriating his intellectual property. I have a feeling you're not going to."

"How about that one?" He pointed to the adjacent table. "Turn that one on."

McCall was similarly disappointed in the crypto-currency, and then the religion status projects.

"All right," he said. "Let's go to your office and talk."

"Sure. I still want to help however I can."

"We'll see about that," he remarked.

Once Zeus wandered in with us—he'd come back from a foray somewhere and was lying in front of the office cabin when we arrived—and we'd settled in chairs, McCall started. "Where were you before Vancouver?"

"Nowhere. That's where I'm from."

"Then why can't we find any photos of you beyond six years ago? How can you explain that?"

"I don't need to. It's not my fault if you can't find things," I said. "But once again, in the interest of cooperation, let me fill you in a little more about me. Not everybody drives, so I've never had a driver's license. And I wasn't involved with anything likely to be online until I started counseling. My photo's on the school site where I worked. You found that, right?"

He nodded. "I'm not concerned with the recent past. We've got that covered. The thing is, you're Canadian, and there's a Canadian angle on this case. Like most of us in law enforcement, I'm not a big fan of coincidences. Were you ever in Montreal?"

"Sure. I spent a summer there when I was a kid—when I was seven. My grandmother lived downtown before she moved to Nova Scotia. I don't remember much about my time there. In fact, my main memory is eating a really delicious corned beef on rye sandwich in a Jewish deli."

"They have those there?" It was almost as though McCall thought this was the part I might lying about.

"Sure. There are large ethnic groups in all the major cities. Quebec City is mostly French-Canadian. There are lots of Jews in Montreal. And Vancouver had a huge influx of Hong Kong immigrants. People in this country don't know much about Canada. It's not all beer, hockey, and bland politeness."

"I don't need a geography lesson, Tobin."

"You asked me a question. I gave you an answer," I told him.

"Fine. I remind you that last time we couldn't trace your past it was because you changed your name to hide something criminal."

"Being in a country without the right paperwork is hardly a crime, McCall," I protested.

"We call you people *illegal* aliens for a reason. The point I'm making is that I wonder if you're doing the same thing again. Maybe you have yet another identity. Maybe that guy's got a connection to the murders."

“Maybe you’re fishing because you haven’t found a viable suspect yet,” I responded. “Maybe you’re thinking I’m somebody who’d be likely to confess if a cop said all this to me. You’re wasting your time here. You can’t intimidate me. We’ve been through this before, haven’t we?”

“You just smell wrong, Tobin. I don’t care what you say.”

“Are we talking about your nose or the DA’s?” I asked.

“Both of us. And we’re a formidable team. Watch your ass.” He stood abruptly, wheeled, and strode out.

Susan had been waiting outside my office. I hoped she hadn’t heard anything.

“Come on in,” I said.

Zeus pulled himself onto his feet and met her by the chair McCall had just vacated. She lowered herself into it and reached up to pat him.

“How did your dinner go?” I asked. “Did you find a kind way to let Mark down?” I’d switched gears verbally, but part of me was still with McCall.

“I didn’t get a chance,” she said. “It was an ambush. I sat down with Mark and then my mother zoomed in and took his place. Next thing you know, she’s interrogating me about you. And then she started harping on the same old things. Why don’t I go back to law school? Why can’t I make it work with Mark? Why don’t I appreciate all she’s done for me? This is why I keep my distance.”

“I’m sorry, Susan.”

“I did find out they’re digging into your past,” she told me. “Is that going to be a problem?”

“No, not at all. Don’t worry about it. In fact, try to put all this out of your mind and focus on your spiritual path. Talk to Martha about what might help you the most right now."

"Okay, thanks."

****

Once again, I felt I needed a break from the case. My encounter with McCall had taken a toll I couldn't have anticipated. Probably, my stress had been cumulative—the way my system responded to a repetitive electronic music track I'd heard once. The throbbing bass line had remained in its initial, unsatisfying pattern, with no shift to a pleasing baseline pitch. Music that never resolves triggers my internal energy to build up without an escape valve.

Merely constructing this metaphor eased my mind a bit, but it wasn't until I'd played badminton against Ralph that I felt like me. He was extremely competitive, which I found amusing, and it made beating him more fun.

There was a lesson built into Ralph's experience, as well. On a spiritual path, being humbled was helpful, and surrendering, however grudgingly, to undesirable events serves an even greater purpose. We all need to accept reality more gracefully. Ralph was challenged in this department. I'd provided an opportunity for him to work on that.

Mostly, though, to be honest, I just enjoyed winning. I'd been a basketball player as a teen. Some things endure no matter how long you meditate.

McCall came back around about five that afternoon with two young deputies I hadn't met before. They found me reading in my yurt.

"Wyatt Barr, you're under arrest for the murders of Althea Curtis and Chloe Valois." He turned to one of the deputies. "Cuff him."

Chapter 17

I sat in the back of a sedan with one of the deputies. He hogged the seat, intentionally inching toward me during the trip. The other deputy drove while McCall swiveled from the passenger seat to talk to me.

Vertical lines divided the area between his eyebrows, his lips were pressed together, and he'd jutted out his lower jaw. McCall seemed to be angry, which struck me as odd. If I were him, and I believed I had caught a killer, I'd have been happy—or at least pleased with myself.

"I'm reading you your rights so we can go on the record with anything you say." He did so, in a controlled, terse fashion.

"Here's what we know," McCall told me. "Before you were Kade in this country or Carl in British Columbia, you were Wyatt Barr. You grew up and lived in Montreal until you were thirty-two. You tutored school kids, and Chloe Valois was one of your students. Her parents were friends with Althea's parents—they all went to college together in upstate New York. Althea stayed at Chloe's house when she visited Montreal—when the girls were twelve. What happened, Tobin? Did you molest them together or separately? Is that why you moved away and changed your name?"

"You've mixed me up with my cousin," I told him. "We look alike. He's the one from Montreal. If you give me a chance, I'll prove it to you."

"That's not all," McCall said. "Someone matching your description—"

"And my cousin's."

"—was seen at Casa Zapoteca with Althea the evening before her death. Her stomach contents are what led us to show her photo at Mexican restaurants in San Jose."

"That was actually my idea, Detective, and I have an alibi for that evening—remember?"

"We'll see about that," he responded. "Here's one more nail in your coffin, Tobin. We know what happened at that ashram you were in before you came here."

"That didn't have anything to do with me," I told him.

"So you say. Here's another thing. We found out that canine seizures don't happen exclusively at night like you said with your dog."

"His usually do," I asserted.

"Bullshit."

No one spoke for the rest of the trip.

I was in trouble. My cousin was a slippery character who had taken even greater pains than I had to stay under the radar—for good reason. I knew he had committed domestic violence. I had no idea he'd molested young girls. I'd claimed I could prove this was a case of mistaken identity, and given free rein, I'm sure I could. Although my parents were dead and I was an only child, childhood friends and teachers could vouch that I grew up in Vancouver. And the fact that Wyatt existed independent of me ought to be easy to prove, as well.

The problem was, how could I do any of that from a

jail cell, and how could I convince the sheriff or the DA to investigate further? If they thought they had their man in custody, why would they work to exonerate him, especially if the DA was Susan Burke's mother?

I could've contacted Phil Karanos—our lawyer member—but I had the only phone on the property in my pocket. When I eventually got in touch with him, he could either do the necessary legwork to prove my innocence or farm that out to a private investigator. For now, I was on my own.

Had anyone seen me get arrested? I couldn't be sure, but I didn't think so. What would people do when they discovered I was missing? I very rarely left the land, and when I did, I always told Jim.

I wasn't worried about the scandal at Baba Ahimsa's ashram. I truly had nothing to do with that unfortunate incident. Being mistaken for Wyatt, though…

****

Susan Burke figured it out, called the sheriff's office to check, and then sent Phil down there. By then, I'd already been interrogated for two hours by McCall and Bill's partner Michael Quinn. It didn't make sense to me that Quinn would be part of the team instead of Bill. All his knowledge of the case had to be secondhand. Maybe they needed Bill to be the one behind the stereotypical two-way mirror.

Other than the mirror, the "interview room"—that's what the sign on the door said—defied my expectations. The ivory-colored walls sported several compact murals depicting historic sites in the county—the Santa Cruz Mission, the lighthouse, the venerable wooden rollercoaster at the boardwalk, and the Mystery Spot. The four black desk chairs grouped around the double pedestal wooden table were quite comfortable. And the recessed lighting was far from the glaring spotlight suspects faced in film noirs.

Even sitting, McCall held himself in a military bearing as if he wished he were standing to better impress the troops under him.

Michael Quinn was another matter altogether. He casually slumped in his chair. His fair skin and short brown hair reminded me of an Irish cop I'd seen in a film. We'd had a founding member with that same look a while ago, too. In fact, it was Frank Dawson, who'd willed his land to us.

Quinn's smallish brown eyes sat below sparse eyebrows and a slightly receding hairline. Oddly, his smattering of freckles and wide smile didn't prevent my receiving a hint of menace from him. When I'd been introduced to him, his grip was firm, but not an invitation to compete for who was the strongest.

Mostly, McCall's questions were redundant in the hope I would contradict myself. When he decided to take a break from repeating himself, Quinn took a turn. If anything, he was even more aggressive than McCall. I didn't know if he shared that personality trait with his boss or just chose to act that way in an interrogation.

Most of the questions could be better described as accusations. "Why did you do it?" "How did you think you'd get away with it?" "When did you decide to start scamming spiritual students?"

The relentless barrage of accusations seemed to be intended to create fear and exhaustion. Why would someone like me say anything foolish or incriminating simply because I was scared or tired?

"You wouldn't last a week in prison, Barr," Quinn

told me at one point. "Molesters don't. Cut a deal now before this goes any further, and you'll stay alive."

McCall tried "We can hold you indefinitely with the evidence we've got." I knew this wasn't so. "Do you know how slowly the wheels of justice turn? It could be a year before you come to trial. Cooperate with us and maybe there won't be one."

On the one hand, the experience was fascinating. The two detectives weren't as skilled as some of ones on TV, but I could see that their methods could work with actual criminals. If I were guilty, they might even have worked on me.

On the other hand, I really was beginning to tire—as they probably were, too—and my continued patience had become an effort. I was doing my best to remain empathetic to their experience of me for the most part—they must've been quite frustrated—but McCall and Quinn had an uncanny knack for inhibiting my effort to remain compassionate.

From what I could gather from the questions and statements that revealed the hand they held, the police thought they could prove I was my cousin. From there, it was a short leap to my being a murderer. I don't think they expected me to confess. Perhaps they thought I'd provide them additional evidence of guilt by the way I answered. Perhaps they just wanted me to suffer.

When Phil finally joined us, Quinn's tone shifted. "We appreciate your cooperation, Mr. Tobin. Now that Mr. Karanos has joined us, I hope we can continue in that vein."

"Sure," I replied. Clearly, that was said for my lawyer's benefit.

Phil put his hand on my arm. "I think my client and

I need to have a chat."

"Of course. We'll give you some privacy," McCall said. He got up and the two men left the room, locking the door behind him.

Phil put a finger to his lips and then pulled a pen and a yellow legal pad out of his attaché case.

"I don't trust these guys," he wrote. "Let's do this on paper."

"Sure," I wrote when he pivoted the pad to me.

The corners of Phil's lips were turned down, not as though he were frowning—more as though this was an expression of sadness or worry. His lowered eyebrows formed slightly diagonal lines pointing to the bridge of his thin nose. And Phil's eyes weren't as bright and alert as usual.

"Why are you talking to them?" he wrote. "Haven't you ever watched TV?"

"I had no way to get in touch with you, and since I'm innocent, I thought talking with them would provide me an opportunity to show them that," I wrote.

"Has it?"

"No."

"There you go. Look, here's how it works," he wrote. "They'll hold a bail hearing tomorrow morning. I'll be there. Be prepared for the worst. Talking a judge into granting bail in a murder case is extremely rare. And Martha mentioned you're a foreign national, which makes you a flight risk in their eyes. Even if the judge sets bail, Jim tells me we don't have the resources to get you out. How do you think you're going to do in jail?"

"I have no idea. I'm curious to find out," I wrote.

"Curious, huh? Well, that sounds like you. Is there anything you need me to do back on the land?"

The slower form of communication allowed me to organize my thoughts more, but it didn't yield any special insights.

"Make sure Zeus is taken care of, and tell everyone not to worry," I wrote to Phil. "This is just a misunderstanding."

"How's that?"

"My cousin looks like me. He's at the center of this."

"How can we prove that?" he wrote.

"Find him."

"I'll try. Write down his name and whatever you think will help."

I did so, taking my time to include everything I could think of. This time, writing instead of speaking helped me remember more.

Then Phil wrote, "I'm going to let the detectives back in and tell them you're done."

"Okay."

****

They put me in my own cell, which I appreciated. The group cell we passed down the hall smelled of alcohol and puke. The guys inside seemed to be mostly sleeping off binges on yellow plastic benches. I rated a cot, a toilet, a small stainless-steel sink, and a wooden table and chair under a barred window. The thinnest off-white towel I'd ever seen was draped over the back of the chair, and a plastic pack of toiletries roosted on the table.

"You missed dinner," the guard told me. "Can I get you anything from the vending machine?"

"That's kind of you, but no. I'll be fine."

"Suit yourself."

I meditated until lights out, and then I slept surprisingly well.

****

The bail hearing was held in a modern courtroom. The decor could've been designed by a newly graduated architect—class of 1965—who'd vowed to come up with something original for his first project. The spiral wrought-iron railings and gate at the front of the room were painted gold, which matched the side walls. Unlit sconces cascaded down from these every twenty feet or so. The light green carpet sported a geometric pattern of brown isosceles triangles.

Within this setting, the traditional dark wooden court furniture looked out of place. Long pews were arrayed horizontally, and the tables beyond the gate matched them. At the front of the room, the dark mahogany witness stand and judge's throne were paneled and gleamed with furniture polish. The jury box on the side wall didn't match either the architect's vision or the other furniture. A grainy, honey-colored railing enclosed black wooden high-backed chairs that sat on two levels. It didn't look as though a short juror in the back row could see over these.

Judge Adkin was a middle-aged African-American woman. A mini-Afro capped a very square head, which, in turn, sat above a voluminous black robe. I liked her face; she looked kind to my eye. Her robe and the rows of pews prompted me to picture her singing in a Baptist church choir. When she spoke, her loud alto voice supported that notion.

Three of us in orange jumpsuits sat in the back of the room with an armed bailiff standing behind us. The other two men had their hearings before mine, which took about five minutes each.

The prosecutor—a young Hispanic woman—spoke for a minute or two in the first case—a convenience store robbery—and then the accused man mumbled something. Bail was set at twenty thousand dollars.

While the accused was trudging back to his seat, I asked the professional-looking defendant next to me if he'd been through this before.

"Unfortunately, yes," he answered.

"Why didn't that guy have a lawyer?"

"He did—a public defender—the guy sitting next to him."

"He wasn't much help, was he?"

They called the second man's name. In his case, his lawyer claimed he was a family man with a thriving law practice. Since the prosecutor had told the judge this was the man's second arrest on fraud charges, bail was set at a hundred thousand.

Then they called Wyatt's name. I didn't budge. The bailiff standing beside the judge's perch tried again. I stood.

"Your Honor, that is not my name," I called out.

"Marion, what's going on?" the judge asked as she turned to her left.

I saw that the DA had come forward to sit next to the junior prosecutor. She stood up. I'd seen photos of Marion Burke online. In person, her burgundy pantsuit—which she wore in all her photos—was not flattering, as it highlighted her substantial butt. On the other hand, the DA held herself with poise and grace, her movements fluid. I theorized that she had been a dancer in her youth, perhaps when her butt had been less substantial.

When Marion pivoted to squarely face the judge, her

high, sharply carved cheekbone created an interesting profile, blocking the middle of her nose. Her hairdo was striking, as well—a tight French braid that resembled vertebrae.

When the DA spoke, it was in a strong, clear voice, with a hint of a New York accent. "The defendant claims that's his cousin's name and that his arrest is a case of mistaken identity. This is not so, and it's not this court's job to adjudicate such a defense. We're here to set bail."

"True," the judge said.

Phil stood at the defense table. "If I may, Your Honor."

"Go ahead."

Phil's gray suit matched his hair, which was about all I could discern since I faced his backside. He was taller than I remembered. How could I forget something like that in twenty-four hours?

He spoke in a clear, confident voice. "We will prove the accused is not who they think he is, but we have not had time to do so. My client was arrested yesterday, and both he and his cousin are Canadian, which complicates our task."

"Thank you, counselor." She beckoned to the bailiff standing behind me. "Bring this man forward, please."

I rose. "That won't be necessary. I was making sure the court knew that I don't answer to Wyatt's name. I had no intention to disrespect the court or be uncooperative."

I slid by the others and strode up to sit next to Phil. From the table, I could smell the lemon scent of the polish on the wooden structures a few paces ahead of me. I was also struck by how spotless the expanse of carpet was.

Marion had remained standing and now she spoke up in a firm, no-nonsense voice. "Mr. Barr is a flight risk, he is the leader of a cult that has many members who would help him evade his duty to appear at a trial, and he may have priors in Canada. We're still checking on that. I would also remind the court that two heinous murders have been committed. That alone warrants a no-bail decision." She sat.

The judge looked at Phil. "Counselor, I can't imagine you have anything to say that will give me a reason to violate the state bail guideline."

Phil stood. "I would just like to set the record straight. The prosecutor has misled the court."

"In what way? And who are you?"

Phil told her his name and continued. "It's true that in the media, the Brethren In Congruence would be referred to as a cult and our property a compound—both loaded terms designed to impugn the intent and values of non-mainstream spiritual communities. In some cases, the derogatory language has been earned, of course. I don't need to list the appalling examples of misguided or outright evil cults that we all know about.

"To be clear, Brethren In Congruence is *not* a cult. This is simply how outsiders might view us. Therefore my client is merely a spiritual teacher who has helped dozens of people with no tangible benefit to himself. I am one of these people. I speak from personal experience."

"That's a lovely speech, Counselor, but I don't care. I'm not ruling on the basis of that or any of the other details Ms. Burke has tacked onto this murder case. What else do you feel compelled to say?"

"You've tied my hands here, Your Honor. Are you

stating that correcting the prosecution's claims makes no difference in this matter?"

"That's exactly what I'm saying. Let's not waste any more time."

"I feel strongly that the matter of the client's actual identity be addressed," Phil said.

"Not here. You'll get your chance. Please sit down. I'm not granting bail. The defendant is remanded to the county jail to await a court hearing to resolve this issue of fact—who he is."

"What's that mean exactly?" I whispered to Phil.

"I'll tell you later. It's a good thing."

An hour later, in a small, plain room at the jail for lawyers and defendants to meet, Phil explained. "Usually the next step is an arraignment hearing, where the state shows enough evidence for the case to proceed and you enter a plea of guilty or not guilty."

"Do accused people get released at those?" I asked.

"Don't hold your breath. It hardly ever happens. Anyway, the judge ruled they'll hold a hearing to decide if you're Wyatt before that. That's when you'll walk, assuming they give us enough time to gather proof. They usually do."

"It will be the same judge?"

"I don't know," Phil told me.

"We need to make a plan about finding Wyatt," I told him. "I gather that if we can't convince the court I'm not him, I'll probably be convicted?"

"No, it's not a slam dunk. There's no murder weapon and very little in the way of forensic evidence. Did they fingerprint you and take a DNA sample?

"Yes," I told him.

"When they come up empty on those, it'll help. And

establishing exactly what happened a long time ago in another country isn't going to be easy. Without that, where's the motive? So far, it sounds like Althea never shared any history of abuse with anyone. Chloe may have. The DA is holding her cards close to her chest about things like that at this point."

"She's allowed to do that?" I asked.

"Yes. Discovery—sharing evidence—is a ways down the road—and only if this heads to trial," Phil said. "There will definitely be a trial if we can't establish your true identity and you plead not guilty. There's no chance of a plea deal here."

"So a plan…" I said.

"We'll hire an investigator up in Canada, and one here if we need to. The entire community is behind you on this. They're chipping in what they can to help. Unfortunately, Jack—our only wealthy member—has left the Brethren."

"Because I got arrested?" I asked.

"Yes."

"Will we need to take out a mortgage on the land?"

"By the time funds come to us from that, it would probably be too late to help, and there's no bail, of course. So you're stuck in jail. It'll be mix of people in there, most of them awaiting trial on drug charges."

"Maybe I can help them on their paths," I mused.

"You might as well try," Phil told me. "It's good to have a purpose of some sort in there."

"That makes sense. Will you look after Zeus?"

"We all will. Don't worry about that," he reassured me.

Chapter 18

The first time I was released into the general population—for lunch in the cafeteria—a young man with long, stringy black hair sat down next to me. His pasty face was dotted with a sparse fledgling beard. One of his eyes was aimed off to the side. He didn't smell great.

"Chet," he said.

"Kade," I told him.

"Cool name. Is that, like, from Europe?"

"Wales." I saw no reason to explain myself to a criminal I didn't know.

"Where's that?"

"Just to the left of England."

"I thought that was Ireland."

"Just to the right of Ireland—across the Irish Sea," I told him.

"So, like, it's in between them."

"Exactly."

He nodded. "I came over because of your aura."

"You see auras?"

"Sure do. You've got a really strong purple one. Are you a warlock or something?"

"Tell me this," I said, sidestepping his question. Once again, I felt no urge to share anything about myself. "How did you come to have this ability?"

"LSD. You should try it. It's amazing."

"Does that have something to do with why you're in here?" I asked.

"Yeah, I was selling it, too. Dumb move. I shoulda just kept my job at the hardware store."

I asked him if he was a spiritual person. The only people I'd ever run across who saw auras had been squarely on their paths.

"Absolutely. This guy told me I'm on the fifth level," Chet told me.

"The fifth level of what?"

"I dunno. That's all he said," Chet said.

"Who was this?" I asked.

"He had a big beard, and he gave a talk at this temple place my friend brought me to. I don't remember his name. It was something weird."

"I can answer any spiritual questions you have," I told him.

"Cool. Let me think about it."

A burly White man in his forties stomped over and hunkered down next to me. There was plenty of room across from Chet and me. Instead, he crowded me and scowled. He smelled awful—like sweat and cigarettes. By comparison, the moldy odor Chet was emitting was pricey perfume.

"What's your deal, new guy?" he asked in a strong Southern accent. His attempt to inject menace into what he'd said was only partially successful. On the one hand, who knows what he'd do if I didn't cooperate? That was in the air between us. On the other hand, his genuine curiosity embodied a child-like quality.

I'd heard it wasn't a good idea to tell other prisoners what one had been arrested for. On the other hand, it was clear this man was trying to bully me and my supposed crime might flip the script. Didn't murderers evoke fear?

"Double homicide," I told him matter-of-factly.

"Nah," Chet said. "Not with that aura."

The man rose without a word and returned to a table across the room, where he sat by himself.

I reluctantly tried to cut my salisbury steak with a plastic knife. If I weren't a vegetarian, I'd have said the meal was better than I expected.

I surveyed the room. Almost everybody looked like a peer of Chet—guys who'd sat in the back of classrooms at school and had trouble following along. In other words, with a few exceptions, including my burly querier, these men seemed to have committed crimes because they suffered deficits that kept them from succeeding in life in mainstream fashion.

Some of the exceptions were notable. Three Hispanic men in their early twenties sat at a table in a corner of the room. Each sported the same jagged tattoo on his neck. Near them, a huge Black man glared at everyone who walked by him. And my courtroom colleagues were present as well—they sat together. The fraudster looked bored. The robber looked scared. I gathered we ate in shifts. Perhaps another shift was comprised of a different demographic.

The room itself resembled an expanded version of my high school cafeteria—if the school staff had bricked up the windows, removed every trace of decor, and added a guard against each wall.

Back in my cell, I found a sheet of paper on my bunk outlining the jail's schedule and what access I had to its various features. I was pleased to see I'd been granted access to the library from one o'clock to three each day.

In the boxcar-like, dimly lit room, several shelves of

well-worn law books sat amidst an array of paperbacks. Most of these were the kind of bestsellers you'd find in an airport bookstore. One wasn't.

This was no coincidence, I thought. The one book Baba Ahimsa had written was wedged between a thriller and a fantasy novel. I couldn't imagine how it got there. *Notes from the Beyond* had been my first exposure to Eastern philosophy.

A prisoner who wore a yellow armband over his orange jumpsuit sat looking at a magazine at a desk against a side wall. Furry sideburns lined his cheeks, and his hair was long and wild. He was probably in his well-worn fifties. I could picture him astride a lowrider motorcycle.

"Can we check out books to read in our rooms?" I asked him, book in hand.

"You wish they were rooms, brother. Yes, you can bring them to your cell, but most people read stuff here."

He gestured at the row of empty white plastic chairs along the other wall. They were the same torture devices I'd hazarded when I visited Janet, the thief.

"Hey," he continued, "aren't you that guy I saw on the news—the one who killed those girls?"

"Yes, and no. You probably saw me on the news, but I'm innocent."

"Yeah, right. And I didn't beat up a low-life in a bar." He winked at me.

"Does the armband denote a special status?" I asked.

"Yeah, I'm a trustee, which means I get to have a job because I've been here long enough without fucking up, so they trust me—with books, anyway. It's better than sitting on my ass all day."

"I'm Kade," I told him, holding out my hand. I

refrained from pointing out that he was, in fact, sitting on his ass. "Is there any other way to get a job?" I asked. "I'd love to be in service while I'm here."

He ignored my hand. "Lucas," he told me. "No, not officially, but you sound like you've been to college. You could write letters for people or teach some of these losers how to read."

"How would I go about that?" I asked.

"Find this guy named Billy and tell him what you want to do. He knows everybody. He'll spread the word. He looks like a stork."

"Thanks," I said. "I probably won't be in here long enough to do much, but I appreciate your help."

"Are you shitting me? You think you're going to get bail on a homicide—no, two homicides?"

"It's a case of mistaken identity," I told him.

Lucas paused to think that over. "If you want my advice, don't tell anyone else that in here. No one's going to mess with you if they think you're a crazed killer. I mean, who kills more than one girl? One is the normal limit around here. If they think you're some slob who got picked up by mistake, that's a whole different deal. And watch out for the Terrores Del Lado Estes, anyway. Those guys are hardcore."

"Eastside Terrors?"

"I don't know, man. I don't speak Mexican. Just watch your ass. They've got lightning tattoos on their necks. You can't miss them."

"Lucas, you've been a big help. How do I check out this book?"

"Just take it. Who cares?"

****

Suddenly, my stay in the jail was going to be much

more bearable. Despite moving on from many of his teachings, I still maintained a heart connection with Baba. Periodically, he reached out to me in dreams, imparting helpful messages. Like all of us, his body was a temporary housing. His essence lives on.

From the first page, my confidence that everything would work out soared. I was reminded of things I knew but hadn't been able to hold onto once I became caught up in the drama of my circumstances.

Baba taught that everything happens for reasons that make sense at the big picture level, no matter how we experience them. Incarceration, freedom, pain, joy, sadness, and even death are just subsets of that which is right, whole, and sacred. You can't judge something complex from its individual parts—let alone something unknowable in the first place.

The blind men and the elephant parable illustrates this. One man touches the side, one the elephant's tail, one the tusk, etc. They could argue all day about the nature of the animal since all their assessments stem from their limited experience of its varied parts.

Another piece of wisdom I encountered in the first chapter was also apt. Buying into the illusion of control in our lives is a major source of suffering and leads us astray. There are too many external variables for us to be in charge of what happens to us, and these are directed by a power greater than us.

Other people, for example, are unpredictable. We can attend a job interview, be perfectly qualified, and perform at a fabulous level. What if the interviewer has been told to hire an African-American lesbian? This actually happened to me. Not only didn't I get the job, I felt like a failure based on the illusion that the outcome was within my control and I'd blown it.

Dinner conversation provided a stark contrast to my reading. Chet sat with me again, explaining which busty celebrity was hotter, until the three Estes gang members swaggered over. The younger prisoner was up and gone in a flash. The three Estes stood across the table from me.

They were a heterogeneous lot, size-wise. Otherwise, in terms of skin tone and their baseline scowl, they could've been brothers. They'd all rolled up the sleeves of their jumpsuits, and the shortest one had also unzipped his, revealing one of the hairiest chests I'd ever seen.

If someone told me the gang members were of Indigenous descent, as opposed to Mexican-American, I wouldn't have argued. Of course, they could easily have been both.

"We heard you were some kind of tough guy," the tallest one said. He was probably five foot nine. "Is that so?" He had no accent, but he slurred his words just a bit, as though he were an elderly man who'd suffered a minor stroke. More likely, he'd gotten hold of some alcohol.

"Not really. I only kill women—so far, anyway," I told him. "I haven't got much to lose, so maybe I'll branch out in prison."

That got me three hard stares, which they held for quite some time before the tall one spoke again.

"Someone else said you were a religious nutcase."

"I guess that fits," I told him, "at least from your point of view."

They sat down across from me, the other two following the talker's lead. He'd mastered an intense stare up to a point, but his eyes weren't dead like the hitmen in movies and his body language didn't fully support his effort.

Close-up, I could see that his skin tone was actually darker than the others and a faded knife scar split his brow above one eye. If he weren't a gang member, I might have settled on another story—standing too close to a golfer? A bicycle accident?

"Here's the thing," he said. "We rule this jail, and we don't need some tough guy messing with what's going on here."

"I have no interest in that," I told him. "I'll keep to myself, catch up on my reading, and wait for my trial."

"You better do that if you know what's good for you."

Once again, he was trying for menace. This time I felt his aggressive energy in my gut. It was nauseating.

"Absolutely," I agreed. "Now is there anything I can do for you?"

"What do you mean?" His raised eyebrows demonstrated his surprise. "Like keeping somebody in line? Is that what you mean? We can do a trade for that."

"No, I mean like letter writing or sorting through your legal situation."

"You a lawyer?" he asked.

"No, but if you've got paperwork, I might be able to help you understand it."

"You calling me a dumbass?"

His fists tightened. One of the other guys sat up straighter. I don't think the third one understood English.

Apparently, the trio's spokesman navigated his way through life looking for an excuse to become violent. I wondered what kind of childhood produced this attitude. I would've expected to be alarmed by the situation, but I wasn't.

"Not at all," I told him. "It's just that I've got a couple of degrees from colleges. I'm good with words."

"Well, okay." He cocked his head, which reminded me of Zeus. I missed him already. "Here's what you can do for us right now," the gang member continued. "Give Jose your salad at lunch and dinner."

"He likes salad?"

"Yeah, I do," said the medium-sized one who'd sat up. "Is there something wrong with that?"

"Not at all. I'm just surprised. I'm not crazy about salad so that'll be easy. You know, I haven't even introduced myself. I'm Kade Tobin."

I held my hand out. To my surprise, and I think to his, the trio's spokesman shook it.

"Call me Jorge. You know Jose's name, and this is Tepehuano." He gestured to the short guy. "He doesn't talk."

"Why not?"

"I don't know."

"So you're sure I can't help with something besides salads?" I asked.

"I guess you could look at this letter I got from my lawyer," Jorge said. "The asshole likes to use all these law words nobody knows."

"I might know. I'd be happy to look. Part of my religion is the idea that it's good to be in service. You keep me safe in here, and I'll keep helping any way I can."

"Deal. I'll meet you tomorrow at breakfast with the letter."

"Sounds good," I told him.

They strode back their table. Chet joined me after they did.

"Man, I don't know if I want to risk being around you now that you sat with that gang."

"Actually, they sat with me," I told him.

"Whatever." Chet's whatever was more rote than an attempt to bury what I'd said, à la McCall. "What did they want?" Chet asked.

"To warn me not to interfere with whatever they're up to in here. And I think to find out who I am. They'd heard rumors."

"Aren't you worried?"

"About them? No."

"You ought to be," he told me.

Chet took off, and a new guy took his place. He looked like a stork. I was proving to be one of the popular kids. Maybe I'd get to take the head cheerleader to the jail prom.

"Lucas said you were looking for me," the stork said. He wore a yellow armband, too.

Tall, skinny, awkward, with a long thin nose, it was easy to see how the man had acquired his nickname.

"You're Billy?" I asked.

"Yeah."

He was probably thirty, with an earnest expression I hadn't seen anyone else displaying in my limited time in the jail.

"I'm a religious nutcase," I told him, "so I'm supposed to help people all the time. Can you put out the word that a college man is willing to help with word things?"

"Word things?"

"Anything that has to do with words," I explained.

"Like telling people things?" he asked. He spoke hurriedly, as if he expected to be interrupted at any moment.

"Sure. I can answer questions on a host of topics. I do spiritual counseling all the time, for example. But I mean written words, too."

"What's spiritual counseling?" Billy asked.

"Helping people understand the nature of the universe, how to live, how to behave true to oneself—things like that. I'm guessing that some of the men in here need someone safe to talk to."

"What about the women?" Billy asked. "I can get the word out to them, too. They might be more interested in something like that. I dunno. Most men in here couldn't care less. What did God ever do for us?"

"Everything," I answered. "But I'm not talking about God, per se."

"Per what?"

"Never mind," I said.

"So what do you think about the women?" he asked. "They're in the other building, but I get to go over there sometimes."

"If the guards will let me, I'd be happy to help women, too," I told him.

"I'll see what I can do," Billy said. "Just watch out with them. There are some really nasty ones. I got bit once in the laundry room."

"Sure. I'll be careful."

****

Phil came to see me the next day. We sat in the same room as last time. Not quite claustrophobic, we nonetheless had to squeeze ourselves into it. At least the chairs were tolerable in there.

"Good news," he told me. "We already discovered some traces of your cousin. Someone named W. Barr checked into a motel in Salinas last month but then didn't stay. And there's a record of him flying out of San Jose the day after Chloe's murder."

"That's great. Where was he heading?"

"Houston. From there, he had a lot of options. It's a hub for flights to Latin America and the Caribbean. Do you have a feel for where he'd head to?"

"Not really," I said. "I know he liked Mexico a lot, so I guess that rules it out. He'd know I'd steer the authorities there once I discovered he'd framed me."

"Speaking of that, why would he? Did you two have a falling out or something?"

"Yes. Any luck up in Canada?"

"Not yet," Phil told me.

"Anything else?"

"Look, Kade, the problem is when my guy showed a photo of you at the motel, the desk clerk who was on duty identified you."

I nodded. "Well, that's the whole problem in a nutshell. Wyatt and I really do look alike. When he came out to visit me in Vancouver once, everyone thought we were twins."

"If we can establish alibis for you when he was at the motel and when he flew, it would go a long way toward differentiating the two of you."

"Right. Check my appointment book in my desk drawer for the dates last month," I suggested. "The day after the second murder—when Wyatt flew out—shouldn't be a problem. I was on the land, and lots of people can verify that."

"Great. I'll get right on it. We have five more days before the hearing."

"That's all?" I asked.

"I had to fight for it. The new judge's attitude is that establishing an identity should be easy and more time would only give us the opportunity to manufacture evidence—bribe people or whatever. He's a really suspicious guy."

"I see. Is there anything I should be doing while I'm here?"

"Keep safe. It won't be long now," Phil told me. "The Canadian angle should do it, and our investigator up there is optimistic about digging up what we need in time. We'll prove Wyatt exists, that he grew up in Montreal, and that you grew up an entire continent away. And once it's established you really have a cousin who looks like you…"

"Thanks so much, Phil."

"It's the least I can do for you. You've helped me so much."

Chapter 19

The days passed. I helped a handful of fellow inmates, including an illiterate woman suffering a painful withdrawal from an unspecified drug.

My digestion was a mess. Suddenly introducing meat into my diet convinced my intestines to stop cooperating.

Chet spent as much time near me as he could because he wanted "to bask in my aura." The Estes approached me for help several times. Phil visited me each day, keeping me apprised of new developments. On the evening before the morning hearing, he told me he felt fully prepared.

At a quarter to nine the next day, a chubby deputy walked me over to the courthouse, which was only two blocks away. The front entrance was swarming with media, so he mercifully took me in through the delivery bay.

Phil met me at the door to our courtroom and led me to the defense table. Once again, Marion Burke sat on the other side of the aisle, flanked by two younger men in dark suits. She wore her burgundy pantsuit, which by now I thought of as her uniform. Phil was back in his gray suit, this time with a white shirt and purple tie.

"All rise for the honorable Judge Perry," the bailiff called before Phil and I had a chance to chat. The deputy had cut it close.

The judge ambled to his raised seat and then told us to sit. He looked about eighty years old, although he probably wasn't. He'd certainly spent too much time in the sun. Aside from his leathery skin, I spied numerous small scars from skin cancer removals on his forehead.

His slight figure was lost in his robe, lending his neck and head a turtle-like appearance. His eyes were sharp, though, scanning the room and noticing what there was to notice.

The judge didn't rap his gavel. I figured he might have already exhausted his available energy, or perhaps pulled one of his remaining muscles.

"Are the two parties prepared to move forward on this matter?" he asked. His voice was much younger than he was.

Phil and the DA answered simultaneously. "Yes, Your Honor."

"Then let's proceed. Marion?"

She stood and held a tablet that she looked at before moving to her podium and beginning. Her pantsuit was wrinkled this time, and her hair was collected on the top of her head in a tight bun.

"Your Honor, there is scant evidence that the defendant is anyone other than the killer," she began. "I believe you'll see how flimsy the defense's assertion is when my esteemed colleague gets his turn. Eyewitnesses have identified Mr. Barr as being with the first victim shortly before the first murder.

"He claims he's from Vancouver—that he was Carl Steubens before he changed his name. We have substantial evidence he's actually from Montreal, where one of the victims revealed to her family that she was molested by him while he was her tutor.

"I could go on, but I prefer not to reveal the details of our case since I suspect we're going to trial. The burden of proof in this case is on the defense to prove Mr. Barr is someone else. Since I know this is not so, I yield the floor to them. Good luck, counselor."

She sat and Phil stood. I was struck by the DA's arrogance. She was so sure of her case, she had hardly tried.

"Your Honor," Phil said in his clear, strong voice from behind his podium, "I'm Phil Karanos representing the defendant. I'm going to begin by simply stating what our investigation has discovered. When I've finished, I'll provide copies of the documents supporting what I've told the court.

"First of all, we can prove that the man in this courtroom is Kade Tobin and was formerly known as Carl Steubens. We have a lapsed Canadian passport with the defendant's photo and original name. We found Mr. Steuben's birth certificate, which states he was born in a hospital in Coquitlam, British Columbia, a city just east of Vancouver. This document was not hard to find, and the prosecutor could certainly have discovered it had they tried to.

"In addition, we have school records showing the defendant's progress from elementary school through high school in Vancouver itself.

"He entered an ashram in Washington State under his original name. We have written statements from others at that site. The teacher there gave him the name Kade Tobin, which has some obscure spiritual meaning. His taking this name was not an effort to hide his identity.

"All of this proves he is not his cousin, Wyatt Barr.

Now let me tell the court how we can prove that a cousin named Wyatt Barr actually exists. If Carl exists and Wyatt exists, obviously they can't be the same person.

"We can thank the DA for telling us that a man with that name may have molested children in Montreal while he worked there. Mr. Tobin's high school records show he was a student in British Columbia at the time of that allegation. I would also point out that Montreal is located well over two thousand miles from Vancouver.

"We have birth and academic documents for Mr. Barr, as well, all in Montreal. He was in trouble with the law beginning in his teens, and he nearly served time after two convictions. Both were downgraded from felonies due to the court being overburdened."

Phil paused to sip water before continuing. "I imagine you know something about that, Your Honor. I have those records, as well, by the way."

The elderly judge dipped his head—half a nod.

"Now let's look at why Wyatt would commit this crime and try to pin it on his cousin, with whom he has a contentious relationship. The first victim told a reliable witness she was in this area to bring someone to justice. The second one, as the DA has told us, has stated she was molested in Montreal. The women were here to confront their molester. This is not Mr. Tobin, as we already established. Perhaps they knew Wyatt Barr was in the area—and we do have multiple sightings of him—or perhaps they mistook Mr. Tobin for his cousin. This would be a natural mistake as the two men are remarkably similar-looking. In any case, Mr. Barr had a clear motive to get rid of his accusers. My client has no motive, as he was unaware of any of this.

"We also have evidence that a man named W. Barr

flew from San Jose to Houston the day after the second murder. My client has an ironclad alibi at that time, which affidavits will show. Your Honor, I could go on. Will that be necessary?"

"I don't think so, counselor. Please bring your paperwork up to the bench and to the DA."

"Certainly."

After doing so, Phil sat down and I put my arm around him. I probably squeezed too hard, but he endured it.

The judge perused the first dozen pages for all of two minutes, and then addressed Marion Burke, whose white face was frozen in place as she flipped through the documents.

"It looks like your people have conducted a very shoddy investigation, Marion. What do you have to say for yourself?"

"Your Honor, give me a few minutes," Marion pleaded.

"I'll give you five, and then I want some answers."

Phil and I whispered our observations about the DA's and his performance, and I poured us each a glass of water from the pitcher on the table. While I drank, the judge studied Phil's paperwork more thoroughly.

"Well?" he finally said to Marion.

"There are parts of the defense's presentation I take issue with," she responded. "But I have to agree with the court that our investigation was incomplete."

"I said shoddy, not incomplete," the judge said sternly.

"Yes, Your Honor. Shoddy."

"I'm going to apologize to Mr. Tobin," the judge told her, "and I expect you to, as well. If I hear that the *former* defendant pursues a civil case against your department, I'll be there to testify on his behalf."

"Yes, Your Honor." Everyone was silent for a moment, then Marion spoke again as she turned to face me. "I apologize, sir. We jumped to conclusions and failed to pursue a vigorous investigation once we settled on you as the perpetrator."

"Mr. Tobin," the judge began, "I have no hesitation in extending this court's deepest apology for how you've been treated."

I nodded my acknowledgement. "May I speak?" I asked.

"Yes."

"I know that everyone connected to this case has been doing their job to the best of their ability. Were I in their shoes, I would've also believed I was guilty. I hope I would've been more open to exploring alternative possibilities, but I understand why the sheriff and the DA's office did not. I will not bring a civil suit. I forgive them. In fact, I thank them for providing me with a fascinating set of experiences in the county jail. Not everyone gets to find out what it's like in there.

"I'd also like to take this opportunity to express my regret that I didn't suspect my cousin after Althea's murder, which might've saved Chloe. I had no reason to, but I'm deeply saddened, nonetheless."

"You're serious about your incarceration?" the judge asked. "You found it fascinating?"

"Yes, Your Honor."

"That's a first. Very well. Would you like to dismiss the charges yourself, Marion?"

"Yes, Your Honor. The county of Santa Cruz requests that all charges against the man currently known as Kade Tobin be dropped."

"Granted."

The judge rapped his gavel and, in fact, almost toppled from the effort.

The gallery cheered. I pivoted and saw most of my community standing and smiling. I smiled back.

Chapter 20

Bill Cullen called my phone a few days later. I was throwing a stick for Zeus in the meadow, who didn't appreciate the interruption.

"I hope there are no hard feelings about my role in your arrest," Bill told me. "Do you forgive me, too?"

"Certainly. You were in the courtroom?"

"Yes. Your attorney was masterful," he told me.

"Thanks, I'll tell Phil you said that."

"Look, Kade, if you want, I can keep you in the loop about our search for your cousin. It's the least I can do after what you've been through."

"That would be great," I said. "Thank you. Any sign of Wyatt?"

"No, not yet, but it looks like the 10K in Chloe's bank account was a blackmail payoff. Althea wanted justice. Chloe wanted cash."

"How do you know where the money came from?"

"We don't. That's the thing. Ordinarily, it would be relatively easy to find out something like that. Someone went to a lot of trouble to hide his tracks. Can you think of a benign scenario where that would be the case?"

"Perhaps," I said. I could think of several. I anonymously contributed to charities on a regular basis, for example.

"Well, there's probably more to it. McCall usually just gives us the highlights. But he's sure."

“That’s interesting,” I said. “So Wyatt paid her off and then went ahead and killed her anyway.”

“She probably asked for more and he realized he’d be paying the rest of his life. Anyway, that’s what McCall thinks.”

“So if you can find out where the money came from, maybe you could get a line on Wyatt?” I asked.

“Yeah, why hide that unless our knowing it leads us to him?” I heard some background voices. “Hold on a minute, Kade.”

He must’ve put his phone down and walked away because the voices receded. After a few minutes, Bill came back on the line. “Listen, I’ve gotta roll. There’s been another homicide. We’ve had none for five months, and now there’s these three. Take care.”

Later, Jim met me in the meadow as I headed to my yurt to meditate after counseling several members.

“Someone’s missing,” he told me. “He didn’t sleep here the last two nights, and nobody’s seen him.”

Jim’s furrowed brow and taut lips told me his worry was more than superficial. His features weren’t particularly mobile. When I could discern an emotion on his face, I knew whatever had catalyzed it mattered to him.

“Who is it?” I asked.

“Wayne Robbins. It’s not like him. Other than when he left a few weeks ago to attend his mother’s funeral out of state, I don’t think he’s ever been off the property.”

“Maybe it’s another family matter.”

“He would’ve told me,” Jim asserted. “And Wayne would’ve wanted to let one of his kitchen staff know they needed to step in and cook. He takes his job very seriously, Kade.”

"What do you know about him?" I asked. "All I know is he's very private, he cooks, he's big, and he's a little rough around the edges."

"Wayne showed up last November in pretty bad shape," Jim told me. "I mean psychologically. He was paranoid—not clinically—but noticeably. I know something about that. You've seen how I get sometimes."

"Yes. How's that going?" I asked.

"The new meds seem to be working. Anyway, I got the sense Wayne had been through something harrowing. After a few weeks, he settled down. He kept to himself. I don't think he has any friends here. He eats like a horse."

"Maybe whatever trauma he endured reared its head," I suggested. "Maybe he got triggered when he went back for the funeral."

"Maybe. I don't know, Kade. I mean, people leave the community without notice sometimes—remember Jennifer Valley."

"I do."

She had disappeared one afternoon after a troubling one-on-one counseling session with me in the morning. I'd been concerned about her well-being until I received an upbeat postcard from Nepal.

Jim continued. "But Wayne left all his clothes and that Giants baseball cap he usually wears. That's worrying, don't you think? Could his disappearance be connected to the murders?"

"Why do you say that?"

"I'm just wondering," Jim replied. "I also wonder if we should report him as a missing person."

"Let's give it a little more time. There's probably a

harmless reason—a drinking binge, a woman, or something along those lines."

"Okay."

****

I called Bill the next afternoon. "Is there any news about Wyatt?"

"Unfortunately, no. We've been busy with this new murder."

"A gang thing? I read something about it online."

"It looks like it, but we're not sure yet," Bill told me. "The victim's prints belong to a fugitive who jumped bail and disappeared last year."

"So he was in a gang?"

"Not that we know of. But we found a gang symbol beside the body."

"What crime did the victim commit?" I asked.

"He was up on a manslaughter charge, and he skipped bail, screwing over his brother who put up the cash. He got into a fight at an Oakland A's game, and when he knocked the other guy down, the guy fell, hit his head on something and died. So the latest victim here—Guy Harrison—was looking at something like five to ten years because he had priors. Anyway, why do you care about that?"

"It was fun working with you—trying to solve a murder," I told him. "I guess I've gotten a bit fascinated by what you do."

"Got it. I better get going. I'll call you when I have news."

"Thanks."

****

Bill and his partner Michael Quinn showed up a couple of days later around two in the afternoon.

"Knock, knock," Bill called out while I was meditating in my yurt.

Zeus was startled awake and darted toward the door before he recognized Bill's voice. Once Zeus heard someone speak for a few minutes, he filed away the person's identity along with all his other canine concerns.

I recognized Bill's voice as well. "Give me a minute. I'll be right out."

When I emerged, Bill and Quinn stood next to where the victims had been found. It was a familiar patch of grass by now. I joined them, and Bill's partner told me he was sorry about his role in my interrogation. I didn't believe him.

Quinn's fair Irish looks and casual clothes provided a contrast with Bill, who wore his shiny blue suit. Quinn's chambray work shirt and black corduroy jeans were what I might wear to meet a computer date if I were still dating. At my interrogation, he'd looked more like a cop.

"What brings you to the land?" I asked Bill.

"I wanted to talk to you again," Quinn answered, "and look around. I need to get caught up on these murders."

"Sure. Let me give you the grand tour. Feel free to ask me anything. Bill, are you along for the ride?"

"I think I'll just go speak to a few of your members," he told me before he strode away.

"So this is where you found the bodies?" Michael asked.

"Yes, I'm sure you know that."

He smiled a wide smile, displaying very white teeth. "I like to start with easy 'yes' questions to get the ball rolling," Quinn told me.

"That works well with some people," I agreed.

"But not you?"

"There's no reason to joust with me, Detective. I'm no longer a suspect, and I'm ready to help however I can."

"Sure, sure. It's just force of habit," he said, waving his hand in the air.

I nodded. "Shall we?"

"Let's."

As we roamed the property, greeting various members in the crisp, cool air, I once again felt grateful and blessed that we were able to be here—that Frank Dawson had given us the property. Despite the run-down appearance of many of the buildings, the land itself was something special, with varied topography and all sorts of flourishing plant life. The redwood trees set it apart from similar forest properties elsewhere.

When I'd first moved to Northern California, I spent a great deal of time communing with the redwoods—sitting against them, walking through them, meditating in their shade. Ours were second growth—the original parent trees having been felled in the 1800s. Those stumps confounded the eye. One was about a dozen feet across. The youngsters—by redwood standards—were no slouches, either. Many were a couple of hundred feet tall. Their needles scattered all over the place, providing soft footing for the pads on Zeus's paws. I've tried not to take the trees for granted since, but I often did. Not that afternoon.

Quinn wasn't particularly interested in anything other than me. All his questions about our community circled back to my role, my history, my feelings about this or that. Most were provocative—to see how I reacted. He didn't care that his charade was obvious and my answers reflected my understanding that.

"So why did you get spiritual?" he asked after twenty minutes of this. We stood beside our well, near the back of the property. "I understand you used to be normal."

"I had a near-death experience after almost drowning." I gestured to the roof of a nearby building. "Take a look at our solar panel array. Impressive, isn't it?"

"Lovely," Quinn said. "So you agree you used to be normal?"

"What's normal?" I asked.

"What do *you* think it is?"

"I know what," I said. "Why don't we each research that and then compare notes a week from Tuesday? After that, we can collaborate on an article for a magazine."

"Touchy, aren't you?"

"Annoying, aren't *you*?" I responded. "And on purpose, too. Why don't you just tell me what's going on? Why are you really here?"

"Tobin, I read your file, I've talked to McCall and Bill, and I've looked into a few things on my own." He paused to stare at me, prison yard-style. I'd been getting a lot of that lately. "Frankly, I don't have a good reason to rule you out for these murders. I don't care what everyone else thinks. I don't care about your so-called alibis. But I can't bring you in for questioning. We've got orders to back off after what happened in court. So here I am."

"Thank you for your candor. I understand. I might do the same thing in your shoes," I told him.

"Oh, shut up. That's bullshit. I'm telling you I'm trying to nail you. I'm your enemy, for chrissakes. Get real."

"Okay, fine. Fuck you, Quinn. Is that what you want to hear?" I wasn't as riled up as him, but I was getting there.

"I don't hear that as any more real," he told me. "You're always in performance mode. You say what you say for the effect it has on people. You've got some sort of mental problem. If there's any authentic person in there, he's buried under a massive pile of bullshit."

I didn't know what to say to that. Quinn didn't seem to be saying it to be provocative. He meant what he said.

"Cat got your tongue, Tobin?"

"You're dating yourself. I haven't heard that idiom in years."

"*That's* your response? I pretty much accuse you of being a sociopath, and you comment on that?"

"What am I supposed to do?" I protested. "You're going to hear anything I say through the lens you've constructed, aren't you?"

"Give me a reason not to," Quinn said. "This is your opportunity to disprove what I'm saying. We're just walking and talking here. What have you got? What's going to change my mind?"

"You can think whatever you want, Quinn. It's not my job to talk you into to a more accurate point of view." I turned to him and glared. As soon as I realized I had, I adopted a half-smile before I continued. "As long as you can't hassle me beyond this visit—and that's all I'm going to tolerate—then why should I care what you think?"

"Okay, fair enough. I'll keep digging on my own if

that's the way you want to play it. And wipe that stupid grin off your face."

"What are you—my third-grade gym teacher? Grow up, Quinn. Since I'm innocent, you can dig all you want. There's nothing to find."

"We'll see about that, Tobin."

I took a moment and took a few deep breaths, which helped a lot, before speaking again. "I suppose Bill is doing digging of his own today—interviewing members again?"

Quinn grinned. "Bingo."

"That's fine. Sneaky, but fine. But it ends today. One call to the DA and you two are toast. She promised me I wouldn't be harassed anymore." I was calm now, but no less firm in my tone.

"What kind of spiritual teacher rats people out?" Quinn asked.

"This one if I need to. Now get the hell off our property, Quinn. And take Bill with you."

He threw his hands in the air and stomped away—back toward our central courtyard.

It turned out that Bill spoke with Phil, Martha, Susan Burke, and an elderly man who knew me back at Baba's ashram. All of them reported that the interviews seemed innocuous—just Bill seeking more background information on our organization. The older member eventually told Bill he was an asshole and walked out.

Chapter 21

The next morning, I couldn't find Zeus. Sometimes after his morning meal, he wandered around the adjacent forest, disappearing for as long as a couple of hours. And one afternoon he'd foolishly chased a coyote across Summit Road into a winding box canyon, where he either got lost or engaged in a prolonged staring contest with his quarry. Generally, after Zeus chased down an animal, he didn't know what to do next. Fortunately, a member of our search party called him from close enough that he raced back to her.

But Zeus had never missed a morning meal. I was concerned. If he didn't turn up in few hours, I'd assemble another team to search for him.

In my office after leading a meditation and giving a brief talk about the importance of radical acceptance of other people, I found a typed note on my desk.

"Look at your phone," was all it said.

So I did. An email from someone whose address was youdon'tgettoknowwho@gmail.com consisted solely of a video. I clicked on it.

A figure in a black balaclava sat cross-legged on a dark hardwood floor next to a sprawled Zeus. The sheetrock wall behind them was bare. He wore sunglasses and had wrapped himself in a red plaid flannel blanket. His arm was across Zeus's shoulders as he stared into the camera.

My gut tightened so much I thought I'd vomit.

"You have a beautiful dog," the figure said in an altered, electronic voice. "I hope he remains healthy."

My pounding heart fought against the sudden tension in my chest. I could hardly breathe, and I felt dizzy.

Zeus looked up for a moment and then decided to go to sleep—cameras weren't interesting. Zeus wasn't drugged; his eyes were clear and alert.

"Here's what you need to do to ensure your dog's health," the man continued. "Admit your fraud. Stop fighting the lawsuit. You have three days."

The video went black.

When my body calmed down—decided not to fight or engage in flight—I considered the meaning of the dognapper's words. The property dispute had raised its head again. When the member who'd owned our land—Frank Dawson—had passed away two years earlier, his will clearly stipulated that the Brethren nonprofit should inherit it. His family fought this on numerous fronts, claiming I had somehow coerced or tricked Frank into changing his will.

I never met any of these accusers, just their attorney once—a quite unpleasant man with a difficult-to-understand Israeli accent. It was no fun having to ask him to repeat his insults.

Thankfully, Phil gathered convincing evidence that Frank had freely changed his will and had explained why. Frank simply believed our community offered a rare opportunity for people he cared about to advance spiritually, and he knew the Brethren couldn't survive without the land. Before Jim took over, Frank kept our books. Even with no rent to pay, at that time our debts had mounted and our donations were slim.

Granted, the short duration between Frank's decision about his estate and his tragic death could be viewed as suspicious. I'd probably wonder about it myself. The authorities, however, were quite certain it was accidental. I mention this because the family's attorney even accused me of murdering him at one point.

In general, spiritual leaders seem to be fair game for this kind of thing. I've certainly been through other, more minor iterations of this lawsuit.

Zeus's kidnapping, then, was probably due to someone expecting to be Frank's heir becoming frustrated when the family's baseless suit never mustered any traction in the legal system. In fact, just two months ago, a judge had tossed it, with an admonition that pursuing it further would be deemed frivolous, resulting in a fine.

I considered calling the police, then realized I didn't need all the Frank drama stirred up again. It had taken up far too much of my time already. And McCall and Quinn were probably itching to have a legitimate excuse to come after me again. I imagined the DA would egg them on, given the opportunity.

On the other hand, I couldn't admit to or reverse any wrongdoing that never happened, and Zeus was precious to me. Would anyone really harm a dog to get his hands on a rural property? Perhaps someone who was already a criminal would.

Frank had spoken of his two siblings and his father on occasion. They were ordinary people—a sister who was a farmer, a cop brother, and a storeowner father. If this was one of them, harming Zeus was bound to be a bluff.

Should I bet my dog's life on it? That was the question. I had no immediate answer. One of the problems associated with my role in the community was a dearth of people to talk to as peers. I was the one others came to for help. There was no one for me to bounce ideas off, let alone help me make the hard choice I was facing.

The closest member to being a peer was Martha, but she wasn't worldly. Tuning into the likes of Frank's family was beyond her experience. Jim was helpful to discuss practical matters with, but his insight was lacking beyond that.

I decided to reply to the threatening email since further contact might yield pertinent information. I started shaking and I needed to breathe deeply for a few minutes to regain my poise. Just the idea of reading more about Zeus's plight was overwhelming.

"Who is this?" I wrote. "If you're related to Frank Dawson, it'll be easy for the police to catch you. If not, what supposed fraud do you mean?"

In just a few minutes the kidnapper replied.

"I forgot to tell you that if you involve the police, your beautiful dog will be shot."

That was significant. "Fair enough," I wrote back. "But I reiterate that I could respond more appropriately if I know what this is about."

"How many frauds have you committed? Is it hard to pick out one?" was the reply. "This is about the land, of course. I'll give you two days to contact the authorities and tell the truth. We'll feed and walk your dog until Thursday at six p.m. After that…"

"Okay. But be aware you're looking at a major felony here."

"Bullshit," the kidnapper wrote. "Dognapping in California is no big deal unless the dog is worth more than $950. Then PC 487e applies—grand theft."

"I see you've done your research. Suppose I tell you I paid $1200 for my dog."

"Zeus? That mutt? Hardly. Now fuck off."

Whoever it was wouldn't reply after that.

I'd learned several important things. The guy knew Zeus's name. I'd been careful not to use it. Very few people outside our community and law enforcement officers knew that. In fact, offhand, I couldn't think of anyone.

Secondly, this wasn't a criminal—someone hired by the Dawson family to do their dirty work. A thug would never have forgotten to warn me about contacting the police. Leaving that out of the video was strictly amateur hour.

Knowing the details of the laws about dognapping steered my thoughts toward Frank's brother—the cop. Of course, this could've just been the fruit of anyone's online research.

The cop notion encouraged me. You'd have to be a major league scumbag officer to kill a dog. That was way over the top. If it was the brother, it stood to reason he was bluffing.

I needed to know more about the Dawsons. Where was the brother working? Where was the sister's farm? Was Frank's father still alive? He'd been elderly while Frank was still alive.

I found Jim in his office. He sat behind his desk, reading a science fiction paperback with a busty astronaut floating beside a space station on the cover.

I raised my eyebrows at that.

"Don't be fooled by the cover," he told me. "This author is brilliant."

"Sure. Is this what you do when you're not working—hole up in your office and read?"

"Pretty much. It's peaceful in here," Jim told me.

I knew that was important to him. His immigrant parents had a Zen garden back in Osaka, and they'd duplicated it in San Diego. Jim had spent a lot of time reading beside it, before the FBI began chasing the family around the country due to his mother's wire fraud.

I looked around at the sparsely decorated, rundown, musty room. If I was seeking somewhere peaceful, it would be out in the fresh air, or at least somewhere we'd fully remodeled.

"What can I do for you?" Jim asked.

"I need a favor," I told him.

"Sure. Anything. What's up?"

"You keep information about members, right—the forms they fill out when they join?"

"Sure," he answered.

"How far do the files go back?"

"All the way. You never know," Jim responded.

"I need to see Frank Dawson's information."

"Okay, why's that?" he asked.

I wasn't prepared to answer that question, so I paused.

"That's all right," Jim said. "I don't need to know. Let me just hunt that up, Kade. The good news is that because of the lawsuit, I dug up a lot about him a few years back—stuff for Phil."

"Thanks."

As always, Jim kept the information as hard copies. And he was sufficiently organized to find Frank's information in short order.

I held the file against my chest as I walked to the projects building to grab a laptop. Susan Burke approached me as I climbed the steps to my office after that.

Her blondish bangs listed to one side, exposing more of one of her elfin ears. The tip of it swooped up at the back. That day, her earrings were customarily garish—dangling feathers that had been dyed bright yellow.

She wore a gray T-shirt with a faded band's name I couldn't read under a silhouette of a guitar player. I was struck again by Susan's amazingly porcelain skin.

"Where's Zeus today?" she asked. "We were supposed to hang out after breakfast."

"He makes appointments and keeps them?" I asked.

"Well, not exactly. He just wanders over on Tuesdays. I think it's because that's the day Geoff makes waffles."

"Waffles?"

"Think about it. Zeus can smell them, so he knows it's Susan day," she told me. "He does the same thing with Martha on Fridays—pancake day. Anyway, where is he? I'm worried."

"He's probably hot on the trail of some terrified animal," I told her. Of course, I wasn't about to share the real story with her. "Try calling him from the bluff."

"Okay. Have a good one."

Frank's file was helpful, sort of. He was from Creston, Iowa, where the family grew a variety of crops on a large farm. He'd graduated from Santa Clara University as a literature major. About that time, the bank foreclosed on the farm, but Frank's parents—second marriages for both—had stashed huge quantities of dried grain—animal feed—in warehouses owned by Frank's uncle.

The family divvied up the sale of this. The father started a hardware store in the nearest town. The mother divorced him and subsequently passed away in Arizona. Frank himself invested wisely in high-tech start-ups and attended an MFA program in creative writing at Stanford. Jim hadn't been able to trace the brother or sister beyond discovering they'd moved out of state. If Frank hadn't mentioned their professions to me, I wouldn't know diddly about them.

All that was interesting but didn't lead me to a dognapper. I googled "Dawson and Creston, Iowa." Zip. I tried "Dawson, police" to find Frank's brother and came up with the town of Dawson's police force and a host of officers around the country with that last name. Quite a few images of these could've been Frank's brother. I had no way of narrowing these down, other than seeing who was most proximate. That proved to be Sydney Dawson, who, unfortunately, was African-American. All the others lived out of state.

I tried "Dawson, farm," and found a few references to the family farm in Iowa. That was it.

Finally, I realized that Frank's obituary would be the best source of information. I found that on the online version of the Santa Cruz Sentinel.

"Frank is survived by his father, Chester Dawson of Denver, Colorado, his sister Mary of San Francisco, California, and half brother Mike of San Jose, California."

Bingo.

I googled Mike Dawson, and a cartoonist came up who wasn't the right age. Anyway, what kind of cartoonist dognaps? Scrolling down, I found a set designer, a football coach, and a musician, among others. None of them lived or worked in San Jose proper, which is only a half hour away. Each had other reasons for me to rule them out.

Mary Dawson proved to an even more common name, and I knew Frank's sister might very well be using a married name, anyway.

Stymied, I considered hiring a private investigator but decided against it. Who could find anyone in a day and a half, and if they did, what could they do then? Would a hired hand be willing to take on dognappers instead of calling the cops?

I watched the video of the masked dognapper and Zeus again, and I'm glad I did. There was no way Zeus would tolerate someone putting his arm across his shoulders unless he knew him. The emailer had known his name, too. If I hadn't been panicked by the video, I would've noticed this right away. Off the land, Zeus was quite standoffish with strangers. I think he may have been abused before I found him languishing in a shelter.

So who could the dognapper be? Zeus would definitely not act the way he did in the video with a Dawson heir. I was sure of that. In many ways, Zeus's behaviors were more patterned—more consistent—than any people I knew.

Could the dognapper be a current member of the community? Why? Several people had been close to Frank, and all of us had benefited from his estate. Where was the motive in any of that?

I thought about the names I'd provided to Bill Cullen—people who might've dumped the victims here. Did any of these potential grudge-keepers have a connection to the Dawson family? I had no way of finding out.

Ann Marin came to mind. Zeus knew her, and his behavior in the video was consistent with the nature of their relationship. He always tolerated her, but he didn't commune with her per se. He didn't seek attention; he didn't back away. That profile was actually rare. It was usually one thing or the other.

Ann had sicced McCall on me, trying to uncover our project—another version of discrediting me. I didn't buy the woman-scorned motivation for her recent actions. And if we were forced off the land, my followers would have nowhere to go to keep advancing along a similar path except for her farm. In time, I might be able to cobble together an alternative living situation. On the other hand, maybe I couldn't.

I was ninety-five percent certain now that the dognapper was Ann. In hindsight, despite how things worked out, I realized risking Zeus's life based on my half-assed conclusion had been arrogant and foolish. What about Wyatt? What about a disgruntled relative of a member? What if a Dawson heir had found a way to befriend Zeus before the snatch? There were any number of other, more dangerous suspects than Ann—people who really might harm him.

I think the idea of losing Zeus was too awful for me to entertain it as a real possibility. This lent a bias to my reasoning.

At any rate, I was left with the "she's bluffing" stance. I couldn't conceive that Ann would ever kill Zeus. Even if she wanted to, Gar Brindisi would never let her. Who would he and his son chase around the farm?

What purpose would it serve, anyway? As a threat, it made sense. To go ahead and do it when the threat didn't pay off? Why? To punish me for not cooperating? That just seemed wildly unlikely to me.

So I let it play out. I did nothing, and Thursday evening Zeus butted his bushy head against my yurt's door. He was no worse for wear.

I hadn't realized how tense my entire body had been until relief washed through me. I hugged him so hard he tried to squirm away. I held tight.

I couldn't be sure Ann was the one who'd released him, but I would've bet a fair amount on it.

Chapter 22

The next day, I had Jim drive me down to the Unity Farm to confront Ann and confirm my assessment. I'd been tempted to head there to rescue Zeus the day before, but I'd worried that would risk his well-being. Why force Ann's hand when I could just let it play out the way it did?

As it was a cloudy day, the countryside we passed through revealed the intricate details of the various landscapes that might otherwise be washed out by harsh sunlight. I could make out the spiral pattern on a goat's horn behind a fence near the road, and, unfortunately, spied a stooped farmworker's ass crack above his muddy canvas pants.

I probably should've devised a plan instead of relying on my in-the-moment sense of what to do. In most situations, that worked out well, but with Ann…

I had Jim drop me off on the road, and I walked in. One of Ann's group who I didn't know directed me to a shed behind the barn. This hulking, muscular guy sat cross-legged on an old tractor tire. He looked more like a pro wrestler than a spiritual seeker. Of course, my own experience told me that sincere aspirants come in all shapes and sizes.

In the small wooden shed, Ann wore filthy denim overalls as she stood in front of a workbench littered with gardening tools. She rolled duct tape around the splintered handle of a trowel and then stood back as though a more distant view would tell her if she'd done a good job.

A familiar scent wafted into my nostril as I sidled in. This was where they'd boarded Zeus. The interior of the shed smelled like oil, hay, and Zeus.

"Hey, Ann," I called.

She whirled, her eyes wide. "Kade! What are you doing here?"

"I wanted to thank you for returning Zeus."

"What are you talking about?" Ann reached behind her and grabbed the nearest tool—a pair of gardening shears. She held them against the bib of her overalls.

"You know what I'm talking about, Ann. This was a very amateurish operation. Clearly, Zeus knew whoever had taken him, and you left other clues. Are you still interested in taking over the Brethren? Is that what's going on here?"

She glared at me. "I want you off our property, Kane."

"What are you going to do if I don't go—stab me with those shears?"

Ann looked down. She hadn't realized what she was holding. "Don't tempt me," she said, pivoting to deposit the shears back on the table.

"I want some answers," I told her. "It's time we settled this."

Ann turned back to face me. "Settle what, exactly?"

"That's what I want to know," I told her.

Ann pursed her lips and paused. "Let's talk in the house," she said.

"Fine."

We passed the tire sitter on the way there. Now he

was slouching against the door of a battered black pickup truck beside the dirt driveway, staring at me without blinking. Why wasn't he working in the adjacent field like the others?

Ann soundlessly led me into her kitchen, where we sat around the same glass-topped table where Bill and I had talked to her. She stared intently into my eyes.

"All right, here's the story. You're like that Teflon don gangster, Kade. Murders don't stick, I can't find your illegal project, and even taking Zeus didn't work. So what the hell. My name's not Ann Marin, and I didn't just happen to join the Brethren."

I nodded, afraid to interrupt her.

"My name is Mary Dawson. You killed my brother, and you stole our land."

"I did not."

"Shut up," she said sharply. "I know you did. But my hanging around the community didn't yield any proof. All those idiots have bought into your bullshit. Even if they knew something, I realized after a while they'd never tell me."

"So next you tried to take over," I said. "To get control of the land."

"Yes, and I almost did."

"The channeling and the energy work? Is that even real?"

"Hell, no," Ann answered. "There's no such thing. It's easy to con people who are inclined to believe what you're conning them about. Even you fell for it."

"In this very room, you told Bill Cullen his partner had recovered from an illness," I protested.

"He wasn't ill," Ann told me.

"How would you know that?"

"Mike Quinn is my half brother. He joined the force here to help me get back our property."

"Jesus!" I thought for a moment. "All this for fourteen acres in the middle of nowhere?"

"What you don't know is there's an underground chamber by that limestone outcropping that looks like the prow of a ship."

"So?"

"It's full of cave paintings that date back to God knows when," Ann said.

"Why are you telling me all this?" I couldn't process the deluge of new, shocking information. Asking questions would keep Ann rolling while I tried to catch up.

"Mike and I decided to offer you a deal. I wasn't going to do it today, but here you are. We'll cut you in for half the value of the land once we reveal the paintings to the world. What do you say?"

"I say you two are insane. Who concocts such a long-term, crazy plan? What were you thinking?"

"We're thinking we're poor, and we could be rich," Ann said, smiling. "Come on, Kade, I know you're a fraud. I know you care about money. Maybe you didn't kill Frank, but I'm sure you talked him into leaving you the land."

"He didn't know about the cave?"

Ann shook her head.

"Why do you?" I asked.

"Martha showed it to me."

"Martha?"

Ann smiled. "Lots of surprises for you today, huh?"

"That's an understatement."

"So what do you say?" Ann asked.

"About selling the land and splitting the money?"

"Yes."

"Well, our non-profit already owns it, doesn't it?" I pointed out. "I appreciate the information you've given me. It explains a lot. But it doesn't give me a reason to split anything with you and your brother."

"You want a cop on your ass, Kade?"

"I already have one, don't I?"

"I've got eleven people on my farm now," Ann said, "including Byron, who you've met."

"Byron?"

"Big angry guy? Sits on a tire? He really likes to punch people."

I shook my head. "How low can you go, Ann—I mean Mary. Physical violence? Isn't there a shred of spirituality in you at this point?"

"Nope. And I can go even lower. Mike can still find a way to pin the murders on you, Kade, What happens if he intimidates whoever provided you with an alibi? Cops are good at that. What if we send someone up to Canada to twist a few arms about your past? There are a lot of 'what ifs' you don't want to discover the answers to."

"I need to think this over," I told her. "This is a lot to take in."

"Sure. We've waited this long. We can wait a little longer. But don't dick us around, Kade. If you do, you'll be sorry."

Ann waved her hand dismissively and turned her back.

I trudged back to where Jim had parked on the shoulder of the country road under a tree. My thoughts were all over the place. Oddly, it was the fact that Martha had shown Mary the cave paintings that popped up the most. Martha? Really?

When I returned to the land, I hunted her up, Zeus ambling beside me. When I ventured off the property without him, he stuck close to me for a while once I returned. I guess you could say he was codependent by human standards.

Martha was meditating by herself in the multipurpose room.

"Have you got a minute?" I asked as I lowered myself onto a cushion next to her.

"Of course." She reached out to pat Zeus when he lay down beside her and beseeched her with his soulful brown eyes.

"The cave. The paintings," I said.

"Remarkable, aren't they?"

"I haven't seen them. That's what concerns me, Martha. You showed them to Ann, but not me."

"Jim said you knew about them, but you wanted to keep the cave a secret. He's the one who showed me."

"I see." I thought that over. "Did you know he was a fine arts major in college—a painter?" I asked.

"No. Wait a minute. You think *he* did them—that they're fake?"

"I don't know what to think, Martha. Apparently Ann and her brother believe they're real, so they're still angling to grab our land."

"That's a shame." She shook her head. "Think of the karmic impact of their behavior."

"I'm thinking more about how to handle this situation. Will you show me the paintings?"

"Sure."

It was a short hike to the far side of the redwood grove past the project building. Zeus initially took the lead, as though he knew where we were going. From the trees, Martha led me along a makeshift trail through scrubby vegetation to the base of a limestone outcropping. When she stopped in front of it, I couldn't see any opening.

"Just a minute," Martha said. She slipped in sideways past a gnarled, dead tree and disappeared behind a buttress of stone. "In here," she called.

I joined her. Zeus didn't. I imagined he smelled the animal that had once lived in the cave and wanted no part of an encounter with a creature that might be even bigger than he was.

We'd forgotten to bring a proper flashlight and my phone didn't do justice to the cavern, but I could see it was about the size of a two-car garage, with a series of paintings along a side wall. The colors were muted, but that could've been the dim lighting.

At first I thought horses were galloping by a herd of wooly mammoths, which would've dated and also discredited the paintings. My recollection is that the Spanish brought horses to the New World sometime in the 1500s. Also, there had never been any mammoths in northern California.

But as Martha and I moved closer, it was clear that the horses were antelopes, the mammoths were some sort of fanciful creature I didn't recognize, and cruder images of people stood in the background. These were vaguely Asiatic-looking men holding spears, wearing what looked like leather dresses.

"I've got to come back with a decent flashlight," I told Martha.

"Good idea. Jim brought one when he showed me. Aren't these magnificent?"

That was a stretch. They could've been done by a kid in a fifth-grade art class. What would make them remarkable is if they were truly painted millennia ago.

If they weren't, perhaps Mike and Mary would back off. I knew they thought they'd been cheated out of their inheritance, but how much was our land worth without the artwork?

As Martha and I walked back and reached the forest, I found a real estate site on my phone that listed the estimated value of pretty much any parcel in the US. I only tripped once on a root. Our property, including all the buildings, would sell for 4.8 million dollars in the current market. I had no idea. Real estate had certainly boomed in recent years.

That was obviously enough money to warrant the family's attempts to wrest the land from us. So did it make sense to have the cave paintings evaluated for authenticity? Would it make any difference one way or another? For that matter, would word get out about them if I brought in an outsider? The last thing we needed were art tourists, or whoever else might flock here.

I needed to talk to Jim. That was the best way to know what the deal was, I realized.

I parted company with Martha by the entrance to the women's dorm and strode to Jim's office, where I found him asleep with his head on his desk.

I needed to shake his shoulders to wake him up. Jim raised his head groggily and blinked a few times.

"I'd dock your pay if I paid you," I told him, smiling to establish a collegial mood.

"I'd talk to HR if we had one," he replied. "Shaking me is just a step below a French kiss."

"Good one," I told him. Jim didn't joke very often,

but when he did, I usually appreciated it.

"What can I do for you?" he asked.

"The cave paintings."

Jim winced. "Uh, yeah. About those…"

I waited him out.

"I did them to get closer to Martha. I'm in love, and I have been for a long time." His face reddened, and he looked down at his lap.

I shook my head. "You know she's still bound by her Buddhist vows, right?"

Jim nodded, still avoiding looking at me. "Hope springs eternal. My plan was to show her the cave so we had a secret we were keeping together, and then eventually—when I worked up my nerve—I was going reveal I'd painted them in order to impress her."

"You thought that would work?" I asked.

"You never know." He looked up, grimacing.

"Where did you even find the time to paint?" I asked.

"I trained Ralph to do some of the paperwork. That amazing memory of his makes him a natural."

"That's fine, Jim, but I wish you'd told me about the cavern."

"Yeah, I should've," he said. "I guess I'm kind of embarrassed about Martha. I know I'm kidding myself, but she's amazing. I've never met anyone like her. Oh, sorry. Except you, of course."

I nodded my acknowledgement of this delayed compliment. "All that's understandable and forgivable, Jim. What you don't know is that Martha showed the paintings to Mary Dawson—Frank's sister—who's been pretending to be Ann."

"Holy smokes! *Our* Ann?" I nodded. "So she was

here to try to get the property?"

"Yup. Now she and her brother want to get hold of it even more because she thinks the paintings are real. If you were her and Martha presented something to you, you wouldn't question it, would you?"

"No, Martha would never lie about anything," Jim confirmed.

"So there we are. Worse yet, Ann's half brother is one of the cops investigating the murders. He could frame me for them. Wyatt already drew up a blueprint for how to do that. It was bad enough when he was doing that without any help. And even if there weren't any paintings, it turns out the land is worth millions—enough to kill for if you're immoral enough."

"I'm so sorry, Kade. I really didn't think it through. I should've explicitly told Martha not to share what she knew. I just assumed she wouldn't."

"Ann is manipulative—and good at it. Martha tends to think the best of people. When Ann was here, she probably pumped everyone for information."

"I feel terrible about this," Jim said.

So I spent some time providing support around Jim's emotions. Already prone to guilt, this was a familiar theme in our one-on-one sessions.

I found the task challenging since at that moment I felt a strong need to process quite a few things myself. Between what Ann had told me about herself, Quinn, and the cave paintings, I still had some serious catching up to do.

When I finally had a moment to myself, I wondered if the cave paintings figured into the murders, as Jim presumed while wallowing in guilt.

What a shitstorm. Just a few weeks ago, it was

business as usual at the Brethren. Zeus and I spent our days in calm service. I counseled and gave talks, and he accepted pats and simply loved everyone. We all meditated—except for Zeus, who slept during meditation time, sometimes noisily. Actually, I suspected an alarming number of members also spent some time asleep. Did they really need to lie flat due to bad backs or achy knees? Some of them, I guess.

Now I had too much on my plate to even sort through. I adjourned to my tent to take a nap. Zeus joined me, lying at the foot of my futon, farting furiously.

Chapter 23

I dreamt that Zeus stole the land by ferreting it away in a backpack and walking on his hind legs to a massive RV. Then he flew away in it.

When I thought about the dream, I decided it represented my anxiety on two fronts: worry about protecting our community and a fear of betrayal.

That the method of the land grab in the dream was absurd reflected the unlikelihood of what was actually happening. And by my subconscious choosing Zeus for the betrayal spoke to how deeply I'd been affected by Mary and her brother. Whatever differences she and I had, I would never have expected anything like what she'd done. And if I couldn't trust a detective assigned to a homicide case, who could I trust?

Bill Cullen had strung me along, pretending to collaborate in a friendly fashion. That was bad enough, but I understood his motive—he was just doing his job. Mike Quinn's motive was venal, at the expense of twenty-three sincere seekers entrusted to my care.

There was no way I was going to enter into a partnership with these snakes. But it might be a good idea to pretend I would. At the least it would stall whatever retribution they'd planned if I didn't cooperate.

I pondered the idea of going to the authorities. My current relationship with Bill was such that he'd tend to believe what I told him, but probably not something so pejorative about his partner. Surely, he had a much closer bond with Quinn.

Perhaps I could bring the extortion attempt to McCall or the sheriff. Marion Burke was another option. I wondered if her daughter knew which of these people would be most receptive.

But all of these options risked making matters worse.

As I lay on my back on my futon and rubbed Zeus's head—he'd instantly realized I was awake—my thoughts went sideways. How could I use Jim's admission against Frank Dawson's heirs? They believed the paintings were real; I knew they weren't. That had to be helpful.

I needed to get into the plotting business, too. I let that sit, confident that if I just went about my business, the universe would steer me as needed. This wasn't faith per se. It was experiential learning. That's simply how it worked—for me at least.

Surprisingly, I slept well that night and woke up refreshed. I spent the morning counseling individuals, and even the member who loved to play the victim and the one who constantly interrupted me couldn't drag me down.

I think knowing what was going on gave me peace of mind. Sure, I didn't know how to handle any of it yet, but awareness is the key to a satisfying life. My teacher once told me that all anyone ever had to do was pay attention. The answers, such as they are, are embedded in the organic flow of our lives.

By chance at lunch, I overheard someone say they were planning to write to Ann to see how things were going on the farm. Here was my first suggestion from the universe—contact Mary. Most people dismissed this sort of thing by calling it a coincidence. What a handy word to help remain asleep to the spiritual substrata that underlies the material world.

It's understandable, though. Opening to this and other nonrational truths is essentially signing up for a wholesale internal reorganization. Only so many of us are either brave enough or in dire enough circumstances to go there. It can feel like psychic suicide when we revamp our core paradigm so thoroughly. It did for me.

I called Mary from my office. "I've thought it over," I told her. "I'd like to discuss the details of collaboration in person with you and your brother."

I have no idea where this statement came from. I must've subconsciously picked up on some earlier choreography.

"We can do that right now," Mary responded. "On the phone."

"It's a nonnegotiable condition to my cooperation."

Ann sighed. "Fine. Where and when?"

I liked that. I was gaining control—setting the terms.

In a sense, counseling entails manipulating people—for their own good, of course. I help members by leading them in what I know to be a positive direction. But sometimes this is tricky, and I need to be sneaky on their behalf. Now I was approaching Quinn and his half-sister with that same skill set, but with the opposite goal. I needed to manipulate them to their disadvantage.

"As you know, I don't drive and I'd rather not involve a member to drive me," I said. "Are you willing to come here?"

She thought it over. "No."

"Are you willing to pick me up and then meet at the

Summit Cafe?"

"Have you heard about ride sharing, Kade?"

"Fine. How about I meet you there at six on Thursday—at the bar?"

"You don't drink," Mary pointed out.

"It's more private."

"How would you know that?" she asked.

"Never mind. If you get there first, take the booth in the back right corner."

"No, I certainly will not. And Mike will frisk you for a wire, so forget about having one on your person, too."

"Ann—Mary, I mean—you've spent a lot of time with me. Have you ever known me to be duplicitous?"

"Besides getting together with me and then dumping me out of the blue?" she asked bitterly.

"While you were pretending to be a seeker?" I responded. "And I never lied to you. I just pulled the plug on something that wasn't working for either of us. You would've broken up with me first if you weren't undercover in the Brethren."

"You know everything, don't you, Kade? You're damned right I would've left you. Hell, I wouldn't have gotten together with you in the first place. You're an arrogant son of a bitch. And convincing Frank to will you the property must've been based on a pack of lies—about you, about the Brethren—about everything."

"Arguing is a subtle form of violence," I told her.

"Fuck you," she replied.

"That counts, too," I told the dead phone line.

Chapter 24

Needless to say, I wasn't looking forward to meeting Mary and Mike. Nor was I all that happy about my plan, despite having a few days to think it over and set it up.

My driver dropped me off early at the bar on Thursday, and I nursed fizzy water at the most isolated table. The shape of the room created a sharp corner, leaving no space for another table near it. I'd met other people there when I wanted to discuss something off the land.

The place was sparsely populated, mostly by work colleagues and a young couple in the opposite corner. The decor was an imitation of a modern brewpub, which it wasn't. Steel beams painted lime green spanned across the elevated ceiling and a new-looking maple floor lent a bit of warmth to the otherwise industrial-looking trappings.

Mary arrived first and sat near the door after she spotted me, pointed to my table, and emphatically shook her head. I waited until Mike Quinn joined her to sidle over to their table.

"Kade," Quinn acknowledged, nodding and smiling incongruously.

"Quinn," I returned, holding my features still.

Now that I knew he was Frank's half brother, I could see the resemblance more clearly. Both were handsome in a bland sort of way, with fair skin, a few incongruous freckles, and markedly sparse eyebrows. Their look would be common in Ireland if brown hair was more prevalent.

Quinn stood and frisked me. A nearby table of techies stared. Then we both sat.

"Let's hear it, Kade," Mary said to me, already impatient. "Get to it," she added when I didn't immediately respond.

"Give the man a chance, Mary," her half brother said. "Calm the fuck down."

If her glare could speak, it would've included at least one "fuck" of its own.

"That's all right," I said. "I understand. You two have an old, unhealthy dynamic that shows up when you're stressed. I don't have a problem with that. Have at it."

Quinn smiled. "You're a hoot, Kade. Everything you say is bullshit. But it's amusing bullshit. You can't make this about us. You can't pit us against each other. We're not idiots like those people in the Brethren."

I nodded. "Okay, fine. Let's get down to it."

We didn't, because right then our young Asian server sidled up to take their drink orders. Both of them asked for Mexican beer. The woman glanced at me. Since I'd forgotten to bring my water over, I ordered another.

I paused once we were alone again, soliciting Mary's impatience, and perhaps Quinn's irritated response. She remained silent.

"Here's my proposition," I began. "I think you'll like it. Basically, you get the cave and I get the rest of the property."

"How would that work?" Quinn asked.

"And is this because you found out the paintings aren't prehistoric or valuable?" Mary asked.

"Quite the contrary. I had an appraiser take a look—a guy who authenticates paintings for a living. He took a pigment sample, and his partner knows quite a bit about this kind of art. He says it's an amazing find."

"How do we know any of that is true?" Quinn interjected.

"Ask him yourself. He's meeting us here in..." I checked my phone. "Five minutes."

Our drinks came and they ignored the proffered glasses, swigging deeply from their bottles as they exchanged glances.

Then Quinn stared at me, studying my face. Mary, in turn, continued to look at him with an indecipherable expression.

"Here's how it works," I told them. "Our property is large enough and the county zoning is such that we can split off part of it. We'll sell you the corner where the cave is for a dollar. Then do whatever you want with it. I'll need some sort of contract where you pledge to relinquish all rights to the rest of the land. We can build in consequences if you violate that. I'll also need a document from you, Detective, that you exonerate me from all criminal charges—at least as far as any investigation of yours is concerned."

"And if we agree to this, there have to be consequences for you, too," Quinn said.

"Of course."

The actor I'd hired walked in the door. "Here's James now," I told them.

As far as "James" knew, I was playing a prank on some old friends. He'd been one of Ralph's roommates in college. My student had vouched for my character.

The bogus appraiser had done his best to look the part. Perhaps he'd researched photos of real appraisers. He already had a full reddish beard, which helped. His silver wire-rim glasses may or may not have been prescriptive. A recent haircut, a dazzlingly white shirt, and a chestnut corduroy jacket lent him both an academic and a professional air.

"Quinn, Mary, this is James McBride," I told them

"Pleased to meet you," he told them.

They introduced themselves.

"Sit, sit," I said to James.

He did. "I understand you're the new owners of the cave paintings," he said to the duo.

Quinn glanced at me. I shrugged.

"Let's see some credentials," Mary demanded.

"Sure."

James produced two business cards, replete with very recently established email and website addresses. He passed them over with a theatrical flourish.

"Anyone can print a card," Mary said.

"What would satisfy you?" I asked.

Quinn typed on his phone. "Well, the website's legit," he said.

"Got any references?" Mary asked.

"Sure," James told her. "But what is this? Why the third degree?"

"Just give us some names and numbers," Mary responded.

"Try Kevin Holcomb at the DeYoung museum. Here, I'll give you his mobile number."

He read it off, she called, and one of Ralph's other friends answered. From Mary's side of the conversation, it was clear this guy was also mustering a passable impersonation.

"Look," I said, before she even hung up. "Let's hear from James about the paintings. You can look him up later all you want. I think you'll want to hear what he has to say."

Quinn nodded, Mary hung up, so I nodded at my co-conspirator. James nodded back.

"The paintings date from a pre-Columbian era—maybe the twelfth or thirteenth century," he began. "The iconography resembles early Chumash imagery, but there are key differences that my partner Jack has never seen before."

"Can you prove any of that?" Mary asked.

"Eventually, once all the lab results come in," James told her. "For now, it's a subjective call that I'd stake my reputation on."

"So they're not prehistoric?" Mary asked.

"No."

"Then what are they worth?" Quinn asked. He was hooked, it appeared.

"The paintings are invaluable—priceless," James told him. "They provide a link between two eras of Mesoamerican art."

"So they're worth so much that you can't even come up with a number? Mary asked.

James looked me.

"Go ahead," I said. "Tell them."

"We have a client. He has very deep pockets and an interest in things like this."

"How much?" Quinn asked.

"Ten figures," James told him.

Quinn whistled, and then turned to me. "You're

willing to let go of something that valuable? That doesn't make sense, Kade."

"Believe it or not, I really am spiritual," I told him. "I really do just want the Brethren to be left alone to do our work on our land. We don't need millions of dollars. In fact, having it would interfere with my teachings."

Quinn looked at Mary. "Yes," she said, "he teaches his sheep not to pay attention to money, which, of course, doesn't make any sense."

"Listen," James said, "I need to get going. You both have my card. Call me. We can promise you a reasonable commission."

"We'll need to meet your partner."

"Of course. Take care." He stood and strolled away.

Bravo, James.

"The thing is," I said, "it takes time to subdivide property and transfer ownership. In the meantime, we need to keep the cave a secret."

Quinn nodded. "If this checks out, you've got a deal, Kade. Right, Mary?"

"Absolutely."

I knew further research would continue to support James's impersonation—up to a point, anyway. Ralph had done a great job implanting information online.

I'd bought time—months, probably. In the meantime, things could change. Or perhaps I'd come up with a more permanent plan.

Chapter 25

At eleven the next morning, McCall appeared in my office doorway. I'd been holed up in there for a couple of hours, catching up on paperwork that Jim had passed on to me.

"Have you got a minute?" he asked.

"Sure. Come on in."

He sat down and peered around as though he was interested in the decor. He wasn't. From the floor, Zeus engaged him in a staring contest and won.

"I've just got a few questions that could help us with our current case," McCall told me.

"This isn't about my cousin?"

"Not directly. The thing is, we've traced Guy Harrison—the victim we found in Boulder Creek—back to here."

"There's no one here by that name. Wait a minute. Do you mean Wayne Robbins? He's been missing for a few days."

"Yes, that's the name he's been using," McCall confirmed.

I shook my head. "I don't know what to say. We had no reason to think he was anyone besides Wayne."

"Do you find it odd that you're connected now to three murders?" McCall asked.

"Very odd. This must be connected to Wyatt. Maybe Wayne saw him bringing one of the bodies here. Wayne might not have wanted to come forward since I heard the victim was a fugitive."

"And it's yet another hidden identity, isn't it?" McCall said.

My mind raced ahead of his words. "Maybe Wayne was blackmailing Wyatt. That's another theme woven into this—blackmail. Have you checked Wayne's bank account?"

"Guy doesn't have one as far as we know, but per a search warrant, my men are currently taking a look at his corner of the dorm. And we'll search anywhere else up here we feel like."

"Aren't you supposed to present a warrant before you do that?" I asked.

"We did, just not to you. According to our research, you don't own this property. A nonprofit does."

"I'm the president of the nonprofit."

"Shut up, Tobin. It's all legal. The question is: what are we going to find?" McCall asked.

"I hope you find evidence that leads you to Wayne's killer. Whatever he did before he came here, he's become a sincere seeker. We'll all grieve for him."

"I can't imagine you grieving for anyone, Tobin. You're a cold, calculating killer, and this time we're going to nail you." His glare backed up his words. I was impressed by the way his energy exactly matched his words and expression, as well.

"So it's like that, McCall," I responded. "You can't let go of how you screwed up."

"Fuck you. There's no Wyatt Barr. I don't know how you pulled that off, but I'll find out."

"This is getting close to police harassment," I told him.

"You're damn right. I'm going to be harassing the hell out of you."

A young deputy poked his head into the room—the same one who'd taken my statement after the second murder. "Detective?"

"Yeah?"

"We found something."

"What?"

"You want me to tell you in front of Tobin?"

"Sure. It would get me great satisfaction to watch him wriggle when we hammer another nail into his coffin."

"I don't wriggle," I told him.

The deputy marched forward. "Here," he said, handing McCall something in a plastic bag that fit into his hand. "It's Wyatt Barr's driver's license—from Quebec. We found it under Harrison's mattress."

They both stared at me, hoping for a revealing reaction. I didn't provide one. "Apparently, my fictitious cousin drives," I said.

"It's probably fake," McCall asserted.

"You just don't give up. Do you?"

McCall waved away the deputy. "Why was this under a murder victim's mattress, Tobin?"

"How should I know? Anyway, wasn't this a gang-related murder?"

"The Estes insignia—their tattoo—is an image of lightning with three bolts," McCall told me. "The lightning carved into the ground next to the body had four. Do you think the colleagues of your friends in the county jail can't count?"

I didn't know what to say to that. Did he really think *I* couldn't count, either?

McCall continued. “We’re asking everyone on your land if they saw you during the time span the victim was murdered. I doubt you’ve had an opportunity to arrange a fake alibi this time.”

“Are you expecting a confession from me? Is that what this is about? You want to catch me panicking while you tell me things? Haven’t we been through this before?”

“Shut up. I’m not done.” He seemed to lose his train of thought for a moment before he continued. “This red herring about your cousin taking off doesn’t make sense. How could he fly to Houston and end up back here to commit this latest murder when there’s no record of his flying back—or to anywhere else?”

“Maybe he rented a car and drove back. After all, you now know he has a driver’s license. Maybe he had to come back to kill Wayne to keep from getting caught. Wouldn’t you drive a long way to do that?”

“It’s about a twenty-six-hour trip.”

“So?”

McCall waved his hand dismissively. “Here’s the thing, we’ve got security footage of Guy—under his own name—getting on a flight from Houston to San Francisco during the time he told your buddy Jim he was in Missouri for his mother’s funeral. What do you make of that, Tobin? Supposedly, Wyatt flies to Texas, and then Guy flies back, and keeps the Wyatt driver’s license under his mattress.”

I didn’t say anything. None of that made sense to me. How did it serve my cousin to arrange all that? As McCall began talking, I realized why my cousin would do it—to frame me again.

“Barr, it’s over,” McCall said. “We’re going to find

traces of mud on your shoes that match the wet ground at the murder site. We'll take DNA there. There'll be some that matches yours. There's more, but the DA asked me not to share it. You're under arrest for the murder of Guy Harrison." He stood. "We'll be adding the other two murders shortly."

"What's my motive?"

"Covering up the first two murders, *Wyatt*."

Chapter 26

Of course, I wasn't granted bail again. This time a different judge presided, and she was considerably harsher, not even giving Phil an opportunity to speak. She also kiboshed a second hearing to establish my identity.

In the jail, Billy the Stork approached me in a hallway as soon as I'd been processed.

"Why are you back? What gives?"

"Now they say I killed three people," I told him.

"Shit, are you crazy or what? You get away with two murders—we saw it on TV—and then you go out and whack somebody else? Jesus."

"Like I said the first time around, I'm innocent."

"You didn't say that to me," he asserted. "Anyway, everybody says they're innocent. That doesn't mean anything."

"What's going on in here?" I asked as we walked to my all-too familiar cell.

"Same old, same old. A few guys got out, a few guys came in. I think everyone you know is still here."

At lunch, the three Estes sat down at my table. As usual, when he saw them coming, Chet took off. The gang's spokesman—Jorge—glowered at me.

"We heard you tried to frame us. What have you got to say?"

He crossed his arms and leaned forward, and Jose

and the silent one with the odd name—Tepehuano—followed suit.

"You know me," I said. "Do you think I'd screw up a detail like the lightning insignia if I wanted to do that? That's pretty stupid, isn't it? Anyway, I didn't kill the guy. Take a look at whichever rival gang profits from getting you guys in more trouble."

The talker looked at the other two. The silent one shrugged. Jose nodded and uncrossed his arms.

"Yeah, okay. That makes sense," Jorge said. "But watch your ass. You're on my radar, Tobin—or whatever your name is."

When I called Phil, he let me know Susan and Martha were happy to once again take care of Zeus in my absence, which was a relief. He'd had a hard time when I was in jail the first time.

****

Since the judge hadn't allowed a hearing about my identity, we went straight to the arraignment where the prosecution presents evidence to warrant a trial and I make a plea.

Phil bought me a gray suit for this, and I changed in the men's room at the courthouse. The sleeves were too short, but he was pleased.

"It'll make a difference with Judge Silverman," he told me. "He's old school. But he's fair."

"Why do they keep switching judges?" I asked.

"Each courtroom serves a different function, and the judges rotate for full trials. We may get one of the ones we've already seen if we go to trial since there are only ten altogether."

While we waited for the judge, I looked closer at the incongruently decorated courtroom. The modern, gold-themed decor enclosing the old, handcrafted furniture was almost offensive—like surrounding a Renaissance painting with photos of kittens clowning around.

Finally, the judge emerged from a door in the corner of the room, and we all went through the usual rigamarole. It was as though judges were royalty.

This one eschewed the black robe the other judges wore. Instead, his outfit consisted of a light green suit with a white shirt and a darker green tie. His ruddy face served as a mask—he was hiding himself behind it.

The judge must've been in his mid-sixties, with a lush head of silver hair, and bushy gray eyebrows. His nose was unusually long but didn't protrude. His eyes were part of the mask. I couldn't read him.

"I've been asked to take over for Judge Silverman, who has had a medical emergency in his family," he began in a firm, no-nonsense baritone. "My name is Martin Harrow. If you don't already know me, you need to know I run a tight ship. No one will waste the court's time. No one will act in any way that doesn't demonstrate decorum. The gallery will remain silent. I'll object myself if one of the attorneys gets out of line and his or her opponent does not speak up. Am I clear?"

"Yes, Your Honor," Phil and Marion Burke said, slightly out of sync. The judge looked directly at me. I nodded and tried my half smile. He frowned and turned to the DA.

"Ready to go, Marion?"

"Yes, Your Honor. We're fully prepared this time. The police have conducted a comprehensive investigation," she told him.

Judge Harrow nodded and waved his arm impatiently.

"Your Honor," Phil said, standing as he spoke. "May I introduce myself?"

"Of course. Where are my manners? You are?"

"Phil Karanos."

"Welcome to my court, Mr. Karanos. I'm sure you heard my rules."

"Yes, Your Honor."

"Marion?" the judge prompted.

She stood, glided to her podium, and faced the judge. "This man is Wyatt Barr. He has murdered three people. And maybe a fourth. We don't need to prove that today. Our burden is simply to present enough evidence for this case to move forward. The defendant slithered out from earlier charges because this department failed in its duties. We will not make that mistake again."

Judge Harrow interrupted. "I certainly hope not."

"Yes, Your Honor. As I was saying, we've put in the work to dismantle the lies and obfuscations that the defense offered several weeks ago. Make no mistake. Mr. Barr has been very clever, setting up his ability to evade responsibility years ago for any future crimes he might commit. But he has not been clever enough.

"Let's start in Montreal, Canada. The records the defense presented last time about that are legitimate. Wyatt Barr was raised there and committed crimes there. I assume you've examined the transcript."

"I have," Harrow said.

"When Wyatt escaped custody and moved to Vancouver, he established a new identity. We can prove this, and we will do so in the trial if that proves necessary. Our belief is that when we hand over our evidence in the discovery phase, the defendant will have little choice but to plead guilty.

"So what does Barr do next after furthering his criminal career in British Columbia? He moves to an isolated spiritual community in the Stehekin Valley in Washington. From there, he moves to this county and cons people into joining a spiritual community of his own, dazzling them with his words, using parlor tricks to convince them of his vaunted status. We have several witnesses who saw through this façade and hastily left the Brethren.

"Among other things—on the land in the Santa Cruz mountains—Kade hired three people to masquerade as students of his in order to run an elaborate, illegal scheme we are still sorting out. Cunningly, he invented mildly inappropriate projects to explain the secrecy surrounding this endeavor."

"Ms. Burke, that's all well and good," the judge said, "but what about hard evidence? Can you tie the defendant to the murder weapon? Is there forensic evidence you'd like to present?"

Marion took a step forward. "I'd be happy to supply more evidence, but we're leery of the defense knowing our case prematurely. Mr. Barr is capable of God knows what, and knowing more might enable him to subvert justice once again."

Phil stood again. "Your Honor!" he implored.

"Marion, get to it. Enough of this," the judge said. "Why should I take these charges seriously—especially after the defendant's first hearing? Give me something concrete."

"Yes, Your Honor. The defendant was seen arguing with the first victim the evening before the murder. His alibi has fallen apart because the third victim supplied it, and this man turned out to be a fugitive hiding out in the

Brethren under an assumed name. Need I go on?"

Harrow paused before responding. "I think one more thing might do the trick—unless, of course, the defendant's attorney can refute any of these accusations."

"Fair enough," the DA replied. "Among other things, Detective Michael Quinn of the county sheriff's department has ascertained that Mr. Barr also stole the land the defendant and his cult members live on. Based on this alone, we request that Barr be held while awaiting trial on the more serious charges."

The DA shot a look at me and then slowly lowered herself in her seat.

"Counselor," the judge said to Phil.

Phil remained seated while I hurriedly whispered to him. Then he spoke as he rose. "My client is *not* Wyatt Barr, and the prosecution has not proved otherwise. His name is Kade Tobin. Moreover, he is a beloved spiritual leader who has helped many people with no reward to himself.

"The prosecution has claimed other things without providing evidence. This so-called illegal project? Why do they assume it's something sinister? The DA herself said they didn't know what it was. Mr. Tobin stole the land? Where's the proof? Detective Quinn has a strong bias against my client. His word is not enough.

"Even more basic is the history here. My client has been harassed, arrested, and impugned by the authorities, which the DA has even admitted in this very courtroom not long ago. The evidence I supplied at that time will hold up in court if it comes to that.

"Another question I have is: why is the prosecution so sure about this other person's—Wyatt Barr's—

history in Canada? Did they send someone to Montreal and Vancouver? Are they trusting random clerks at these respective courthouses? Why isn't Ms. Burke providing paperwork about all this?"

The judge turned to her. "That's a fair question, Marion. Why aren't you?"

"I've explained, Your Honor. Our strategy is to present just enough evidence to ensure the proceedings move forward, and not a bit more. Mr. Barr ruined the lives of at least two young girls in Canada and murdered at least three people here. We're looking into a fourth—the member who willed his land to the Brethren. Barr is a monster. We are dedicated to not giving him anything to help him escape justice this time."

"You are required to provide the defendant's attorney with all they need to mount a viable defense," the judge pointed out.

"Not now. Now we get to choose what we share in an open hearing."

"Yes, that's true. But you're setting a tone that supports the defense's allegation that you and the sheriff's department are biased against the defendant. Is he not presumed to be innocent until proven guilty?"

Phil spoke up. "I'd like to address that point, if I may."

The judge nodded.

"Ms. Burke's daughter is a member of Mr. Tobin's community. Clearly, that's a conflict of interest that explains her zest to lock up Mr. Barr."

"Is this true?" Harrow asked Marion.

"Yes, my daughter is a member of the Brethren. No, that's not what's driving this vigorous prosecution. That's due to the heinous nature of these multiple murders."

Phil jumped in again. I was surprised the judge let him. "And Detective Quinn—do you know his ties to Mr. Tobin's community?" he asked the DA.

Marion Burke looked flustered as she turned a page and gazed at her notes. "I am not aware of any connection."

"His brother Frank willed the land to the Brethren."

She paused and took a deep breath. "That's irrelevant."

"I'll decide what's relevant," Harrow said sternly.

"Yes, Your Honor."

"Let me ponder this question of conflict of interest in my chambers. I want everyone to remain in the courtroom while I do. See to it, bailiff."

"Yes, Your Honor."

Phil and I huddled. I told him more about my cousin, Quinn, and Mary, and possible lines of defense. I probably should've been more comprehensive in our conversations prior to the hearing, but I had no idea the authorities had constructed such elaborate fictions. I'd expected the case to be dismissed. Perhaps it was naive of me, but I assumed that if I was innocent, I wouldn't be subjected to a trial.

"Apparently," I told Phil, "Quinn has framed me to create leverage—to get his hands on the land without having to honor an agreement I made with him."

"That's unfortunate. It's hard to impeach the testimony of a law enforcement officer—let alone a senior detective." Phil smiled grimly as he shook his head.

"We can dispute what he claims to have discovered. Truth banishes lies," I said.

"If we could find Wyatt, that would settle things, wouldn't it?" Phil responded.

I nodded.

The bailiff announced we were all to stand. The judge strode in and took his place on his mahogany throne.

"Be seated," he told us. "Clearly, there are multiple conflicts of interest here, but it would be an insult to Marion and Detective Quinn to suggest that these will keep them from doing their jobs properly. If anything, they are likely to work that much harder. Plus I know both of these dedicated public servants, and I have confidence in them.

"Let me warn you, though, Marion, if the trial judge finds a hint of impropriety, he'll dismiss this case. I'll be letting him or her know what the situation is. Under these circumstances, you will have no leeway. Are you willing to proceed on that basis?"

The DA nodded her agreement.

"Now on the other hand," the judge continued, "I shall require the prosecution to offer more evidence in light of what the defense has presented. Are you prepared to do that, Marion?"

"If I must."

"You must."

The DA consulted her notes again. "How about this," she said, walking first toward Phil and then the judge with a document in her hand.

We looked it over. It was a reproduction of a Montreal newspaper article, with a grainy photo of Wyatt being led into a police station in handcuffs. Of course, he looked like me, although at that time I had long hair and a mustache. Wyatt's hair was carefully trimmed and he was as clean shaven as I was now, making the resemblance more marked.

“That is the defendant,” Marion asserted.

The judge looked up at me and Phil. “Counselor?”

“It has been our assertion all along that Wyatt Barr closely resembles the Mr. Tobin. This confusion has been the root of this bogus investigation and arrest.”

“Nevertheless,” the judge pronounced, “it’s enough for me. The defendant is remanded to custody until his trial. How do you plea, Mr. Tobin, or Barr, or whatever your name is?”

“Not guilty, Your Honor.

“Very well.” He rapped his gavel, and a policeman I didn’t know grabbed my arm and pulled me up as I attempted to talk to Phil.

Chapter 27

Back to jail—my second home.

That evening, as I finished a meal of boiled hot dogs and mashed potatoes—ugh—Jorge approached me on his own.

"I'm getting out tomorrow," he told me as he sat across from me.

Slouching, Jorge looked even shorter. He'd abandoned his tough guy act to some degree with me, now looking more like a bully in a high school parking lot than a killer. Mostly, that was due to a softening of his dark, widely-spaced eyes and a new baseline configuration of his mouth—the scowl was gone.

"That's great," I replied. "What have you learned?"

"What do you mean?" he asked combatively. When Jorge didn't understand me, his response was always aggressive.

"What would you do differently next time so it wouldn't turn out the same way it did this time?" I explained.

He thought for a moment, his brow furrowed. "I dunno. Not get caught?"

"That sounds good. What did you get caught doing, anyway?"

"I got another DUI, and then they found a knife in my car."

"You can't have a knife?" I asked.

"It was part of my probation," Jorge told me.

"I see. Well, what can I do for you before you leave?"

"I need money, so it's what I can do for you on the outside," he told me. "I heard some cop has it in for you."

"Where'd you hear that?" I asked.

"Some guy who was waiting for his hearing today said he'd trade his info for Jose's dessert."

"It's true that a detective has treated me unfairly, Jorge, but you don't want to mess with a cop."

"I will if the price is right," he told me, nodding emphatically.

"What are we talking about here?" I asked.

"Well, I don't disappear people anymore," Jorge told me.

"That's good."

"Yeah, I promised my mother. But I could mess him up pretty good," he told me matter-of-factly.

"That's a tempting offer, Jorge, but no. Let me think things over, though. There may be something else I could hire you for. After all, I'm stuck in here and my spiritual students don't operate in your world."

"What are you talking about? There's only one world." His tone was fierce again. So many of the criminals I was sharing space with were literal thinkers.

"I just mean my students aren't effective at getting things done the way that you are."

Jorge grunted before continuing. "Okay, let me know by noon tomorrow about paying me to do something—or you could tell my boys, I guess. They're both in here for four more months. They know how to get hold of me."

"Sure."

Chet returned to the table once Jorge left. His stray eye was aimed at my potatoes while the other one looked at me. His attempt at a beard had come along a bit but was never going to fill in all the way.

"What did that guy want?" Chet asked.

"It doesn't matter. Let's talk about something else," I suggested. I'd been trying to help Chet for days without much success, but I wasn't ready to give up.

"Like what?"

"What are your aspirations?"

"What are those?"

Unlike Jorge, when Chet didn't understand me, which was often since I was having trouble adjusting my vocabulary to match jail standards, he was never abashed to ask what I meant. I think this was because of it happening so regularly. He was fully accustomed to what his minimal education dictated.

"What are your goals once you get out?" I tried.

"First thing, I'm having a beer. I'm torn between Bud and Miller. Then I'm gonna go find a nice-looking hooker—maybe at one of those massage parlors with the happy endings."

"You've done that before?"

"No, but this old guy in the yard said he did. He likes Asian chicks and lots of them do that. He says they like it."

"Why would they like it?"

"I dunno, man. What's with all the questions?"

"I'm just passing the time. Have you got something you'd rather do?"

"No, but if your aura wasn't like it is, I don't think I'd hang out with you."

Eventually, I convinced Chet to go to the jail library

with me to look up careers that might interest him. He was drawn to becoming a shepherd, a longshoreman, or a circus performer, which was not on any of the lists we found.

I had more luck helping an older prisoner make out his will. He was grateful enough to bequeath me twenty dollars.

These people fascinated me; I was thoroughly enjoying myself.

****

I found Jorge in the courtyard after breakfast the next day. He peeled off from his two pals when he spied me coming. They were intimidating an effeminate young guy—invading his personal space and getting him to flinch by feinting punches. The poor guy held his hands up in front of him in a futile attempt to ward them off. As I met Jorge under the lone pine tree at the edge of the open area, I saw Tepehuano knock one of the young man's hands down.

"Tell those guys to cool it," I told Jorge.

"Why should I? They're just having a little fun." He was genuinely puzzled that I cared.

"It's a condition of my hiring you."

"Okay, then." He whistled and then gestured to the other two gang members to move away. They did. "So what's the deal, Kade?"

His orange jumpsuit was filthy, but he was clean within it—the cleanest I'd seen him.

I told him what I'd come up with, and he said it wouldn't be a problem. He wanted a thousand dollars to do it, but I bargained him down to two hundred. Enough said. I just hoped it would make a difference.

That afternoon, Phil visited. Someone else was

using the consultation closet, so we sat in the visitors room, surrounded by other prisoners, wives, and a couple of guys in cheap suits. Now that Phil wasn't in court, he wore his customary jeans with a forest-green fleece sweater.

Dark circles sat under his weary eyes, and he hadn't shaved for a couple of days. I'd only seen him like this one time before—when he'd contracted Covid.

"I don't have any good news," he told me. "Our investigator hasn't been able to disprove anything the DA said, and in fact, he uncovered some additional things we hope they haven't discovered. I'm not sure our original case will stand. After the first hearing, it sure looked like it would."

"That's a shame. Besides Wyatt, at least I know who else is framing me now. That's progress of a sort."

"You mean Quinn?"

"Yes. Suppose we focus on him and prove this is a vendetta to grab the land and the cave. Then whatever evidence he supposedly dug up would be null and void, right?"

"What cave?"

"Oh. I'm sorry I didn't tell you sooner, Phil. We've been keeping it a secret, and I thought it wouldn't be relevant."

"Kade, you need to tell me absolutely everything. I want to know your GPA in college. I want to know your shoe size. I can't do my job if you withhold information."

I didn't like being schooled by one of my students. And I didn't like that I didn't like it, for that matter. I felt petty as my words tumbled out. "My GPA was 3.4, I'm an eleven wide, and there's a cave on the property with paintings in it," I told him.

"Like in France? Cave paintings?"

"Jim did them to impress Martha. Then she showed them to Ann—I mean Mary Dawson."

Phil was silent for quite a while. "That's surprising. Do you think that Quinn and Mary think they're real—that this is what motivated them to ramp up their efforts to seize the Brethren's land?"

"It's a strong possibility. Would you disbelief Martha?"

"Good point." He thought for a moment, his eyes far away. "Kade, since you're innocent, who really committed the murders? Are you saying it's Frank's siblings now—not your cousin? I find that hard to believe. Cops and farmers don't turn into serial killers over a land dispute."

"No, I'm not saying that. It was definitely Wyatt. Everything you presented at my hearing after the first arrest is true. Quinn just capitalized on Wyatt's frame-up. It didn't stand up on its own, but with a detective's intervention..."

"So Quinn is risking his career—and prison, for that matter—to get the land?" Phil asked

"That's my assumption," I told him, nodding.

"If that were the case, it sounds like he definitely believes the paintings are historical. They'd be worth a fortune if they are, right?"

"Yes. So can you get your guy to do a deep dive on Quinn? If he's capable of this, maybe there were other transgressions wherever he worked before. Maybe he's got bribe money squirreled away or a platoon of luxury cars in a barn somewhere."

"Sure, we'll look into it." He paused again, and then leaned forward. "Look, the main reason I came is that I want you to rethink your decision for a speedy trial. I can't mount a comprehensive defense in just a few weeks. There's so much more we need to find out."

I shook my head. "I can't be away from my students for months on end. Look what happened when I had the flu for a week and a half. Greg took Adam out for a driving lesson and wrecked one of the vans. Chuy left the Brethren and signed up for Scientology. *Scientology*, Phil."

"Yeah, there's that," he conceded, "but if you focus on our welfare at the expense of your own, you might not be around to keep working with us. Didn't you say once that compassion is a 360-degree phenomenon—that we needed to administrate it wisely, including ourselves in the equation?"

My words came back to haunt me again. On paper, Phil was right. My intuition told me otherwise in this instance, and that overruled the general principle.

"Nevertheless," I told him, "I'm not changing my mind. Just do the best you can, Phil. However it turns out is how it needs to be. We can't second-guess the universe, no matter how much we try to promote a particular outcome."

"Whatever you say, Kade. Since you're not second-guessing the universe, I guess I shouldn't be second-guessing you. Just don't make a habit of ignoring my advice when we come to trial."

"Sure. You're the expert, Phil."

Chapter 28

Besides meeting with Phil, I passed the time before the trial reading, helping anyone who requested it—including several guards—and meditating as best I could amidst the din of the jail.

By the time I needed to climb back into my suit and walk to the courthouse, I'd gathered half a dozen men who I met with each morning. Mostly, we focused on how they could improve their lives. Sometimes we discussed spiritual matters, usually in the context of how these might be helpful in real-life scenarios.

Several times I needed to redirect Chet in the group, who believed that if he became better at reading auras, he could achieve his dream of performing in a circus. He'd discarded shepherding and working at the docks as career paths when someone told him these were boring.

This time, a chatty guard accompanied me to the cluster of county buildings across the street. Kevin was the one who monitored our discussion group.

He was built like an inside linebacker—someone even a powerful running back wouldn't want to meet if he got past the line of scrimmage. The gentle giant stereotype manifested itself in the way he spoke. I could imagine him teaching a fifth-grade special ed class. When I asked him once how ended up being a guard in the jail, he changed the subject.

"I've heard you talking to the other prisoners about

your philosophy," he said, "so I have a question. How can you be spiritual and also be so crazy that you kill people? I just don't see how those two can go together. My first thought was that the spiritual stuff you say was just bullshit, but it all makes so much sense I can't dismiss it."

"People aren't one thing or another," I told him. "We're brought up in a very dualistic culture—everything is either this or that. Plenty of spiritual people—even teachers and gurus—are advanced spiritually, but also creepy or outright crazy. Tuning into realms beyond logic can be destabilizing to the psyche. The most common version of this is grandiosity. I don't fit the bill here because I'm innocent and I've worked through that phase of my path, but there's your answer. Life is nuanced—complex—and well beyond our superficial, conditioned responses to what we encounter."

Kevin nodded as we approached the back door to the courthouse. "Thanks. That's all good food for thought except for the innocent part, Kade. You're guilty as hell, and everyone knows it."

He'd dropped his soft tone, his condemnation obvious. I could understand why. If I thought someone was a multiple murderer, I'd have a hard time maintaining civility, too.

Enterprising journalists had camped out behind the building. They rushed over. Several thrust microphones in my face. Two men supported video cameras on their shoulders. Others shouted out questions. I pointed to a guy directly in front of me. If he'd garnered the best spot, perhaps he was the most accomplished of the lot. Plus his tie was the least garish.

"What do you have to say about these charges?" he asked in a Boston accent.

I hadn't rehearsed any answers to questions since I expected to be able to sneak into the building again.

"What does it matter what I say?" I responded. "Words are just words. I know it's typical for someone in my position to endeavor to appear wholesome and righteous, or even outraged that he's being subjected to prosecution. But I understand that the authorities are sincere and working hard to do what they think is right. They have been fed inaccurate information by the real murderer and an unscrupulous detective with ulterior motives. And we will demonstrate that in court. I forgive all these people. They are simply enacting their life curriculum, as we all are. Life is a series of lessons, tailored to our karmic needs."

The journalists ignored my answer and shouted out other questions as Kevin ushered me past them. I hoped my impromptu speech would be aired. It might prove helpful to someone.

Phil met me in the hallway, where a bailiff took over Kevin's role and escorted us to the defense table. It was capable of seating four and looked as though it could withstand a major earthquake. I felt oddly safe with the table between me and what I faced—the judge's roost, the witness box, the court reporter's desk, and the jury box. None of these were as shiny as they had been last time I'd been in the courtroom.

Phil and I had walked through a crowded gallery where I saw a lot of familiar faces—Brethren members—and others who wore expressions of disgust, hate, or fear. One older woman in a red muumuu gave me the finger.

Phil and I chatted for a few minutes before we were interrupted by the loud soprano voice of another bailiff—a waif-like young woman I hadn't seen before.

"The courtroom will come to order," she announced. Her auburn hair was whirled on top of her head like a soft-serve ice cream cone. I liked her eyes, which were dark blue.

After everyone stood, Judge Harrow strode in and assumed the dominant position in the room. I'd been told we'd get the judge who'd first heard Phil's case of mistaken identity. That guy was probably disposed to think better of me than any of the others.

"Yikes," Phil whispered. "This is not good. Harrow didn't do us any favors last time."

The judge was in a robe this time. He must've shaved shortly before the trial, and it looked as though he'd gotten a haircut since last I'd seen him. I wondered if he was going to allow news cameras in the courtroom. Why primp otherwise?

"Are you ready to begin jury selection?" he asked Marion, ignoring Phil.

"Yes, Your Honor."

The judge nodded to the bailiff. "Bring them in."

"Yes, Your Honor."

The first twelve jury candidates filed in. They all looked unhappy to be there, except for one elderly man who peered around with great interest.

"We need to keep the old guy," I told Phil.

"I'll try."

We had discussed jury selection at length in the jail. Phil believed it was the most important element of a trial. We both agreed that potential jurors who didn't want to serve would be likelier to vote against us. It was easy to settle quickly on guilt following the prosecution's first dibs on presenting a case. And when getting back to one's life is a priority, a juror tended to rush to judgment.

Phil felt we'd do better with men than women. He reasoned they could identify with me more easily. I needed to be a real person in a juror's eyes, not so different from them that I was just a two-dimensional character in the horror story the DA was likely to concoct.

I wasn't sure about this. It seemed to me that any general policy based on something as basic as gender couldn't take into account the particulars of an individual's attitude. Phil agreed to play it by ear.

As far as age goes, we reasoned that younger was better, although neither of us could explain why. The main thing was to go with our gut as we watched each juror. As in poker, people had "tells" that gave away their inner experience and what they were likely to do.

Judge Harrow provided the jury instructions, which were almost exactly the same as the script of a movie I'd seen. Perhaps he'd seen it, too. He told them the witnesses would be sworn in and under oath, that if he sustained an objection, they were to ignore what had been said, and other trial basics. No surprises there.

Candidate number one wasn't related to a cop, had no criminal background, and had never been the victim of a crime. The judge asked him about all that.

The forty-something man looked like a Texas rancher or someone who'd tried to pose for a Norman Rockwell painting but was rejected because he wasn't quite wholesome enough. This potential juror wore jeans and a black western shirt with white trim and mother-of-pearl snaps.

"Don't you get a chance to question these people?" I asked Phil.

"I certainly hope so."

Having checked out a few other elements that might disqualify the candidate, Harrow turned things over to the attorneys. Marion interviewed the man first. Her questions seemed rather pedestrian—what was his occupation, education, family, hobbies, etc. Perhaps she was expert enough to ascertain more than I could from this. All I learned was that number one was as ordinary a person as he could be. Even his dog was named Dog. I didn't think someone with so little imagination and creativity would help us.

"This juror is acceptable to the prosecution, Your Honor," Marion announced when she'd finished.

Phil rose to question him next. "Thanks for coming, sir."

"I didn't have a choice, did I?"

"Do you resent being here?"

The man shrugged. "Not really. I'm just saying there's nothing to thank me for."

Phil smiled. "Okay, I take it back. Let's start over."

Number one liked that. "Sure." His smile endured until the next question.

"What do you think about spirituality?"

"I don't."

"You don't think about it?" Phil asked.

"That's right. It doesn't matter to me. I think about things that do."

"So it's not BS to you?" Phil asked.

"BS?"

"I can't say that word in court."

"Oh, I get it." He shook his head. "No, like I said, I

don't have an opinion about it."

"Have you read the papers or seen the news about this case?"

"A little bit, but that kind of stuff doesn't…"

"Matter to you," Phil finished.

"Exactly." Another smile appeared. The man had great teeth—white and even—like a line of well-trained soldiers on parade.

"Do you think you can be fair and not rush to any conclusions about the case until it's over," Phil asked.

"I dunno. I'll try if they pick me."

"Thank you," Phil said. "Oops, no thank-yous for you."

The guy smiled yet again. Clearly he liked Phil and he was, at best, indifferent to Marion.

"Your Honor, may I consult with my client before I decide whether this juror is acceptable?"

"Certainly, as long as you keep it brief."

"Take him," I said when Phil leaned over the table. "He's honest, straightforward, and he likes it when you use humor."

"I agree."

So we took the guy. Since Marion had already accepted him before she knew how he'd react to Phil, we were ahead of the game already.

The day consisted of a long series of back and forths as we tried to construct a jury that suited us and didn't suit the prosecution. Ultimately, as the last juror was sworn in around 4:30, Phil turned and smiled.

"We did pretty well all in all, Kade. I wish we hadn't gotten stuck with number six and I think eleven is iffy, but I'll bet Marion is disappointed. She wasted a rejection on that sailor who would've been on her side, and we fooled her into thinking we wanted the college kid."

"He was too arrogant to really listen," I said.

"I agree."

"It's a fascinating process, Phil. Was it hard to give this up to join the Brethren?"

By now, the judge had climbed down and a prison guard—Kevin again—was approaching me.

"Not at all," Phil told me. "Working trials is such an adversarial thing. It goes against who I want to be."

"And that is…?"

Kevin clamped his hand onto my upper arm and led me away.

"Kind!" Phil called. "I want to be kind through thick and thin!"

Chapter 29

I spent an uneventful evening and night in my cell by myself. For some reason, they'd never saddled me with a roommate. The next morning, I was back in court.

"Are you ready to make your opening statement?" the judge asked Marion Burke.

"Yes, Your Honor."

Today, Harrow was back in a suit—a dark gray one—and he'd switched to a light-yellow shirt and a black tie. I wondered what was up with his clothing choices. I had to admit he looked pretty spiffy this time. He could've been the owner of a luxury jewelry store or even a network news anchor.

Marion had abandoned her burgundy pantsuit. Her white blouse with small ruffles at the neck and her black slacks made her look like a server at a snooty restaurant. She'd donned higher heels and put on more makeup than the day before. I wondered if this constituted some sort of strategy. Was looking more feminine an advantage?

Judge Harrow turned to the jury. "Opening statements are not evidence. They are simply a way for the attorneys to preview what's coming from them—like a movie trailer without all the gunplay." He smiled, pleased with himself.

"I've been told he always says that," Phil whispered.

"So take what is said with a grain of salt," Harrow continued. "You might hear some facts mixed in, but basically it's one person telling you the defendant's guilty and the other one telling you he's innocent. If that's all you use to make a determination here, heaven help us."

He watched the jury for a moment, assessing the impact of his words, then turned to the DA. "Please proceed, Marion."

While she shuffled papers, I whispered to Phil. "Didn't he basically discredit both of your opening statements?"

"Yup."

"And he's calling the DA Marion and using your last name?"

"He is. Get used to the justice system, Kade. There's not a whole lot of justice in it."

Unlike the TV version, the attorneys were required to stand behind a low podium just in front of their tables. Marion's posture was erect and she spoke without notes once she positioned herself behind it.

"The defendant would have you believe he is someone else. He would also have you stretch your imagination and believe there is a conspiracy against him, led by an outstanding senior detective in our sheriff's department. That's just for starters. There is a wealth of evidence we have painstakingly gathered that his attorney—Mr. Karanos—will attempt to discredit. He won't be able to. It will be a simple, common-sense decision that Mr. Barr is guilty of at least three vicious murders, including two young girls with bright futures ahead of them.

"The defendant's character will also be on display in more minor matters. He has hoodwinked a slew of sincere spiritual seekers. He stole the land his community lives on. He's involved in a project to bilk investors. And he lied repeatedly to the police. All of this—and more—adds up to a cunning criminal mentality—a pattern of heinous behavior that will turn your stomach as we detail it to you.

"The state is not asking you to do anything extraordinary here. You don't need to be students of the law. All we ask is that you pay attention. That's it. Pay attention to the evidence we present. Pay attention to whether Mr. Karanos makes sense as he goes to ridiculous lengths to convince you of wildly unlikely things."

"Your Honor!" Phil interrupted.

"Marion," the judge said. "I will not have you disparaging your adversary. Stating that his defense will be ridiculous is not acceptable."

"Sorry, Your Honor. May I continue?"

"Certainly."

"We have a clear motive. Mr. Barr was trying to suppress the fact that he had committed major crimes in Canada and is a fugitive from Canadian justice. Moreover, these crimes were—"

"Once again, Your Honor," Phil interjected, "the district attorney is venturing into inappropriate territory. Where she is going with this is clearly inadmissible—assumed prior acts that impugn the character of the defendant."

"If I may, Your Honor," Marion asked.

"Shouldn't we discuss this in your chambers?" Phil interrupted.

"I run a largely transparent courtroom, Counselor. Go ahead, Marion. There's no harm in the jury learning more about the law."

"Any prior acts that speak to motive are admissible, no matter how they might reflect on a defendant's character," she stated. "In the case of prior crimes in which a case has been made, the law is unwavering."

"That is correct," the judge said.

"There has been no case made in this country," Phil protested. "How would this play out if an official in, say, Nigeria said a defendant there had done something wrong. Should that open the door to prejudicing a jury here?"

"Hmm," the judge mused. "I see your point. Marion, what sort of evidence do you have about any crimes Mr. Barr may have committed in Canada? Can we be sure these would merit convictions here in the United States? And can you substantiate your claim that whatever happened there speaks to motive?"

"May I approach the bench, Your Honor?" the DA asked.

"Yes. Counselors?"

Phil and Marion walked up and stood shoulder to shoulder as the DA produced several documents, which Phil and the judge perused. Then the judge waved them back.

"I'll allow Ms. Burke to continue her statement," he announced, "and Mr. Karanos, I'm sure you are aware that you cannot object to an opening statement. If the district attorney says anything she's not allowed to, please let me handle it from now on."

"Yes, Your Honor."

I whispered to Phil. "So she's the one creating problems and the judge is making you look like the bad guy here, isn't he?"

"Yup. We can expect more of the same, I think."

Marion detailed Wyatt's sexual abuse of Chloe—the prosecution had dug up police files in Montreal. Several members of the jury gasped at the graphic descriptions.

Marion's tone maintained its mix of outrage and repugnance as she continued. "As I was saying, escaping justice for this horrific crime—and others—has been Barr's motive for the murders he is on trial for.

"Make no mistake. We have motive, means, and opportunity regarding these more recent crimes. Those are the three elements of any prosecution. When I served on a jury, I drew three boxes on a sheet of paper and checked them off as the trial proceeded. That's all I needed to do to arrive at a guilty decision.

"The defense will assert that the defendant is someone else—that Wyatt Barr is a cousin of the man you see at the defense table," Marion continued. Several jurors looked at me. I employed my half smile.

"We have ironclad documentation that Mr. Barr is who we say he is," Marion continued. "We'll present that as the trial proceeds. When we are finished, none of you will have any doubts about that.

"As Judge Harrow has told you, opening statements are not evidence. I'm telling what to expect—that you will see and hear clear-cut facts that will make your job easy. It will be a slam dunk that the defendant is guilty when we are finished.

"Mr. Karanos will do his best to chip away at the evidence, both in his cross-examination and his defense witnesses. Don't be fooled by this. The truth is the truth, and no amount of tomfoolery changes that."

She sat down.

Phil stood, sidled to his podium, and stood behind it. "Hello. My name is Phil Karanos. I know the defendant—*Kade Tobin*—well. He has helped me in many ways over the past few years. You could say I'm a big fan. Frankly, I'm working on becoming more like him every single day."

Phil turned and solemnly bowed to me, which I thought was a bit over the top.

"I'll do my best to avoid tomfoolery, by the way," he continued, "although I'm not certain what that is. Likewise, I shall refrain from saying anything ridiculous, wild, or tricky. That's not my job. I want the truth to be your guide, so my job is to show you what that is on behalf of my client. I remind you that he is innocent unless proven guilty *beyond a reasonable doubt.* That's a very important phrase. If you have doubts at the end of this trial, you cannot vote guilty.

"Both the defendant and I agree that the man who molested this girl in Canada and killed three people here is a monster—the worst kind of monster. If Kade Tobin were his cousin—Wyatt Barr—I would hope he would be summarily locked away in a particularly nasty cell for the rest of what I hope would be his short life. I know my feelings are leaking through here. I suspect they're the same feelings all of you had as Marion Burke described Barr's crimes in detail. It's disheartening to think that any human being could act this way."

Phil did his best to look disheartened, and I deemed his effort to be about an eight on a sincerity scale of ten. My guess is that most of the jurors bought it.

Phil's expression morphed into "I'm not so disheartened now, but I'm still being damned serious here."

"What you don't know is that Kade's cousin—Wyatt Barr—is a dead ringer for the defendant," he told the jury. "Their entire life they have been confused for one another. Many people thought they were twins. So what better way for Wyatt to once again escape justice than to frame his look-alike cousin as he eliminated witnesses to his prior crimes.

"Make no mistake. Wyatt Barr has been very clever about this, and the prosecution has fallen for it. In their eagerness for a conviction to enhance both the sheriff and the DA's reelection, they've tried to convince the world they've wrapped up the case with a big red bow.

"Speaking of prior acts, let me tell you about the prosecution's behavior in the recent past."

"Your Honor!" the DA implored.

"Turnabout is fair play, Marion. This information goes to *your* motive, and I'm well aware of where this is going." He nodded to Phil.

"As I was saying," Phil continued, "the sheriff's department and the district attorney's office arrested my client two months ago on the same charges. Let me read you a transcript of the hearing in which Ms. Burke addressed my client.

" 'I apologize, sir. We jumped to conclusions and failed to pursue a vigorous investigation once we settled on you as the perpetrator.'

"These are the words of the prosecutor sitting before you today. If I had her on the stand, she would acknowledge this or face a perjury charge. Here's one more quote: First the judge speaks, then Ms. Burke.

" 'Would you like to dismiss the charges yourself, Marion?'

" 'Yes, Your Honor. The county of Santa Cruz requests that all charges against the man currently known as Kade Tobin be dropped.'

"As you can imagine, this unprofessional behavior greatly embarrassed the authorities. As a result, they have focused on vindicating themselves at the expense—once again—of my client. If he is now found guilty—a very unlikely possibility, you'll soon see—then they will have exonerated themselves in reference to their earlier harassment. By the way, Mr. Tobin publicly forgave them and promised not to bring a civil lawsuit as most people would.

"The most egregious example of bias on the part of law enforcement is Detective Michael Quinn's behavior. We shall prove beyond a shadow of a doubt that his motivation for maligning Mr. Tobin goes far beyond this initial prosecutorial travesty. Quinn's half brother, Frank Dawson, was a member of the spiritual community that my client leads. You'll notice that no mention was made by the prosecution that this is Mr. Tobin's commendable avocation.

"Frank Dawson willed the property to the community which still lives on it. For several years, Quinn and his half sister—who went undercover within the community to spy on it—have strived to discredit their brother's legal will. That failed in court, so now they've come up with framing Mr. Tobin to grab the land.

"Detective Quinn is in a perfect position to create, suppress, and tamper with evidence. In fact, he is one of the law enforcement officers working this case. How about that? If that's not a conflict of interest, what is?

"So first we have Mr. Tobin's cousin framing him for his crimes. That didn't work. As you heard, the charges were dismissed. And now Quinn and Mary Dawson are giving it another try.

"Oh, I forgot to mention that Marion Burke's daughter is also a member of the Mr. Tobin's spiritual community. What a coincidence. Imagine how you would feel if you were a mother hoping for a law career for her daughter, only to find she is a student of a spiritual teacher instead? Could you be neutral and fair under these circumstances?

"Forgive me for the length of this statement—the longest one I've ever made. When you hear the evidence supporting everything I've said, you'll understand why I'm outraged by what's happening in this case, and why I feel a need to be thorough. Thank you."

Chapter 30

I slept well that night, pleased with both the jury selection and Phil's performance. He was my lawyer because he was a member of the Brethren and was working pro bono. I'd actually had no idea if he was proficient in trial law.

Kevin and I chatted about mindfulness en route to the courthouse the next morning. I recommended several books and told him we could do a brief mindfulness exercise later that day on the way back to the jail.

Marion Burke began her questioning with one of the forensic team whom I'd spied from a distance after I'd found Althea.

As he marched to the witness box, no longer wearing his white coveralls and blue booties, of course, I saw he was a nervous-looking, skinny guy wearing purple glasses. His bowl-cut haircut did nothing to increase his attractiveness, nor did his two sizes too big navy blazer.

A series of straightforward questions quickly established that Althea Curtis and Chloe Valois had been murdered, the means the killer had used—a large-caliber handgun—and the locations of the bodies. For the latter, the prosecution had prepared a slide presentation showing the property from a drone that hovered overhead and then lowered itself for a ground level visual. The jury liked that. Nothing in this testimony implicated me beyond the fact that I was in my yurt nearby.

Then Phil cross examined the man, whose name was Greg Knaught.

"Mr. Knaught, can you tell us more about the murder weapon? You stated it was a large-caliber handgun. Is that correct?"

"Yes."

"Can you describe what it looked like? Was it a revolver? A pistol? Perhaps some of the members of the jury have never seen this particular type of gun."

"No, I cannot."

I expected a nervous-looking person to act nervous when cross-examined on the stand. Knaught was oddly calm. It was almost as if he had no stake in the outcome.

"Why is it that you can't describe the gun?" Phil asked, continuing a friendly tone.

"We have not located the murder weapon itself."

"Oh, really? No murder weapon? Isn't that usually a key element to finding the perpetrator of a murder?"

"Yes, it is," Knaught affirmed.

"But nada in this case, huh?"

"That's correct."

"Does that worry you?"

"Worry me? No. It would be helpful, of course, but my wife can tell you that, as usual, I'm sleeping like a baby."

"All the babies I've known repeatedly wake up and cry during the night," Phil said. "Is that what you mean?"

The judge broke in. "That's enough, Counselor."

"Yes, Your Honor." He turned back to Knaught. "So tell us more about where the victim was killed."

"That hasn't been determined. As I said in my

earlier testimony, where we found the body was—"

"Yes, yes, we know all about that. Thank you for filling us in. I'm asking you about the site of the crime itself. That's also an important element in investigating a crime, isn't it?"

"Yes." Knaught's confidence was fading. His equanimity had been a façade.

"And your team has nada there again. Correct?"

"Yes."

"Is this unusual—to have no murder weapon and no idea where a violent crime was committed?"

"No, it is not." Knaught was pleased he could dispute the point that he believed Phil was making.

"How about in successful prosecutions? Is it common in those circumstances?" Phil followed up.

"I'd have to say no." Now Knaught looked sad. He had transformed from an impassive professional to someone who seemed to have emotional regulation difficulties.

"So exactly what is it you found at the scene on the Brethren's land that anyone else here couldn't discover?" Phil asked. "I think we all could see a big hole in someone's head, couldn't we?"

"I suppose so."

"You mentioned fibers. I don't think I could've found those, so that might be an exception," Phil said, seemingly throwing Knaught a bone.

"That's right." Knaught brightened a bit. "Even if you did, you wouldn't have the proper equipment to analyze them."

"I certainly don't. So I guess those fibers tied in to my client somehow. They must've implicated him, correct?"

"No, they didn't." Now Knaught could've been the poster boy for the word "crestfallen."

"I see. Then what did you find that led you to believe Mr. Tobin was guilty of this crime?"

"That's not my job. I just collect evidence."

"I didn't ask you what your job was," Phil reminded him. "I asked what you found that caused you to believe my client was guilty. Would you like the court reporter to read the transcript of my question?"

"No, that's okay. It's just that you're making an assumption here."

"Oh, what's that?"

"You're assuming that I developed an opinion about the defendant's culpability when we first investigated the murder." Knaught had regained his poise.

"By culpability, you mean guilt?"

"Yes."

"So you're saying that, based on what you found, you didn't have a reason to even suspect my client?" Phil asked.

"I wouldn't put it that way."

"What way would you put it?" Phil injected a bit of sarcasm into his tone.

"Well, he was nearby where we found the victim's body, and he found her as well."

Even I could see Knaught had fallen for Phil's trap.

"So now you're saying that you do more than collect evidence—that your job also entails drawing conclusions about who happens to be nearby?"

"That's not what I meant."

"But it's what you said isn't it? Which is it? Is your job limited to forensics or should we give weight to your opinions about other things? You're up here to provide expert, professional facts and opinions, right?"

"Yes," Knaught agreed.

"Are you an expert about who is guilty in this case?"

"No, I'm not. I misspoke."

"Hmm, do you think it's possible you 'misspoke' about other things here today?"

"No. I stand by my testimony," Knaught asserted.

"Some of your testimony, you mean?"

The judge broke in again. "That's enough, Mr. Karanos. Let's not belabor this. You made your point."

"Yes, Your Honor," Phil responded. "Let's take a look at things like fingerprints and DNA samples, Mr. Knaught. You didn't mention these during the prosecution's questioning, did you?"

"No, I did not."

"Why is that?"

"I wasn't asked about them. I'm up here to answer what I'm asked, aren't I?" Knaught had decided that pushing back might be the best strategy to recover his credibility.

"Fair enough," Phil conceded. "Was there any evidence generated by these elements that implicated my client?"

"No."

"I have no further questions for this witness."

"Marion, any redirect?"

"Yes, Your Honor. Mr. Knaught, did you find a shred of evidence that exonerates the defendant—anything that leads you to believe he was innocent?"

"No, I did not."

"And are you, in fact, an expert in the field of forensics?"

"Yes."

"So we have no reason to doubt what you've told us that relates to the physical evidence at the scene on Mr. Barr's land?"

"Objection, Your Honor," Phil called. "It has not been established that my client—who is not Wyatt Barr—owns that property. In fact, he doesn't."

"I believe," the judge responded, "that Marion stated he did in her opening."

"Erroneously," Phil told him.

"Then who does own it?"

"It's owned and administered by a nonprofit."

"I see. Objection sustained. Marion, let's stick to known facts."

"I'm sorry, Your Honor. Now, getting back to my question, Mr. Knaught, can we trust what you've told us about the physical evidence where the victim's body was found?"

"Absolutely."

"I'm finished, Your Honor," Marion announced.

"You may step down, Mr. Knaught. Marion, call your next witness.

"The prosecution calls Matt Hernandez."

The first cop to show up on our property did his best to project professional competence on his way to the witness chair, but his slight limp rendered him more human than cop. Hernandez was in his uniform, which he'd washed and ironed—or somebody had, anyway. He held his hat under his arm as though it were a truncated baguette.

After he was sworn in, Marion began. "Officer Hernandez, you are a Santa Cruz County sheriff's deputy?"

"That's correct."

“How many years have you served in the department?”

“Eighteen.” His pride was evident in his tone.

“So it would fair to say you are a veteran officer, well-experienced with responding to crime scenes?”

“Yes.”

“On the morning of the discovery of Althea’s body, were you the first officer to arrive at the scene?”

“Yes, along with my partner,” Hernandez confirmed.

“What did you find?”

“Exactly what Greg Knaught told you—a body in a meadow with a bullet hole in the back of her head.”

“Where was Mr. Barr at that time?” Marion asked.

“He walked toward us when we arrived, and then led us to the body and stood next to it.”

“And his dog was with him?”

“Yes, a very large dog. We asked Mr. Barr to have him stand down, and he complied.”

“I see. Did you subsequently interview the defendant in his office?”

“Yes.”

“And what conclusions did you draw from that conversation?”

“Objection,” Phil called. “This one’s kind of obvious, isn’t it? The question calls for a conclusion.”

“Sustained.”

“Let me ask you a different way,” Marion said. “What stood out for you? What do you remember now that might help us sort all this out?”

“His dog didn’t bark the night of the murder, and Barr is the boss of a bunch of so-called spiritual people.”

“Your Honor,” Phil objected. “Facts not in

evidence. Describing my client as a 'boss' is inaccurate and prejudicial. And the term 'so-called' is inappropriate, as well."

"Sustained. Deputy Hernandez, please limit yourself to what you heard and saw. Let the jury draw their own conclusions about that."

"Yes, sir."

"Yes, Your Honor," the judge corrected.

"Yes, Your Honor."

"Tell us more about the dog," Marion said. "Why did you mention that?"

"The murderer dumped the body where Barr found it by his tent, and his dog was outside all night, but he didn't bark."

"How do you know that?"

"Mr. Barr said he hadn't woken up," Hernandez explained.

"I see, and this seemed significant for what reason?"

"If Barr's dog didn't bark, there's a good chance he was familiar with the murderer, which therefore could be Barr."

"Did you explore other reasons why the dog might not have barked?" Marion asked, trying to preempt Phil asking that.

"We tested him for drugs, and it came out clean."

"Let's move on. Did the defendant seem upset by finding the victim? It was a messy scene, wasn't it—blood and gore?"

"It certainly was," Hernandez agreed. "It was hard to look at. Mr. Barr didn't seem to mind any of it."

"And by that you mean…?"

"He didn't seem to care," the deputy said.

"Objection," Phil called. "Once again, drawing a

conclusion with no supporting evidence."

"Sustained. Mr. Karanos, you're batting a thousand on your objections, but try to limit yourself to the ones that are essential to your case."

Phil nodded his acquiescence.

Marion continued. "Did the defendant show any sign of distress?"

"No."

"He wasn't visibly upset?"

"No," Hernandez repeated.

"Did you find that odd?"

Before Phil could interrupt again, she continued. "In your many years of investigating crimes, do people who discover grisly crime scenes usually act unperturbed?'

"No. They're always shook-up."

"Thank you. That will be all, although I'm sure Mr. Karanos will have some questions for you."

Phil turned to me. "I'm going to have a field day with this clown," he whispered.

"Deputy Hernandez," he began, "did you know that my client worked as an EMT in a major city?"

"No."

"Would you agree that people in that line of work are exposed to a lot of gory sights?"

"I suppose so," Hernandez conceded.

"So would you agree that this explains why my client didn't look distressed to you?"

Hernandez squirmed in his seat. I hoped the jury noticed.

"I wouldn't know about that," he responded.

"I think the rest of us do. Can you tell us how many murder investigations you have participated in?" Phil asked.

"Uh, one, actually."

"Were you the first on the scene in that case?"

"No."

"So would it be fair to say that you are actually quite inexperienced with the type of crime in this case, as well as in your role as a first responder to murder?"

"I guess so."

"Yes or no, please."

"Yes." He had to force the word out. Phil was doing great.

"Do you think you misled the court about this a few minutes ago?" Phil asked.

"I just answered what she asked me."

"Okay, fair enough. Now let me ask you this. It seems to me you were accusing my client when you spoke of his dog's behavior. Is that correct?"

"If the shoe fits, counselor. If the shoe fits."

"Very colorful, Officer, but perhaps a yes or no might once again be more appropriate," Phil told him.

"Okay, yeah. It occurred to me that the dog wouldn't bark if his master was the one who brought the body there."

"You checked for drugs," Phil said. "Did you check to see if my client was a sound sleeper, or his dog had been hunting that night in the adjacent forest, or was engaging in coitus with another dog somewhere else, or any other number of explanations for his not having barked?"

"Uh, no. How would we do that—I mean the dog part. He can't tell us anything, can he?"

"So you don't know if any of those possibilities—or a host of others—might be true?" Phil asked.

"No, that's not something we could know, assuming

that coitus means having dog intercourse."

A few of the jurors smiled at that, and someone in the gallery guffawed. It sounded like Ralph.

"It does mean exactly that," Phil told him. "So your idea about the dog and my client isn't exactly rooted in fact, is it?"

"I guess not in some ironclad way, but it was reasonable to consider it at the time."

"Fair enough. Here's my next question. Don't many deputies who have been in the department as long as you get promoted to detective or another position higher on the career ladder?"

Hernandez squirmed again, more visibly this time. "I wouldn't know about that."

"You don't know what happens in the sheriff's department after eighteen years? I find that hard to believe. Would you like to change your answer?"

"Okay, sure. Some people move up, some don't. It's like any workplace."

"Fair enough," Phil said.

I liked his "fair enoughs." They kept him from sounding unreasonable—as though he was trying to challenge everything Marion's witnesses said.

Phil continued. "Why would you say you've remained a deputy for all these years?"

"Probably because I'm so good at my job." Hernandez pushed his chest forward as if that might back up his words. It came off as unconvincing bravado.

"Ah, thank you for opening that door, deputy," Phil said, smiling. "Your Honor, I'd like to offer exhibit A into the record. It relates to this officer's competency and the reason why he has not advanced in his career."

"Objection, Your Honor," Marion called.

"Your witness did indeed open the door, counselor," Harrow told her. "I'll allow it subject to my perusal of the paperwork."

Phil strode to the bench and handed several pages to the judge, and then to the DA.

"Would you like to see this as well, Deputy?" Phil asked.

"No."

"Do you know what's on these pages?"

"Maybe." Hernandez's tone was pugnacious now. He knew what was coming.

Phil returned to his position behind his podium. "Why don't you tell us about what happened nine years ago outside Watsonville."

"Lots of things happened nine years ago, and I don't remember where they all were."

"Shall I refresh your memory about the incident that got you suspended for six months?"

"No, that's okay," Hernandez replied. "I made a mistake back then. That's all there is to know about it," he asserted.

By refusing to divulge information, the deputy was digging an even deeper hole. He was about to fall down it, and I doubted he could climb out.

"And what was the nature of that mistake?" Phil asked, unwilling to be stymied.

"I arrested my brother-in-law."

"Did he commit a crime?"

"No." Once again, Hernandez had to force himself to say this word.

"Then why did you arrest him?" Phil asked, as if he were genuinely puzzled.

"He owed me money and nothing else I tried got him

to pay me," the deputy answered.

"Are you aware that what you did was against the law?"

"I was suspended, that's all," Hernandez said.

"Did the department try to fire you, but your union intervened?" Phil asked.

"I wouldn't know about that."

"Would you like to see the paperwork I have about your transgression?" Phil asked.

"Okay, yeah. The union saved my ass."

I knew our research hadn't turned up some of this. Phil was an expert bluffer, aided by Hernandez's reluctance to read about his misdeeds.

"Let's move on," Phil said. "Let's take a look at the interview you conducted with Mr. Tobin on the morning the body was found. Was the fact that your daughter recently joined a spiritual group you consider to be a cult a factor in what you asked Mr. Tobin about?"

"Who said I consider those people to be a cult?"

"At the moment, I'm saying it," Phil responded. "Do I need to produce witnesses about what you've said in the past about this?"

Phil was bluffing again.

"Okay, yeah. I don't like cults. That's normal. And the Brethren is a cult."

"What gave you that idea? Do you have experience sorting through spiritual communities and determining which are benign and which aren't?"

"No, I found out what the story was by questioning Tobin—I mean Barr. I gave him a chance to tell me about the place."

"And was he, in fact, humble and helpful? Remember, you're under oath."

"Yeah, I guess so."

"In light of your testimony on this topic, would you say you had a bias against my client before you even met him?"

"I don't let my personal feelings intrude on my work."

"Unless it's someone who owes you money, right?"

"Objection, Your Honor."

"Strike that," Phil responded. "I don't need to say anything more about this deputy's integrity. Obviously, the jury can draw their own conclusions concerning that."

"Mr. Karanos," the judge admonished. "You know better—or I hope you do. I direct the jury to disregard the defense's last remarks. Does the defense have any more questions for this witness?"

"No, Your Honor."

"Any redirect, Marion?"

"No, Your Honor."

She knew Hernandez was a lost cause. The sooner she got him off the stand, the better.

"The witness is excused," Judge Harrow said, "and we'll take a lunch recess for an hour."

****

Phil returned to his seat next to me. "That was a major mistake on Marion's part. She should have known what a lousy witness Hernandez would be."

Everyone besides the bailiff began filing out of the courtroom.

"Is it possible the DA does know, and this is a strategy of some kind?" I asked.

"Well, she's certainly saving her best people until later. Bill Cullen is sixth on the list, and he's the one I'm most worried about."

"Don't underestimate McCall."

"I won't. He's supposed to be up right after Cullen."

"I'm starving," I said. "What are we doing about lunch?"

"Martha's bringing sandwiches. She should be here soon. We're insulated from reporters and the public if we stay in the courtroom."

"You're doing an amazing job," I told Phil. "It seems to me we're winning so far."

"I agree, but it's early. It doesn't mean a whole lot, Kade. A lot of prosecutors go through the motions with basic testimony and then accelerate the case presentation with star witnesses. It sets us up to become overconfident and not prepare properly for the latter stages of a trial. Also, juries are more likely to become invested in a verdict when they've flipped from one side to the other."

"You mean if they start liking our side and then switch to the prosecution's, they don't keep an open mind after that?"

"Yeah, it's an interesting phenomenon. There's a lot of psychology at work in a trial. I know about it and so does Marion. It's like a chess match. In essence, Marion sacrificed a few pawns today. We'll see what she has up her sleeve by the third day, I'd guess."

Martha arrived and ate with us. As usual, she wore her denim overalls with a white waffle-knit undershirt. I wondered what Judge Harrow would've done if I showed up in that outfit.

She was probably the only African-American in the building. There hadn't been any in the gallery. The county was about half White, a third Hispanic, and only four percent Black. Not for the first time, I wondered what that was like for Martha.

She'd made peanut butter and jelly sandwiches on hefty slices of homemade whole wheat bread. I ate two and most of a pint of Greek yogurt. We were all able to meditate for about twenty minutes after that, which I found nourishing. It was always so noisy in the jail.

"Court is back in session," the bailiff called once Martha had departed and the room filled up again.

After we all stood and then sat down—a waste of everyone's energy—the judge asked Marion to continue, and she called Mary Dawson.

"Your Honor," Phil called. "This witness is not on the list the prosecution provided."

The judge looked at the DA.

"Ms. Dawson has just come forward."

"In the last hour? You couldn't notify the defense at all?" Harrow was incredulous.

"We tried, Your Honor. We called Mr. Karanos's office during the lunch break."

"Your Honor," Phil said. "That could not be true. I don't have an office."

Harrow frowned at Marion. "Be that as it may, the defense does need prep time to conduct an effective cross-examination of each witness. You know that, Marion." He shook his head."Mr. Karanos, how much time will you need?"

"Actually, we are prepared to proceed. Based on the DA's past behavior, we didn't assume the list was accurate. We anticipated Ms. Dawson's testimony."

"Watch it, counselor. I didn't let Marion characterize you negatively and I won't have you doing it either."

"Yes, Your Honor."

Harrow paused and narrowed his eyes. "Counselor, why did you even bring this up if you were prepared to proceed," he asked Phil, his irritation evident. "You heard my admonition about wasting the court's time."

"I felt it was important to draw attention to the way the prosecution is operating. As you probably know by now, an element of our defense is highlighting the bad-faith efforts of the authorities in this case."

"Fine. Let's move on. Where is this witness?"

"Here, Your Honor," Mary called from a seat behind the prosecution's table.

"Come on up and be sworn in," the judge told her.

Mary's business-like attire had probably been supplied to her by the prosecution, much as my suit had been by Phil. I wondered if the DA herself had lent her the gray pantsuit. They were about the same size.

Moreover, Mary had trimmed her spiky black hair so that it resembled a hedge instead of a porcupine. Her thin mouth and lips were pursed as she strode to the stand. I couldn't decode that. Determination?

"Miss Karanos, what is your relationship with the defendant?" Marion asked.

"We were lovers. Now we are estranged."

"I understand you were once a member of the Brethren of Congruence, as well—Mr. Barr's group."

"That's correct."

"Why aren't you still a member?" Marion asked.

"I came to understand how manipulative, exploitive, and self-serving Barr is."

"Objection," Phil called.

"Sustained," the judge said.

"Mary, tell us what you directly observed that caused you to make those judgements," the DA asked.

"Well, for one thing, he doesn't do any work. Everyone on the land takes turns buying groceries, cleaning up, and so forth. Not Barr."

"What else?"

"He acts like he knows esoteric things other people don't—like he's special. He sits on a pillow and tells everyone what they should think," Mary asserted.

"You mean he brainwashes people?"

I glanced at Phil. Surely that was something he could object to. He didn't. I'd watched enough TV to know the DA was leading the witness.

"I wouldn't go that far," Mary answered. "He just tries to convince them to switch over to the way he looks at things. It's arrogant to think you have all the answers, and that one size fits everybody when it comes to spirituality."

"Your Honor!" Phil finally called.

"Ms. Dawson, your judgements about character are not relevant. Please refrain from sharing them."

She nodded. "I guess what I mean is that he says things with so much certainty that it shapes his members."

"Shapes them?" Marion asked.

"They turn into junior Barrs."

"And you think that's a bad thing?"

"Don't you? Do you want to be like him?"

Marion smiled. "I certainly don't. Now tell us about this dispute over the property ownership. What's the story there?"

"My brother Frank was a member before I was. In fact, he and Barr were roommates at another ashram in Washington State before Barr started his community on Frank's land in the mountains."

"An ashram is a spiritual community?"

"Yes, it's a Hindu word—or Sanskrit, I should say. I looked into all that when Frank took off to start 'seeking.' Anyway, Frank has always been gullible. Once when we were kids I convinced him one of our cows could count, and another time when he was in his mid-twenties, he fell for a conman selling phony stock. It was supposed to be a company making pizzas out of compost material. Can you believe that?" Mary shook her head slowly. Several jurors mirrored her movements.

"So you think he was vulnerable to what Mr. Barr does with people?" Marion asked.

"Absolutely. I know he was," Mary asserted.

"What did you do at that time—when your brother joined the defendant's group?"

"Everything I could think of to get him out of there, but he was hooked. Barr has big, sharp hooks. They hurt. I can vouch."

"Objection," Phil called.

"Sustained."

"Are you trying to tell us that the defendant hurt you?" Marion asked.

"It's a metaphor, but he certainly hurt me emotionally. He dumped me for no reason at all. That's what he does when he doesn't have a use for someone anymore."

"He's done this with other people?"

"Yes," Mary asserted.

"Now tell us about how the defendant acquired the property the Brethren live on."

"Objection," Phil said. "How many times do I have to correct the DA as to who owns the land? It is not my client."

"Let's not get too fussy, Counselor," the judge admonished. "All these petty interruptions slow us down."

"Yes, Your Honor."

Mary spoke up. "Barr convinced Frank to will it to him—to his nonprofit—then my brother just happened to die a few months later."

"You're suspicious about the circumstances of your brother's death?"

Mary raised her voice. "You're damned right I am. Who falls off a cliff except a drunk or someone with some sort of physical problem? Frank wasn't a rock climber or anything. It just doesn't add up."

"This is a serious accusation, Ms. Dawson. Do you have proof?"

"No, but even if it was a natural death, you've still got the inheritance being withheld from our family. We have a right to it. It would be ours if Barr didn't steal it out from underneath us."

I whispered to Phil. "Why aren't you objecting to all this?"

"It doesn't reflect well on Dawson, the judge told me to cool it, and I'll use some of it against her on the cross. Trust me."

"So if you were to summarize what you're telling the court today," Marion continued, "what would that be?"

"I guess I'm kind of an anti-character witness. I know Barr, and I know what he's capable of. If it was in his interest to kill someone, I think he'd do it."

The judge looked at Phil and raised his eyebrows. Phil shook his head. No objection. The judge shrugged, clearly puzzled.

"Your witness, Counselor," Marion told Phil.

"Thank you. Mary, we know each other, don't we?"

"Yes."

"Was this while you were using a different name, pretending to be a different person?"

"I needed to join the Brethren to find out how to get our land back."

"Is that a yes?" Phil asked.

"Some questions don't have yes or no answers."

"This one does," the judge told her. "Answer the question."

"Yes, I was using another name."

"So you lied to two dozen sincere spiritual seekers for your own personal gain?" Phil asked.

"No, of course not."

"I'm confused. It sounded like that was what you said a moment ago. You came to a community pretending to someone else, you did so to find a way to seize land that was legally owned by a nonprofit organization, and then you seduced the leader, entering into an intimate relationship, once again for personal gain. What have I said that's inaccurate, Ms. Dawson?"

"He seduced *me*. And this was never about what you're calling 'personal gain.' It's about righting a wrong—getting things to be the way they ought to be."

"Has a court ruled on this matter?"

"Yes." Mary wasn't pleased about where this was going.

"What was that ruling?"

"Barr and his lawyer—*you*—were clever. You set it up so the judge couldn't do the right thing."

"And the ruling was…?"

"Against us."

"Us?"

"My half brother and myself."

I smiled. I knew what was coming. Another door had opened.

"Are you referring to Detective Quinn—one of the officers investigating these crimes?"

"Yes." Mary's shoulders drooped. She knew she'd screwed up.

"So you can verify that Detective Quinn has been involved in a lawsuit against the Brethren?"

"Yes."

"For how long?" Phil asked.

"Two years."

"I imagine you both must've become very frustrated," Phil said.

"Imagine all you want. That's not a question."

"No, it isn't. Here's one: you use the word 'right' a lot. Why do you think your opinion about what's right ought to supersede what the legal system has decided? And for that matter, why is your brother's express wish to leave his estate to the Brethren nonprofit wrong in your eyes?"

"The courts screw up all the time," Mary stated. She glanced at the judge and grimaced. "Sorry. And like I said before, Barr talked Frank into things."

"Yes, about that. Do you have any proof? For that matter, is there even one other person besides you and Detective Quinn who believes that?"

"That doesn't matter."

"Please answer the question," Phil said.

"No, there's no one else, but I know what I know. There's just no one brave enough on the land to come forward and tell it like it is."

"So now you know what's right or wrong better than everyone else, and you also know that two dozen people are all cowards because they don't agree with you. Is it possible that your arrogance is the problem here?"

"Objection."

"Sustained."

"Sorry, Your Honor. Now, Ann—I'm sorry, *Mary*—you stated that Mr. Tobin broke off your relationship for no reason. But that's not correct, is it?"

"Sure it is," Mary asserted.

"Isn't it a fact that he told you he wanted to be celibate—for spiritual reasons?"

"He'll say anything to get what he wants."

"Do I need to repeat the question?" Phil asked.

"Go ahead if you want to."

Phil turned to the judge. "Your Honor?"

"Ms. Dawson," he said, "you are required to answer these questions. You are wasting the court's time."

"Fine. Yes, that's what he said."

"Thank you for your cooperation," Phil responded, creating a contrast between his cordial tone and her truculence. "Was there a time when you attempted to take charge of the brethren—a coup d'état of sorts?"

"I wouldn't call it that."

"Okay, did you try to depose my client as the leader of the community?"

"Yes," Mary conceded.

"Was this another attempt to acquire the land you did not own?" he asked.

"It would've been good for everyone up there."

"That's not an answer to my question. Did you do this to get the land?"

"Yes," Mary admitted.

"Do you have any legitimate interest in helping people on their spiritual paths?"

"It's all bullshit," she declared heatedly.

"Your Honor?"

"Answer the question, Ms. Dawson. I'm getting very tired of this song and dance, and I think the jury is, too."

I saw several of them nod their heads. They did not like Mary. Phil had told me that if they didn't like a witness, they gave less credence to what she said. Among other things, that was why he was pushing her.

"I'm an atheist," she told him.

The jurors did not appear to like atheists. Several frowned, and one woman slowly shook her head.

"Let's move on to some other things you've said today. You stated that your brother Frank was not a rock climber. How do you know that?"

"He was scared of heights," Mary told him.

"Are you aware that he saw a therapist and worked on this and several other phobias?"

"No."

"Are you aware that when Frank Dawson's body was found, he was wearing a rock-climbing harness?" Phil asked.

"Barr put that on him afterward."

"How do you know that?" Phil asked.

"It stands to reason. He had to come up with something to make it look like an accident."

"So you have no evidence to support that?" Phil asked. "It's just your idea of what happened?"

Mary didn't answer.

"That's fine. You don't need to answer that one. I think we all know what you'd be compelled to say.

Here's one last question: why would anyone associated with the Brethren need to kill Frank for the land? They already had it, didn't they? Your brother didn't charge rent and he paid the property taxes. There was no real advantage to the nonprofit owning the land, was there?"

"Objection," Marion called. "Calls for speculation."

"Sustained. Mr. Karanos, I hope that really is your final question. My son has a soccer game at five thirty."

"It is. Thank you, Your Honor."

"Court is adjourned."

Chapter 31

Phil paid me a visit that evening, which I actually discouraged. His spiritual growth was already being compromised by his return to a profession that had held him back for years. He didn't need to tack on extra work hours.

"Don't let this trial be all-consuming, Phil," I told him. "Let's keep this meeting brief."

"That's fine. I just wanted to get your thoughts on how things went today. What's your read on Marion and the jury?"

"I found it alarming that Marion didn't seem disheartened by your cross-examinations—at least not visibly. What is she planning that made your eviscerations low-magnitude events?"

"We'll see, won't we? I'm beginning to think she may just be incompetent. She was elected, and that wasn't necessarily because she's the strongest trial prosecutor in the department. She could be taking the case herself just to boost her visibility for the upcoming election. After all, she totally bungled trying to nail you the first time, and I haven't seen anything out of her that impressed me yesterday or today."

"That would be handy," I said, "but I'm not going to count on it."

Although we were sequestered in the attorney room, a ruckus in the hallway interrupted us.

"Fuck you!" someone shouted.

"What did you say?" someone else replied. It sounded like Billy the stork.

"You heard me, bitch."

"Fuck you."

"No, fuck you."

Phil and I exchanged glances. As their voices receded. I continued speaking.

"As far as the jury goes, I think it's looking good. I've been watching them. Two or three seem checked out most of the time, but they came to life when you homed in on the witnesses. Another couple of them don't appear to be impressed with you. I think that's a bias at work—thinking I'm probably guilty and the DA must know what she's doing. The others nod and smile when you talk, and frown or grimace when the prosecution's witnesses get caught out. So all in all, I think it's going well, don't you?"

"Yes, I do," Phil agreed.

We discussed other details for another fifteen minutes, and then I finally convinced Phil to return to the land to meditate and then sleep.

At court the following morning, Marion called someone to the stand I'd never heard of before seeing the witness list. Joe Lombardi was an investigator whom several counties used off and on.

His stocky frame had been hard to jam into a suit, and his thick neck suggested he was a gym rat. No one was born with a neck wider than their head. Lombardi's face reminded me of a Sicilian I'd known back at Baba's ashram. Swarthy, with black, bushy eyebrows and a hawk-like nose, the investigator wasn't someone I'd want to meet in a dark alley. Perhaps this uncharitable thought derived from the plethora of gangster movies I'd seen.

"Mr. Lombardi, can you tell us something about yourself?" Marion asked after he was sworn in.

"I'm a licensed private investigator currently working for your department. I've been doing this for twelve years. I'm good at it."

Phil spoke up. "In the interests of keeping things moving, Your Honor, the defense will stipulate that this man is who he says he is, and if he says he's good at his job, that's good enough for me."

The judge nodded. Phil had scored points with Harrow by keeping things moving. Also, he appeared to be a fair-minded guy to the jury.

Marion continued. "Did the prosecution send you to Montreal and Vancouver, Canada, to ascertain certain facts related to this case?"

"Yes."

"Would you share what you found there?"

"Certainly. I discovered proof that the defendant is Wyatt Barr. which verified the documents the Canadian authorities sent you."

"Your Honor," Marion said. "I'd like offer exhibits A, B, C, and D into the record."

"Granted."

She walked over to the court reporter and handed her a manila file, then she gave one to Phil. He opened it and began scanning its contents.

"At a later point in Mr. Lombardi's testimony," Marion told Harrow, "we'll show them on the screen for the jury and everyone else to see."

"That's fine," he told her.

"Specifically, who did you interview to ascertain

what you just stated?" Marion asked her witness.

"I got it from the horse's mouth. I talked to—"

Before he could continue, I heard someone call out from the gallery, "Which horse was that—specifically?"

"That's enough of that," the judge admonished.

I was surprised he didn't toss whoever it was. Perhaps Harrow couldn't tell who'd said it or he didn't want to interrupt the testimony any more than necessary.

"Can you explain what you mean when you used that idiom?" Marion asked Lombardi.

"*Specifically,* I spoke to the arresting officer in Montreal, I saw Barr's mug shots at the police station, and I found school records, which are all part of the exhibits. I also interviewed a dozen people associated with Barr, including a former employer and a former lover. There's zero doubt in my mind about any of this."

"Now when you say there was an arresting officer, can you tell the court about that?"

"Barr was convicted of statutory rape in Montreal while the police continued to investigate more serious charges."

"What were those?" Marion asked.

"Sexual abuse of a minor, sexual battery, and lewd and lascivious acts."

"What happened next?"

"Barr escaped from custody while being transported from the court to jail. After that, he successfully disappeared."

"Until now?"

"Exactly. He's sitting over there." Lombardi pointed at me.

"Objection," Phil called. "Facts not in evidence."

"Sustained."

"What else can you tell the court about this elusive Mr. Barr?"

"I found no evidence that he has a cousin, as I understand the defendant claims."

Phil turned and looked at me. "There's the frame," I whispered. "Quinn must've paid this guy off. It would've been easy to find. All he had to do was talk to our relatives up there. The family knows we're cousins."

"What did you find in Vancouver, Mr. Lombardi?"

"I was informed that before Mr. Tobin named himself Tobin, he claimed he was Carl Steubens, a resident of Vancouver. So I looked into this identity to determine what the deal was. Carl Steubens died some time ago. A man who looked exactly like Wyatt Barr began living under this name, eventually becoming a counselor in a middle school. This age group coincides with Barr's preferred victims' ages in Montreal."

Phil looked at me again. "Not true," I told him. "We need to get someone up there to refute all this."

"Your Honor," Phil said, "may we approach the bench?"

He waved him up, and Marion joined him. In a couple minutes, he returned to the defense table.

"What's happening?" I asked.

"I argued that this evidence was prejudicial, represented prior acts, and didn't have enough probative value to warrant inclusion. It's one thing to talk about all this in an opening statement. It's another one to offer testimony about it. You're not on trial for any crimes committed elsewhere."

"What did the judge say?"

"He was inclined to agree, but he wanted to read case law before he made a final decision. Marion made the argument that this line of questioning goes to motive—that the murders were to escape consequences from the earlier crimes. That may be upheld. This is a close call. For now, Harrow ruled that Marion won't get to project her documents for the jury to see, which is a big plus for us."

"They can't unhear all that, though, can they?" I asked. "Why didn't you object sooner?"

"I'm sorry about that. I wanted to hear what ammo the prosecution had. I didn't realize it would be so damning."

"We need to reiterate that I'm not Wyatt."

"Yes."

The judge spoke. "I think I've given the defense enough time to confer. Members of the jury, we are going to suspend the rest of Mr. Lombardi's testimony until I rule on a technical matter. Please draw no conclusions from the partial testimony you have heard."

"Your Honor," Phil said. "It would be a breach of the court's rules not to let me cross-examine Mr. Lombardi based on what we've heard so far."

"Hmm, that's true. Marion, are you okay with this?"

"No, Your Honor."

He thought it over. "Nonetheless, go ahead, Mr. Karanos."

"Thank you, Your Honor." He stood and faced Lombardi. "Are you being paid for this testimony, sir?"

"Yes, of course."

"I don't mean for your time investigating. I mean sitting here saying these things that help the prosecution's case."

"The answer is still yes." Lombardi spoke confidently in a smooth baritone voice.

"How much are you being paid to speak to me right now?" Phil asked. He knew the amount would seem exorbitant to jurors.

Lombardi turned to the judge. "Do I have to answer that?"

"Counselor," the judge said. "Where are you going with this?"

"I'm establishing that the witness is hardly a non-biased source of information. He's been hired to come up with things that please his masters. The amount he's being paid might well be proportional to the amount of bias he has. After all, if he doesn't come through for the prosecution, one of his main sources of income dries up."

"I'll allow it," the judge decided. "Answer the question, please."

"Five hundred dollars an hour."

I saw a lot of raised eyebrows in the jury box.

"And you think having a business relationship on that scale creates no ethical problems?" Phil asked.

"I do."

"Would it surprise you to know that others don't?"

Marion stood to object, but when Lombardi didn't answer, she sat again.

"Okay, let's move on," Phil said. "You stated that the police in Montreal were, and I quote, 'continuing to investigate more serious charges.' Is that correct?"

"Yes."

"So Mr. Barr—my client's cousin—was not charged with any other crimes?"

"He was in the wind. There was no one there to charge."

"Is that a yes or a no, Mr. Lombardi?"

"Obviously, it's a no, due—"

"Thank you. Do you see how naming crimes that someone was never charged with could be prejudicial? What if I said I was considering charging you with treason? Would that be appropriate to mention in a trial?"

"Of course not, but—"

"Thank you. Now you say you found no evidence that my client had a cousin. Is that correct?"

"Yes."

"Did you ask his relatives about this? His uncle, for example?"

"No, I did not."

Phil was bluffing again. I knew he had no idea if there was an uncle in the picture. I didn't myself.

"Do you think the family would be the best source of information about who has a cousin?" Phil asked.

"Sure, but—"

"Thank you. So after an investigation that was not comprehensive, and did not entail contacting the best source of information, do you think the lack of evidence is meaningful?"

"I'm not sure what you mean."

Lombardi was stalling. It was there in his voice and his body language—an unnatural stiffening.

"Let me clarify my question," Phil said. "I'm wondering if you want us to believe that your lack of evidence about a cousin counts as evidence. Because you didn't personally find something out—and your due diligence was apparently lacking—does that mean a cousin doesn't exist?"

"Listen, I tried to—"

"Are you heading to a yes or no, Mr. Lombardi?"

"Objection," Marion called. "He's badgering my

witness."

"Sustained. Let the man speak, counselor."

"Certainly." Phil turned back to Lombardi, switching gears quickly. "Tell us about your relationship to Detective Quinn."

"He's on the team that has been investigating this case."

"So he's a colleague?"

"Yes," Lombardi told him.

"Has he spoken to you about what he believes?"

"About the case?"

"Your Honor," Marion said. "Hearsay."

Phil responded. "I'm not asking him *what* Quinn said. I'm asking *if* he said things."

"Overruled, Marion."

"What was the question?" Lombardi asked.

"Let me put it another way," Phil said. "Is it possible that Quinn's conflict of interest has bled onto you?"

"I don't know what you're talking about."

"You're investigating this case and you're not aware that Quinn's brother left his land to the Brethren?" Phil asked. "Quinn and his sister have been trying to get it for years now. They consider the defendant to be an enemy. They want to get him out of the picture."

Marion spoke up. "Counselor is testifying."

"Sustained. The jury shall ignore the latter part of Mr. Karanos's remarks."

"You're unaware of this?" Phil asked Lombardi.

"That's right. None of that has anything to do with what I was hired for, and I resent this 'bled' thing. My integrity is not in question. Ask the DA. She'll vouch for me."

Lombardi's red face and clenched fists were surely

visible to the jury. Although Phil had uncovered the fact that the investigator had a temper, I was still surprised at how quickly Lombardi had gone from zero to sixty.

Most of the jury looked at Marion, who nodded vigorously in support of her witness.

"So you're involved in this case as an investigator and a highly paid witness," Phil continued, "and you're not aware of at least one major relevant fact about a colleague. Is that correct?"

Lombardi raised his voice. His frustration was evident. "I have no reason to know anything about Quinn. I went to Canada. I gathered evidence. That's what I was hired to do."

"Are there other important elements of this case that you don't know about?" Phil asked.

"How can I tell you about things I don't know about? That's a ridiculous question."

Phil smiled. "You've got me there. I guess that was a little silly. Let me try again. Would it surprise you to know that the prosecution has failed to inform you of other aspects of the case that are very important in these proceedings?"

"That's just a sneaky way for you to introduce an irrelevant idea to confuse the jury—that whole 'would it surprise you?' deal. This isn't my first rodeo, Mr. Karanos."

"So you'd rather not answer my question? Why is that?"

"There you go again. You say everything in order to make me look bad. I've done great work on this case and nothing you say can take that away." His fists tightened again and he tensed his shoulders. Phil was certainly getting under Lombardi's skin.

"Do you have a temper, Mr. Lombardi?" Phil asked.

"When I'm pushed hard enough, *Counselor.*"

"Like I'm doing?" Phil asked.

"Now that you mention it, yeah. I'm not your punching bag."

"Would say you have problems with authority?"

"When they act like horse's asses." Lombardi was out of control. I expected Judge Harrow to step in, but he didn't.

"You interacted with quite a few authorities in Canada, didn't you?" Phil asked.

"I see where you're going with this. No, my temper didn't enter into it," Lombardi asserted.

"You probably had to wait on lines, listen to a lot of bureaucratic BS, and maybe get pushed around by all the rules they have up there, right?"

"That's my job."

"You're telling us you have a temper, which you've demonstrated in here, that you have problems with authorities, and that none of that showed up while you were investigating this case?"

"That's right. That's exactly what I'm saying." Lombardi turned to the judge. "I'm done," he told him. "That's all I'm going to say."

"You're done when I dismiss you," Harrow told him. "Now sit there and answer any question the defense asks you unless you want to be held in contempt of court."

"I'm in contempt of this lawyer," Lombardi said, jerking his thumb at Phil.

"That's enough," Harrow rebuked sharply.

"Your Honor," Phil said, "owing to the volatility of this witness, I think it's best if I stop. I'm not sure what might happen if I drill down any further."

"Very well. You are dismissed, Mr. Lombardi."

"Redirect, Marion?"

"No."

"Court is adjourned for an early lunch. We will reconvene in an hour."

Chapter 32

A Canadian cop was next on the list; he was going to testify on a secure video link. Susan Burke was due after him, which I found bizarre. What could her mother garner from *her* testimony? And why all this focus on Barr's Canadian criminal history? This was a murder case. Why wasn't the DA focused on the murders?

Phil told me during lunch—sandwiches again, toted in by Jim—that if the DA didn't call Quinn to the stand, he would. Quinn wasn't on the current witness list.

"If they don't want him up there, there's got to be a reason," Phil explained. "I can call him up and try to ferret that out. When he gives me a hard time, which he will, I can get him declared a hostile witness. That gives me a lot more leeway."

"Why didn't you do that with Mary or Lombardi?"

"We can only do it with our own witnesses," he told me after swallowing a massive bite.

"Ah. Lombardi did a lot of damage, didn't he?"

"He was a lousy witness, as it turned out, but the documentation he provided in those exhibits is really damning. If we can't show they're false, we might be screwed. In fact, if I didn't know you, I'd think—based on those—I had a guilty client."

"What are the odds our guy can locate the real Wyatt?" I asked. "That would solve everything."

"At this point, I'd have to say pretty low, and

everyone else has stopped looking."

"So for now I guess we have to find a way to discredit Quinn," I said. "He must've spoon-fed the supposed facts to Lombardi or paid him off."

"I don't think Lombardi is dishonest," Phil stated. "That's not my read on him. It's more likely Quinn set things up for Lombardi to find—bribed the people he talked to. Let's try to trace Quinn's movements. I'll ask our guy up there to pass around Quinn's photo, and hopefully he can also check into the financials of everyone mentioned in Marion's exhibits."

"That sounds good," I told him.

At that point, a young man entered the courtroom, traipsed down the aisle, and handed Phil a sheet of paper. "It's a revised witness list," he told him in a high squeaky voice.

Phil read it as the guy walked away. "Good news," he told me. "Quinn is now up next. We can find out some of what we need to know from the horse's mouth."

"Which horse—specifically?" I asked, smiling.

Then I borrowed Phil's phone, which he'd purchased shortly before the trial. I made a quick call in the men's room and hoped there would be enough time for what I had in mind.

****

"Detective Quinn, thank you for being here today," Marion began. "You have been instrumental in gathering evidence in this case, have you not?"

"Yes, I have."

Quinn's dark suit contrasted with his pale complexion. His white dress shirt and thin black tie completed a funeral director look, marred only by black running shoes featuring light yellow stripes.

When I studied Quinn's brown eyes, I could see I'd underestimated him in the past. There was cunning there, and a strength of character to follow through with whatever he'd planned. I suddenly felt unconfident about his testimony. He'd certainly covered the bases up in Canada when he'd set out to frame me. He'd probably do so with what he'd say on the stand as well.

Tearing my eyes away from my nemesis, I looked to the back of the courtroom and a familiar face waved at me. I felt a bit better.

"You directed Mr. Lombardi in his efforts. Is that correct?" Marion asked Quinn.

"Yes."

"His reputation has been under attack this morning. Do you have complete confidence in him?"

"I do. He's not the world's best witness, but he's a crackerjack investigator, and I'd trust him with my life."

"Wow, that's quite an endorsement," Marion said, glancing at the jury to drive the point home.

"Objection. The DA is testifying."

"Sustained."

"When did you first suspect the defendant?" she asked.

"While I was out on medical leave, my partner filled me in about the case. We both immediately suspected Tobin, or should I say Barr?"

"You should."

"Objection."

"Sustained."

"Why did you deem Mr. Barr to be the murderer?"

"There were a number of things," Quinn replied. "For one, he found the body. You'd be surprised how often whoever that is turns out to be the killer. Then the body was found near his tent, Barr had a shaky alibi, he wasn't using his real name, he was unnaturally calm, over-interested in our investigation…I could go on and on."

"I think that will be sufficient. Earlier today, before you arrived, we heard testimony which was halted for reasons—"

"Marion, tread carefully," the judge warned her.

"Yes, Your Honor. Detective Quinn, I'm going to ask you about what you and Mr. Lombardi found concerning the defendant's true identity. I'd like you to do that without mentioning anything about any crimes he may have committed in Canada."

Quinn nodded. "Sure. I can do that."

"I understand that in Vancouver someone assumed the identity of a dead man."

"That is correct. Carl Steubens."

"In your experience as a law enforcement officer, why would someone do that?" Marion asked.

"To escape whatever negative consequences are associated with their original identity."

"Are there other reasons?" she asked.

"Not really—unless you count spies or something like that," Quinn answered.

"Was there a spy in this case?" Marion asked.

"No."

"Who was it that assumed this false identity?"

"We determined that the man was Wyatt Barr—the defendant." Quinn pointed to me with a straight arm, accentuating his gesture.

"How did you do that?" Marion asked.

"Photographic evidence, interviews with former coworkers, and other authoritative evidence. Once we knew there was no cousin, the rest was easy."

"Is all this evidence in the exhibits I showed you and then entered into evidence?" Marion asked.

"Yes."

She turned to the judge. "Your Honor, I'd like permission to project the exhibits at this point."

"Marion, we talked about that. It'll have to wait until I've made my ruling. My clerk is researching the matter. There is material in there that may be inadmissible."

"Understood."

I took a moment to whisper something to Phil. His surprised expression was something I expected.

"Detective, we've heard that you've been in a dispute over land," Marion continued. "I'm sure the defense will be asking you about that. Can you explain?"

"Certainly. My half brother owned the land the Brethren live on. He willed it to that group instead of to his family. When he died, we contested the will, as most people would."

"That's all there is to it?"

"Yes."

"Enough said. Why don't you walk us through your investigation step by step? I think the jury needs to understand all the timelines and procedures."

Quinn painstakingly detailed his investigation, frequently referring to a small spiral notebook. I saw two jurors eyes glaze over and one kept nodding off and then jerking awake. Unfortunately, the others paid rapt attention. Here was their chance to match up reality to all the police-procedural TV shows they'd seen.

Phil and I whispered for several minutes while Quinn talked about forensic evidence that the first witness hadn't mentioned. We both had ideas about how to cross-examine Quinn.

Finally, it was Phil's turn to question Quinn. "Detective, what was the nature of your medical leave?"

"Objection," Marion called. "Relevance, plus HIPAA laws apply, too. Medical information is owned by the patient."

"Mr. Karanos?"

"We have evidence that Mr. Quinn did not have a medical problem—that instead he was taking time off to create a bogus case against my client."

"That's outrageous!" Marion exploded. "Your Honor, I've put up with a lot in here, but this…"

"Mr. Karanos, if you have evidence of that, you may present it when it's your turn to call witnesses. Until then, you are not to slander the prosecution's witnesses, nor will I let you slip in innuendos or insults."

"You asked me a question, Your Honor, and I answered it. That's the reason I am asking the detective about his leave."

"I don't care. There will no more of that."

"Yes, Your Honor. So where were you during your leave?" Phil asked Quinn.

"What do you mean?"

"It's a simple question. Did you stay in bed? Did you seek medical treatment somewhere? Were you out and about locally—going to the movies, eating in restaurants? Fill us in. And be aware that we have our own investigator and your career will be over if you commit perjury."

"It varied from day to day," Quinn said.

"Objection," Marion called. "Once again, what is the relevance of this line of questioning?"

"I'm curious about that, too," the judge said. "Let's

wait and see where this goes."

"Did you, in fact, travel to Canada?" Phil asked.

"Yes, later."

"It wasn't while you were out on leave—while you weren't on duty?"

"It may have overlapped with that period of time. I was investigating Barr's history," Quinn said.

"I thought Mr. Lombardi was doing that. Why would the department hire him when you were already doing the same thing?"

"You'd have to ask the DA." Quinn's tone was hostile now. He was actively resisting where Phil was leading him. I watched several jurors frown. As with other witnesses, this kind of thing didn't reflect well on someone's testimony.

"That's an interesting idea," Phil responded. "Perhaps I will. If I did, would she say she or the sheriff had authorized your visit to Canada? The *part* while you were off-duty?"

"No, they wouldn't," Quinn admitted.

"Why is that?"

"As you know, my zeal to hold Barr responsible for his crimes pushed me to work above and beyond my usual duties. I worked the case even while I was ill."

"So you're admitting you're motivated by strong personal reasons?" Phil asked. Quinn's attempt to spin his behavior as exemplary was backfiring.

"Sure. Before these crimes, I already knew Barr was a sleazy fake."

Phil turned to Harrow and raised his eyebrows.

"The witness will refrain from such remarks," Harrow admonished. "Just answer the questions."

"Yes, Your Honor," Quinn responded. "The point I

was making is that my zeal was justified. It has actually aided the investigation and this prosecution, too."

Phil continued. "So you think personal, residual feelings have a place in a criminal investigation?"

"Sometimes."

"And you get to decide what those times should be?"

"For myself, yes." Quinn nodded furiously. I don't think he understood how that came across.

"Okay, let's move on," Phil said. "I think the jury gets the picture here. Tell us about the cave."

Quinn paused momentarily and frowned as though he'd thought hard about it, but just couldn't come up with an answer. Unfortunately, when someone did this in the first few seconds of being asked a question, the act was wholly unconvincing.

"What cave?" he finally said.

"The one on the Brethren's land. You are aware of it, are you not?"

"I heard something about there being one. That's it," Quinn claimed.

"I can produce a witness who told your half sister—Mary Dawson—about it."

"I'm not my sister, am I?" Quinn's hostility manifested again.

Marion spoke up. "Your Honor, I'd like the court to consider relevancy again. Why should the court care about a cave, or a pond, or any other features on the Brethren's land?"

"I'm getting to that," Phil said. "I'm attempting to impugn this witness's testimony.

"Get to it soon," Harrow told him.

"Yes, Your Honor. So Detective, you don't know about the paintings in this cave that might prove to be extremely valuable? This isn't a factor in your so-called *zeal*?"

"Oh, I know there are fake paintings intended to con my half sister and myself. By the defendant, in fact."

He pointed at me again. In case any eyes turned to me, I kept my features neutral this time. I knew that overusing my Buddha smile would dilute its effectiveness.

"Can you prove this allegation?" Phil asked. "And what's a fake painting, anyway? Either something is a painting or it isn't one. Isn't that right?"

"I mean Barr said they were by done an Indian tribe centuries ago, but they weren't."

"He told you this himself?" Phil asked.

"Well, no," Quinn admitted. "He brought a fake art expert to a meeting and had him tell us."

"So your sister was there at the time, as well?"

"Yes," Quinn said.

"So let me get this straight. On the one hand, you stated that you had 'heard something about there being a cave,' and now it turns out you met with your sister and some third party to talk about the paintings in it? How do you reconcile those two statements?"

"I said I'd heard about the cave, and now I'm going into detail about what I heard."

"You weren't trying to mislead the court?" Phil asked.

"No."

Phil shook his head in disbelief. "All right. Can you produce your so-called fake art expert to verify what you're telling the court?"

"No. We've tried."

"You're a detective with all the resources that

entails and you can't find someone?" Phil asked.

"He covered his tracks well."

"So we have to take your word for the existence of this phantom expert? And if such a person does exist, you think we should accept your assumption that Barr convinced him to pretend to be an expert? To what end, Detective? That's a lot of faking, isn't? Why would someone do all that? It sounds to me like a real painting would only increase your *zeal* to seize the land, which would be against my client's interests."

"Which question do you want me to answer? I can't even remember them all," Quinn said.

"I'll simplify this for you. Why? There's a one word question I think you can remember. Why would my client do any of this?"

"Objection. Badgering the witness."

"Sustained."

"To reiterate, Mr. Quinn, I think asking the one-word question 'Why?' is perfectly civil."

"You'd have to ask Barr."

"Perhaps I will. Kade Tobin, I mean. You've suggested I call the DA and my client to the stand. Do you think they'd validate your testimony?"

"How should I know?" Quinn said quickly.

"Fair enough. So you didn't try to cut a deal with my client about the cave and the land?"

"I don't know what you're talking about," Quinn protested.

"I'm talking about your threat to frame him if he didn't turn over the portion of the land that contained the cave," Phil told him. "This was when you believed the paintings were authentic."

"That's bull. I certainly didn't do that."

"Yes, you did!" a voice called from the back of the court. "I was there. He's lying!"

Jorge came through, bless his heart. If Quinn could play dirty, so could I. I couldn't very well produce Ralph's actor friend, but I could still cast doubt on what the detective was falsely claiming.

"Bailiff, show that man out of my courtroom."

Fortunately, Jorge wasn't under oath, and it looked as though the judge wasn't going to slap him with a contempt charge. He'd made two hundred dollars for three sentences.

I didn't feel entirely comfortable paying for a public lie. On the other hand, prison would definitely be even more uncomfortable, and certainly wildly unjust.

"That's a lie," Quinn asserted. "That man's a known criminal."

"Your Honor," Phil protested.

"Detective, you have to limit yourself to answering the defense's questions," Harrow told him. "You are not permitted to say that."

"Sorry, Your Honor. No one likes to be accused of being a liar."

"I understand. I apologize on behalf of the court for that man's behavior. Now let's get back to your testimony.

"Thank you, Your Honor," Phil said. "Mr. Quinn, do you—"

"*Detective* Quinn."

Sorry. Detective Quinn, do you think your testimony and the events in the courtroom cast doubt on your motives, your actions, or your veracity?"

"I don't know that word."

"Veracity? Truthfulness," Phil told him.

"Absolutely not."

"Do you think the jury might disagree with you?" Phil asked.

"You'd have to ask them," Quinn said.

"I guess we'll find out at the end of this trial, won't we?"

"Is that a question?"

"I guess it isn't," Phil conceded. "Here's one. Were you able to match my client's fingerprints to those of Carl Steuben—who is, in fact, my client?"

"He isn't, but no, we weren't able to do that."

"Why not? In this country, employees of public schools are fingerprinted in order to do background checks."

"It's probably different in Canada," Quinn said. He was grasping at straws.

"In fact, it isn't. What's the real reason no fingerprint evidence has been entered in this case? Is it because the prints do match—and the prosecution asked you to withhold that fact? After all, if they're identical, then my client definitely couldn't be Wyatt Barr."

"No, of course not. We just weren't able to get hold of Barr's prints from when he was pretending to be Carl Steuben in Vancouver."

"Did you forget to contact the school? That would be pretty shoddy investigating, wouldn't it?"

"I think Lombardi was going to do that," Quinn said.

"At your direction?"

"I don't remember who told him to."

"If I recalled Mr. Lombardi to the stand, would he verify what you've told the court?" Phil asked. "Never mind, I know the answer to that one—'You'd have to ask him,' right?"

"That's right." Quinn smiled grimly.

"Were you coached to answer my questions that way?" Phil asked.

"The sheriff's department gives us training on how to be an effective witness."

"I see. Our investigator is in Canada right now. What further surprises about you is he likely to find? What else did you do up there besides conduct a normal investigation?"

"Well, I went to hockey game," Quinn said.

I had to smile at that myself.

"You were in both Montreal and Vancouver?" Phil asked.

"Yes."

"Did you find any evidence in either city that was in the defendant's favor—other things you're withholding?"

"I'm not withholding anything," Quinn said.

"You're presenting evidence to help the prosecution convict my client?"

"Of course I am."

"Then it only stands to reason that you're not volunteering anything that would help Mr. Tobin's defense, correct?"

"That's the way trials work, counselor," Quinn responded. "You should know that. And that man"—he pointed at me—"is definitely Wyatt Barr."

"That's your opinion, Detective."

"That's a fact."

"I'm through with this witness, Your Honor."

"Very well. Let's adjourn for the day."

Chapter 33

Phil didn't stop by for a post-mortem, which was fine with me. I chatted with Chet at dinner, who told me all about his high school baseball career. When the silent gang member sat down across the table, Chet hastily departed as usual.

Tepehuano pulled a piece of paper out of his pants pocket and handed it to me. In blocky, hand-lettered penmanship, it read:

"I can do things for you too for money."

"I appreciate that. If I think of something, I'll let you know," I told him. "Did you get that? I don't know if you understand English."

He nodded. Then he pulled another piece of paper out, which read:

"For two like Jorge."

"Okay. We'll see."

He stood abruptly and joined Jose at the gang's customary table. I wondered which of the two was in charge now that Jorge had been released. Could someone run the show without speaking?

****

The next morning, Marion once again requested that the judge allow her to show her exhibits about the Canadian investigation.

"I'll have my ruling after lunch," he told her. "You may be able to present them all or you may need to redact certain parts. We'll see. Be patient. This is an important ruling."

Then Marion sprung another surprise witness, which Phil told me wasn't allowed except under special circumstances. She made her case to Harrow. The Canadian cop had been delayed and another last-minute witness had reached out. Harrow allowed it again.

"Your Honor," Phil protested. "This could be grounds for appeal."

"You'd lose," the judge responded. "I will not pause the trial."

"How much r*eaching out* do we have to tolerate?" Phil asked. "I need prep time."

"If I see you unable to effectively defend your client with this witness, I'll grant you a long recess. That's it."

The witness was Chet.

He wore his orange jumpsuit, which surprised me. Perhaps his testimony had been too last minute to allow a change of clothes. His long black hair was stringy and greasy-looking, and Chet slouched in the witness box to the point that I wondered how he stayed in his chair.

Once again, it seemed that Marion had chosen a poor witness. I wondered why. I whispered to Phil, letting him know who Chet was.

"Mr. Novak, how do you know the defendant?" Marion asked.

"We're both in the jail. We hang out."

"Why are you in the jail?"

"Drug charges," he told her.

"What can you tell us about Mr. Barr?" she asked.

"Well, he calls himself Kade, and he told people there he killed those girls."

"He told you personally?"

"No, he told me he didn't," Chet admitted. "But then he told everyone else he did. People are scared of him in there."

"What else can you tell us about the defendant?" Marion asked.

"I dunno. What do you want to know?"

"Mr. Novak, we talked about this. Remember?"

"Oh yeah, sorry. Kade's in with the Estes," Chet said.

"The gang in the jail?"

"Yeah. Talk about scary."

"These men are violent?" Marion asked.

"Oh, yeah."

"I'm going to show you a picture my staff captured yesterday," Marion told him. "Your Honor, I'd like to offer it as exhibit E."

"Let's see it," Harrow said.

"Of course."

The judge looked at it, handed it back, and told Marion to show it to us. It was Jorge, on his way out of the courtroom.

Marion handed the photo to Chet. "Do you know this man?"

"Sure, that's the leader of the gang—at least while all of them are in jail, he's the leader there."

Marion looked at the judge. "May I give the photo to the jury so they can see for themselves that this is the man who called Detective Quinn a liar yesterday."

"Yes."

The jurors passed it around. I wondered why there was only one copy.

"Is this man's name Jorge Rodriguez?" the DA asked Chet.

"I guess so."

"You guess so?"

"Sorry. Yes, it is. That's what you told me," Chet said.

"Objection. Hearsay."

"Sustained.

"Now when you say the defendant 'was in with' with gang members," Marion began, "I assume Mr. Rodriguez was one of those people? And the defendant spent time with him?"

"Yeah, the guy in the picture was the main one. I saw them talking a few days ago away from everybody else in the courtyard."

"Did that look suspicious to you?"

"Objection. Calls for speculation."

"Sustained."

"Let me put it another way, Mr. Novak. What did you observe when you watched the two men conversing?"

"They talked real low so no one could hear them, and this Jorge guy smiled when they were done." Chet paused and smiled. "Like that," he said, "only the dude's was creepier."

"Objection, Your Honor," Phil called.

"Sustained.

"Did you see Mr. Barr and Mr. Rodriguez together after that?" Marion asked.

"No, Rodriguez got out later that day, but maybe they talked on the phone."

"Why do you say that?"

"Mostly, Kade didn't care if you overheard him," Chet told her, "but yesterday he made sure no one was around when he called someone."

"I see. Do you think it's possible that Kade arranged with Mr. Rodriguez for him to interrupt the court yesterday and impugn my witness?"

"He was here?" Chet asked.

"Yes."

"What does impugn mean?"

"He called Detective Quinn a liar."

"Is he?" Chet asked.

"Is he a liar?" Marion asked.

Chet nodded.

"That's for the jury to decide, but I certainly don't think so. Be that as it may, Mr. Novak, does your experience of Mr. Barr lead you to believe he would be capable of hiring or coercing Mr. Rodriguez to disrupt this court?"

"I dunno. You'd have to be pretty dumb to mess with the Estes. Kade isn't dumb. He's the smartest guy in the jail."

Seeing that she wasn't getting anywhere with this, she passed her witness on to Phil. He'd been taking notes, and I'd whispered more information to him. I was confident Chet would turn out to be an even weaker witness than the others.

"Chet—may I call you Chet?"

"Call me whatever you like, just don't call me late for dinner. That's what my grandmother always said."

He was off-script, and I knew his impulse control was poor.

"Okay, Chet it is. You mentioned a gang in the prison. I'm picturing a few dozen hardened criminals. Is that the story?"

"No, man. There's only three. Well, two now."

"And you saw this man Jorge Rodriguez being

violent?"

Well, no. But he threatened people, and once he stole Kade's salad to give to this other guy."

The gallery laughed, and I saw several jurors smile.

"Is it common for inmates to threaten one another?" Phil asked.

"Well, yeah," Chet said.

"Did you ever know Jorge to lie?"

"No, man, I kept my distance."

"Do you know why he was in jail?" Phil asked.

"Somebody told me he was a hitman," Chet replied.

"So you'd be surprised to learn he was sentenced for driving under the influence of alcohol, as well as a parole violation?"

"Yeah, that would surprise me. That's no big deal. Is it true?"

"It is."

"Weird," Chet said.

"So you have no personal knowledge to discredit what Jorge might say in a courtroom, correct?"

"Well, I haven't *personally* seen him do anything bad, but there was that meeting I saw."

"Yes, let's take a look at that," Phil said. "Had my client been helping Jorge sort through some legal paperwork?"

"Yeah."

"Although you said the other prisoners were frightened of my client, hasn't he been helping a lot of people while he's been in custody? Hasn't he helped you?"

"Yeah, that's true," Chet conceded.

"You're even in a discussion group he leads, correct?"

"Yeah."

"I'm puzzled why you concluded my client and Mr. Rodriguez were discussing something nefarious in the courtyard. Could Kade have simply been helping Jorge again?"

"Nefarious?"

"Secretive, criminal," Phil explained.

"Oh. Well, they were talking real low."

"So you couldn't hear anything."

"That's right," Chet agreed.

"So you actually have no knowledge of what they were saying, correct? Is it possible they simply wanted to keep their conversation confidential for other reasons? It could've been something embarrassing or something other prisoners might exploit, couldn't it?

"I guess so."

"Let's take a look at how you ended up in court today," Phil said.

"Okay."

"The prosecutor said you reached out to her department. Is that true?"

"Not exactly," Chet said. "One of the guards heard me talking about Kade, and he must've told them because next thing I know this guy in a suit showed up."

"Did he offer you a deal for testifying?"

"Yeah, he said they'd reduce my sentence."

"And that's the reason you're here today?" Phil asked.

"Yeah, plus it's nice to get out of jail for a day. It's totally boring in there."

"So to be clear, you didn't come forward because you had damning evidence against your friend Kade. You did it to get free sooner."

"That's right," Chet agreed.

"Does that mean you're lying to the court today?"

"No, no. I only said what the DA said I could. She didn't tell me to lie."

"You are a criminal, though, Chet. Is that fair to say?"

Chet shook his head. "Not really. I'm just a regular guy who made a mistake."

"Is the jail full of 'regular guys'?"

"I'd have to say no."

"So what makes you different?" Phil asked.

"C'mon, man. Why are you giving me such a hard time? I'm here doing what the guy in the suit said was my civic duty, and you're breaking my balls."

"Language, son," the judge admonished.

"Sorry."

"I'm asking these questions because it's my job," Phil told him. "You signed up for this when you took the stand."

"Well, I didn't know it would be like this."

"Chet, isn't it true that you were arrested for possessing and selling drugs?"

"Yeah, that's what I mean about how it was just a mistake—not like a real crime. Nobody got hurt. I didn't steal anything. It was what my public defender said was a victimless crime. He said it was an antiquated law, too, which means it doesn't make any sense anymore."

"Since you're in jail, I assume those arguments did not affect the outcome," Phil said.

"No. I wish they had," Chet replied. "The dude was Mexican or something, so nobody listened to him."

"Chet, did you lie to the officers who arrested you, as well the prosecutors who questioned you?" Phil asked.

"Sure. I mean, who wants to go to jail?"

"So you're admitting that you lied in a legal proceeding for personal gain—to not go to jail in your drug case?"

"Yeah, like I said, who wouldn't?" Chet responded.

"So why should we believe you now?" Phil asked.

"Hey, I'm already in jail. I can't do anything to stay out now."

"But you can get out sooner. That's a similar situation, isn't it?"

Chet though that over, but didn't answer.

"Just a few more things," Phil said, "then you can be on your way. You said that one time Kade wanted to talk on the phone without being heard. Is that correct?"

"Yeah."

"Can you think of reasons why he'd want to do that that had nothing to do with gangs or Jorge or what happened in court yesterday?"

"Sure. I'm not stupid. I can think of lots of things," Chet told him.

I glanced at Marion, who rolled her eyes. She was one step away from putting her head in her hands.

"Then why did you bring up this incident to make my client seem guilty?" Phil asked.

"This other guy in a suit told me to think of everything that *might* be suspicious. I needed to come up with a certain amount of stuff to make my deal."

"So you don't think the phone call was to Jorge?" Phil asked.

"I don't know, man. I'll tell you, jail is starting to look good compared to this."

"I understand. Sometimes it's hard for me in here, too. One last question. Do you see auras?"

"Objection!"

"On what grounds, Marion?"

"Relevance, as well as character assassination. The witness is not on trial about his beliefs."

"Mr. Karanos?"

"I'm seeking to impugn the witness's testimony by illustrating how out of touch with reality he is. If I were questioning someone who was hallucinating or delusional, wouldn't I be allowed to explore that? All I want to do is ask the witness about himself. If what I'm suggesting is not so or doesn't affect his testimony, he's free to tell us that."

"Marion, he has a point. Mr. Karanos, be careful."

"Yes, Your Honor."

"Chet, I'll ask you again. Do you see people's auras?"

"Yeah, I've been able to do that since my bike accident."

"Why is that?" Phil asked.

"It's cuz I'm really spiritual," Chet told him.

"How do you know that?"

"A guy with a beard in a big temple told me."

"I see. Are you seeing auras right now?" Phil asked.

"Sure."

"What does mine look like?"

"Objection," Marion called.

"On what grounds this time?"

"Honestly, I'm not sure. It just doesn't feel like any of this is appropriate in a murder trial."

"Obviously, that's not a valid objection," Harrow told her. "Plus, I'm curious about this aura thing. Answer the question, Mr. Novak."

"I'll do the lawyer first, then I'll do you, too, Judge,

if you want."

Harrow smiled. "Go ahead."

Chet looked at Phil for a moment. "Yours is kinda green and kinda blue. It sticks out about six inches."

"What does that mean?" Phil asked.

"I don't remember. I've got a book about it back in my cell."

"All right," the judge said. "I think we've heard enough. Is that all, Counselor?"

"Yes."

Chapter 34

"I'm confused," I told Phil while we once again ate lunch in the empty courtroom. This time the bailiff got egg salad on white bread for us from a vending machine in the basement. Why anyone voluntarily chose bread like that was beyond me. I was tempted to scrape the filling off into my hand. "Would you have put Hernandez, Mary, or Chet on the stand?" I asked Phil. "I wouldn't."

"I agree. It doesn't make a lot of sense. And she hasn't addressed the meat and potatoes of whatever they have on the murders themselves. It's all been about identity—evidence from Canada—and other peripheral things. Where's any testimony about Althea or Chloe? Hell, Marion hasn't even referred to the third victim—the guy we knew as Wayne. It's strange."

"You know, another thing I don't understand is that the judge said at the outset that he was strict," I said. "It doesn't seem like it. He's letting the DA do all kinds of things."

"Yes, that was bullshit. He's let me do all kinds of things, too. Marion could've objected quite a few more times, but she knows that would irritate Harrow. Like he keeps saying, he wants to keep things moving."

"So back to the crappy witnesses," I said. "Is Marion sandbagging us—waiting to pounce?"

"I suspect so. Susan Burke filled me in about her

mother's career last night. She's won a ton of cases, going back ten years."

"Who do you think will be her strongest witness?" I asked.

"Bill Cullen. Not only does he know the most about the case, he holds up well in court. I've cross-examined him before. I can't attack his integrity because it's rock solid. And he's a damned good detective."

"So what *can* you do?"

"Create doubt about the content of his testimony," Phil told me.

"Sounds good."

The judge made Marion wait even longer to find out about his documents ruling since the cop from Montreal was only available right after lunch. He needed to go to dialysis later—a damned good excuse.

The witness turned out to be a retired detective who wheezed after everything he said. He identified me as Wyatt, and although he'd been admonished not to discuss the nature of the crimes he'd investigated, he was allowed to talk about everything else he'd discovered about Wyatt. Of course, he didn't see us as two separate people.

He verified almost all of what Lombardi and Quinn had said. Clearly, he was in on the fix, but Phil couldn't shake him or portray him in a bad light. I liked the guy myself. I just didn't like his lies.

For the first time, I realized I could be convicted. I'd maintained a naive faith in the system, our investigator's abilities, and Phil's expertise as a trial lawyer. The latter was certainly being demonstrated to me, but it might not be enough.

If the universe required me to go to prison, I'd

willingly go, and make the most out of it, much as I was doing in the county jail. On the other hand, the Islamic phrase, "Trust in God and tie up your camels," seemed apt. I needed to continue to do everything in my power to keep serving my community.

When the cop's testimony and cross-examination were through, the judge ruled against us. All the exhibits and any testimony Marion wanted to present about prior crimes was fair game. He also accepted all her other exhibits and told her she could project any or all of it onto the court's screen.

"Your Honor," she told him, "I hope it would not inconvenience the court if I delay sharing the exhibits?"

He sighed. "First you rush me, and now it turns out you want to wait. So be it. Are you prepared to call your next witness today?"

"Yes, you honor. I call Susan Burke."

A few people gasped. Susan herself seemed baffled. After she'd walked to the stand and was sworn in, Marion began.

"Hello, Susan. You're probably wondering what you're doing here."

"I am."

"Let's start with the basics. Are you my daughter?" Marion asked.

"Yes."

"Are you a member of the Brethren of Congruence community?"

"I am."

"Are you in a unique position to know relevant information about both Wyatt Barr and myself?"

"I suppose I am. But the defendant's name is Kade Tobin," Susan asserted.

"Have I ever acted with prejudice, bias, or in any other unfair way to the Brethren or the defendant?"

"No, not to my knowledge."

Susan was clearly versed in trial law. She was keeping her answers as concise as she possibly could. Volunteering information or elaborating on her responses opened the door to a prosecutor's probing.

"Do you know about the so-called project the Brethren runs out of an outbuilding on the land? I don't mean the one for public consumption. I mean the real one."

"Yes." Susan cast her eyes down.

I didn't understand why this should make her ashamed. We weren't robbing banks or stealing from orphans.

"How did you find out?" Marion asked.

"I overheard a conversation between Jeremy Kasco and Greg Cowen."

Phil leaned over and whispered. "How did Marion find out what Susan knows?"

"I have no idea," I told him.

"These are other members of the community?" Marion asked.

"Yes, supposedly."

"Objection!" Phil called. "Hearsay. Whatever these people said is inadmissible."

"There are exceptions," Marion said.

"And yours is…" asked Harrow.

"Reputation concerning character."

The judge paused a moment and then allowed Marion to continue.

"Would you tell us about this endeavor?" she asked Susan.

"I'm sure Kade doesn't know anything about it."

"Susan, you know that isn't what I'm asking. Please tell the court the nature of the secret project."

She took a deep breath. "It's essentially a Ponzi scheme."

Phil turned to me, shock on his face.

I'm sure my shock was just as evident. "I had no idea," I told him. "I thought we were pursuing a campaign to get a zoning change so we could build a restaurant. I suspected Jeremy and Don were using unethical methods, and I didn't stop them. That's on me. That's it, I swear."

"Some of the jurors might not be familiar with that term," Marion told her daughter. "Please tell us more."

"People invest money to get an unusually large return back—as much as twenty percent."

"This is like a high-paying CD or a stock that does well?" Marion knew perfectly well it was more than that.

"It's a much higher rate than any legal investment out there—guaranteed. In this case, it's supposed to be a mutual fund."

"It isn't ?" Marion prompted.

"No."

"How can they afford to do that and stay in business?"

"They keep getting an influx of investment funds from new people," Susan explained. "The money they pay out comes from that. They keep all the rest without investing it at all."

"It sounds like that only works as long as the criminals keep signing up investors."

"Yes, there's always a day of reckoning when the Ponzi schemers can't pay out any more. Usually, they take off and live in luxury in South America, New Zealand, or somewhere like that."

"How is it that you know so much about this?"

"Your sister—my aunt—was swindled out of half a million dollars by Bernie Madoff. That's how I know about Ponzi schemes. And I broke into the project building on our land and hacked several laptops to find out about this one."

"I see. I imagine you were very alarmed," Marion said. "What did you do?"

"Well, I didn't want to do anything while Kade is on trial. I knew that would look bad, so I was just going to wait until this was all settled to tell the police. I expected the trial would be done by now. I didn't know all the details."

"You've been in the courtroom for the trial?" Marion asked.

"No. Another person who was here has been telling me about it."

"Do you think the defendant is guilty?"

"Your Honor!" Phil called.

"I withdraw the question," Marion said. "Your witness, counselor.

"Hello, Susan," Phil began once he'd stood behind his podium. "It's nice to see you, even under these circumstances."

"Thanks. It's nice to see you, too."

"To be clear, we're both members of the Brethren, and we know each other well."

"That's right."

"Was there anything on the laptops that implicated Kade—any mention of him at all?"

"No, there wasn't," Susan answered.

"Do you have other reasons to think that members conspired behind his back?"

"I do. I know Kade to be the kindest, most helpful, most *advanced* person I've ever met. And I'm not some gullible, naive schoolgirl. I've known Kade for three years, and I've never seen him speak a harsh word, or lie, or be anything other than be an inspiration to our community."

"How do you feel about what your mother has done today—calling you to the stand to testify against your mentor?"

"Super crappy. It was an ambush," Susan said.

"What is your relationship with your mother like?"

"Estranged. This isn't the first time she's done something like this."

"Objection," Marion called.

Phil responded before the judge could. "The district attorney opened the door when she asked this witness if the DA herself ever acted with prejudice."

"Overruled," Harrow said.

"How does she feel about your being a member of our community?"

"She hates it," Susan said.

"Does she hold my client responsible for your choice to do so?"

"Yes."

"Would it shock you if you found out that behind the scenes—unknown to you—your mother turned a blind eye to others who acted in bad faith?"

"I probably would be shocked, but either I have to believe Kade is being framed or I have to throw away years of personal experience and an entire belief system. Which one would you pick?"

"The same one as you, Susan."

"You Honor!" Marion called.

"Move on, Counselor," Harrow commanded.

"How do you think your mother discovered that you knew about the project?" Phil asked.

"I have no idea."

"Nor do I. I hope it was something legal."

"Your Honor!" Marion protested again.

"I'm done with this witness," Phil announced before the judge could speak.

"Redirect, Marion?"

"Yes, Your Honor." She stood and clasped her hands together at her waist. "Susan, do you really think I would do something unethical or dishonest in pursuit of my duties as the district attorney?"

"No, not really. But somebody's framing Kade, and you're the one in charge of the department, so I think you bear some responsibility about that."

"That's hurtful," the DA told her daughter.

Sussan shrugged.

"Have I been that terrible a mother?" Marion asked.

"Objection," Phil called. "This line of questioning is touching and who wouldn't to ask things like that to a child under oath, but obviously it's irrelevant to the matter at hand."

"Sustained. Marion, perhaps you could have this conversation over dinner some time."

The DA nodded and sat down.

"Court is adjourned," Harrow pronounced.

Chapter 35

Chet apologized to me at dinner and then complained at length that my lawyer had been very mean to him. Tepehuano came around with another note. This one told me his brother lived in Sacramento but could come down to do things for me outside the jail like Jorge did. The syntax was challenging to sort through.

I lay awake that night, worried about what might happen the next day in court. If Bill Cullen testified in support of the conspiracy to frame me, I'd likely be doomed—unless we found Wyatt or exposed Quinn for the snake he was. What were the odds that would happen in the next few days? After all, our investigator hadn't managed much along those lines in three weeks.

I had yet to meet the private detective, who was slated to be our first witness. Phil had told me he was the guy he'd want working for him if he were on trial, which was good enough for me.

For a moment, I felt like hiring Jorge or Tepehuano's brother to beat the truth out of Quinn and shanghai Wyatt if he could find him. The moment passed. I meditated. Eventually, I fell asleep.

Back in court. Bill Cullen wore his customary blue suit, and he'd shined his shoes. His jacket was tight around his wide shoulders. The otherwise slim detective looked even slimmer than he had when I'd first met him. His long face enhanced this impression, and on this occasion also lent him a hint of Scandinavian heritage for some reason. His green eyes steadily surveyed the courtroom, ostentatiously avoiding mine. Cullen sat bolt upright in the witness box.

"Detective Cullen," Marion began. "I'm going to move on from the question of the defendant's identity and character and start looking at the recent murders. You've been working on these cases since the first body—Althea Curtis's—was discovered, correct?"

"That's correct. I met the defendant and started working that case the morning after that murder was committed."

"Can you summarize what you and your team uncovered during the initial phase of the investigation?"

"Certainly," Cullen replied. "And I'd like to say I've given you all the paperwork—the hard evidence—about the case, and that includes our recent discoveries. You've told me you will display that today."

"That's right. I'll be showing exhibits that support your testimony when you've finished testifying. Please proceed."

"Chloe Valois—the second victim—came out here to make Barr pay for what he had done to her in Montreal. I mean that literally. Her goal was to blackmail him. And she did—to the tune of ten thousand dollars to start with.

"She learned his whereabouts from Althea Curtis. They'd remained in contact following Althea's trip to Canada when she was twelve because their parents were old college friends.

"Althea saved money from a part-time job and hired a crackerjack private investigator, who tracked Barr down. Her goal was to bring him to justice for molesting her, but before she could, she confronted him at a restaurant, and then she was murdered.

"Chloe upped the ante in her blackmail scheme now that she could provide evidence that Barr was not only a sex offender, but also a murderer. So she had to go, too.

"Barr planted the women's bodies nearby so he had a reason to become involved in the sheriff department's investigation, keeping track of its progress and misleading us whenever he could. If the department began to unravel his elaborate, fictional backstory, Barr would know and could flee once again before he was apprehended.

"In his arrogance, it didn't occur to the defendant that after the first few days, I was stringing him along while our team gathered evidence against him. More on that later.

"Now about the third victim—a member of Wyatt's community—Guy Harrison. The man Guy trusted to lead him along his spiritual path found out he was a fugitive and blackmailed him into helping to trick the authorities. Guy provided alibis as necessary—we had no reason to suspect these were false at the time. Barr's appointment book seemed to confirm that the two men were in counseling sessions when we wondered if Barr was offsite.

"Guy Harrison also flew to Houston, Texas, using Wyatt Barr's old driver's license from Montreal, which the defendant had kept up to date in case he needed it for such a purpose. Guy did his best to disguise himself to resemble the defendant, but CC footage our department retrieved revealed his true identity. The TSA agent who allowed him to pass security did a shoddy job. Later, Guy returned under his own name, creating the illusion that

Wyatt had taken off for parts unknown.

"Then Guy turned things around when he realized he too could prove Wyatt was guilty of murder, so he blackmailed *him.* Then he had to go, too.

"I know this convoluted tale would be hard to believe without ironclad proof. But know this. We have it. The prosecution has it. The court will see it soon. This so-called spiritual teacher is a ruthless murderer and molester. Wyatt Barr is a monster who must be locked away for the safety of all of us."

"Why aren't you objecting?" I hissed at Phil.

"You're guilty, aren't you, Kade?" he replied, turning to stare me in the eye.

"Of course I didn't kill people, Phil. How could you think that?"

Marion continued questioning Cullen. "Mr. Barr stated to the police that he doesn't drive, which would make it challenging for him to have committed the murders of the young women off his property, as well as transporting the victim's bodies. Is that true?"

"No, he does drive. The driver's license we found in the defendant's real name speaks to his ability to do so, and we have substantial evidence that he drove a car the night Althea Curtis was killed."

"Could you tell us about that, Detective?" Marion asked.

"A man who lives about a mile from the Brethren's land noticed that the mileage in his car was off when he went to tell his insurance company what it was. This was a lucky break for us."

"What did you mean by 'off'?"

Cullen didn't miss a beat explaining. "The man wrote down the mileage two days before the murder, then the morning after it, he double-checked it and found there were seventy-eight additional miles on the odometer."

"Your Honor," Phil said. "Relevance?"

"Marion?" The judge asked.

"This line of questioning speaks to the defendant's modus operandi—how he employed a vehicle to commit the crime."

"I'll allow it."

"Detective, why would this man check the mileage twice? Didn't that seem odd to you?" Marion asked.

She was once again employing the strategy of anticipating the defense's questions and addressing the subject on her terms.

"It did seem odd. It turns out the man has obsessive-compulsive disorder—OCD—so he checks everything multiple times."

"I see. And how would you know about all this?" the DA asked.

"Another fortunate thing is that the man holds a grudge against a teenaged boy who lives near him. He reported the situation to the sheriff's department because he thought that boy had taken a joyride in his car. He hoped to get the boy in trouble."

"And this man is a reliable reporter? Apparently, he has a mental illness and a grudge. Did you suspect he might be fabricating this story?"

"I did at first, but it checked out," Cullen told her.

"I understand the owner of the car reported this event some time ago?" Marion asked. "Why the delay in your tying it to this case?"

Her continued exploration of the potential holes in Cullen's testimony was effective, making both her and

Cullen seem reasonable and fair-minded.

"Once again," Bill responded, "we were lucky we heard about it at all. When the owner reported it, he wasn't satisfied with the investigation, which immediately cleared the neighbor boy—he was staying at a friend's house that night. The deputy looking into it decided the car owner—who is elderly as well as challenged by his disorder—had simply been mistaken."

"So then what happened?"

"The owner was driving past the Brethren's land and saw a different deputy's car in the driveway," Cullen told her. "When he stopped and complained about how he'd been treated, our man put two and two together."

"I see. Now tell us how this man's discovery led to evidence against Mr. Barr."

"His car was a 2023 model which has GPS tracking built in."

"In other words, the car can tell someone where it has been?" Marion asked.

"Exactly. We discovered the car had been driven to a location near the hostel where the first victim was staying, and then to a remote location off Highway One north of Santa Cruz."

"What did you do when you found this out?"

"We drove to the second location and set our forensic team loose to examine the area surrounding where the car had been."

"And what did they discover?" Marion asked.

"They found blood residue on the ground and on redwood needles on top of the ground."

"Did this blood match Althea's?"

"Yes," Cullen said. "It was the same type and shared several other characteristics."

"Is this proof positive that the first victim had been killed at this site?"

"No, not in and of itself, but there's more."

"Please continue," Marion said.

"We also found shoe prints that matched the sole of Mr. Barr's shoes."

"By this, you mean it was the same brand of shoe?"

"Yes, with the same wear pattern, as well," Bill told her.

"Is this absolute proof? Could there be other people who wear the same type of shoe and wear it down in a similar fashion?"

"It's possible, but highly unlikely in my experience."

"Is there more, Detective?"

He smiled. "We found the gun there—buried a hundred yards away."

"The one that killed Althea?"

"Yes, the lab confirmed that." Clearly, finding the gun was the element Cullen believed to be the most significant.

"So let me see if I've got this straight. A car was stolen and then returned a mile from Mr. Barr's residence. While stolen, the car traveled to where the victim was staying, and then to the crime scene, where you found damning evidence that—"

Phil spoke up. "Damning, Your Honor?"

"Sustained. Marion, please refrain from characterizing the evidence. Stick to the facts,"

"Yes, Your Honor. I'll be more specific. Are you stating that in addition to what I just said, you also discovered the murder weapon, footprints matching the defendant's, and blood that was consistent with the first victim's?"

"That's correct," Cullen confirmed.

"I imagine the defense will ask you several more questions about your testimony, so I'll ask them now instead. I'm sure you'll be able to give more helpful answers when no one interrupts you or tries to skew what you say."

"Marion," Harrow admonished. "That's enough of that."

"Yes, Your Honor. Detective, could you tie the murder weapon to the defendant?"

"No, not directly. It was registered to a man who reported it stolen from the glove compartment of his car last year."

"Who is this man?" Marion asked.

"His name isn't important. What's important is that he is the brother of a member of the Brethren."

"And who is that member?"

"Martha Sutherland," Cullen told her.

"So you see that fact as significant because it might explain how Mr. Barr had access to the weapon?"

"Yes."

"Could it be a coincidence?" Marion asked.

"Of course. But it isn't."

"Why do you say that?"

"The preponderance of evidence that Mr. Barr committed felonies in Canada, stole the car, and killed the victim indicate that 'coincidence' is not a viable explanation."

"This is your expert opinion as a veteran law enforcement officer?"

"It is," Cullen said.

Marion continued. "Another line of questioning the

defense might want to explore is why aren't we hearing about the crime-scene forensic evidence from a forensic expert, and why only now?"

"Our expert didn't do so well when he testified. I'm a better witness. If need be, I'm sure you can recall him to the stand. Anyway, all Greg would say is what I've said plus what you're going to show on the screen here later. As for the timing, we just got all the lab results yesterday."

"Are there any other recent findings that this court hasn't heard yet?" the DA asked.

"Yes. Detective Quinn has headed back to Canada, where he found a man who'd altered documents in Vancouver after being bribed by Mr. Barr. Quinn is hunting for more compromised officials. Since Barr set up his false trail some years ago, this has proved to be a challenge."

"Does this eliminate all doubt in your mind that the defendant is guilty of Althea Curtis's murder."

"It does," Cullen asserted.

"Now, about the other murders. Do you have similar evidence in relation to those?"

"We do, but you requested that I let you present that yourself in your exhibits."

"Why did I tell you I wanted to do that, Detective?

"Objection. Hearsay."

"Sustained."

"Do you believe the evidence in the exhibits will speak for itself?" Marion tried. "Do you think it's a good idea for me to present the additional evidence this way?"

"Objection," Phil called. "Leading the witness and calls for speculation.

"Sustained."

I thought it was strange that almost every objection by both parties had been sustained in the trial. Perhaps Phil and Marion, in their efforts not to annoy Harrow by slowing things down, were only raising the ones that were slam dunks.

"Detective," Marion tried, "in your expert opinion, do you understand my strategy in this matter?"

"Objection. The witness in not an expert in trial tactics. The question still calls for speculation."

"Give it a rest, Mr. Karanos. Overruled."

Ask and ye shall receive, I thought. That was the first overrule I remembered.

"Detective?" Marion prompted.

"I understand, but actually I think juries prefer to hear the facts from a person," Cullen told her.

"Is it correct that you yielded to my judgment in this matter after I explained that juries can absorb facts better when there's a varied medium of presentation—that long verbal testimony can be boring?"

"Your Honor," Phil objected. "We don't need to hear the prosecutor justify her trial strategy. She is sneaking this in the backdoor by pretending to ask the witness about it."

"And so your objection is…"

"The DA is testifying."

"Quite right. Sustained. The jury will disregard these references from the prosecution to itself. And jurors, I want to thank you for your attention. As far as I can tell, none of you are the least bit bored." Harrow nodded to Marion. "Please continue."

"Thank you, Your Honor. You don't need to answer my last question, Detective. Is there anything else you'd like at add to your testimony?"

"Yes, our tech guy investigated what Susan Burke testified about—the Ponzi scheme being run by the Brethren."

"I almost forgot that. Thank you for reminding me."

Phil whispered, "The hell she did."

"Can you tell the court what your expert discovered?" Marion continued.

"Yes, once he was able to get into their computers, he found evidence that verified your daughter's testimony."

"Your Honor, "Marion said. "I'd like to offer into evidence exhibits F, G, and H, which support all the new evidence presented by this witness."

She distributed paperwork to the judge and Phil, who kept his eyes trained on Cullen.

"The exhibits are accepted," Harrow said after glancing at them. "Marion?"

"Detective Cullen, were you able to find evidence beyond what Susan found that implicates the defendant in the Ponzi scheme?"

"Yes. That would be exhibit H."

"This scheme is a major felony, isn't it?" Marion asked.

"Yes, this kind of crime is prosecuted to the letter of the law. It's a massive fraud ruining countless lives."

"Thank you, Detective. I'm finished, Your Honor," Marion declared.

"Is the defense ready to cross-examine?" the judge asked.

"May I have a minute to confer with my client?" Phil asked.

"Yes. Be brief."

"Look, I don't know for sure who you are or what

you've done," Phil said. "I'll do my best on this cross, but consider a plea deal if they offer one. I can see the writing on the wall. Almost all the evidence I presented at the first hearing has been discredited—or will be soon. And if Cullen says there's ironclad proof coming, there's going to be ironclad proof. Even based on what we've heard today so far, you're going to be found guilty."

I was stunned into silence. What could I say to that? Even Phil doubted me now. And prison loomed. Who else on the land might've walked down the road and commandeered that car? Who else could've committed the crimes beside Wyatt?

"I'm ready to cross," Phil announced to Harrow.

I came to my senses in time to whisper, "I've been missing a pair of shoes, Phil. Ask about that."

"Go right ahead, Counselor," the judge responded.

Chapter 36

"Hello, Detective Cullen. You seem awfully sure of yourself. Don't all criminal investigations contain an element of uncertainty—of conjecture or nuance?"

"I think it's fair to say that most do," Cullen replied. "This one doesn't, and I'll tell you why." He seemed happy to have been asked that question. "After the DA's office bungled their case the first time around, my department was instructed to gather far more evidence than was necessary to arrest Mr. Barr in order to guarantee there would be no screw-ups this time around. We didn't move until we were absolutely positive about the facts."

"Isn't that a form of discrimination—singling out a suspect to be treated differently?"

"Sure," Cullen agreed. "We prioritized a multiple murder case with a suspect who'd gotten off the first time. We *discriminated* this perp from the one who drove recklessly, and the one who held up a convenience store, and the one who withheld his child support payments, and the one who—"

"We get it," the judge intervened.

"Anyway, Counselor," Cullen continued, "it's our job to make the world safe from monsters, and we did it. Pick at this all you want. That's the bottom line. Nobody else is going to be killed by the defendant."

"You say the prosecution has proof of your words,

and we'll see it soon," Phil said. "Why not tell us now? You've said you disagree with the DA about delaying. Is there a hidden reason—something that favors Mr. Tobin?"

"No, there isn't. I'm along for the ride when it comes to the prosecution's strategy."

"Do you think *she* has a hidden motive?" Phil asked.

"Objection. Calls for speculation."

"Sustained."

"Detective, did you mislead my client to make him believe you were his friend—that the two of you were working on the case together?"

"I sure did. It was legal, and it paid off."

"So you're telling the court that you lie when you're fulfilling your duties as a detective?" Phil tried.

Cullen laughed. "So now you're implying I'm lying under oath? Is that where you're going? Dream on, Counselor. It's standard operating procedure to trick suspects, lie during interrogations, and otherwise do what's necessary within the limits of the law to lock away criminals. We're not looking at an integrity or a character issue here. We're looking at a cop doing his job."

"Did you investigate the murder weapon further?" Phil asked.

"What do you mean?"

I couldn't tell if Cullen was stalling to think about how to answer or he was genuinely stumped. Then I realized that he'd probably been trained not to answer any vague or overly general questions.

"Were there fingerprints on the murder weapon?" Phil explained. "Who else had access to the car's glove compartment? Did Martha's brother keep his car locked?

Do you have anything at all along those lines?"

"Sure, we checked into things."

"So let's go through my questions one by one. Were there any fingerprints?

"No."

"Who else had access to the gun in the car?"

"We don't know exactly."

"Less than ten? More than ten? More than a hundred? Give us a ballpark figure, Detective."

"I couldn't say."

"Isn't it true that an unlocked car on a public street might be an attractive target for a car thief?"

"Yes."

"And that therefore everyone walking by an unlocked car could be said to have access to it?"

"I suppose so, but I didn't say the car owner leaves his vehicle unlocked," Cullen protested.

"You didn't say he locks it, either, did you?"

"No."

"The fact is, you didn't even try to find out any of this, did you?" Phil asked.

"It wasn't necessary," Cullen claimed.

"Would you estimate that an unlocked car on a public street would be vulnerable to hundreds of people in just a few days?"

Marion objected. "Calls for speculation."

"Your Honor," Phil responded, "this witness implied that my client stole the murder weapon from a car. We are impugning this testimony by pointing out other explanations concerning this theft."

"I'll allow it."

"Detective?" Phil asked.

"Sure, plenty of other people could've stolen the

gun. But only one of them lived on the same property as the gun owner's sister."

"Yes, the sister—Martha. Did you interview her about this?"

"Of course," Cullen immediately replied.

"How did you experience her?"

Cullen frowned. "That's kind of vague, don't you think?"

I'd been right about the coaching detectives received.

"You're right. I apologize," Phil said. "Did you find anything suspicious about her?"

"No."

"How long was this interview?"

"I don't remember the exact duration," Cullen replied.

"Give us a ballpark figure. Two hours? Ten minutes?"

"It was a brief interview," Cullen said. "We asked about her brother, and she helped us find him."

"Why don't you tell us about the brother—the original gun owner?" Phil asked.

"What do want to know?"

"When you talked to him, what observations can you tell us about?"

"He is a much different kind of person than his sister," Cullen said.

"How so?"

"He has a record, for one thing."

"You mean a criminal record?" Phil asked, knowing the answer, of course.

"Yes," Cullen confirmed.

"Is that why he owned a gun?"

Marion spoke up. “Calls for speculation.”

“Sustained.”

“Did this brother lie to you?” Phil asked.

“Yes.”

I smiled. Phil had lucked out with this question. He’d only been fishing.

“About what?” Phil asked.

“Several things,” Cullen replied.

“And those things are…?”

“He told us he owned no other weapons, but he did. He said he’d been out of state at the time of the first two murders, but he wasn’t. And he claimed his sister—Martha—had been a criminal before she became spiritual.”

“That was also a lie?” Phil asked.

“We could find no record of criminal activity,” Cullen reported.

“No arrests, no convictions?”

“That’s right.”

“Is it possible Martha’s crimes were committed elsewhere, or under a different name?” Phil asked.

“Counselor, you know this woman. Can you even begin to imagine that?”

“I’m asking the questions,” Phil responded. “Is it possible?”

“Sure. Anything’s possible,” Cullen replied.

“So did you consider either the brother—a lying criminal—or the possibly criminal sister to be suspects? After all, the sister could’ve walked down to borrow the car, just as anyone else on the Brethren’s land could. And it was the brother’s gun that killed Althea, and you say he didn’t have an alibi.”

“No, I didn’t say that. I said the brother claimed to

be out of state. He had a local alibi that he didn't want to tell us about."

"Why was that?" Phil asked.

"He was in bed with a co-worker's wife."

"Ah, another black mark against his character and integrity."

"Counselor," the judge warned.

Phil nodded his acknowledgement. "And Martha? Didn't she tell you in her initial interview that she'd been outside the night of the murder? Combined with her easy access to her brother's gun, and his report of her criminal history, didn't that make a her a suspect?"

"We have so much evidence against Barr, we really didn't have any need to pursue anyone else."

"Ah," Phil said, smiling. Once again, a prosecution witness had opened a door that served us. Phil turned around and hunted for a piece of paper. "I'm going to read from the transcript of the hearing associated with my client's first arrest, Detective. I'd like to hear your thoughts on this passage."

"Don't bother," Cullen told him. "It's true that the DA stopped looking for other suspects prematurely last time. I'm not her. I haven't done that."

"And you expect us to take your word for that?"

"I do." Cullen's voice and tone were rock steady.

"Well, I guess the jury can decide if *they* do," Phil said.

"Mr Karanos," Harrow admonished.

"Sorry, Your Honor."

"Stick to asking questions."

Phil nodded. "Let's take a look at this convoluted, unlikely car story. You referred to it several times as lucky, correct?"

"Yes."

"In previous cases, when you've encountered a series of amazingly *lucky* circumstances that point to a particular suspect, are these often crafted by a guilty party?"

"I wouldn't say often," Cullen replied.

"Have you learned to be cautious about accepting major coincidences when working a case?"

"Yes," Cullen admitted.

"So you didn't readily accept this car owner's story?"

"No, I didn't.'

"Why should we?" Phil asked, gesturing to the jury box. "You said the owner 'checked out.' What does that mean, exactly?"

"We ran a background check, and he came out clean. He is a veteran with a stellar record in the Navy. And he passed a lie detector test."

"Are those tests one hundred percent reliable?"

"No," Cullen admitted.

"In fact, haven't quite a few cases been tossed out of court because the test was deemed invalid?" Phil asked.

"I wouldn't know."

"Well, it's a fact. Could someone have bribed the car owner to concoct his story?"

"Once again, anything's possible, but—"

"Thank you, detective. Did you check the car owner's financials?"

"No."

"Why not?" Phil asked.

"The car owner refused to allow us to."

"Could he have something to hide? Could he have been paid to concoct this story?"

“He said it was none of our business. And it isn’t,” Cullen asserted. “The important thing is that one way or another, we found the location of the first murder and gathered vital evidence there.”

“So you’re telling the jury to ignore the car element—that it’s not important, and perhaps not even true?” Phil asked.

“You’re putting words in my mouth. Of course I didn’t say that. I said the most important part of the completely legitimate car evidence is what it led us to.”

“You don’t find it awfully convenient that one thing after another led you to this evidence—evidence that just happened to implicate my client?”

“Nope. Sure don’t,” Cullen replied.

“Could this evidence have been planted at the scene of the crime to frame my client?” Phil asked.

“I don’t see how. If you do, please fill me in.”

“That’s your job, Detective. Did you look into that? Why haven’t you made us aware of alternate explanations about the evidence at the murder site? Even if you eventually dismissed other possibilities, aren’t you supposed to explore them?”

“I think I’m a little more in the know about what I’m supposed to do, counselor.” Cullen’s voice was steely now. “Are you saying you know better than an experienced detective about how to handle a crime scene?”

“I’m merely asking questions,” Phil said. “Why are you being so defensive?”

“You Honor!” Marion called.

“That’s not an appropriate question, Mr. Karanos.”

“Sorry. Detective Cullen, did you know that my client has been missing a pair of his shoes for some time now?"

"You mean, according to him."

"I mean is that something you asked about—investigated?"

"No," Cullen said calmly.

"Why not?"

"There was no reason to."

"I see." Phil glanced at the jury before continuing. "Let's explore another weak point in your testimony. Is my client on trial for what someone is doing to defraud people—this Ponzi scheme?"

"No."

"You said you have evidence that 'implicated' Mr. Tobin, is that right?" Phil asked.

"Yes."

"By definition, an implication merely suggests something may be so. You don't have proof, do you?"

"No," Cullen admitted.

"How does this fraud evidence relate to this murder trial?" Phil asked.

"You'd have to ask a lawyer," Cullen replied.

"I'm asking you. How many times have you testified in court as an expert witness?"

"I couldn't say."

"Couldn't or won't?"

"I just don't know, exactly," Cullen explained.

"Okay, tell us inexactly. Ten? Fifty? Five hundred?"

"Maybe a hundred-ish."

"And in all those appearances, you haven't learned what evidence relates to a given case and what doesn't?" Phil asked, raising his eyebrows.

"Fine, here's my take on it. I'd say that although Barr hasn't been charged with this particular crime at this time, it speaks to what sort of person he is, and whether he has been masquerading as a spiritual teacher when he's actually a criminal. Part of the state's case here is that he's not who he says he is."

"Would you be surprised to learn that your arguments won't hold up in this court once the defense presents its witnesses?"

"There's that 'would you be surprised' lawyer tactic," Cullen said. "What surprises me and what doesn't isn't relevant here."

"Let's move on," Phil said. "Is my client on trial for crimes committed in Canada?"

"No."

"Then why all this commotion about anything that happened there? It seems like the DA has been focused on that for days."

"I couldn't say why she's doing what she's doing. I can only speak for myself. Mr. Barr has asserted that he is Carl Steubens, AKA Kade Tobin. To prove this is not so, we needed to investigate his crimes in Canada, which are in the public record there. In addition, we ascertained that concealing these crimes was Barr's motive for the murders."

"Do you think a juror could remain unbiased after he or she heard about the nature of the Canadian crimes?"

"Objection. Calls for speculation.

"Sustained."

"Detective, have you ever been suspicious of your partner—Detective Quinn? We heard him misrepresent quite a few things when he testified here. I wonder what you've observed."

It hadn't occurred to me that Phil might ask this. It

could yield something that helped us, or it might elicit a ringing endorsement. I figured that given all of Quinn's and Cullen's testimony, Phil believed he didn't have much to lose.

Cullen smiled. "Once Michael ate half my sandwich and then said he didn't."

A few jurors laughed.

"Thank you for the comic relief. I think we all need a little of that at this point. You know I mean something more serious, don't you?"

"Well, since I'm under oath, I have to admit that sometimes Michael cuts corners."

Phil had hit pay dirt again. "And by that, you mean…"

"He doesn't always follow procedures," Cullen explained. "He came to us from a very loosey-goosey department in the Central Valley."

"Can you give the court an example?—not the most mild one, something typical."

"Sometimes Michael gathers evidence that might not be admissible if his methods were known."

"Has that been a problem for you?" Phil asked.

"Yes. I believe in going by the book."

"I understand that Detective Quinn has had several cases thrown out of court for similar behaviors."

"Yes," Cullen said.

"In your expert opinion, is this reprehensible behavior?"

"Your Honor," Marion broke in. "This man is not an expert about what is reprehensible."

"Sustained."

"Detective, does Detective Quinn's past behavior in his capacity as a law enforcement officer cause you to wonder about his role in this case?"

Cullen looked at Marion. "I'm sorry," he said. "Yes, it did. Not so much now."

"In what way did you wonder?"

"He didn't tell me or anyone else he was up in Canada instead of being ill. He found out a lot very quickly about Barr's history when that's not usually possible, even here in the States. And I saw him on the stand in this trial. I could tell he lied several times. I know him well."

"Thank you for your candor, Detective. I imagine you feel very uncomfortable talking about your partner this way."

"Yeah, I do," Cullen agreed.

"So you wouldn't do it unless you thought it was an important element in this case?" Phil asked.

"No, I'm doing it because I'm under oath. I wouldn't perjure myself for my own mother."

Phil smiled. "Does this information you're sharing create doubt for you concerning some of the evidence in this case?"

"It does, but there's so much other evidence I gathered myself that it doesn't matter. I know Barr is guilty."

"Does some of the suspect evidence unearthed by your partner have a bearing on my client's identity?"

"Yes, most of it," Cullen conceded.

"So perhaps Mr. Tobin is not Mr. Barr?"

"I didn't say that. There's plenty of other information coming to us from Canadian authorities that has nothing to do with Michael."

"How do you know that? How *could* you know he isn't involved in what reaches you?" Phil asked.

Cullen shook his head and didn't answer.

"Are you concerned that you are currently weakening the prosecution's case?"

"Yes," Cullen responded.

Phil paused quite a while before speaking again. I was surprised the judge let him. "Is it possible that Detective Quinn had a hand in what you found locally—that he 'cut corners' in some way detrimental to my client—things that misrepresented what happened?"

"I don't see how," Cullen said.

"I'm not asking you if you currently are aware of a possible mechanism. I'm asking if it's possible."

"I don't know."

"So that's not a no? You haven't ruled it out?" Phil asked.

"There has been no reason to examine that, so I don't have a point of view about it."

Phil paused again. This time, Judge Harrow told him to get going. I could sense that Phil was at a loss as to how to chip away further at Cullen's testimony.

"Here's an odd question, Detective," he finally mustered. "I'm at a bit of a loss as to what to ask you next. If you were me, what would you ask?"

"Objection," Marion called.

"On what grounds?"

"Calls for speculation. And it's just plain weird, isn't it?"

"You know," Harrow responded, "this is the first time I've heard that question asked in my courtroom. I think Detective Cullen can handle himself, and I'm curious what he'll say. Proceed, please."

"Counselor, if I were you, I'd convince Barr to take a guilty plea. Anything you ask besides what you asked about Michael Quinn is just going to bury him deeper. And when I'm through testifying, what Marion projects onto that screen over there will be the final nail in Barr's coffin. You know me. You know I don't say things like this if they're not true. Give it up."

Clearly, that question had been a mistake. Or was Phil throwing me under the bus? Had he lost interest in exonerating me?

Phil paused again and then spoke to Judge Harrow. "Your Honor, would it be possible to dismiss this witness for now so we can view all of the prosecution's exhibits? I'm finding it difficult to question this witness further without all the facts to use as a guideline. I'll be happy to recall Detective Cullen and elicit the rest of the detective's testimony after that."

"Marion?"

"That's fine, Your Honor."

Cullen casually ambled to the back row of the courtroom, perhaps to demonstrate that he wasn't rattled by Phil's questioning.

Once again, I wondered if Phil's request was an attempt to bury me. The thought was almost too disturbing to consider.

"Very well," Judge Harrow said. "Marion, the floor is yours after a lunch break. Members of the jury, I apologize for such a late lunch. We needed to hear uninterrupted testimony this morning. Court adjourned."

Phil abruptly stood and marched out of the courtroom without a word. I hoped he was rushing off to prepare our defense or figure out how he'd continue to cross-examine Bill Cullen later that day.

I feared he was too angry to even talk to me. And at that moment, it seemed to be even odds he no longer believed in me—that he found Cullen's testimony so compelling that I'd reached monster status in his eyes. How could he defend me if that were the case?

Phil had said as much at one point. I initially attributed that to an emotional reaction when he was surprised by some of the testimony. Now I wasn't sure.

I found Cullen's condemnation of Quinn to really move the needle back over to our side, but there was now a plethora of circumstantial evidence against me. If the jurors—and Phil—couldn't accept that a frame could be so comprehensive, I was a goner.

Chapter 37

Susan brought me a container of cold spinach lasagna and an iced tea for lunch. Her pinched face, the psoriasis outbreak on her neck, and her rumpled peasant blouse spoke to her stress level.

"Are you okay? I asked.

"I'm hanging in there. Getting questioned was pretty brutal."

"And the others?"

"The ones watching the trial in the gallery are having the roughest time," she told me. "Hearing all that crap about you seems to be pretty hard to take. Plus, they have to line up early in the morning to get a spot."

"And how's Zeus?"

I took a bite of the lasagna, which smelled like oregano, but tasted as if someone had added salsa to the tomato sauce.

"I can tell he really misses you," Susan responded, "but he's eating okay and everybody's taking him on walks and playing with him. The other day, he tossed a stick out of his mouth to get Ralph to fetch it. It was hysterical."

Susan smiled and looked like herself for a moment.

"Did he do it?"

"Of course—several times—until Zeus decided squirrel hunting was more fun." She pulled a can of soda and another plastic container out of her backpack.

"Where's Phil?' she asked. "I brought him his favorite. The poor guy is working so hard. And how'd it go today?"

"I don't know where Phil is, and I'd have to say it didn't go well. The afternoon promises to be worse."

"Are they going to be able to lock up those guys running the Ponzi scheme?" she asked. "It's so awful they were doing that right under our noses." She opened the soda, took a sip, and then grimaced. "Ugh. How does Phil drink this stuff?"

"I assume they've caught them by now," I replied. "And I don't know why anyone wants to drink carbonated chemicals."

Susan shook her head. "Those con artist assholes took off the day after you were arrested this time. Several other members have left the Brethren, too."

"That's a shame. I hate to think that what I'm going through has had a ripple effect on our members' spiritual growth," I told her.

"Yeah, that's what I thought, too." She looked me in the eyes. "But it has."

"And we have to accept that," I said. "Like everything else."

"Sometimes I wish my mother wasn't who she is," Susan said, looking toward the empty prosecution table.

"What do you mean?"

"If someone else was the DA, would it be like this?"

All I could was shrug. There was a teaching moment in there somewhere, but I didn't have the energy for it.

Susan had a doctor's appointment, so she took off, and I was left with my thoughts and the bailiff assigned to keep an eye on me. After I finished eating, I meditated to banish my unhelpful rumination, reaching an odd state that wasn't as tethered back to the physical world as usual. Even when the gallery and the attorneys filed in, and I tried to return to a normal state, a part of me involuntarily remained in the subtle realm. That wasn't going to help.

****

"All right, Marion," Judge Harrow said once we'd all gone through the usual rigamarole to get the trial started again. "Please proceed with your presentation."

"Thank you, Your Honor."

One by one, reports, documents, lab results, interview transcripts, and the like scrolled down the huge screen that had been rolled out in front the witness box. Quite a few of them had apparently been faxed from Canada. The local ones were just as damning. All of it could've easily have been tampered with by Mike Quinn. I hoped the jurors could see that, too.

Marion read everything out loud for about forty-five minutes, her voice faltering by the time she was through. I gradually returned to the world from my altered state, so I missed details of the early portion of her evidence. The jury was still rapt when I was alert enough to notice. But soon after, quite a few jurors looked bored or distracted. It had probably been a mistake for her to inundate them with so much information.

When Marion finished, she announced that the prosecution rested. Her smug tone indicated she didn't feel any need to present more evidence to win the trial. I didn't blame her. If I didn't know better, I'd have voted for a guilty verdict at that point.

"Are you ready to proceed, Mr. Karanos?" the judge asked Phil.

"Actually, no. We need some time to absorb the

district attorney's presentation and prepare a robust defense."

"Robust, eh? Weren't you given access to the content of the presentation as part of the discovery phase?"

"Yes, Your Honor," Phil responded. "But seeing it written is different from hearing it read. I need to consider the impact on the jurors of my opponent's intonation, the words she emphasized—things like that."

"Very well. It's Friday afternoon. Do you think you can be prepared by Monday morning?"

"Absolutely," Phil assured him.

"Marion?" Harrow said. "Any objections?"

"No, Your Honor." In fact, she looked relieved. Her shoulders relaxed, and the corners of her mouth loosened.

The judge rapped his gavel. "Court is hereby adjourned."

The jailer who'd been assigned to escort me back to my cell wasn't someone I knew. As the gallery filed out, he made his way against the flow and approached our defense table before I had a chance to chat with Phil. I introduced myself.

"I know who you are," he told me. "I'm Ronald Gutiérrez. I appreciate what you've done to help the other prisoners."

His friendly, open face matched his words. It was hard to picture him wading into a jail fight with a baton in his hand. On the other hand, he was quite tall and wiry strong, with vein-popping forearms and an athletic stance. Perhaps that alone did the trick in hairy situations.

"Ronald?" Phil said, glancing across me at the man.

"My mother admired Ronald Reagan. Don't ask me why."

"We haven't met, have we?" I asked.

"No, I'm filling in from the women's side of things. There are a few men working there. Don't ask me why about that, either. It doesn't make much sense to me. Listen, if you two need to talk, I can wait to bring you back. I need to reply to some texts, anyway."

"That would be very kind," I told him. "I'll take you up on that."

He marched to the back of the courtroom and hunkered down onto a bench in the last row. It looked as though he were sitting in a kid's chair during parent-teacher's night.

"So, Phil," I said, "intonation, emphasis? Really?"

"That was just bullshit to give us time. I've got some things I need to pursue."

"I appreciate your willingness to still do that," I told him.

"I haven't given up on you, Kade. Whether you're guilty or not, you're still owed a thorough defense."

"That's not exactly a ringing endorsement, is it?" I pointed out.

"It's the best I've got right now. But keep your fingers crossed." He held his hand up and crossed his own. "I may be onto something that puts me squarely back into the 'my guy's definitely innocent' column."

"But you don't want to tell me what it is?" I'm sure my frustration was leaking out in my tone.

"I don't want you to get your hopes up," Phil said, "and if I put you on the stand, it's better if you aren't aware of some things."

"I hope you're not planning anything contrary to our

shared value system," I told him, still unsatisfied by Phil's answers.

He shook his head. "No, it's nothing like that."

I couldn't help but wonder what Phil was up to as I strolled back to the jail with Ronald—sans handcuffs. Halfway there, he began telling me about a troubled friend who'd lost his faith. I let go of my personal concerns and offered words I believed would help Ronald and his "friend"—who I suspected was Ronald himself. Perhaps my escort had been lenient with me in the courtroom to establish an unnecessary quid pro quo.

The weekend passed in the same way virtually all my time in jail did. That was probably the hardest aspect of being there—the unrelenting sameness of one day to the next. Most of the prisoners were profoundly bored, which created a breeding ground for misbehavior. Other prisoners vicariously enjoyed whatever conflict arose—anything to relieve *their* boredom.

At any rate, I heard from Phil late Sunday evening when Ronald passed me a note. I was finishing a game of dominos with Chet.

"All systems are go, my friend," it read. "You are innocent, and I think I can prove it. Hang in there. Phil."

Until I read it, I hadn't realized how tight my gut had been for weeks on end. When it suddenly relaxed, the release of third chakra energy zapped up my spine, energizing my heart and mind. I didn't feel whole compared to my baseline configuration, but my emotional state and mood shifted significantly toward the positive—toward hope.

I let Chet beat me at dominos. The guy needed something to feel good about, too. I had something now.

****

Back in court on Monday morning, I had no chance to find out more from Phil since he entered the room only seconds before the judge. He was winded, and a few drops of sweat dangled from his eyebrows. His dark suit hung on him, and I realized he'd lost a lot of weight since I'd been arrested.

"Trust me," he whispered as we stood to honor his honor. "It's all good."

"Counselor," Harrow began after his gavel rap—an especially loud one. "Are you ready to call your first witness?"

"Yes, I am. I call Marion Burke."

Stunned, neither the DA nor the judge uttered a word. Marion broke the silence first.

"Objection. There's no precedent for this. It's completely inappropriate."

She sat ramrod straight, speaking as if she couldn't possibly be anything but absolutely correct.

The judge nodded his agreement. "Mr. Karanos, what are you thinking? You're wasting the court's time with this."

"Actually, Your Honor, there is precedent. The best example is the State of California versus Fletcher. In that case, much as my opponent has done, the prosecuting attorney personally presented information to advance his case without a witness's presence. In essence, this designated the prosecutor as a witness himself. As such, the defense was entitled to a cross-examination."

"If this is true…" Harrow called to a young African-American man in a charcoal suit in the front row behind Marion. "Jesse, go look this up."

"Yes, sir."

The judge faced Phil. "You're sure about this? Even

if it's allowed by law, it might not serve your client's best interests. What could Marion say that would help you?"

"I'll take my chances, Your Honor."

"Your Honor," Marion protested, standing and pointing at Phil. "The defense set me up. It was a trap. I'd been planning to introduce the slide presentation while I was questioning Detective Cullen. Mr. Karanos encouraged me to present the evidence myself."

"And whose fault is it that you chose to do that, Marion?" Harrow's tone and stern frown expressed his impatience. "Are you afraid to get up there? Is that it? Maybe it's time you experienced the other side of the witness box."

"Your Honor!" Marion exclaimed. She sounded like a scandalized churchgoer—more shocked than truly offended. Her comrade had turned on her.

Phil and I exchanged grins. This was great stuff.

Harrow continued in an even gruffer voice. "I get sick of attorneys whining in my courtroom, Marion. I don't care what you think is fair. *I* care about the law."

The judge looked down at his phone, which was sitting on the raised desk in front of him. Then he looked up and spoke. "My clerk found the precedents. Come on up, Marion."

The DA rose slowly and walked even slower to the witness seat. Her dark brown pantsuit matched her hair, rendering her a monochromatic look, like a sepia photograph. After she was sworn in and Phil settled behind his podium, he began.

"I'd like to explore the sources of the so-called evidence you presented. Is that all right with you?"

"Objection," Marion snapped. "So-called is an

improper opinion."

"You can't object, Marion," the judge told her. "You're a witness right now."

"So he can do whatever he wants? Really?" She'd raised her voice. Her outrage seemed authentic, unlike some of her other maneuvers during the course of the trial.

"Calm down. I'll keep an eye on things," Harrow told her. "Do you have any other prosecutors in the room? If you do, you can designate them to object."

"No, there's no one."

"All right, then. Trust me." He turned to Phil. "Go ahead, counselor."

"Getting back to your sources," Phil began in a calm, clear voice, "according to my notes, a 'Detective Boucher' faxed you quite a bit of paperwork from Canada. Is that correct?"

Marion nodded. "Yes, he's been very helpful."

"And you ascertained his credentials?"

"Absolutely. He's with the Montreal police force, and he has two decades of experience," Marion reported confidently.

"Who is it that put you in contact with Boucher?"

"I believe it was Detective Quinn."

"I see. Did you know that Boucher is currently under investigation for corruption?"

"I doubt that," she replied, shaking her head. "He was thoroughly vetted."

Phil pivoted and selected a document from the defense tabletop. "Permission to approach the witness, Your Honor."

"Granted."

Phil handed Marion the sheet of paper. "Would you

read the highlighted sections, please."

She looked beseechingly at Judge Harrow. "Must I?"

"You must."

"Fine," she said, meaning it wasn't fine at all. "Here's what's highlighted: 'From the desk of Montreal Police Commissioner Jenkins. Dear Mr. Karanos, in reference to your inquiry about Bernard Boucher on behalf of your client accused of murder, I cannot share details, but I would be remiss to let a miscarriage of justice stand unchallenged. I understand that Boucher provided information to the authorities in Santa Cruz County, California. We strongly suspect that he has done so in other cases in which the information has proven to be false. Our forensic accountant is currently examining Boucher's finances. He is under suspension. Please let my office know if there is any other way we can help you arrive at the truth.'

"Thank you, Marion," Phil said. "May I call you Marion?"

"No."

Phil paused to let her hostility sink in for the jurors. "Very well. What do you now think about the information this detective provided to you?"

"I'll have to verify your letter is real," she said.

"I assure you it is. Would you like to call the phone number on the heading to check?"

"No, that's all right." Marion waved her hand.

"Maybe it would help if I rephrased my question. If this letter is real, would that change how much confidence you have about the accuracy of some of your presentation?"

"Of course."

"Who else sent you so-called evidence from Canada?" Phil asked.

"Your Honor," Marion said. "You said you'd intervene if he said this again."

"Marion, I think 'so-called' turned out to be spot on the first time around. Let's just wait and see if it is this time."

"Shall I repeat my question?" Phil asked.

"No, I remember. Another source was an officer named Desmond McPherson. That's the only other one I remember offhand. I'm a prosecutor, not a policeman. You can call one of them to the stand if you want to know more about this."

"That won't be necessary," Phil responded. "That's the man I'm interested in. What do you know about him?"

"Only what I was told."

"By whom?"

"Detective Quinn."

"Hmm, his fingerprints seem to be all over this case."

The judge spoke up. "The jury will ignore that remark."

"I apologize, Your Honor," Phil said. "Ms. District Attorney, would it surprise you to learn that McPherson is no longer with the force in Vancouver, Canada?"

"I don't see why that matters. What he told us goes back to when he was."

"How do you know that? No, never mind. I get it. That's what you were told by you-know-who."

"Counselor," the judge admonished.

"Sorry." Phil turned back to Marion. "Do you know why McPherson is no longer with the police force?"

"No, I don't."

"Do you think you should?"

"Like I said, it's the responsibility of law enforcement to investigate matters like that," Marion answered.

"So you don't care if he was dismissed for what authorities in Canada are calling 'gross misconduct'?"

"Of course I care. Is that true?"

"Yes. Would you like to see the documentation about that?" Phil began to turn around again.

"No, that's all right. You'd never practice law again if you forged documents."

"Yes, that's true. By the way, Your Honor, I'll enter all the exhibits I've gathered when I'm through with this witness." Phil paused to take a sip of water. "Let's take a look at where we stand with your presentation," he said to Marion. "How confident are you about what you read to us now?"

"Obviously there are parts that may be inaccurate. I'll definitely be reading the riot act to whoever's responsible."

"It looks to me like that's Detective Quinn. Do you agree?"

"You might be right. We'll see." Marion gathered herself and sat up straighter. "The thing is, you've only impugned a portion of the evidence. There's a lot that I still stand behind."

"Did you stand behind everything you read to us before?" Phil asked.

"Of course." As soon as she said this, she winced.

"So how much weight do you think we should give to your judgment now?" Marion didn't respond. She held her features still, her eyes locked on Phil. "That's okay," he continued. "You don't have to answer that."

Phil turned again to gather some notes. I gave him a thumbs-up, and he smiled back at me before pivoting back.

"Has there ever been any chicanery at the Sheriff's department?" he asked.

"What do you mean by chicanery?"

I couldn't tell if Marion was genuinely puzzled or just stalling while she considered her answer.

Phil explained. "Intrigue, illegal activity, successful lawsuits against the department—things like that."

"Of course. That's true of any department," Marion said. Her tone implied that he'd asked a stupid question—one with an obvious answer.

"Can you tell us about the deputy you prosecuted in 2023?"

She blinked rapidly and then turned to her right. "Judge, is this relevant? I'd object if I could."

Phil spoke up quickly. "Your Honor, this is just an end run around your ruling that the DA is only a witness and can't object. And the integrity of law enforcement is a theme today, isn't it?"

"Yes," Harrow replied. "Answer the question, Marion."

"I successfully prosecuted Allan Gifford for taking bribes to remove evidence against a local gang."

"So you know things like that happen?" Phil asked.

"I already said that, didn't I?" Marion rebuked sharply.

Once again, Phil paused. Marion's frustration—her powerlessness to direct things—was leaking out and that reflected poorly on her.

"Let's go a step forward with this," he began. "Is it

possible there's chicanery going on right now in the sheriff's department that you will have to prosecute?"

"I have no idea," Marion said.

"So you're not denying the possibility?"

Marion didn't answer.

"That's all I have for this witness," Phil told the judge.

"Very well. You may step down, Marion," he told her, and then brought his gavel down. "The court is in recess for twenty minutes. I have other business to attend to. Do not be late returning. Mr. Karanos, please submit your exhibits to the court reporter."

"Wow, Phil," I said when he returned to the defense table after turning over his documents . "Great job. How did you find all that out?"

"I'll tell you later. I need to make a few calls. There are even better things coming, Kade."

He retreated to the far corner of the courtroom and leaned against the wall as he brought his phone up to his ear. He also received several phone calls during the recess, and he texted furiously following each. What could he be doing?

I sat, breathed, and cultivated calming energy. Witnessing my own trial was exhausting. And it continuously tested my equilibrium.

When the session began again, Phil was once more the last one in his seat, drawing a glare from the judge this time. Phil whispered to me hurriedly. "I'm putting you on the stand to stall for time and distract the jury while—"

"Get to it," Harrow commanded in a no-nonsense tone.

"You'll see," Phil said to me, and then he stood. "I

call Kade Tobin to the stand."

The gallery murmured in unison, with a few loud whispers mixed in. I endured the usual rigamarole to become situated in the witness chair.

"You've heard the evidence against you, Kade," Phil began. "What do you make of it?" He leaned forward against his podium.

There was an open-ended question if there ever was one. I took a moment to think how best to answer it. "I'm impressed," I finally said.

"Impressed?"

"Yes, my only exposure to someone being framed for crimes they didn't commit has been in the media, and I can't recall any plots in which the false case has been so elaborately and skillfully crafted."

"Can you tell us more about that?" Phil asked.

"Trying to prove I'm someone else isn't an easy task. Bribing officials in another country isn't, either. And manipulating a district attorney's office is—"

"Objection," Marion called. "Facts not in evidence, and it's prejudicial as well."

"This is the defendant speaking, Marion, not his attorney," the judge reminded her. "I think we're all interested in what he has to say, whether or not it fits the facts as we know them thus far."

Phil asked me to continue, so I did.

"I know I'm innocent, yet quite a bit of the evidence against me is seems strong at first glance. I think Wyatt Barr and Mike Quinn have done an exemplary job of framing me."

Marion stood to object. The judge anticipated this and told her to sit down before she could speak.

"I see," Phil said. "What about the credibility of the

prosecutor's sources and witnesses? After I questioned her witnesses, didn't you find most of them incompetent or unreliable? Doesn't that belie what you're saying about the evidence being strong?"

"Objection," Marion called out. "Is the court going to allow the defense to keep characterizing my witnesses like that? These are seasoned law enforcement officers who have earned our respect."

Harrow paused before speaking directly to Phil. "Given that the defendant is on trial for his life, I'm going to give you some leeway, counselor. But please rephrase your question so it's acceptable to this court. And jurors, be aware that the answer to this and earlier questions are what the defendant would have us believe—not factual evidence."

I saw several heads nodding, but one older woman frowned. Perhaps she shared my point of view that the judge had basically told them to ignore what I said. I wondered if something like that was grounds for appeal.

"Kade, here's my revised question," Phil began. "What is your impression of the prosecution's witnesses?"

"I think the witnesses themselves have been weak, except for Detective Cullen. You've done a great job demonstrating their fallibility, and I appreciate that. Nonetheless, the material they presented has been compelling at times."

"Speaking of appreciation, I applaud your candor, Kade."

"Your Honor," Marion called.

"Let's stick to questions," the judge admonished.

"Yes, Your Honor."

I heard a minor commotion at the back of the

courtroom, but kept my focus on Phil as he swiveled his head to look and then turned back to face me to ask his next question. "Do you think you might be convicted?"

He smiled as he asked this, which struck me as incongruous. Why the sudden good cheer?

"It's a real possibility," I answered.

Marion spoke up again. "How is any of this relevant, Your Honor? Leeway is all well and fine, but there's a limit. The defendant's comments, as you said, are not evidence. He's simply expressing his opinions, which are surely driven by self-interest. "

The judge looked at Phil. "Counselor?"

"I'm giving the jury a chance to get to know my client—to see what kind of man he is."

"That's why we have character witnesses," the judge replied. "Defendants only get to reveal their character while answering relevant questions. Objection sustained."

Next, Phil asked me, "Would you recognize your cousin if you saw him? My understanding is that he resembles you, so that wouldn't be too hard, would it?"

"Calls for speculation," Marion stated. "And once again, relevance, you honor."

"I'm inclined to agree, Marion," the judge said. "Where are you going with this?" he asked Phil.

"With the court's permission, I'd like to provide a demonstration to answer that question."

"What sort of demonstration?"

"Unfortunately, if I explain it ahead of time, its impact may be nullified."

Marion spoke up. "You can't give the defense carte blanche to do whatever he wants, Your Honor. It was bad enough that I couldn't stop him when I was on the witness stand."

Harrow scowled. Marion was not winning any brownie points with him lately. "I don't need you to tell me what I can and cannot do," he told her. "Go ahead, Mr. Karanos. I'll stop you if you're acting improperly or you're exceeding my patience."

"Thank you, Your Honor."

Phil beckoned to Martha, who sat in the second row of the gallery. I saw that behind her, in the last row, a burly man sat between two uniformed policemen with his head down. What was going on there, I wondered. A new witness? Someone from the jail? Was that what Phil had been arranging during the recess?

Martha brought Phil a partially filled grocery sack and then returned to her seat. She grinned at me from there, which I took to be a good sign. Even if it weren't, her wide, toothy smile always boosted my mood.

"Permission to approach my witness?" Phil asked.

"Go ahead."

He handed me the sack. "Put these on," he whispered.

"Counselor," the judge said, "while the defendant is on the stand, anything you say to each other belongs on the transcript—the public record. Please repeat what you told him so that all of us can hear."

While the judge was talking, I pulled on a blond wig. While Phil repeated himself, elaborating to give me time, I slipped on black frame glasses and began affixing a false goatee to my chin with the two-way tape inside its mesh.

Everyone stopped what they were doing and stared when I'd finished. Marion was clearly taken aback and not sure whether to object or ride it out. The judge's expression was complex. He frowned with his mouth, but his eyes indicated interest, as though he'd been presented with a puzzle he thought he'd enjoy figuring out.

"Well, this is a first," Harrow finally said. "What's up, Counselor?"

"I'd like to call my next witness now."

"You're finished with the defendant? You don't want to do anything with this new look of his?" His raised eyebrows and widened eyes accentuated his surprise.

"Not at this time," Phil told him.

"Marion, are you prepared to cross-examine?" Harrow asked.

"Uh, no, Your Honor."

"Then why don't you call your next witness, Mr. Karanos, and we'll come back to whatever this is all about later."

"Perfect. Thank you."

"You're dismissed for now," the judge told me.

I stepped down and began to pull off the itchy beard.

"Please keep that on," Phil said.

So I did. I thought I had an inkling of what he was up to now. He must be planning to show a photo of Wyatt in a similar getup to drive home our resemblance.

In a louder than usual voice, Phil faced the jury. "The defense calls Wyatt Barr to the stand." He turned and faced the gallery.

One man in the jury box said, "Holy smokes," and a woman in the gallery let out a stifled shout.

I couldn't see the value of calling a witness who wasn't there. Perhaps by getting the jury to look behind him, Phil could trick them into acknowledging Wyatt might actually exist.

Slowly, the man sandwiched between the two policemen in the last row was pulled up by the hand cuffs attached to his wrists as one of the officers stood. The man tilted his head up and stared daggers at me. He had a goatee, straggly blond hair, and black frame glasses. It was Wyatt.

My mouth literally dropped. I'm sure I looked like a cartoon character at that moment. I tore my gaze away to look at the jury. Their eyes were darting back and forth between us. Obviously, they saw how alike we looked.

"Bring the witness forward," the judge ordered.

The police officer led Wyatt to the witness stand, uncuffed him, and then strode back to his seat as his charge sat, still glaring at me.

"Your witness, Counselor," the judge prompted Phil, who had paused for dramatic effect.

Marion rushed to her feet. "Your Honor, this witness was not on the list we were provided by the defense, and there's no proof he's Wyatt Barr, or, for that matter, if such a person even exists."

"Perhaps I can help with that," Phil said. "Mr. Barr was apprehended by the Santa Cruz city police yesterday afternoon, and that just came to my attention a short time ago. If I'm allowed to question him, I believe I can clear up any confusion about who is who."

"Of course you're allowed to question your witness, Counselor. Sit down, Marion. And Mr. Tobin, you may remove your disguise now. You've made your point."

"Yes, Your Honor."

I was heartened by his referring to me by my name, which he hadn't done before. It certainly wasn't lost on the jurors, who must've been thinking of me as Wyatt for most of the trial.

Phil locked eyes with Wyatt. "You are Wyatt Barr, are you not?"

"No." His voice was lower-pitched and hoarser than I remembered.

"Who do you purport to be?"

"My name is Gary Farber."

Wyatt's loud declaration rang out in the packed courtroom. He had an accent now, as though he'd spent some years in the south—maybe Texas.

"And you have ID to that effect?" Phil asked.

"The cops took it."

"Why is that?"

"You'd have to ask them," Wyatt said.

"Do you deny that your license was forged and when you were fingerprinted today, those prints matched the ones on file from Canadian extradition documents for Wyatt Barr?"

Wyatt was silent.

"Answer the question," the judge commanded.

"That's what they say," Wyatt grudgingly admitted.

"Now, why were you arrested today?"

"I don't know." Wyatt shrugged dramatically, as though he were in a school play directed by a hammy drama teacher.

"Would you like me to tell you why?" Phil asked.

Wyatt shrugged again, less emphatically this time. His feigned indifference wasn't convincing. His tight lips and the furrows between his darting eyes revealed his stress.

Phil gestured to one of the officers who'd accompanied Wyatt. The slim, older man walked up the center aisle and handed him a manila file.

"Let's see," Phil began. "You were parked outside a middle school playing field, correct?"

"Sure. That's not illegal, is it?"

"And girls were playing soccer in gym shorts and T-shirts?"

"So?"

"What were you doing in the car at that time?" Phil asked.

"None of your business."

I saw that Wyatt's pugnacious replies didn't sit well with the jury. Most of the jurors refreshed their frowns after each of his answers.

Phil turned to the judge. "Permission to treat this man as a hostile witness."

"He certainly is. Go ahead."

"Mr. Barr, isn't it a fact that whatever you were doing, it caught the attention of an undercover policeman who had staked out that area based on complaints from the school? Remember, I have the police report in my hands and there are stiff penalties for perjury."

"Yeah, that's what happened," Wyatt admitted.

"And this officer discovered you had outstanding warrants under the name Gary Farber."

"We're talking about minor shit here."

"Language, please," the judge admonished.

Wyatt just stared at him. The judge stared back.

Phil continued. "Would you like me to read what happened when you were brought to the police station?"

"No."

"I will, anyway. That way you'll have a chance to refute it—to explain your side of the story. Does that seem fair?"

Wyatt was silent again.

"Here we go," Phil began, looking down at the open folder. "This is from a report filed by Officer Winn. 'The suspect was uncooperative in every respect upon apprehension. He refused to voluntarily submit to fingerprinting and two deputies had to force him to do so. Although the suspect was wanted under the name of Gary Farber, the prints revealed his true identity to be Wyatt Barr, a person of interest in an ongoing sheriff's department investigation. Sergeant Glover called and spoke to Captain McCall, who came down to the station and interrogated the suspect. Captain McCall also ascertained that the suspect's prints matched the ones on file for a man named Kade Tobin, which could not be possible. McCall called his station to have someone investigate the chain of evidence in his murder case to determine why Barr's prints were filed as Tobin's. The result of that investigation is unknown to us.'" Phil paused. "How am I doing so far, Mr. Barr? Does this match your experience?"

"You already know the answer to that, don't you?"

"No, I don't. Your Honor, could you instruct the witness to answer my question?"

"You will answer," the judge told Wyatt.

"I can't prove anything different," Wyatt conceded.

"Let's just go ahead then and say you're Wyatt Barr," Phil asserted. "I think that's been proven, hasn't it?"

Wyatt grunted and looked away.

"So that would make you Kade Tobin's cousin, correct?"

Wyatt paused for a long stretch and Phil let him. I could sense we were at a turning point. If Wyatt admitted who he was, everything shifted.

"Yeah, he's my cousin," Wyatt said. "But he's the murderer."

"Why do you say that?"

"Cuz I didn't do it. I can't even drive a shift."

"I'm not sure what you mean," Phil said.

"That neighbor's car—the one Kade used—it's a manual transmission, isn't it? I don't know how to drive one of those."

"*That's* your defense?" Phil asked, raising his eyebrows and widening his eyes. "Claiming you lack a particular skill? That doesn't mean much, does it?"

"There's lots more," Wyatt asserted. "That's just off the top of my head."

Phil moved away from his podium to hunt up some notes on our table. When he returned, he was smiling.

"Did you know, Mr. Barr, that there's been no mention of what type of transmission that car has in the media?"

"Uh, I must've heard something about it at the police station."

"I see. Let's move on. Why is there an extradition order for you from Canadian authorities?"

"You'd have to ask them."

"I'm asking you," Phil said. "Are you saying you don't even know why you're a fugitive?"

"Okay, okay. It was a misunderstanding up in Quebec. Those French people…"

"Isn't it true you are wanted or are a suspect for statutory rape, sexual assault, and several other charges?"

"It could be," Wyatt said.

"Do I need to produce documents to prove that?"

"No, I guess that's about right."

By now, Wyatt's tone embodied resignation, with a touch of hopelessness.

"Mr. Barr, you've admitted to multiple lies and misrepresentations while you've been on the stand. Why should we believe anything you say?"

"I'd rather be a liar than a murderer."

"Me, too," Phil told him. "That's probably the only thing we have in common."

"Counselor," the judge warned.

"Sorry, Your Honor. It's hard to stay civil when I'm dealing with someone like this."

The judge glanced at Marion, who'd been objecting to similar remarks throughout the trial. She shook her head.

"Let's move on," Phil said. "Mr. Barr, you know Mike Quinn, don't you?"

"Who?"

"Detective Quinn—you know, your co-conspirator."

Again, the judge looked at Marion, who once again shook her head.

"Never heard of him," Wyatt said.

"What would you say if I told you we have a witness who can testify that the two of you have been in contact?"

"Go ahead," Wyatt replied. "Tell me that. That's how you'd find out what I'd say." Wyatt leaned back in his chair and smirked. He'd gotten his second wind, mood-wise.

"I think I just did," Phil told him "Let's not play games. I'm letting you know that lying about you and Quinn isn't going to fly. You know him, don't you?"

"I'll take the fifth on that," Wyatt said.

"You refuse to answer?"

"Yeah."

"Do you know how that comes across to a jury, Mr. Barr?" Phil asked.

Wyatt didn't respond.

"Are you willing to tell us about your relationship with Kade Tobin?" Phil tried.

"Sure. I don't have one. I haven't seen him in years."

That was the first truthful thing Wyatt had said, and I was glad it was. Who needed a monster in his life?

"You bear no ill will toward your cousin?" Phil asked.

"No," Wyatt asserted. His exaggerated head shake didn't bolster his credibility.

"Do you think most people would be angry or resent a relative who may have turned them in to the police?" Phil asked.

"Calls for speculation," Marion muttered.

"Oh, give it up, Marion," Harrow told her. "Go ahead and answer, Mr. Barr."

"How the hell should I know?" Wyatt said, throwing his hands in the air. He probably didn't. Narcissistic and amoral, Wyatt really didn't have a clue about other people's feelings or attitudes.

"Let me put to this way," Phil began, "is it normal to forgive what feels like a betrayal? Are you telling us you're the most forgiving man in the world—the one person who doesn't mind that?"

"That was a long time ago. And who says Kade ratted me out, anyway?"

I hadn't had the opportunity or I would've, but Phil's questions and Wyatt's answers certainly implied I'd done so.

"I see," Phil said. "Mr. Barr, since you're being allowed to speculate, what do you think is going to happen to you?"

"I don't know." Wyatt's bluster was gone. He sounded like the teenager I'd known.

"Do you think you're going to be a free man?" Phil asked.

"I guess not."

The judge broke in. "Mr, Karanos, if you have more questions for this witness, and I hope you do, let's save them for tomorrow. And Mr. Barr, I strongly suggest you obtain legal counsel before the defense continues questioning you."

"I have no problem stopping for the day," Phil responded. "In fact, with the court's permission, I suggest we give the prosecution a few days to clear up things on their end. I think they need some time to absorb this new development and decide whether to continue the trial."

"Very well. That's a good idea. Marion, I expect you to do your homework. Talk to the police. Get the story here."

"Yes, Your Honor."

He rapped his gavel. "Court is adjourned until Thursday at nine a.m."

Chapter 38

On Thursday morning, Marion dropped the charges against me, Wyatt was charged with multiple murders, and Mike Quinn was indicted on other felony charges.

I later discovered that Quinn's half sister provided details of the crimes she'd committed with him in order to obtain a reduced sentence. Quinn himself ratted out Wyatt. Phil was certain they would all be convicted one way or another. Even with reduced sentences, neither of Frank Dawson's siblings would be loose in the world for a very long time.

All along, Quinn and Ann/Mary had been using information fed to them anonymously—by Wyatt—to frame me more thoroughly. Quinn surely knew the source had to be the real killer. The conspirators might have succeeded if not for Wyatt's perverse sexual addiction.

It took years, but karma finally bit Wyatt in the ass, simultaneously resolving what went awry in my life. I think the definition of infinity in action is the way in which everyone's karma is simultaneously administered in a complementary fashion with everyone else's. We work out our karmic bindings from previous lives in relationship to one another. That which I need to do is that which you need to have done. And vice-versa.

****

Our community endures—the most committed

members still live on the land. Several local therapists volunteered their time when I was exonerated, and quite a few members have taken advantage of their services to process their trauma. The erosion of their spiritual focus also needed addressing, as did mine. For weeks, I'd been self-absorbed—in survival mode. The return to teaching re-anchored me to my essential self.

What I mean is that deep down, we are far greater than our circumstances, our personalities, and our triumphs and troubles. We are not simply the person who was wrongly accused, the person who was murdered, or the person who committed crimes. And we all embody the possibility of realizing this—of anchoring back to our ineffable essence.

****

Farewell, my friends.

My parting words (I am a teacher, after all): Become the wondrous creatures you truly are. Own your magnificence. Try your best to live congruently, and embrace everything that entails. Try your best to gracefully accommodate failing to do so. Yield to what is. If I add a comma to the Wicked Witch of the West's skywriting, here's a summary of what I mean: "Surrender, Dorothy." (I watched *The Wizard of Oz* a zillion times as kid.)

Why not give this a try—see if it works out better for you than your current modus operandi? Have you got anything better to do? I don't.

A word about the author...

Verlin Darrow is a psychotherapist who lives with his psychotherapist wife in the woods near the Monterey Bay in northern California. They diagnose each other as necessary. Verlin is a former professional volleyball player, country-western singer/songwriter, import store owner, newspaper columnist, wedding photographer, and spiritual teacher. Before bowing to the need for higher education, a much younger Verlin ran a punch press in a sheetmetal factory, drove a taxi, worked as a night janitor, shoveled asphalt on a road crew, and installed wood floors. He barely missed being blown up by Mt. St. Helens, survived the 1985 Mexico City earthquake, outran a tornado, and (so far) has successfully weathered his own internal disasters.

For more about Verlin's books, visit
www.verlindarrow.com/

Thank you for purchasing
this publication of The Wild Rose Press, Inc.

For questions or more information
contact us at
info@thewildrosepress.com.

The Wild Rose Press, Inc.
www.thewildrosepress.com